THE DOPPELGANGERS

THE
DOPPELGANGERS

PART 3 THE NUN

DAVID RAY

THE DOPPELGANGERS
PART 3 THE NUN

iUniverse books may be ordered through booksellers or by contacting:

iUniverse
1663 Liberty Drive
Bloomington, IN 47403
www.iuniverse.com
1-800-Authors (1-800-288-4677)

ISBN: 978-1-5320-5804-2 (sc)
ISBN: 978-1-5320-5805-9 (hc)
ISBN: 978-1-5320-5803-5 (e)

Library of Congress Control Number: 2018913062

Print information available on the last page.

iUniverse rev. date: 11/13/2018

Contents

Dedication

A special shout out to all the believers and
dreamers…past present and future.
"…Dreaming births imagination,
believing fuels desire,
Keep on dreaming…never stop believing."
Lastly, to my wife Jackie…. who put up with me all the
while I finished this project …. let's take a vacation!

David Ray

Preface

The modus operandi for a person's reality depends on his or hers perception and understanding of how they interpret what they see based upon what they've been taught.

Occasionally, a tear, or a rip emerges in that tightly woven fabric of their existence, giving way to another perception, another reality.

Point in case, repetitious and seemingly endless and twisted mirrors of darker, and strange things can be substituted and forced to become one's reality.

The native people of this land believed in the existence of dreams, and visions and in other realities, as a significant part of their belief structure, and not to become so jaded in their perception of what they daily saw and or experienced.

Just as it was true in the beginning of their time, so it remains in ours.

The residents of Columbus and Port Clinton, Ohio will soon discover that behind each reality, lies something else. Behind each interpretation, a door into something else.

Just because the date on a calendar changes, and the passing year is replaced by another, doesn't change things which were in existence before the world was young.

One of mankind's failure is in the belief that only his intellect governs, rules and controls this reality, not giving way to the possibility of older intellects, ruled and operated on this earth long before man.

All around man, things and properties operate without man's knowledge, awareness or intervention, yet only a few dare ask the questions leading to a true understanding of all things.

Some time ago, a few started to ask the questions, started to search the truth, but somehow, somewhere along the way, man's arrogance blinded him to what has been and is now.

Introduction

Ohio like any other state, experiences months of cold and snowfall, undergoing the process of winter, to the emergence of spring.

Expecting to go from the cold and snow to the first signs of spring, is the norm, but things aren't always what they seem.

Signs in the home improvement stores and people pulling from garages, attics, and basements, last year's many yard trinkets.

The occasional School buses starting and stopping and the sounds of children's laughter, and the signal of the end of a day and the promise of a new, fill the streets.

A solitary lawn mower is heard in the distance and then one after the other, along with the sporadic parents calling their children in for supper.

These sounds along with the occasional dog barking all spell the sound of normalcy, which was only masking something else, something a little out of the norm which was rearing its head.

That's when a different darkness and coldness was ushering in for the residents of the towns of Port Clinton and Columbus, Ohio in two-thousand-twelve.

Had the residents of these cities been more concerned with their surroundings instead of their manicured lawns, yard floral design, and bland existences of the back-yard parties and cookouts they would have seen the coming darkness and felt a different spring approaching.

Columbus, Ohio
German Village 1911

German Village in the mid seventeen hundred in Columbus, Ohio was both the beginning of a promise for the immigrants of Europe and a curse for the newly developed city.

By the early eighteen hundreds, many German immigrants arrived daily to Columbus, Ohio from Europe, and by eighteen-fourteen, the 'Alte Südende' settlement, commonly referred to as German Village was born.

By mid-eighteen hundred, thousands of Germans escaped the economic disasters of Europe and migrated to Columbus, Ohio in the hope of new dreams and a fresh start for their families.

Some of the most prominent and first places in German Village was Saint Francis Xavier Roman Catholic Church, Schiller Park Town Hall, Hahn's fish market, the local farmer's market and F & R Lazarus Department store.

During the early twentieth century, the short mid-east-side of Columbus saw newcomers from eastern Europe as well as Hungarian immigrants, resulting in a vibrant and thriving German-Hungarian community.

Along with this dual neighborhood of immigrants, revealed a dark dual religious system. A religious system of German Roman Catholic faith mingled with Gypsy practices.

While the Roman Catholics had an established religious order, the Hungarians practiced a darker, paganist order, full of spells, witchcraft, curses and human sacrifices.

As the two communities began flourishing in Columbus, Ohio so were many strange and unexplainable occurrences given birth to.

The most talked about place in German Village in the mid-eighteen hundred was, the enormous church at Four-Twelve Rhinegeist and Studer streets.

Along with the introduction of many customs and practices such as Halloween, Fasching and Krampus Eve, came many rumors of missing children, strange noises and screams heard, all hours of the nights, as well as rumored sights of horned creatures, lurking the church grounds.

Of all the mysterious places in German village, Saint Francis Xavier Roman Catholic Church carried its share of whispered secrets.

The church leader was Monsignor Frederic Klaussstein, a fifty-nine-year-old Berliner and fifty-eight-year-old Sister Mary Jacalyn Mayer from Nuremberg.

As the German-Hungarian community was flourishing, so were the rumors and unexplained events.

One of the first programs put in place by Monsignor Frederic Klausstein, was the School for Prospect Nuns, headed up by Sister Mary Jacalyn Mayer.

In every place, and in every corner, everything that happened in Columbus, had to be approved by the church, and there was always Sister Mary Jacalyn Mayer in the background.

Her parents were from Nuremberg German, while her grandparents were from Eger Hungary, a secret she kept hidden from the church. As much as Sister Mary Jacalyn's bloodline was mixed, so were her ideals, thoughts and practices even, her loyalties were divided.

Sister Mary Jacalyn's main duty in the church was to interview and assist young girls between the ages of fourteen to sixteen-year-old, who were brought to the church by their parents to be taught in the German-Roman Catholic order of Nuns.

Sister Mary Jacalyn was slightly over five-feet-eight-inches tall, with a masculine staunch to her posture.

Her demeanor was an unusual characteristic to pin down, a cross between one who is strict and one who is on the verge of a major sanity leak.

Sister Mary Jacalyn was sent to assist Monsignor Frederic Klausstein, after she was discharged by the church in Nuremberg with many accounts of sexual deviance with young girls and inappropriate liberties with small children.

One of the conditions placed on Sister Mary Jacalyn was that she was to have no hands-on contact with young girls, yet she found herself in charge of young girls by Monsignor Frederic Klaussstein.

Within the first six months of heading up the young girls project, multiple rumors and whispers circled around Sister Mary Jacalyn, by some parents of the girls, nonetheless Sister Mary Jacalyn's behavior was never called into question.

In the spring of eighteen-sixty-nine, the community of German Village, due to the war saw a once thriving community on the verge of collapse and void of hope.

In order for many families to eat, the community's young daughters were given over into the care of the Church to be prepared in the order of Nuns. The church would then provide daily meals and allow members of the families to farm and tend one of the many empty fields that the church owned.

To the early immigrants of Columbus, Ohio this seemed like a great opportunity. The men could look for meaningful work, while the women and the young sons would tend the fields, but...

Something was happening, something far more sinister than anyone imagined was happening at the church and in the fields. A hand was being dealt... a hand of distorted realities, a hand from where there would be no shuffling or redealing.

Monday, May 16, 1869
Saint Francis Xavier Roman Catholic Church.
4:45 a.m.

The first sign that something was wrong in the now over populated community of German Village was when Mrs. Klum, a German immigrant went to St. Francis' to deliver a message to her daughter that her father had just died of influenza.

When Mrs. Klum turned her daughter over to the care of St. Francis's, she was informed that the children were to have no visitors from the outside community for six years, no letters, nor visitor's, but Mrs. Klum felt surely, a message such as this would be accepted...but it was not.

Upon meeting Sister Mary Jacalyn at the front door of the church, Mrs. Klum spent the better part of an hour explaining to Sister Mary Jacalyn that her daughter, Kathryn needed to know this as she was very close to her father.

Sister Mary Jacalyn explained to Mrs. Klum that while her daughter was not available to personally take the message, that it would be delivered.

Mrs. Klum accepted the explanation of a delivered message, which she would live to regret her actions of leaving without demanding to see her daughter that day.

Sister Mary Jacalyn closed the door and tore up the message, discarding it into a trash can, without reading its contents.

Sister Mary Jacalyn made her way to the office of the Monsignor and after knocking, entered saying...

"We have a problem, Monsignor."

The Monsignor listened to Sister Mary Jacalyn and then replied...

"No Sister, you have a problem...I entrusted into your hands, all of the day to day things, now if you can't handle this I'm sure I can find someone who can.

All I expect from you is, for you to ensure that I get my bed time services, without pause."

Walking away with a scowl look upon her face, Sister Mary Jacalyn by-passed her room and entered through a door at the end of the hall on the second floor.

The stairs led to a massive hall with several rooms. Removing a large key ring from her pocket, Sister Mary Jacalyn opened a door and entered a room which held a dozen young whimpering girls shackled to the walls and beds.

Hungry and scared, these girls were all crying out to Sister Mary Jacalyn for food and water, of which she ignored.

Of all the girls crying, Sister Mary Jacalyn walked towards the end of the room to the bed of one girl who lay silent.

A red-haired girl with freckles, kind of a homely looking girl, with deep green eyes and a not so nervous look upon her face.

Sister Mary Jacalyn approached her bed and after gently caressing her face, took out a pin from the hem of her dress and pricked the girl's finger.

Sister Mary Jacalyn then, smeared blood from girl's finger on the little girl's cheeks and then unlocked the shackles which kept her bound and the two of them headed towards the door...past the other girls, past the cries and whimpering into the outer hallway.

Sister Mary Jacalyn and this young girl climbed the stair well which was dimly lit until it revealed a single door, which Sister Mary Jacalyn unlocked.

The door opened to a hallway, riddled with cobwebs and a musty and moldy smell. Sister Mary Jacalyn led the little red-head girl down the hall and into a small room off the right of the hallway.

Lighting a large candle which sat on a small table near the door, Sister Mary Jacalyn led the little red-head girl into the room and over to a chair which sat in the middle of the room.

Before closing the door, Sister Mary Jacalyn pointed the young girl to a basin of water and a cake of lye soap, telling her to wash and afterwards, to dress in a white bed dress draped on the bed.

Sister Mary Jacalyn brushed the red headed girl's hair and instructed her to sit on the bed and wait.

With the swell of immigrants pouring into Columbus Ohio... proper meals and housing was hard to come by, not to mention that the

Church was an all-powerful-necessity with the immigrants, and never has anything bad ever been tied directly to the church...but something was wrong at Saint Francis Xavier German-Roman Catholic Church, something was terribly wrong.

Sister Mary Jacalyn left the room after several minutes and locked the door behind herself and headed to the Monsignor's room.

Sister Mary Jacalyn knocked on the door and within minutes the door opened and there was Monsignor Klausstein, standing, wearing nothing but a white night shirt and a red pair of slippers.

Monsignor Klausstein welcomed Sister Mary Jacalyn in and after she took a seat, poured her a glass of wine saying...

"Well now Sister, do you have my bed services ready?"

Sister Mary Jacalyn rose to her feet and after finishing her wine, poured another and said...

"Yes, she is fourteen years of age, pretty, freckles and green eyes with red hair."

Licking his lips and combing his hair while touching himself, Monsignor opened his legs, and while playing with himself, said...

"Is she a screamer, or will she just lay there, because you know I like them screaming."

Sister Mary Jacalyn sat her empty glass down on the table and said...

"I told her to be a Nun in this holy order, she has to get rid of all worldly desires and the only way to show the Monsignor that she has, is to show him that her body is free and belongs to the Monsignor's service."

Monsignor Klausstein leaned back in his chair, looking at Sister Mary Jacalyn as she walked towards the door, saying...

"As a matter of fact, I also picked out a twelve-year-old dark hair Hungarian girl. She's a juicy and plump young girl, with small lips and big brown eyes who I promised would be stationed in Rome itself if she did as you asked...she shall be yours as well, as soon as I am through with her."

As Sister Mary Jacalyn left the room, Monsignor Klausstein said...

"Oh, by the way, make sure Boris burns and disposes of all of their belongings when he gets rid of the bodies..."

The door shut as Sister Mary Jacalyn *said...*

"Of course, Monsignor."

Over the next fifteen years, this scene continued to play out over and over, night after night. The desperate residents, bringing their young daughters to the church for a few dollars, food and the promise of training their daughters in the order as a Nun, when they were really trained as sex slaves for devious minds, and discarded in the middle of the night.

This misuse and abuse by Sister Mary Jacalyn couldn't go on, or could it? Many parents came close to reporting the despicable things which they believed were happening to their children, only to be threaten by the church, or to have wagons of meat and other foods appearing at their front doors in exchange for their silence.

After fifteen years, of rape and abuse and hundreds of missing or murdered children, the parents received a break...one of the young girls escaped from the church and hid out at her uncle's house at the edge of German Village.

When she was convinced that it was safe for her to tell her story along with her parents, she presented her case not only to the local Dispatch news, but to a group who called themselves the 'Rights Group' who were in disguise the city's largest anti-Catholic group.

The enormous pressure by the 'Rights Group' prompted an immediate investigation into the church's' activities. Monsignor Klausstein and Sister Mary Jacalyn, upon learning that an investigation was ordered, and the Police were standing at the gates, protecting the church, attempted to destroy all evidence and to hustle the remaining young girls off in one of the secret passages, until they could be smuggled off in middle of the night to be sold or worse.

Unfortunate for Monsignor Klausstein and Sister Mary Jaclyn, they were eventually captured, tried and convicted, but were never punished.

Monsignor Klausstein and Sister Mary Jacalyn were remanded to the confines of the church, but one day they both disappeared into the night.

It was rumored that Monsignor Klausstein, with the assistance of the church in New York, was whisked away on a freighter bound for Europe, and Sister Mary Jacalyn, suffered a total mental collapse and was confined to a mental asylum, somewhere in New York.

In the spring of eighteen hundred and ninety-eight, while making rounds of the patients in the asylum, it was discovered that Sister Mary Jacalyn escaped and was never seen again.

Several inquiries were made into the disappearance of Sister Mary Jacalyn, but nothing led to the capture of Sister Mary Jacalyn.

The only clue which remained behind at all of the sightings, of Sister Mary Jacalyn, was a skeleton key, with a red ribbon tied to it, and on the wall, a picture of a toad near an oven and under it, the word....

'Kinder'.

Prologue

When we last read, David Blue was being released from the Veterans Psychiatric Hospital in Columbus, for believing that he was seeing people who were not there and claiming that his friends were disappearing.

David and his friends, plus many other residents of Columbus are being visited by a Nun, named Sister Mary Jacalyn. As this story continues, they discover that Sister Mary Jacalyn is more than what she appears to be.

Sister Mary Jacalyn is neither dead nor alive, she is neither flesh nor spirit... but she possesses one very unique ability, which, all who come in contact with her, will soon discover.

One by one, David & Deanne's five friends were either tormented or killed, along with some of their neighbors, while David and Deanne and their friends, are confronted by beings, spirits and things uninvited, whose purpose remains a mystery.

Lastly, David and Deanne's neighbor on the farm in Port Clinton, proved to be much more then they seemed, as they and a large man in a Ballerina's Tutu, chased them and a host of other people relentlessly all over David and Deanne's farm in what proved to be a deadly game of cat and mouse, or is it?

One of David and Deanne's friends has opened a portal into another reality, thereby drawing a dangerous being from another reality into theirs. This being, has the power to alter one's reality and perception into whatever she chooses, whenever she chooses.

David, Deanne and their friends have but a little time to figure out, who opened this portal and close it, or else, along with the residents of Columbus and Port Clinton will be doomed to relive multiple realities over and over, until they become a part of another realm, another place.

I
Wake Up

David awakened from sleep and found Deanne's hand and kissed her fingers as Deanne squirmed and moaned saying...

"Oh Blue, good morning."

David Blue continued to kiss and caress Deanne's hand and neck saying...

"Oh babe, I had the weirdest dream ever...I dreamt about a man in a Ballerina's Tutu and that..."

Cutting him off, Deanne said...

"We were at the farm and Wendi was dead."

David replied...

"Omg.... Were we dreaming the same dream babe, how weird is that..."

Deanne looked over at David saying...

"Weird or not all I can say is that I'd bet anything that there's some truth to it, I mean, I dreamt that Wendi was dead, and Kristin and Mary were tortured beyond belief, and you dreamt the same thing..."

Deanne started humming the sound to the Twilight Zone, as she headed to the bathroom while David went downstairs saying...

"Hey sweets, coffee will be ready in a bit, you want me to fix you a cup or do you want to pour own?"

"No babe, I'll pour my own...give me about fifteen minutes."

David headed into the kitchen and then hollered...

"DEANNE!"

After calling Deanne a second time she emerged in the kitchen to see David standing near the refrigerator and her best friend Wendi sitting at the table in her robe drinking coffee.

With looks of bewilderment cemented on the faces of David and Deanne, Wendi turned sipping her coffee saying...

"Morning you two?

Deanne and David stood frozen *in their tracks and visibly shaken.*

Deanne slowly walked towards Wendi saying...

"Wendi, when did you get here and how long have you been here?"

Wendi sat her coffee cup down and said...

"Oh, I came down early in the morning, around two, but I didn't wanna wake you or Dave, so I just used my key... by the way Dave, you didn't have problems parking last night did you, the rain was coming down so hard when I got here...all I could do was get from the car to the house...I didn't see your car at all."

David and Deanne looked at one another and then at Wendi with a disturbing gaze, they all felt that something far sinister had just happened, when Wendi said...

"I would've poured you all coffee when I heard you two stirring, but it's not coffee I'm drinking, I'm drinking vodka, and I'm going to have another cup when this one is done."

As Wendi started to refill her cup Deanne handed her two cups and said...

"You'd best pour us a cup too."

Wendi filled the first cup and then the second saying...

"A man in a truck followed me near here and then I think he murdered me, and then I woke up here, alive...I couldn't have dreamed it...it happened I know it did.

I was driving to you Deanne, and the next thing I know I'm being chased by some big man. I remember he had me in the woods then he killed me."

David Blue took a large swig from his cup saying...

"I'm going to call Tim and Mary and see if they're alright, I remember that Mary was beat pretty bad."

David dialed Tim and Mary's number and as it was ringing Deanne said...

"Okay, we just went through some creepy stuff, how likely is it that all three

of us dreamed the same thing...but how did we get back here and why do we remember the same thing?"

David began leaving Mary and Tim a message on their answering machine and turned to Deanne saying...,

"Hey, it doesn't matter as long as we're back ...right?"

Wendi walked over to David saying...

"Don't you see...we at least got back, what if this shit happens again."

Just then Deanne's cell phone began ringing.

Deanne left the kitchen for the living room for a little privacy, and when she returned she said...

"Looks like we're going to have a little company, that was Mary, she said her, and Tim were leaving the farm, heading to Columbus."

David walked over to Deanne as she handed him the phone as David also read the message.

Giving Deanne the phone back David said...

"What in the hell are they doing at our farm?"

Wendi interrupted...

"The farm.... who's coming to the farm?"

Deanne was explaining the phone message to Wendi, when Wendi jumped, forgetting that her cell phone was on vibrate in her pocket.

Wendi answered her phone to a most welcoming voice, her husband Steve, who was on a hunting trip.

"Hello babe."

Steve said nervously.

Wendi waved her hand to motion everyone to quiet their voices and said...

"Oh, hi sweets, I didn't call because you told me not to call you while you were hunting, is everything alright?"

Steve took a couple of deep breaths saying...

"I'm alright, I'm going to be leaving here in a few minutes, I just wanted to know where you were."

Wendi walked over to the opposite side of the room saying...

"Baby, I'm with Dave and Deanne at their condo..."

Steve was about to ask Wendi what made her take a three-and-a-half-hour drive to Port Clinton, when his voice broke and he softly told Wendi...

"Wen, something happened up here and I'm not sure about some things... just stay there, I'll be there by noon, okay?"

Wendi asked Steve...
"Baby are you sure everything's alright...the tone in your voice is scaring me?"
Before hanging up Steve said...
"Look let me speak to Dave really quick."
Wendi walked over to Deanne and David handed him the phone saying...
"Here Dave, he wants to talk to you."
David took the phone and said...
"Hey what's up grunt dog?"
Steve tried to disguise the fear in his voice as he replied...
"You know me...kicking ass and taking names. Dave, I'm leaving the wildlife area and I told Wendi to wait there...something happened up here man, and I-I-I need to run some things past you, I'll be there in five hours...okay?"
Before handing the phone to Wendi, David said...
"Sure, thing dude, but were not at the farm."
Handing the phone to Wendi, David said...
"Wow, I don't believe that shit.?
Both Wendi and Deanne said together...
What?"
David walked over to the table and sat down saying...
"Something must really have him all jacked up because, I served with him in the Nam and this is the first time that I've ever known him to be rattled."

Deanne walked behind David and as she massaged his shoulders, said...
"You know, come to think of it...Steve was part of this whole ugly nightmare, I bet he is finally figuring the same things out that we are, that's what I think."
Wendi stood over by the window looking out and saying in a somber voice as Deanne came over to her...
"This is all messed up, we were all at your place, Deanne, in Port Clinton, with this nasty old man and the big fucker in the Ballerina's Tutu, and then

suddenly we're here in Columbus...how can stuff like this be happening, I mean shit like this only happens in the movies or on Twilight Zone...pardon my French."

Rubbing her shoulders, Deanne said...

"Look girl, don't apologize, I think...we all earned the right to curse if we want, besides I feel what you're saying, how did all this shit start anyways."

As Deanne and Wendi walked over and sat on the sofa, David stood in front of them saying...

"You wanna know how this started and all, but nobody listened to me when I said I was seeing all this creepy shit...now you'll believe me from now on."

Looking at David, Deanne replied...

Honey how were we or anyone for that matter supposed to believe in some weird shit like that, I mean if I came to you saying the kind of shit you were saying would you have believed me?"

Wendi joined in saying...

"Yeah Dave, but you were talking about seeing things and people that weren't there and all of that, not to mention being admitted into the psychiatric ward...how were we or anyone else supposed to have taken you seriously...huh?"

David walked over to the wine rack and pulled out a bottle of Chardonnay and after pouring a glass said...

"Well, you were supposed to consider the source, and, in this case, it happened to be me."

"I believe that ship sailed, when you talk about believing in you...I just don't get how and why these spirits are picking on us, I mean there are lots of other people who deserve to be fucked with."

Lifting his glass too fast to his mouth, David spilled his wine on his shirt and tried wiping it off as he said...

"One of the Doppelgangers told me, eighty years ago a Nun named Sister Mary Jacalyn, was investigated over the same kind of stuff that happened to us, but everything was abandoned because she just up and disappeared like a fart in the wind."

"So, this kind of shit has happened to other people before...why hasn't none of this be in the news or papers?"

Wendi replied as she noticed Deanne's preoccupation with her nails.

Taking a big long sip of wine, David said...

"Haven't you ever read those magazines in the checkout stands in the supermarkets, not all of the stuff in there is BS."

Deanne looked over at David saying...

"Blue how about pouring me and Wendi a glass, I'm tired of being sober and dealing with this."

David stood up and headed for the kitchen when Wendi said...

"No wine for me, but I could go for a double vodka...with the shit were dealing with, wine ain't gonna do it."

David handed Deanne and Wendi their drinks as Deanne said...

"Blue, why haven't you said anything about this before, this is the first time I'm hearing this."

David refilled his glass and when he came back in the living room, he said...

"For starters, I didn't know anything about this until the Doppelganger said so up at the farm. Hell, I looked it up on the internet, that's how I found out about it, besides I kept trying to tell all of you, but no one listened."

Wendi sat her drink on the coffee table saying...

"The question I have is...what are we going to do about this, heck I wouldn't even know who to report this to, so what do we do...just sit here waiting for it to happen again?"

Deanne turned to Wendi saying...

"I can tell you this, Tim, Mary and Steve are on their way here...let's wait until they get here, and then we can figure something out."

Deanne and Wendi noticed that David was looking all around the living room and not talking, when Deanne asked...

"What is it Blue?"

David said...

"Shone, where the hell is Shone. OMG!!! We're at the farm again."

Deanne walked over to David saying...

"Earth to Blue...I left Shone with Clara and Bill in Columbus...don't go squirrely on me Blue, and why wouldn't we be at the farm?"

Monday

Clara and her husband Bill Scott got up early Monday morning to take their daily morning walk with their dog.

Their neighbor, Deanne had left a message with Clara that they had an emergency at the farm and that they had left Shone in the house, and for them to look after her until they returned Monday afternoon.

Clara met up with Bill, who was trying to cover up the fact that he had just sneaked a puff or two of a cigarette.

Bill Scott is a retired Firefighter and Clara, whose real name is Clarissa is a Certified Public Accountant, who works from home.

Clara caught up with Bill who was standing near a large oak tree one block away as both dogs greeted one another with wagging tails and smelling one another.

Shone is a two-year-old Golden Retriever and Charles is a four-year-old white and golden rough Collie, very much like Lassie, of the television series, but a short version.

Shone and Charlie were well liked dogs by just about everyone who lived in the neighborhood and every time both Charlie and Shone were being walked together the neighbors would comment on how pretty the two dogs looked together.

Mercy park is a medium sized park complete with all the comforts of your normal large city parks...play area for children, small pond with ducks, gated pet area, and the two-mile walking trail.

Like all parks, pets had to be on a leash and the owner had to carry with them a pet waste bag.

Clara and Bill missed their opportunity to go walking over the weekend because it rained both Saturday and Sunday and decided to take advantage of the cool but dry Monday morning.

The weather was mild for Clara and Bill's walk, partly sunny, a light breeze with temperatures holding steady at fifty-five degrees.

Clara and Bill lived on Pecan Drive ever since the sub division was developed twelve years ago and knew almost everyone in the neighborhood.

It was rumored that their subdivision was originally several burial sites of the Mohican Indian tribe back in the early eighteen hundreds and some neighbors have even reported seeing strange lights in the middle of the night and hearing drums and singing in the distant open fields.

The area where the subdivision is located, was ten miles from the nearest business, so if you needed anything, your best bet was to shop before getting home, because if you tried coming back into the area, you had to face hundreds of cars coming from all over to that one small area.

The nearest business near the Alum Creek sub-division is a two-year-old strip mall which was developed to serve the residents in the Alum Creek sub-division, however people from all over Columbus and the surrounding area flooded the small Alum Creek strip mall, making it difficult for the sub-division residents to shop without making it an all-day event.

Clara had plans to head to the strip mall, do whatever shopping she needed to do for the morning and then spend the afternoon working on several accounts in her office, while Bill was going to be packing up and storing all the patio furniture in the outside shed while the weather was half-way decent.

After leaving Mercy Park, Bill and Clara walked Shone and Charlie through the sub-division and after two hours of walking headed back to their home on Pecan Drive.

Once Clara and Bill returned home from their morning walk, they noticed David and Deanne's car in the drive, but decided to keep Shone with them, thinking Deanne and David needed sleep.

Clara went into her office to check her messages while Bill let Shone and Charlie out into the back yard, unaware that there was something else in the yard moving just underneath the surface of the ground.

As Bill turned his back to go inside he noticed Shone and Charlie racing and barking to several spots in the yard and frantically digging.

As Shone and Charlie were digging up the grass and dirt in one area, something underground caused the turf to pop up in the air, making the dogs yelp and jump.

Bill hollered for the dogs to quiet down, when Clara tapped Bill on the shoulder saying...

"What are they doing?"

They're digging holes in the yard...I guess I'm going to have to get some mole bait and set them out."

Bill said as he closed the door.

Clara followed behind Bill sipping her tea and stated...

"Moles...we've never been bothered with moles."

Bill turned and as he did he took the cup from Clara's hand and took a sip of her tea as Clara said...

"Hey...go make your own."

Bill kissed Clara and stated...

"I like yours better."

Clara walked into her office and sarcastically replied...

"No, you don't...you're just too lazy to make your own."

Bill headed for the kitchen and said...

"Okay...when Mr. lazy makes eggs, pancakes and sausage, don't come sniffing around my plate either."

Clara turned and blew Bill a kiss saying...

"Mmm, pancakes, sausage and eggs...sounds yummy, I want my eggs over easy."

Before going in to make breakfast, Bill should have paid more attention to what was causing Shone and Charlie to behave so erratically.

Had Bill paid a little more attention he would have notice that it was not moles which had evaded his yard...but something else, something far worse than moles.

Bill and Clara sat down to a hearty breakfast of eggs, pancakes, sausage and orange juice when Bill heard Shone barking and growling and Charlie letting out a large yelp.

Cramming an entire sausage link into his mouth Bill got up and walked towards the kitchen window with his glass of orange juice, saying...

"Now what!

Bill looked out the window and at first, all he saw was Shone barking and then at the far end of the yard he saw Charlie with both of his front legs sticking in what he thought were holes in the yard.

Turning to Clara who was on her feet, Bill said...

Damn...it seems that Charlie's front legs are stuck in a hole that they were digging...I'll be back in a minute."

As Bill walked out into the back yard, he could easily see that Charlie's two front legs were deep inside of two holes or a large hole as Bill thought...

"*How in Skippy did they dig a hole that deep?*"

What Bill didn't know was that Charlie didn't accidentally get stuck in the holes, but something underneath the ground grabbed Charlie and was holding onto to him, trying to pull him in the ground.

Bill got up to Charlie who was yelping and whimpering when Bill cried out...

"*C'mon Charlie...C'mon boy.*"

Bill saw Charlie's back legs kicking and clawing in the dirt as he got down on his knees to pull Charlie's legs out of the holes.

Clara came running out the back door, when Bill hollered to her saying...

"*I can't believe it...grab Shone, don't let her come over here!*"

Clara grabbed Shone's collar as she stood watching Bill struggling to free Charlie's front legs from the ground.

Bill jumped to his feet and ran past Clara to the outside shed and grabbed a shovel and raced back to Charlie saying to Clara.

"*I can't believe it...something is actually pulling Charlie's legs!*"

Clara shouted to Bill as she held onto Shone's collar...

"*What-What do you mean something is holding onto Charlie's legs, that doesn't make sense!*"

Bill began digging large shovels full of dirt all around Charlie's legs as he hollered back at Clara...

"*I know that sounds crazy, but...*"

Bill stopped talking because something in the hole which he had just dug near Charlie's legs caught his attention.

Bill shouted over to Clara...

"*Let Shone in the house and get over here...hurry!*"

Clara opened the door and let Shone in and ran out into yard. Clara screamed as she looked in the hole that Bill dug...

"*WHAT THE HELL!*"

What Clara saw startled her at first and then made her afraid. Clara saw that the blade of the shovel was pinning what looked like fingers against the dirt.

Bill turned and looked at Clara and said...

"Do you believe this shit...these are fingers, what the hell!"

Bill's grip of the shovel started to slip as he placed his right foot on the shovel for more pressure.

Suddenly the fingers which were gripped onto Charlie's legs disappeared, as Charlie ran as fast as he could to the house with Bill and Clara following him.

Bill and Clara stood looking out the back door as their back yard suddenly began moving up and down like the shape of waves in the ocean, then the entire ground returned to normal, not even the hole that Bill dug was there.

Bill and Clara sat in the living room checking Charlie's legs while Shone lay huddled near the front door.

As Bill and Clara inspected Charlie's legs they noticed deep finger claw marks to his right leg, nothing serious but Clara cleaned the cuts with hydrogen peroxide to prevent infection from setting in.

Bill turned to Clara as he walked to the kitchen window saying...

"Honey what in the hell just happened? I know I'm not imagining things, but did we just see..."

Clara interrupted Bill saying...

"Don't say it...I'm too freaked out to think about it right now...did you see the ground moving and all that?"

Bill stood nervously looking out the window and said...

"Damn, I don't know what to think, but I can tell you this...this shit is way too messed up."

Uncertain and unsure of what to do, Bill called one of his neighbors, Russell Locklear who lives two doors down the street and asked him to come over.

Russell Locklear and his wife Tonya are originally from Scranton Pennsylvania, and while they are both from Scranton, they met one another a year after moving to Columbus, Ohio.

At fifty-two, Russell Locklear who started out in the janitorial department with General Motors, is a poster boy for how hard work pays off by being promoted to finished products production manager.

Russell's wife Tonya began her career in Scranton, Pennsylvania as a mail carrier for the post office twenty-four years ago, and after a messy divorce transferred to Columbus, Ohio, where she met Russell.

Russell and Tonya are two-time divorcees with a total of six children between them.

While Russell is only two years older than Tonya, he never misses an opportunity to act as if he is much older, which when he does... pisses Tonya off.

How Bill and Russell became and remain good friends is a mystery. Bill is relatively quiet, but direct when he's engaged in conversation, while Russell is loud, arrogant and assuming, yet they both feed off one another.

Tonya and Clara are somewhat different. Clara and Tonya are both forty-nine, prior divorcees with several children and that is where the similarities end.

Tonya is a Charismatic Christian while Clara is a practicing Buddhist. Bill and Russell try to have weekly invites especially during the football and baseball season but have found it a challenge to get together without having both Clara and Tonya in the same room.

Tonya seizes every opportunity to interject her belief of 'claim it and speak it', while Clara counters with 'you are who you were, once you've been enlightened'...and thus the battle wages on from there.

Whenever Clara and Tonya are in the same room together, Bill and Russell try as best they can to tune them both out...believing that during those times, that they are both full of it.

Bill is a member of the Baptist faith and attends church services during the holidays such as Easter Sunrise, Christmas and occasionally Mother's Day services, while Russell rarely attends services at all.

Russell finds contentment with observing the philosophy of treating his fellow man with kindness and honesty and enjoying a good movie and a six pack of cold beer.

Bill will appease Clara with an occasional appearance at her church, simply to avoid Clara's non-church attending Christian ..." you're going to hell" conversations.

Shone and Charlie were both asleep in the dog room, while Clara was checking her phone, wondering why Deanne and David hadn't come to get Shone, since they're home.

Bill laid the daily newspaper down and picked up his phone and dialed Russell's number.

Bill was about to hang up the phone when Russell answered it saying...

"Afternoon Bill, nasty little storm we had last night huh...so, what's shaking?"

Bill cleared his throat and then walked over to the kitchen window, looking out into the back yard and said...

"Hi, how ya doing buddy, you got a few minutes...I need to show you something can you come right over?"

Russell responded...

"Can do...I'll toss a six pack in a plastic bag and head right over."

Russell should have asked a few more questions before agreeing to come right over, if he had he would have changed his mind and stayed at home...or for that matter left the state altogether.

Russell put his sneakers on and placed a six pack of beer in a plastic bag and headed for the back door.

Russell held the bag in the air and hollered to Tonya...

"Bill wanted me to come over to show me something, he sounded a little serious so I'm heading over there to see what's up."

Tonya reached up and pulled her hair into a pony tail and looking at the plastic bag of beer said...

"Looks like you guys plan on making it an all afternoon thingy."

Walking over to kiss Tonya goodbye, Russell said...

"No don't worry... this is for later, you know Bill's not a beer drinker, so I'm bringing my own...besides, I don't plan on spending all day there."

As Russell headed out the door, Tonya said...

"Don't forget, you promised to take this cute white ass out to eat tonight."

Russell headed out the back door saying...

"Yea-yea-yeah I know."

Russell headed down the steps and then out the back gate. It was only a half a block from Russell's house to Bill's. Bill and Clara lived at the end of the cul-de-sac on Pecan Drive, while Russell and Tonya lived at the beginning of Pecan Drive Ct.

As Russell walked towards Bill's house he noticed the warning rain clouds circling above his head and thought to himself...

"I could catch a break and get out of going out to eat tonight if it waits and then storms hard enough."

Russell hurried down the street to Bill's house and as he did, he paid no attention to the neighboring yards he passed, but if he had he would've noticed that the ground and grass was moving up and down as if something barely underneath the ground was about to surface.

Bill saw Russell coming up his walkway and came outside to meet him. Both men stood on the front walkway talking for a few minutes when Russell said...

"Okay you got me down here so what is it that you wanted me to see?"

Bill motioned with his hand saying...

"Back here...me and Clara were out here earlier this morning with the dogs...let me show you."

Bill arrived at the spot in the back yard where Charlie's legs were stuck in the ground and pointing to the spot, he said...

"It was right here."

Russell looked down to where Bill was pointing and then all around saying...

"Okay, I'm looking but what am I supposed to see except the fact that you need to cut your grass."

Bill squatted down and looking up to Russell said...

"Charlie and Shone were digging around here and the next thing I know is, Charlie's two front paws were stuck in a hole and when I went to pull his legs out, I felt something..."

Russell cut Bill off saying...

"Either I need one of these or you do because I don't see a hole...hell, I don't see anything."

Raising his voice, a little bit Bill said...

"Look I know how this sounds but if you think I'm full of it, you can ask Clara she was out here with me when all of this happened. I'm telling you, there was something underground pulling on Charlie's legs."

Russell snapped the tab off a beer and knelt beside Bill and feeling all around the ground said...

"Look pal, there's nothing here. The grass is solid, are you sure you weren't..."

Bill stood up saying…

"Aww man c'mon…do you think I'd call you down here for some bullshit. Damn I'm trying to tell you something was really pulling on Charlie's legs…the least you could do is not to patronize me…shit!"

Russell stood up and offered Bill a beer saying…

"Bill, I'm not trying to come off like an ass but, I mean what do you expect…do you think that I'm supposed to believe that there is something underground pulling on your dog's legs…I mean how messed up is that?"

Bill took a swig of beer and looking at the beer can, said…

"First, why can't you buy something worth drinking and secondly all I was asking was for you to listen and you can't even do that.

I'm telling you…look, when I grabbed the shovel and dug around the hole there were these creepy ass fingers holding on to his front legs."

Chugging the rest of his beer down and looking around the yard, Russell said as he wiped his mouth…

"Bill I'm not trying to deal with stupid this early in the day, but don't you know how ridiculous this sounds…I mean what if I came at you with something like this, what would you say?"

Just at that time Clara came out of the house and as she approached Bill and Russell she said…

"Hey, you two…what are you doing?"

Russell turned as Clara came up to Bill and hugged him saying…

"How ya doing Clarissa, Bill was just telling me about a little excitement you two had out here."

Bill leaned into Clara and kiss her and then said…

"Clara, will you tell Russell about the creepy ass hands that were holding down Charlie's legs and about the ground moving?"

Clara looked at Bill and said…

"Honey, what are you talking about. Who was holding Charlie?"

Letting his beer drop to the ground and pointing down to the ground, said…

"Now come on Clara, you mean to stand here and say that you don't remember that something was holding onto Charlie's legs. Are you going to say the ground wasn't moving either!"

Clara took a step backwards and looking at Bill said…

"*Remember! There's nothing for me to remember, what the hell is all of this about Russ?*"

At that moment, Bill walked off and went into the house leaving Clara and Russell standing in the back yard when Clara said...

"*I'm sorry about all of this Russ, Bill's been having headaches and bad dreams for the past couple days and...*"

As Clara was apologizing for Bill, Russell said...

"*It's alright you don't have to explain...I mean maybe he tied a good one on and imagined the whole thing.*"

Clara and Russell turned and walked towards the house and while Russell exited through the side gate he stopped and said...

"*Tell Bill I'll call him a little later.*"

Clara waved at Russell as he walked down the walkway, as Bill stood inside the house watching through the window.

Clara walked into the house and noticing Bill standing at the window said...

"*Baby are you feeling alright...what was all of that about?*"

Bill turned around and started to walk away from Clara when she grabbed ahold to Bill's arm as he jerked away saying...

"*I can't believe you Clara...why in the hell did you tell Russell that bullshit about not knowing that anything was wrong with Charlie when you were right there and saw everything!*"

Clara threw her hands in the air saying...

"*What are you so pissed off about...talk to me Bill.*"

Bill stopped at the door and turned and said...

"*For starters, I'm not pissed off...I just don't understand why you said what you said.*

Clara walked up to Bill and as she reached for his hand said...

"*Bill, I know you're pissed off, because you called me Clarissa...now whenever you call me Clarissa, that means you're pissed off at me. Look, I don't have a clue as to what you're saying...I don't recall anything happening to Charlie, did you have another bad dream or something?*"

Bill was still visibly upset as he walked to the kitchen with Clara following him. Bill stopped at the window and pulled the drapes back and pointing saying...

"Are you going to stand there and tell me that you don't remember holding onto Shone while I was trying to get Charlie's leg out of the hole in the back yard?"

Clara stepped up to the window and looking out said...

Bill, I'm telling you the truth...I don't know anything about what you're talking about; if I saw something, then I would say I did...I'm not going to agree or disagree with something, when I don't know anything about it."

Bill walked over to the refrigerator and pulled out a bottle of wine and poured himself a glass saying...

"So, the next thing you're going to tell me is that I was hallucinating, or I was remembering a nightmare or some dip shit stuff like that?"

Clara reached her hand out and grabbed the glass of wine Bill had and took a sip and then gave the glass back to Bill, who said...

"Do you want me to pour you a glass, or are you going to just drink all of mine?"

Clara shook her head no, saying...

"No baby, I thought by me doing that, you'd think I was acting sexy...but I will say, you did have a few of them last night before you went to bed...maybe..."

Bill finished his glass and said as he walked over to Charlie and examining his legs...

"Clara, I'm sorry for blowing up, but I'm positive it wasn't a dream...I don't know, maybe it was a nightmare...but damn it was so real...I couldn't have been imagining all of that."

Clara walked up to Bill and kissed the back of his neck saying...

"Bad dreams, too much wine, not enough sleep, no sex, hell...I'm surprised you didn't see the Easter Bunny too... look I have a taste for some ice cream, I'm going to run down to the store...you need anything?"

Bill sat down on the sofa and laid his head back saying...

"Thanks, but no thanks...I'm good."

Five minutes after Bill laid his head back when the phone rang, picking up his phone Bill answered...

"Hello."

It was Russell calling Bill to see if he was alright as he said...

"Hi Bill, it's me Russ, I was calling to see if you were okay."

Bill took a deep breath before responding, saying...

"Yeah Russ, I'm good. I think I had one too many last night and I must have had another bad dream on top of that...sorry 'bout everything."

Russell assured Bill that it was nothing to get a jacked up about and as the two of them continued talking Bill looked down at his phone and noticed that Clara was trying to call him.

Bill ended his call with Russell saying...

"Hey Russ, I'm going to have to call you back sometime tomorrow...Clara's trying to call me...talk to you later."

Bill hung the phone up and tried answering Clara's call, but she hung up before he could switch over to her.

Bill instantly called Clara who answered her phone saying...

"Bill I just called you, would you do me a favor...I tried calling Deanne and David but I'm not getting either one of them to pick up, would you mind calling, and ask them, when do they want us to bring Shone over?"

Bill grabbed his glass and headed into the kitchen to pour another glass of wine saying...

"Sure, I can do that...but I'm sure they'll be down when they get up."

Clara entered the store and her phone began cutting in and out as she said...

"Bill...Bill look I'm going to hang up, my phone's cutting in and out."

Bill heard only a small portion of what Clara said as he hung the phone up and tried calling David's cell phone.

After several unsuccessful attempts, Bill tried calling Clara to let her know that he tried calling David but could not get through to him but kept receiving a message saying that the 'party he was trying to reach was not his service area'.

Bill sat back sipping on his wine and eating some cheese and crackers saying...

"That's ridiculous, how can Clara not be in our service area...the daggone store's not even a mile away."

Just then Charlie and Shone walked up to Bill wagging their tails and going back and forth from the front door, letting Bill know that they needed to get outside.

Bill walked over to the washing machine and removed the double leash and after putting it on Charlie and Shone started for the back door when he stopped saying…

"Oh, no you don't… there's no way in hell I'm going out there, especially at night and alone…no way!"

Bill turned around and after grabbing a jacket from the closet, walked the dogs to the front door.

As they went down the steps, Bill could tell that they were in for a storm later that evening. The wind was blowing and as Bill glanced up he saw that the clouds were dark and menacing.

Bill decided he was not going to go too far from the house in case they got a sudden downpour.

Bill and Clara have kept Shone for Deanne and David on numerous occasions and understood when Shone hears thunder or firecrackers, she heads for the bed and it takes hours before she'll come out.

With that in mind, Bill wrapped another piece of Shone's collar around his hand, and turned the corner onto Mound Street, one block from the house when he heard ominous rumblings of what was to come in the distance.

Mound Street was a short cul-de-sac with just four houses, so Bill decided once they made that circle that they would head home in seconds.

Twenty minutes after leaving the house Bill was headed back, when he looked up ahead and noticed Clara was heading up the steps to the house when he saw a bright flash followed by what sounded like a sonic boom.

Instinctively, Bill hunched his shoulders when suddenly and without warning, Shone took off jerking Bill so hard that he almost fell face first.

With Shone running at full speed and Charlie trying to keep up, Bill was being dragged up the steps to his house.

The clap of thunder was so loud it scared Shone and Charlie until both dogs nearly knocked down Clara who had just opened the front door.

Bill was doing everything that he could to hold onto both dogs as they darted past Clara and into the living room.

Clara slammed the door shut saying…

"Gosh you guys, it's just a little thunder…you just about knocked me the hell down, Bill?"

Bill was holding onto Charlie and trying to remove his section of the leash as he let go of Shone who had crawled under one of the living room chairs.

Bill reached under the chair and as he unhooked Shone said...

"What...was I supposed to do, you know how Shone is when she hears loud noises, besides that, I was doing everything I could to keep from being dragged by both of them."

Clara sat the bag with her ice cream, and strawberries down on the table and after kicking off her shoes, grabbed a bowl from the cabinet and walked towards the bedroom saying...

"Don't even think about it Bill, I can see you eyeing my bowl."

Bill folded the double dog leases up and placed them on top of the kitchen counter and after getting a bowl down for himself hollered...

"Aww C'mon Clara...you mean to tell me you're going keep all of that to yourself?"

Clara disappeared into the bedroom, softly shutting the door and turning on the television, to a movie.

Bill, opened the fridge and picked a few strawberries from the fridge and plucked them into his mouth, watching the storm as lightening lit up the night sky and the thunder crackling and popping, signaling a long night lay instore for the residents of Columbus.

Bill and Clara had gas heat, as Bill walked over and placed several logs in the fireplace and started a fire.

Grabbing another glass of wine from the fridge, Bill sat down in the recliner besides the fireplace and settled in for the evening.

Bill pulled his cell phone from his pocket and checked it for any missed calls. He was particularly looking for a call from Deanne and David regarding when they were going to pick up Shone, but there were no missed calls.

Little did Bill know, there was not going to be any calls from Deanne or David...at least not tonight.

Without realizing it, Bill's eyes were a lot heavier than he realized as his head fell back into the recliner and his eyes shut tight.

If Bill knew what was in store for him, he would have never fallen asleep. Bill woke up to the sounds of Shone and Charlie yelping and whining and to the sounds of something scratching.

As Bill opened his eyes, he glanced all around the living room and only seeing Shone and Charlie, stretched out his arms and yawned deep as he walked to the bedroom to check on Clara.

To Bill's surprise, when he opened the bedroom door Clara was not in bed asleep as he hoped she would be, so Bill walked into the bathroom thinking she was using it, but as he turned on the light, Clara was not there either.

Scratching his head and going from room to room, Clara was nowhere in the house. Bill looked out the front room window to see if Clara's car was there...and it was.

Next Bill walked back into the bedroom and upon entering he saw that Clara's cell phone and her purse and keys were laying on the nightstand next to her side of the bed.

"Where is she?"

Bill thought to himself as he stood in the middle of the living room scanning the entire area and then walked over and inspected both the front and the back door and found that they were locked, thinking...

"Okay...Clara's keys are upstairs in the bedroom, both doors are locked, so there's no way Clara left because she'd need her keys to lock the doors...but where in the hell is she?"

Again, Bill cut on all the lights on in the house and searched room after room calling Clara's name, but he got no answer. Bill picked up his cell phone and thought for a minute before using it...

"Now who in the hell am I going to call?"

For the second time that day, Bill was speechless and had no clue as to what to do. Almost every scenario played through Bill's head, even that Clara was hiding in one of the closets waiting to scare him.

Bill stood clueless in the living room, Shone and Charlie continued to whine and yelp when the scratching noises, which seemed to be coming from the front room window started up again.

Bill walked slowly over to the window and as he did he got this eerie feeling about what he might discover, when Shone yelped making Bill jump.

Bill could hear the rain pounding on the roof and against the window, as he inched even closer to the window.

Bill's hand slowly reached out for the drapes and as he was just about to grab it and pull it back, something cold, wet and hard pressed against his leg, making Bill turn and holler…

"SHIT!"

Looking down on the floor was Charlie who was scared at the reaction of Bill and hunched down with his paws on either side of his face.

Bill reached down to pat and ruffle Charlie as Shone remained underneath the chair whimpering.

Bill turned his attention once more to the window where he'd heard the scratching noises and as he approached the window, he turned to make sure that Charlie was staying put.

Seeing that Charlie had laid down near Shone, with two fingers Bill grabbed the drapes and pulled it back slowly.

Bill looked out and all that he saw was the hard rain beating against the window, and when he had placed his face closer to the window, something jumped out at him.

It was Clara! Clara was standing in the rain, hair soaked and lying on the side of her face, as Bill ran to open the main house door, and as he did he yelled…

"What the Fuck…what the Fuck!

Bill opened the door to see Clara standing on the top step soaking wet waiting for Bill to open the screen door and let her in.

Once Bill opened the screen door, a very soaked, mad, and crying Clara entered.

Clara walked over to the closet and grabbed a large beach towel from the self and as she began wiping her face and drying her hair, Bill walked over to Clara with a bewildered looked on his face saying…

"Honey, what the hell were you doing outside?'

Clara finished hand drying her hair and balled up her fist and as hard as she could, and punched Bill in the stomach, saying…

"Damn you Bill! What the hell were you thinking about…I told you to stand at the door and wait while I turned my head lights off on my car and then as I'm heading up the steps, you slammed the door, what the hell was that all about?"

If Bill was in a state of shock over seeing Clara standing outside in the rain, what Clara just told him made him even more shocked. The last thing that Bill remembered was Clara was in bed and he was sitting in the recliner having a glass of wine.

Clara removed her wet clothes and wrapped the towel around her and then headed upstairs saying...

"Bill, I wouldn't come up here if I were you...I'm way to fucking pissed off to deal with you!"

Clara turned as she heard Bill following behind her saying...

"Honey hold on a sec, you don't think..."

Clara stomped her right foot on the step and yelled...

"Seriously Bill, I'm not fucking playing with you, if you come up here I swear I will walk the hell out of here and never come back...I'm serious Bill!"

Bill stood looking lost and confused at the bottom of the steps as Clara went into the bedroom slamming the door.

Bill walked back over to the living room and sat down on the sofa, trying to figure out what in the world had just happened.

In between Bill's thoughts, thunder continued crashing in the night sky, sometimes with a crackling sound and other times it sounded like a sonic boom.

Bill wanted so badly to walk upstairs and talk to Clara, but he knew to leave well-enough-alone too. Bill got up and walked over to the living room closet and pulled a linen, a blanket and a pillow down and prepared to sleep on the sofa.

Once Bill finished with making his bed for the night, he walked into the kitchen and poured himself a large glass of wine and put the leftover house Lo Mein noodles and an egg roll into the microwave and walked into the living room.

All during the night as one storm raged outside, another storm was brewing inside Bill's house.

Bill stood looking out of the living room window at the rain which was showing no signs of letting up.

Bill glanced down at Charlie and Shone whom were asleep in their dog beds on either side of the fire place, as Bill thought to himself...

"Damn will you look at this...I bet Deanne and Dave saw this coming and decided to wait till morning."

As Bill was watching the storm, the microwave sounded, alerting Bill that his late-night snack was ready.

Bill turned to go into the kitchen when the lightening flashed, and the thunder roared, drawing Bill's attention to the vacant lot across the street.

Closing the drapes, Bill walked towards the kitchen for his food and as he approached the steps which led to the upstairs, he glanced up at the bedroom door and noticing the light was out, continued into the kitchen.

The beginning of a movie which Bill was going to watch still had twenty minutes before it came on, so Bill decided to eat in the kitchen, just in case Clara came down stairs.

Clara had a thing about eating all over the house and even when their two children were staying with them, she preferred that the kitchen was the only appropriate place to eat.

Clara originally grew up in a rural area in the West Virginia mountains, and when she was a small child had memories of their small two-bedroom house and how they had a terrible problem with roaches being everywhere.

Clara and Bill's four-bedroom house was extremely immaculate, and Clara worked extremely hard to keep it that way.

Clara had a habit of cleaning every room, washing all the linen, including the table cloths and dresser coverings, even in the rooms of their two college children, who came home twice a year, during Thanksgiving and Christmas.

Bill was already on Clara's bad side, and for her to find him eating on the sofa in front of the television would have only signaled world war three.

Bill wolfed down the Lo Mein noodles and the egg roll and after wiping the table clean placed the container and egg roll wrapper in the trash and started for the living room when the thunder cracked and lightening momentarily lit up the sky in the back yard.

With one hand, Bill pulled one side of the kitchen curtains open and as he did something caught his eye.

Bill reached over and turned on the back-yard flood lights, which partially lit up the back yard, but enough for Bill to see most of the yard.

As Bill looked he saw the ground right where Charlie's legs were stuck hours earlier and two figures emerging from the ground.

Bill removed his glasses and wiped his eyes and after he put his glasses back on, noticed that the figures were a little girl holding on to the hand of what appeared to be a smaller boy.

Bill opened and closed his eyes several times and each time he opened them, the figures were there, not moving just standing still in the rain.

Suddenly, the little girl reached down to the ground and picked up a handful of mud and shoved it into her mouth.

She leaned her head back and with a quick thrust spit out a large chunk of mud which came flying towards Bill, hitting the kitchen window where he was standing, causing him to jump backwards.

Bill inspected the window wondering why it hadn't shattered as the mud ran down the window, and that's when Bill noticed it.

Bits of teeth were embedded in the mud, and as Bill looked a little closer he jumped as something tapped him on the shoulder.

Bill turned and as he did, noticed that Clara was standing behind him.

It looked as if Clara had been crying because of the redness of her eyes.

Clara reached out and rubbed Bill's back saying…

"I'm sorry baby, nothing should've made me snapped at you like that…and I'm sorry, what are you looking at?"

Bill was pointing at the mud which was still running down the window and as he turned to look at Clara, he expected a response from her regarding the mud against the window, as Clara said…

"Yeah it looks like this is going to mess up a lot of people's plans…huh?"

As Clara continued rubbing Bill's back, she leaned in a little closer to the window saying…

"Well, I can see that I'm going to be washing all of the insides of the window's tomorrow."

Bill tried not to make a big deal out of it, but said to Clara as he continued pointing…

"Inside, Clara…the muds on the outside."

Clara looked at the area where Bill was pointing to, saying…

"What mud…you better get your eyes examined, there's no mud on the window."

Bill turned to look at the window as Clara started walking out of the kitchen saying…

"Are you going to stand there looking at the weather, or are you coming to bed?"

Bill could not believe what had just happened, and as he turned out the kitchen light to follow Clara upstairs he said…

"I guess Deanne and Dave decided to wait till morning…huh?"

As Clara reached the top of the stairs she headed into the bathroom to brush her teeth saying...

"That's odd you know what I mean, Deanne or Dave should've called by now, and when I tried dialing her number...it went straight to voicemail; oh well, we'll probably hear something from them by tomorrow."

As Bill climbed the steps he turned to look at Charlie and Shone who were sound asleep. Bill turned the hall light out as Clara left the bathroom and came into the bedroom. Little did either of them know it, but the back-door knob of their house slowly started turning until it quietly opened.

The sound of the rain muffled the squeaking of the door as several figures entered the kitchen.

Though Clara and Bill had been married for quite some time, they still enjoyed making love to one another with the same kind of passion which bought them together twenty-two years ago.

Clara was by no stretch of the imagination a very gorgeous and shapely woman. She proudly displayed the prettiest pair of feet and legs, not to mention that for a woman in her late forties, she could still turn heads whenever she wore blue jeans.

Bill had paid attention and did his homework over the years because he still knew how to make Clara hot, wet and excited with the slightest touch.

Clara loved the times that she and Bill made love; Clara kept a small chest under the bed with a variety of adult toys designed to achieve maximum pleasure.

After thirty minutes of raw, passionate love making, Clara and Bill fell fast asleep. Both Clara and Bill were light sleepers and on any other given night would have heard the slightest of noises, but the rain provided the perfect cover...and maybe it was a good thing that they didn't awaken out of their sleep.

Perhaps it was a good thing that they stayed sound asleep in their bed, elsewise they would have discovered the muddy footprints leading from the kitchen, and into the living room and up the steps.

Clara and Bill lay sleeping not able to see the figures which surrounded their bed. Suddenly the lightening flashed, and in the instant Clara opened her eyes and saw for a second, faces surround her and Bill and let out a scream.

The sound of Clara's scream woke Bill up who as he raised up, saw Clara sitting up in the bed, when he said...

"Hey sweets, what's the matter...you going to let a little thunder and lightning keep you up?"

Clara put her finger up to Bill's lips and said...

"Shhh...there's somebody in here."

Bill slowly reached over to the nightstand and turned the lamp on, which did not come on...whispering to Clara, he said...

"The bulb must have blown...cut on your lamp."

Clara turned on her side and as her hand felt for the lamp in the darkness, she screamed as something grabbed her arm and yanked her out of bed and on to the floor.

Bill scrambled to Clara's side of the bed and cut the lamp on and as he did, saw Clara sitting on the floor with one of her house slippers in her hand and said...

"Gosh Clara, what are you doing on the floor, and what's with the bed room slipper?"

Clara looked around the bedroom and upon seeing that there was no one there, got up off the floor and said...

"Bill I'm telling you, I went to cut the light on and something grabbed me by my arm and yanked me out of bed."

Bill motioned with his hands as he glanced around the room saying...

"Clara, there's no one in here, you probably just fell out of bed...hell, I've done it once or twice myself..."

Clara cut Bill off before he finished his statement and showing him her arm, which was covered in mud, said...

"What about this...how did all of this mud get on my arm if no one else is in the house?"

Bill grabbed the towel which was draped over the back of the chair and began wiping Clara's arm saying...

"What the Fuck!"

Quietly Clara said…

"Listen, do you hear that…s-somebody's in the bathroom, the shower curtain rings just moved."

Bill slid his feet into his slippers and he took the gun from his nightstand and slowly walked towards the master bathroom saying…

"You are trespassing, and I have a gun…if you don't want to get shot, you'd better come out of there."

With one quick motion, Bill turned on the bathroom light and pointed his gun in the direction of the shower.

The master bathroom was an open area with one of the old style free standing bath tubs with the attached shower curtain circling it.

The shower curtains were closed, and Bill could hear the water running and saw a faint image of someone through the shower curtain, and said…

"Alright now, whoever you are…I said I have a gun pointed at you and you'd better stop playing games and come out right this instant!"

Bill could see several figures through the shower curtain, moving but could not make out who or what they were.

Bill inched closer to the bath tub and as he did he put the muzzle of the gun against the shower curtain and pulled back the curtain, keeping his gun trained on the figures.

As the shower curtain opened and to Bill's surprise there was no one in the bath tub. The hot water was running, steaming up the bathroom but the tub was empty.

Bill inspected the bath tub and the muddy foot prints on the top of the tub and leading away from the tub to the bathroom door.

Bill looked at the muddy foot prints and thought…

"Wait a minute…I just came through that door and there were no prints a minute ago, what the hell!"

Bill turned his attention back to the bath tub and as he reached to cut the water off something brushed up on the back of his leg, scaring Bill and making him bang his knee against the side of the tub.

Bill turned to see what or who it was when he heard Clara's voice calling him as he said…

"What in the— Clara, you could have at least made some noise."

Bill gave Clara a look of frustration when Clara said…

"Bill, I'm starting to freak out...what in the hell is happening, who was in here?"

Bill put the gun's safety back on and shrugged his shoulders saying...

"Well I'm glad you see this...earlier today when Russ was here you said you didn't see anything...made me look stupid."

Clara walked and stood next to Bill and said...

"Look I'm sorry for doubting you earlier, but I didn't see anything out in the yard...this time we've both seen and heard the same thing, but what are we going to do Bill...I'm not staying in this house tonight Bill."

Walking towards the door Bill turned and said...

"Look I can't explain it either Clara, but I'm not about to let somebody scare me out of my own house, I mean c'mon this isn't some late-night movie or something."

Clara held on to Bill's arm as Bill followed the muddy footprints from the bathroom down the steps and to the kitchen, as he cut on every light.

In all the commotion, Charlie and Shone thought that they were going to get fed, as they stretched and followed Bill and Clara into the kitchen.

Upon entering the kitchen and following the footprints which went out the back door, Bill slammed the door hard and turned, saying...

"Charlie and Shone lay back down, it's not time to eat...I shouldn't give either one of you anything to eat...you let people walk all up in here and not even one bark, heck a growl would have been good."

Clara slapped Bill's arm saying...

"Bill don't say things like that to them...and answer my question...what are we going to do?"

Bill walked over to the wine rack and grabbed a glass, when Clara said...

"You'd better bring me a glass too, heck my nerves are shot all to pieces."

After pouring Clara and himself a glass of wine, Bill unplugged his cell phone from the charger and said...

"First thing I'm going to do is call the Police, and tell them we had a break in...let them see the muddy prints...will that give you peace of mind?"

Bill and Clara sat on the living room sofa near the door and waited on the Police to arrive, constantly looking towards the kitchen when Clara sprang to her feet saying...

"Did you see that!"

Bill turned his head towards the kitchen and said...

"What! I don't see anything, C'mon Clara you're starting to get all jumpy and shit...so why don't you just sit down...here finish my wine."

Clara obliged and finished Bill's glass of wine saying...

"Look I wouldn't be jumpy or freaking out, if someone had paid attention to me and took me to a hotel until this gets figured out."

Just then the doorbell rang, and as Bill went to the door he could see the front room drapes.

As Bill opened the door, there stood two uniformed Officers whom Bill let inside. The Police Officers greeted Bill and Clara and Bill took the Police Officers upstairs to the master bathroom.

Police Officer Don Willis signaled to his partner Officer Patrick Johns, to the muddy foot prints leading away from the bath tub to the steps. Next Bill led them into the bedroom, where Clara said she was yanked out of bed.

Bill told the Officers that he pulled his gun from the nightstand, which was still in his pocket, and went into the bathroom and then down the steps.

While both Police Officers watched Bill's movements, Officer Patrick Johns asked Bill which pocket of his bathrobe the gun was, and then while Officers Johns had Bill place both of his hands on the bed post, Officer Willis took Bill's pistol from his right pocket and after removing the clip, placed it in the bedside drawer.

Clara who was standing a few feet from Bill turned to Officer Willis saying...

"Hey, why are you treating him like he's the criminal...my husband just told you someone was in our home and you..."

Officer Willis motioned with his hands for Clara to calm down as he said...

"Look Mrs. huh..."

Clara looking irritated said...

"Scott...Clara Scott."

Officer Willis replied...

Mrs. Scott...this was for your husband's protection as well as ours. We don't know you or your husband, and if he's got a gun in our presence, we needed for it to be secured, until we checked things out."

Bill removed his hands from the bed post and putting them around Clara said...

"It's alright Clara, they're just doing their jobs."

Bill and Clara led Officers Willis and Johns downstairs to the kitchen so that they could get a look at the muddy footprints exiting out the back door.

Officers Willis and Johns followed the foot prints through the kitchen and out to the door, as they stopped and turned saying...

"Judging from the prints it looks like a medium and a small child...you say they were in your bath tub?"

Bill stood holding onto Clara and nodding his head when Officers Johns said...

"I admit it is a little odd but judging from the fact that nothing is missing, and the only prints were found were in the bathroom, I'd say it was a homeless mother and a small child looking for something to eat and maybe a hot bath or something."

Bill and Clara looked at one another in disbelief, as the Officers walked calmly towards the front door, when Officer Willis turned and handed Bill his card and said...

"Look I doubt if they'll be returning tonight or any other night...we'll cruise the area, two people out walking in all of this weather can't be too hard to spot. In the meantime, if you have any problems or see anything call us.

As Bill and Clara watched the Officers get into their patrol car circling the block Clara said to Bill...

"Did you hear that...'Mama Walton and John Boy' wanting food and a hot bath...that's stupid, what were they going to do after getting cleaned up, go back out in the rain?"

Bill locked the front door and said...

"It does sound a little crazy, but I mean what else could it have been. When I went into the bathroom, I must have scared them, and they ran off, or something."

Something is right...but exactly what kind 'something' was it, this is a question that Bill and Clara were going to find the answer to in the strangest way.

Even though the Police provided a believable explanation for the night's events, Bill placed his gun back in his robe pocket as he and Clara cleaned the muddy prints from the bathroom and then in the kitchen.

Bill laid his gun on top of the nightstand and decided to keep the light on as he and Clara laid in bed listening to the storm and the sounds of the night.

With each sound of thunder Bill thought about getting up and going to the window, but the thought of what he might see if he did, so he laid in bed looking at Clara who had just gotten up and walked over to the window.

Bill's eyes were getting heavy when he looked over at Clara who had just closed her phone and said...

"Still no word from Deanne or Dave?"

Clara let out a sigh and said...

"No, no nothing...it's not like her not to call, I mean every time she leaves Shone with us she at least calls to check up on her, I hope they're alright."

Bill yawned and said...

"Yeah...they probably saw the weather report and decided to hunker down and wait until morning."

Clara stood by the window looking out as the lightening flashed and the rain poured, when she jumped as something touched her shoulder.

Turning around it was Bill who was motioning for her to come to bed.

The thoughts Bill had about Deanne and Dave, on any other night would have rang true, but little did he know that Deanne, Dave and all the other guest at the farm were anything but alright...as a matter of fact, things on the farm were growing very wrong, very fast.

2
Marcia & Denise

Denise Long and her partner of four years, Marcia Mims sat on the bed discussing the recent murders of two women near their subdivision. Denise is a marketing consultant and Marcia is a sub-contractor and co-owner with her brother, Charles of their home-make over business.

Denise is originally from Arizona and Marcia is from Chicago. Both women met one another four years ago, in the Easton Mall.

Denise is forty-four years old and Marcia is forty-two. To look at Marcia, you'd never think that she was handy with a nail gun let alone all the other tools of the carpentry trade.

Standing a mere five-foot-six, Marcia weighs a hundred and thirty-nine pounds' soak and wet, with long dirty brown hair which she maintains in a ponytail, until it's time to throw on a dress for evenings out.

Denise is an attractive slim five-foot-eight inches tall, one hundred and fifty pounds with the greenest eyes and auburn shoulder length hair.

Neither Marcia nor Denise considered themselves a part of the gay community, but after sharing an apartment for over a year, they both discovered they were more than attracted to one another.

Three years earlier, Marcia and her brother Charles were contracted to renovate one of the homes in the sub-division where they currently live and through default on the home owner who contracted them, sold Marcia and Denise the house.

Life for two female couples has not always been easy, as a matter of fact Denise and Marcia almost considered moving away from the subdivision after only a year of living there.

The neighbors of the subdivision were outrageously bitter and mean-spirited towards Marcia and Denise to the point of being ridiculous.

It was during their third year of living in the subdivision that the neighbors accepted them as neighbors and their treatment of Marcia and Denise changed.

One summer during the first-year Marcia and Denise lived in the subdivision, the temperature soared to an unbelievable hundred and five for several days. Denise and Marcia had walked down to the swimming pool in the subdivision to take advantage of the water and to escape the sweltering heat.

Several of the resident's children were in the pool until their parents showed up and made their children leave the pool, all the while talking under their breath about the pool being contaminated and that their kids could come back only if the pool was completely drained and sterilized.

That happened a year earlier, and it was also the last time Marcia and Denise used the pool, even though the resident's attitude towards Marcia and Denise had changed.

Marcia and Denise explained that if they were in the pool the possibility of remembering that incident and the faces of those who said it, might give way to hard feelings.

Denise and Marcia were two very classy women who never displayed public affection, preferring to keep their emotions to the confines in their house.

Marcia and Denise sat painting each other's toe nails and tenderly discussing the two murders which occurred earlier in the week.

Marcia gently lifted Denise's foot and while blowing her nails dry kissed her feet saying...

"Denise, I know you sometimes get in a little late but promise me, if you're going to be late that you call me...don't have me worried about you or else..."

Denise scooted close to Marcia and after affectionately kissing her said...

"Or else what?"

With her right hand, Marcia slapped Denise on her ass saying...

"You make me worry and someone is going to get spanked."

Locked in a warm embrace Marcia and Denise hugged one another while Denise's small nose found Marcia' ear and her neck.

Slowly moving her tongue from Denise' ear to her neck, Denise let out a soft moan as her hands fondled Marcia's long hair.

Love making with Denise and Marcia was always one of passion and intensity, climaxing in screams of excitement.

The two women collapsed into each other's arms, their love making-soaked bodies revealing the intensity of their desire they shared for one another.

Denise lay asleep in peach panties and a long white tee shirt, lightly snoring while Marcia lay comfortably in her University of Illinois jersey, stroking Denise' hair and kissing her forehead before laying her head on the pillow beside Denise.

The two women lay close to each other, Denise lay on her left close to Marcia, with her right arm draped over Marcia...the two women lay soundly asleep not knowing that something frightening entered their house and was slowly making its way towards their bedroom.

Marcia was the first to awaken when she felt cold water drops landing on her cheek. At first, she wiped her cheek and turned over on her back only to feel more cold water drops on her neck.

Marcia started mumbling in her sleep saying...

"Damn...roof has a leak."

Unaware that something or someone had come out of the rain leaving wet tracks all through the house and was now standing over the two ladies watching them as they slept.

Suddenly Marcia begin sniffing and smelling something very foul and opened her eyes.

Marcia screamed in fear because when she opened her eyes, she saw the most hideous face just a few inches from her nose.

Denise jumped up calling Marcia's name saying...

"What's wrong, what are you yelling about Marcia?"

Marcia was sitting up in the bed with her back against the headboard when Denise turned on the bedroom lamp, saying...

"I know you're going to say that I'm dreaming, but I was not dreaming... there's someone in here Denise, a creepy old ass woman was right there!

Denise climbed out of bed and walked over to Marcia's side of the bed saying...

"Hey sweets, you just had a bad nightmare...and why is your side of the bed all wet, you didn't."

Marcia snapped as she climbed out of bed...

"C'mon get a grip Denise...hell no, I did not pee in the bed...gosh, I don't believe you went that way.

Denise replied to Marcia saying...

"Spilled water, I was going to say spilled water."

Reaching in the closet and grabbing the flash light, Marcia headed out of the bedroom with Denise following her saying...

"Now where are you going?"

Stopping short at the steps Marcia shone the flashlight on the top steps and then down the steps whispering...

"I told you someone is in here, look at the muddy wet shoe prints coming up to the bedroom...I didn't go outside, and I was asleep before you were."

Denise walked over to the wall and tried flicking the switch to turn on the lights, but nothing happened.

Whispering in Marcia's ear Denise said...

"We're going to have to trip the switch on the circuit breaker...storm must have knocked out the power."

Marcia shone the flashlight all around as they headed down the steps. Just as they reached the bottom steps the lightening flashed, making both women jump and scream.

As the two women crept ever so slowly towards the back door, where the circuit breaker was, Marcia said...

"Go ahead, I'll keep the light on you."

Keeping the light trained both on Denise and the circuit breaker, Marcia did not see the dark figure easing up behind her.

The strangers hand extended and was inches from grabbing Marcia's panties, when the lights came on and Marcia screamed.

The two women inspected the house. The back door and front doors were locked, but there were muddy foot prints leading from the back door to the stairwell...someone had been in the house, but Marcia and Denise noted that both doors, back and front were locked from the inside.

Marcia turned off the flashlight and laid it on the table and started to wipe up the muddy prints when Denise stopped her saying...

"No don't clean them up, its evidence...I'm going to call the Police, and you better stand beside the door incase whoever it is, is still in the house."

With the intensity of the storm and it being in the early hours of the morning, Marcia knew it would take the Police a while to get there, especially for a break in, especially since the nearest substation was a good ten miles away.

Denise made coffee for her and Marcia and asked...

"You want a little 'Jack Daniels' in yours too?"

Holding her cup towards Denise, Marcia replied...

"Normally I'd say no, but I think I need something to settle my nerves.

The two women sat on the love seat facing the stairs, and watching television and waiting on the arrival of the Police when Denise whispered as she turned the volume to the television down...

"Did you hear that...listen!"

Marcia turned around scanning the room saying...

"Hear wha...?"

Before Marcia could finish her statement, Denise placed her hand over Marcia's mouth saying...

"Shhh."

Then as Denise removed her hand, it became apparent what Denise had heard. It sounded like scratching noises coming from the living room window, when Marcia whispered...

"It must be a tree branch scraping against the window."

Denise whispered back...

"Remember, the only trees in our subdivision are the ones which were planted six months ago, out near the side walk and they're only four-to-five feet tall."

Marcia and Denise heard scratching noises coming from the front door and then all along the sides of the house.

The scratching noise continued all the way to the back door and grew louder when suddenly there was loud pounding on the front door causing Marcia and Denise to experience more fear.

Denise and Marcia approached the front door slowly and peeked out of the front door drapes at the welcoming sight of the Police car's lights, and two uniformed Officers climbing the steps to their house.

Marcia opened the door and welcomed the Police Officers inside saying…

"Hi, thanks for coming out in all of this crappy weather, my name's Marcia and this is my partner Denise…and we think someone broke into our house a little while ago and might still be upstairs hiding."

As the two Officers walked in closing the door behind them, the first Officer said…

"My name is Officer Don Willis, and this is my partner Patrick Johns… and you say someone broke in?"

Denise reached out to shake their hands and said…

"Excuse me I'm not trying to be smart or anything, but you two look awfully young to be Police Officers."

Officer Johns replied…

"We get that all the time, but we're really Police Officers with guns, Tasers and everything…heck we even have hand cuffs and a badge."

Marcia walked Officer Willis over to the muddy prints leading from the back door to the steps saying…

"I woke up to someone standing in our bedroom, and then they ran out or something."

Officer Johns walked up the steps to the bedroom while his partner Officer Willis was inspecting the downstairs and back door.

Officer Johns came down stairs and joined Officer Wills on the back porch, and after several minutes, they both came inside saying…

"Well there's nobody in the house and there's nobody standing around outside…at least we didn't see anyone. It's apparent there are a couple of homeless people in the area looking for shelter….this is the second call like this tonight in this area."

Officer Johns opened the back door and turned to Marcia and Denise saying…

"Is there anything missing, and when you two came downstairs which door was opened?"

Marcia pointed to the muddy print by the door and placed her small size five and a half foot next to the print saying...

"You guys can clearly see that we didn't make these prints, they've got to be at least a size ten or eleven."

Officer Willis and Johns stood in the living room and as Officer Johns pointed to the muddy prints he said...

"There are two things that's not adding up, number one...there are no jimmy marks at either door, and two, the muddy prints start here at the door...and."

Officer Willis interrupted...

"And...the prints start at the back door and go up the steps."

Marcia walked over to Officer Willis and said...

"Meaning?"

Officer Johns pointed to the back door saying...

"The prints only go one way, and you said the doors were locked when the both of you came downstairs...so how did they get out without disturbing their prints and who locked the door behind them?"

Denise came up to Officer Johns saying...

"Are you saying they're still in the house!"

Officer Johns stated as he walked over to the stairwell...

"We can check upstairs again if you like, but I didn't see anyone upstairs earlier."

Marcia stood next to Denise rubbing her shoulder and said...

"This is all messed up...how did somebody get in and get back out again, I just don't get it."

Officer Johns looked over at Marcia and said...

All I can say Ms...."

Marcia snapped...

"Mims, my name is Marcia Mims."

Officer Johns handed Marcia his card and continued...

"All I can say Ms. Mims, when we leave... lock all your doors and make sure the windows are all locked, and we'll patrol the area, if you have any problems give us a call."

Officer Johns and Willis left and walked down the steps and into their patrol car as Denise said to Marcia…

"Well that was a big fucking help, and I saw that young Officer…. huh Johns, yea, he was looking more at your 'twins' than he was anything else."

Marcia reached up and gently kissed Denise saying…

"My…is someone a little jealous?"

Denise stood in front of Marcia with her hands on her hips saying…

"Oh please…he doesn't have anything I want."

Marcia and Denise began locking and checking all the doors and windows and poured another shot of Jack Daniels into their coffee cups before heading upstairs.

As Denise sat down on the bed Marcia walked into the spare bedroom and came out with an aluminum baseball bat which she held in a batter's stance, saying…

"Let your creepy old lady come up in her and WHAM…she gets it…right upside her head."

Marcia sat on the side of the bed and after sipping her coffee said…

"My creepy old lady…why all of a sudden is she my creepy old lady?"

"Well if I recall…you're the one who saw her."

Denise started massaging Marcia's shoulders and neck, then took the bat from Marcia and slowly let it drop to the floor, then gently bit Marcia's ear whispering…

"I don't wanna talk about her anymore…umm…is this all I get to massage?"

Marcia crossed her arms and slowly removed her tee shirt revealing her well sculptured figure and pulled Denise close to her and in a soft sexy voice, whispering…

"Do you want me to wave a white flag saying that I surrender, or ring the dinner bell saying, 'come and get me'?"

Denise gently pushed Marcia down on the bed and turned the bedroom lamp out and began caressing and kissing Marcia. Starting at her feet, kissing and smelling them, and then making her way up Marcia's sexy legs until Marcia grabbed Denise by the hair bringing her closer to her wetness, as she softly moaned…

"Ooh…oh yes."

While Marcia and Denise were deeply into each other's needs, someone or something else was standing on the roof paying attention to them through the bedroom window.

Police Officers Willis and Johns parked their patrol car at the end of the cul-de-sac watching Marcia and Denise's house as well as the rest of the neighborhood.

Officer John's was a smoker and Willis was not, so whenever Officer Johns wanted to smoke he would normally step outside of the patrol car, but not on this night and especially not in all the rain which began intensifying.

Officer Willis looked over at Officer Johns and said...

"Go ahead...just crack the window and I'll turn the air up, so that I'm not all smoked up."

Officer Johns looked in the rearview mirror and said...

"If you can reach in the back seat, I have a can of air freshener in my bag."

With the defrost blowing on high, Officer Willis sprayed a small amount of freshener in the air while Officer Johns lit his cigarette, taking deep drags and blowing the smoke out of the cracked window.

Once Officer Johns had finished his cigarette and discarded the butt out of the window he said...

"I appreciate this Will, I know how smoke bothers you."

Officer Willis sprayed another shot of freshener in the air and said...

"Hey, look partner, it's no big deal...my girlfriend smokes, and heck there was a time when I was going to take up smoking but after hearing my grandfather coughing up half of his lungs...it just stayed a thought and nothing more."

Officer Johns rolled the window completely down and after sticking his hands out of the window wiped his face with his rain-soaked hands saying...

"What say we head and get something to eat, there's nothing happening over here...I think perhaps one of those ladies probably had a boyfriend to sneak in and was trying to make up an excuse for his muddy foot prints being discovered."

Tossing the air freshener can in the back-seat Officer Willis said...

"Sounds like a plan Stan, but you're wrong about the two ladies back there, the impression I got was they, they are one of huh."

Officer Johns tried drying his hands as best he could and said...

"You mean they are lovers.... see that's what gets me...all of that going to waste, no wonder I can't find a woman,"

As Officer Johns placed the car in drive Officer Willis said...

"Naw...the reason you can't find a woman is because you're too busy being a whore-dawg. Women can spot a guy who's only about the short game."

Just as the patrol car pulled away from the curb Officer Johns slammed on brakes saying...

"Hey...did you hear that?"

Officer Willis turned around towards the rear window saying...

"What noise...all I can hear is the rain."

Officer Johns turned off the engine and said...

"That noise, don't you hear it...it sounds like scratching...like somebody's finger nails scratching the back seat, you don't hear it?"

After Officer Willis repeatedly told him that he did not hear anything, Officer Johns pulled away from the curb and headed for Livingston Avenue.

Officer Willis would later regret not taking Officer Johns' concerns a little more serious before the night was over.

As Officer Johns headed towards the expressway he looked in the rearview mirror when something caught attention and he said...

"Hey...what the hell!"

Officer Johns saw something in the back seat which made him slam on brakes, sending the patrol car skidding off the road, and into a ditch and crashing into a tree.

The patrol car's rear wheels rested unevenly in a depression off the side of the road with the wheels spinning and smoke coming from the smashed hood.

Officer Willis had just come to when he looked over at Officer Johns who was face down in the steering wheels' air bag.

Officer Willis reached over to see if and how bad his partner was injured when he began coming to.

Officer Willis said...

"Pat...Pat are you okay buddy?"

Officer Johns raised his head and looking at Officer Willis said...

"Oh, my head...I'm okay but my right knee is screwed up."

Officer Willis reached up on his right shoulder for his radio to call for assistance, when Officer Johns yelled...

"Oh Fuck...me!"

Officer Willis let go of his radio just in time to see a menacing figure emerging from the back seat, scratching and ripping apart the iron prisoner grate barrier.

Officer John's grabbed the shotgun which was in between Officer Wills and himself and tried to point it towards the back seat when the figure grabbed the tip of the barrel and pulled it, pointing it upwards through the damaged grate opening.

Officer Willis struggled trying to get the door opened and trying to radio for back up when he noticed Officer John's had pulled his 9mm Luger from his holster and fired multiple shots in the back seat!

Because of the intense rain and the cracking of thunder the only evidence pointing to the Officers being in trouble was the gun-shot burst of light.

As Officer John's fired six rounds into the back seat the shotgun lay motionless between the front and back seat.

Officer Willis finally got his door open and as he exited the patrol car, aimed his Glock-thirty-eight and walked slowly towards the rear door.

Officer Johns approached the opposite rear door, and as he did he reached inside of his coat pocket for his radio to call for backup, but all he heard was static on the line.

While the weather was mild, the rain was not only packing a punch, but was unseasonably cold, which made trying to accomplish anything difficult not to mention intolerable.

Officer Johns could hear in the distance the sound of dogs barking against the backdrop of the rain. With one hand shinning a light in the back seat and his other hand on the rear door handle, Officer Johns tried peering into the driver's side back window which was fogged up good.

Just as Officer Johns reached to open the door he heard a faint scream and when he looked through the window again to where his partner was standing on the other side of the car, all he saw was a huge trail of blood running down the window.

Officer Johns took a few steps back and then slowly walked around the rear of the car with his gun drawn and as he came in view of the side of the car he noticed the window was smashed and his partners hat and gun lying on the ground near the rear door.

Officer Johns wondered what had happened to his partner looking at the window, when he said to himself...

"Damn...I didn't hear any noise and I didn't feel the car move...surely with the window being smashed and all, I would have heard or felt something."

Within moments of thinking that, something came up from behind him and grabbed him by the back of the neck and lifted him four feet off the ground.

Officer Johns first thought was, to try and aim his gun behind him and fire, but the crushing grip on his neck was so tight, that Officer Johns ended up firing nine shots at the ground.

Just then, whatever had Officer Johns, dropped him to the ground and as he got to his feet he began running towards the row of houses hoping to get away from whatever or whoever it was, and call for help.

Officer Johns didn't bother looking behind him as he ran, because the pouring rain made seeing anything almost impossible.

Officer Johns ran to the first house he came upon and as he did he noticed all the lights were off with the mailbox over flowing with mail.

Figuring that no one was home Officer Johns noticed that the house next door had its inside lights on and ran down the steps and up on the porch and started knocking on the door.

Officer Johns nervously turned and twisted and looked in every direction as he pounded on the door of Tony and Diane Smith's house, not knowing that the curtains had just slowly and carefully moved.

Officer Johns caught a glimpse of the moving curtains and shoved his badge in the window.

The howling of the wind and the barking of the dogs in the distance caused Officer Johns to look to his right as the door knob under his hand turned and opened, causing him to nervously jump.

A towering figure over six feet-five inches stood in the entrance as Officer John showed his badge to the man standing in the door...

"Can I help you Officer?"

Officer Johns placed his badge back upon his jacket and took one step inside the door as Tony closed the door.

"Look, I'm Police Officer Pat Johns and I need to use your phone to call the precinct for help. My partner's been hurt, and our radio doesn't work".

Officer Johns wiped the rain from his face as Tony pointed towards the phone on the end table next to where his wife Diane was sitting, saying...

"You're more than welcomed to use the phone...oh, I'm sorry this is my wife Diane and I'm Tony...Tony Smith".

Officer Johns nodded his head as he picked up the phone and dialed the number to the precinct.

Diane got up from the sofa where she had been sitting and her and Tony walked over to the window to give Officer Johns some privacy.

Tony and Diane were watching the storm and then their attention was drawn back to Officer Johns, he cried...

"Who the Fuck is this!"

Diane grabbed Tony's arm as Tony walked over towards Officer Johns saying...

"Trouble Officer?"

Officer Johns looked down at the phone and as he redialed the number said out loud...

"I just called my precinct and got..."

Tony stood in front of Officer Johns as he redialed his precincts number saying...

"You dialed the number and got what?"

Officer Johns held up his hand to ask Tony to be quiet as the number was ringing, when he saw a shock and horrified look on Tony's face. Officer Johns handed the phone to Tony saying...

"Listen...do you hear that?"

Tony grabbed the phone and put it to his ear and turned to Officer Johns and said...

"Okay...what am I supposed to be listening to?"

Officer Johns clearly heard the number ringing, but when Tony placed the phone on speaker, there was a busy tone, as Officer Johns said...

"Look man, I heard this creepy ass voice on the other end."

In disbelief, Tony ended the call saying...

"I didn't hear anything except the phone ringing...I'm calling nine -one-one, you said your partner's hurt...where exactly is he?"

Officer Johns stood shaking his head, not believing what was happening and said...

Willis...my partner is at the corner, across the street on the other side of the patrol car...I don't know if he was breathing.... I-I ran to get help because we wrecked, and I dropped my weapon...and I need back up."

Tony looked over at Diane asking...

"What were they doing out in all this weather anyways for?"

As Tony was dialing nine-one-one, the thunder cracked, and Tony held the phone away from his face saying...

"Damn this storm.... I lost signal!"

Tony attempted to redial as Diane approached him saying...

"Tony, I don't like this...my phone's dead too!"

"I think you'd best go check on your partner and see if he's still alive.

Tony said as he leaned over and checked out Diane's phone.

Tony looked at Diane's phone as she held it out, and just as Tony was about to reach for her phone, all the windows in the house began cracking and breaking one-by-one.

Diane began screaming as the glass shattered and smashed all over the living room, as Tony grabbed Diane and fell to the floor covering her face and head.

Tony looked at Officer Johns who was on the floor scrambling towards them from the window.

Diane, Tony and Officer Johns all let out a loud yell as the thunder crashed and the lightening cracked...

"Man...that was close; it seemed like the lightening hit the house."

Tony said as he was picking the glass out of Diane's hair and placing it on the coffee table.

The wind and rain was beginning to come through the busted windows as Tony and Officer Johns got up from the floor, as the curtains being blown from the curtain rods and tossed all over the living room.

Diane clung to the arm of Tony and began crying...

"What's going on Tony.... what's going on?"

Tony scrambled to the end table and removed his gun from the drawer and shouted at Officer Johns...

"What the hells out there?"

Officer Johns crawled close to Tony and Diane and said...

"I don't have clue one as to what is going on, my partner and I were attacked by something or someone, I didn't see who or what it was, after I saw blood on the squad car window I ran over here."

Tony placed the clip in his gun and chambered a round and said...

"So, you left your partner out there?"

"No...I didn't leave my partner, one minute he was there and the next minute he was gone."

Officer Johns shouted, as the remaining downstairs windows busted out and the ceiling chandelier began to shake at the sound of heavy footsteps.

Diane began screaming louder and louder as she clung tighter to Tony's arm, shouting...

"OMG Tony, what the fuck.... what the fuck!"

Tony and Diane had two young adult children and were supposed to be at their daughter and son n law's house for dinner but had decided to wait until after the rain let up.

Officer Johns noticed that Tony and Diane were crawling towards the door which led to the carport when he yelled...

"Are you crazy...if you go out there, then whatever or whoever it is out there is surely going to get you. Your best bet is to stay inside, find somewhere safe until the storm lets up, and we can get a cell phone signal."

Diane stopped and looked at Tony and was about to say something when Tony shouted...

"Safe! You want us to stay in here, after whoever it is has smashed all the windows...look, we are going to the car and we're getting the hell out of here, now you can come with us or stay here.'

Tony and Diane stood up and made their way to the door, while Officer Johns was still attempting to dial the precinct's number.

Tony activated the garage opener and as Diane got inside the car, Tony remembered that he did not have his keys with him, so he ran back inside to get them.

Upon entering the kitchen and retrieving his keys from the hook on the side of the cabinet Tony was met by Officer Johns who had changed his mind and decided to go with Tony and Diane.

Tony grabbed the keys and yelled to Officer Johns...

"Well...C'mon if you're coming!"

Tony and Officer Johns approached the car when Officer Johns said to Tony...

"Excuse me but, where's your wife?"

Tony walked over to the driver's side of the car and opened it and said...

"She's...D-Diane!"

Tony snatched open the rear door of the car and then walked to the garage door as Officer Johns followed, shouting...

"Diane—Diane!"

Officer Johns stood at the garage door opening looking around in every direction as Tony frantically called out for Diane, when Officer Johns said...

"Say, maybe she went back inside the house."

Tony looked out at the wind and the rain and the darkness and then turned to Officer Johns saying...

"No way...I was standing right in the kitchen, I would have seen her if she went in the house."

Tony headed for the house and turned to Officer Johns saying...

"Stay right here, I'm going to search the house."

Officer Johns replied...

"I though you said she didn't go in the house!"

Tony took the gun from his pocket and turned to Officer Johns saying...

"Look I don't know, she's not in the car and I know she didn't go out in all this weather...she wouldn't have done that, just stay here."

Tony ran into the house leaving Officer Johns in the carport.

Many things crossed Tony's mind as he ran upstairs looking for Diane...

"Perhaps she had to use the bathroom or went to grab her purse".

Tony thought to himself as he searched the bathroom and then both bedrooms, when he heard Officer Johns yelling...

"Tony...hey man, down here!"

Initially Tony didn't hear Officer Johns' calling him and then after several calls from Officer Johns, Tony ran downstairs and then emerged from the kitchen and into the doorway of the carport to see Officer Johns holding Diane who was soaked from the rain and crying.

Running over to Diane, Tony embraced her and said...

"Honey...what happened-where were you?"

Diane grabbed and held onto Tony when Officer Johns said...

"I-I dunno man, I started calling her name and then from out of the storm she just walked in, wet, cold and shaking."

Diane looked up at Tony, shaking and crying and said...

"Oh Tony, get me out of here...I'm cold Tony."

Officer Johns opened the car door as Tony climbed in the driver's seat and started the car after helping Diane in the back seat.

Officer Johns climbed into the passenger seat as Tony put the heater on and placed the fan on high to give Diane some much-needed warmth.

Turning around to Diane and notice her shivering and shaking, Tony said...

"Honey where were you, what happened... we were looking all over for you?"

Calming down but still shivering Diane said...

"Tony—I w-was sitting in the car and the next thing I know, I was outside side in the rain walking...I don't know."

Tony locked the doors of the car, put his foot on the brake pedal and tried to put the car in reverse, but the gear selector would not move.

Officer Johns leaned over in his seat asking Tony...

"Now what's wrong?"

Tony tried putting the car in reverse, and then he tried all the other gears, but it was no use, the transmission would not shift out of park.

Just then Diane pointed at the back window behind her and screamed.

Officer Johns turned in time to see two figures emerging from the rain and stopping just short of the rear of the car when Tony jumped out of the car pointing his gun and yelling...

"Okay that's far enough...who the hell are you?"

The two figures stood a few inches from the rear of the car with their heads pointed towards the ground.

Officer Johns turn as he noticed Diane running past him and into the house.

Turning his attention back towards the two figures, Officer Johns saw that they were about four to four and a half feet tall and wearing hoodies, but the noticeable thing about the two figures was, though they came out of the storm...their clothes were all dry.

Officer Johns thought to himself...

"What the Fuck...they came out of the rain, but their clothes are all dry."

With his gun still pointed at the two figures, Tony made his way over to Officer Johns and whispered at him...

"*Get in the house man...were sitting ducks out here.*"

Officer Johns snapped...

"*Look if we go inside we're not going to be any safer, I say we take our chances out here.*"

Tony walked past Officer Johns saying...

"*Do what you want, I've got more ammo inside and a shot gun in the den plus I got to check on Diane, I saw her run inside.*"

Officer Johns turned his attention from Tony to the two figures who were now several feet from him.

Officer Johns knew that running back in the house meant that they were trapping themselves inside and he was determined to stay out in the open.

Suddenly the two small figures wearing hoodies stood before him.

Their heads were down, and their hands were behind their backs when slowly they lifted their heads up towards Officer Johns, and in unison said...

"Little pig, little pig, let us in, let us in,
you can't get out, and you can't run
It's no use, just you wait and see The Nuns coming!

Officer Johns took one step towards the two figures believing that they were simply teenagers, playing some kind of joke...perhaps runaways, until he saw their faces, but more importantly their eyes.

Officer Johns noticed that their complexion was abnormally pale but figured they were just cold and wet until he saw their eyes.

Their faces were of normal size, but their eyes...Officer Johns saw that there was no other color to their eyes, only two large oval black eyes.

Not knowing who or what they were, Officer Johns backed into the kitchen doorway and slammed the door, locking the door knob and the master lock.

Tony came into the kitchen shouting to Officer Johns...

"*Who the hell are they...are they still out there?*"

Officer Johns rested his back hard against the door as Diane slowly backed into the kitchen with a look of horror on her face.

Officer Johns pointed to Diane and looked at Tony, saying...

"Hey, what's the matter with her?"

Tony turned to look at Diane when she pointed and murmured...

"OMG...l-look!"

Tony and Officer Johns turned to see what had Diane in a state of terror and as they did, they noticed that standing in the living room were the two small kids wearing dark hoodies.

Tony removed his gun from his pocket and pointed it at them saying...

"I don't know who the hell you are and what you're doing in my house, but you'd best be getting the hell out of here NOW!"

Tony had no more than pointed his gun in their direction when the two kids removed their hoods from their heads and lifted their eyes to look at Tony, Diane and Officer Johns, when Diane screamed...

"AAAAH!"

Tony and Officer Johns looked in horror as the kids revealed their faces. Their heads were completely bald, not the type of bald head you'd expect to see if one had shaved their head...but eerie waxed looking bald heads, with unusually large bulging veins.

Their complexion was a grayish, milky tone and their eyes...their eyes were solid black. Tony cocked his gun at the kids and as he did one of the kids turned and looked at Tony and opened his mouth letting out an ear-piercing scream.

The kid's mouth opened unusually wider than what you'd expect, his jaw seemed to dislocate and stretch downward as the pitch of the scream grew louder.

The pitch was so ear-piercing that Tony dropped his gun and dropped to his knees, cupping both hands over his ears.

Diane and Officer Johns were on the floor cupping their ears and screaming and writhing in pain.

The second kid approached Diane and then Officer Johns and then Tony, spewing a black thick tar-looking liquid from his mouth which covered their faces and filled their mouths.

Somewhere during the screaming, all the lights in the house went out, leaving nothing but the wind, darkness and cold.

Somewhere during all of this, they lay unconsciousness.

The sun peeked through the windows as Tony emerged from the kitchen with a cup of coffee, yelling upstairs to Diane, saying...

"Do you want a cup of coffee babe?"

Diane, stood at the top of the steps, saying...

"Tony...what's happening?"

As Diane came downstairs, Tony handed her a cup of coffee, saying...

"What are you talking about, what do you mean, what's happening?"

Diane started walking through the house, inspecting every room, and then asked Tony...

"Now wait a minute, I know I'm not dreaming, but the last thing I remember, we were in the living room with that Police Officer on the floor, and the two hooded kids were screaming."

Tony took a sip of his coffee and said...

"Honey, I don't know what you're saying, and what Police Officer are you talking about?"

With a blank look on her face, Diane said...

"Don't mess with me Tony, it's way too early for that, are you saying that you don't remember what just happened with the Officer and those creepy kids?"

Tony sat down on the arm of the sofa saying...

"Honestly honey, I don't know what you're talking about, we just both got up and I told you I was going to make coffee, and you came down and the next thing I know you're talking about the Police and some kids."

Walking over to the living room window, Diane looked out, saying...

"Tony, it should be night right now, and the windows on both sides of your recliner should be busted out and..."

Tony interrupted Diane, saying...

"Whoa honey, it's eight-thirty in the morning, and as you can see there's nothing wrong with the windows or anything else in here...you must have had a bad dream or something, I mean, you were tossing and turning all night."

Diane walked away from the window, and went to the door in the kitchen, which leads to the garage, and after opening it said...

"Tony, come here."

Tony walked into the kitchen, stood behind Diane, kissed her neck, and looked into the garage, saying...

"*Okay, I'm here honey, so what am I supposed to be looking at?*"

Diane turned facing Tony and said...

"*The garage door. Tony, last night...I don't mean last night, I mean it was night time not too long ago, and those two creepy kids were trying to get at us and were behind the car, which should be backed in.*"

Tony and Diane walked away from the door to the kitchen table and sat down, as Tony said...

"*Honey, I was following you, but you lost me...there were no creepy kids or nothing last night. We went to J.P.'s and ate, then we came home and looked at television until we went to bed. I'm telling you, you had one hell of a nightmare.*"

Diane screamed out, slamming her fist on the table saying...

"*I don't know what's going on, and I didn't have some goddamn nightmare or anything because we didn't go to sleep. I'm telling you we were sitting on the sofa and some Police Officer named Johns came to the door for help and then two kids wearing hoodies were trying to get into our house, and the next thing I know, it's morning and we're drinking coffee.*"

Tony lifted his head and took a deep breath, saying...

"*Diane, dreams can seem so real, that sometimes we wake up believing that what we dreamed actually happened. I'm telling you, you had a bad dream, nightmare or both, cause, none of that stuff happened, look around you...isn't it daylight?*"

Diane raised her voice and yelled at Tony saying...

"*Damnit Tony, stop patronizing me and acting like I'm a stupid cow or something, I know what happened...it was storming like crazy, we were on the sofa until the Police Officer banged on our door, and then two kids wearing hoodies got into the house, and we tried to leave but couldn't.*"

Trying not to over react to Diane's outburst, Tony took Diane's' hand, saying...

"*Honey, I'm not trying to make you feel stupid or anything like that... look, come here...*"

Tony took Diane by the hand and they walked to the front door as Tony opened it saying...

"You see honey, it didn't rain last night, the grass and driveway is as dry as anything."

Tony walked Diane half way down the drive way, and picked up the newspaper and then walked over to the garage and keyed in the code and as the garage door raised, Tony said...

"Diane, there's no wetness, water or damage to the door. I hear what you're saying, but it didn't happen here honey."

Diane didn't say anything as she and Tony walked in the house, shutting the garage door.

Tony and Diane then walked over to the kitchen table and sat down, as Tony picked up the phone and called the Columbus Police department, saying...

"Hello Columbus Police? Can you connect me with an Officer Patrick Johns please?"

After a moment of silence, a voice answered, saying...

"Hello this is Officer Johns; how can I help you?"

Tony talked with Officer Johns briefly and after hanging up the phone turned to Diane, who asked...

"Well, what did he say, or let me guess...he didn't come out here last, right?"

Tony walked to the living room table and after getting his coffee which he left, returned to the kitchen table and sat down, saying...

"Oh no, he said he remembers coming out here yesterday."

Diane interrupted saying...

"Whew... see there, I told you so...I thought I was losing it for a second, what else did he say?"

Tony looked at Diane and said...

"Honey, Officer Johns remembers coming out here, but he said he never came to see us...but to another family who lives a few blocks over."

Tony could see how upset Diane was over this and decided to get her out of this by taking her to the Easton Mall and a drive, for an afternoon of shopping, since they both had the day off.

Diane was always happy any chance she had to go shopping especially with Tony, but this shopping trip she was a little less enthusiastic.

On the way to the Easton Mall, Diane had very little to say, and

Tony tried making conversation as much as he could without forcing a conversation that neither one was interested in.

Mile after mile, moment by moment, Diane began to loosen up until she was engaging Tony in whole sentences, and before either of them knew it, they were pulling into Easton.

Tony explained to Diane that there were a couple of things he wanted from the Men's Shop which was located at the entrance and agreed to get what he wanted when they were leaving the Mall.

Diane initially told Tony she was only going to grab a few things, until she got inside the Mall and noticed all the things which were on sale.

Tony normally would've huffed and puffed under his breath, having to go here and there and there again, but he wanted to try anything he could because he loved Diane and knew if he was going to be happy, Diane needed to be happy.

The shopping trip was going well for the three hours, they were shopping until Diane went into the dressing room to try on an outfit at the last shop before the Men's Shop.

Tony had waited on Diane to come out of the dressing room for almost an hour when he began to become a little worried.

Not knowing which room Diane was in, and not knowing if he should go inside, he located a sales associate and asked her to check on Diane for him.

Fifteen minutes after the associate went to check on Diane, she came out and told Tony that Diane was sitting and crying hysterically, but that her supervisor was called to talk with her and that she was calming down a little and should be coming out any minute.

Tony managed his composure and remained calm but sat on edge until he saw Diane and a lady emerging from the dressing room area.

Tony raced to Diane and hugged her, saying...

"Honey are you alright! I was really getting worried and I sent someone in to check on you."

Diane grabbed a couple of her bags from Tony and said...

"I'm sorry honey, can we please just leave."

Without saying a word, Tony reach and kissed Diane on her forehead and took her hand as they left the mall.

Tony was not interested in stopping at the Men's Shop, because he wanted to get Diane home and find out what was going on.

The drive home for Tony and Diane was far more intense than the drive up. Diane just sat looking out the right-side passenger window while Tony kept his eyes forward, occasionally glancing at Diane.

As Tony pulled into the drive way and waited for the garage door to open, Diane unbuckled her seat belt and repositioned the bags in her lap.

Just as the garage door was half way up, Diane jumped, saying...

"EEK!"

Diane's reaction startled Tony who stepped on the brakes, jerking the car and saying to Diane...

"It's alright honey, it's just the Snowman Christmas decoration."

Diane sat shaking her head and then said to Tony...

"After I put all this stuff away, I'm going to take that damn snowman and put his ass up in the storage area...it scared the shit out of me."

Tony stopped the car and turned off the engine, saying...

"Honey, that's alright I can take care of that."

While Diane went inside, Tony lowered the rope and let down the storage ladder to the excess storage area and placed the few remaining Christmas decorations into the storage area, and then came into the house.

Diane was sitting on the sofa looking at all the things she had purchased from the mall, when Tony asked...

"Can I get you something?"

Shaking her head, Diane said...

"No."

Tony sat beside her and gently asked...

"You want to tell me what's going on. What happened in the Mall that got you so upset?"

Diane looked at Tony, took a deep breath and said...

"Promise you'll just hear me out first before you stick me on the short bus?"

Tony took hold of Diane's hand, saying...

"Honey just tell me what's going on, I promise not to get all jacked up."

Diane took a deep breath and sighed and said...

"You know when I asked all those questions this morning about Officer Johns, and said I saw a creepy Nun and two creepy kids wearing hoodies?"

Nodding his head, Tony said...

"Yes, I remember."

Squeezing Tony's hand, Diane said...

Well, I took two outfits into the dressing room and hung them on hangers and was trying the pants and vest on, when someone was rattling the dressing room door handle, like they wanted to come in.

In a calm voice I said, 'someone's in here'. I thought they'd left and I was looking at myself in the mirror when the door opened up and there was this creepy Nun again, in a dirty Habit smiling at me".

Tony interrupted Diane, saying...

"Honey, why didn't you call for help?"

"I did, do you think I'd just let someone come up on me like that and not do anything?"

Diane said as she shifted her body in the chair. Tony motioned for her to go on, saying...

"Okay, so this Nun barged in on you in the dressing room, then what, did she do or say anything?"

Diane placed her index finger on Tony's lips and said...

"If you'd stop interrupting me, I'll get to that part, anyways, when she came up on me so fast, I was so scared that I couldn't say or do anything, not to mention her hand was covering my mouth.

I was so damn scared, that I almost peed on myself. This Nun put her face close to mine and started sniffing me, I mean I tried to scream, but I couldn't make a sound. Then she licked my face and said..."

"I'm Gonna come for you tonight."

Tony had a disgusting look on his face as he said...

"Eww."

Diane sat back in her chair, saying...

"After that, someone knocked on the door, and when I looked up in the mirror...The Nun was gone, I mean, she wasn't there anymore, and she didn't use the door, because another woman was knocking on it."

Tony sat there with a look of disbelief on his face, when Diane said...

"I know you don't believe me but, I just screamed and then I lost it for a few minutes, until some woman broke the dressing room door open."

Tony remained speechless for a minute and then he said...

"Honey, I'm not saying anything, because I'm trying to think of the right thing to say, I mean Nuns don't go around doing stuff like, I mean they pray and hold bingo and all that kind of stuff, unless she's a pedophile."

Diane broke and gave a smile and a small chuckle and said...

"Deviant, Tony, deviant is what you'd call her, I think a pedophile is an adult who is attracted to small children. Besides, it's more than that...I mean this Nun just vanished...I don't think she's human."

Tony got up to get something to drink, saying...

"You see, that's the only part I'm having an issue with...the vanishing part."

Diane followed Tony in the kitchen saying...

"Don't you think I know that too, but there's still one more thing though?"

Tony lifted his head from the fridge, saying...

"And what's that?"

Diane said...

"She said she was coming for me tonight...if she does, what are we gonna do?"

Getting grapes, cheese and pouring a glass of wine, Tony replied, saying...

"Let her creepy sick self-show up...let me deal with it?"

Diane snapped back, saying...

"Tony, I'm telling you, that I don't think she's human."

Tony sat down in the kitchen and cut a slice of cheese and took a sip of wine and said...

"C'mon get serious honey, I was simply saying, I will be with you every minute and if she shows up, watch, I'll deal with her ass."

Diane turned to Tony, saying...

"Will you pour me one of those...I think I'm really going to need one, maybe two of three of those about now. Baby, that Nun said she was coming for me tonight...what the hell does that mean, what did I do to her?"

Tony replied, saying...

"All I can say is, you need to call a couple of your friends from your church to be here with you tonight, praying and whatever; and if that doesn't do the trick, well then, 'Smith and Wesson' will."

Diane grabbed the cell phone out of her purse and called several of her friends and explained to them what was going on and, surprisingly, they agreed to meet at Tony and Diane's later that evening.

On the phone, one of Diane's friends suggested that Tony be everywhere Diane was, and to not be alone until they get there.

Tony and Diane went upstairs so that Diane could get her Bible and Rosary Beads, and they came straight downstairs, cut on all the lights in the house and sat on the sofa, when Diane said...

"OMG, I can't believe we're acting like this, if you'd asked me yesterday if I believed in this kind of crap...I'd told you hell no, but now look at us, and I tell you all of this weird stuff with The Nun and all, had better be real, because if it's not I'm checking in at the nearest nut house."

Tony took Diane's hand and said...

"Look I've never known you to lie, and as wild as this whole thing is, I'm right here and if it helps, I have my pistol under this cushion."

Just then the front door bell rang, startling Diane and Tony. Both Diane and Tony got up to answer the door, as Diane said...

"It's probably, Robin or Michelle."

Tony peeked out the window and turned to Diane and said...

"No, it's a man...I wonder who this is?"

As Tony fully opened the door a man, in his thirties, about six feet tall, casual dressed revealed his badge and said...

"Hello sir, my name is Patrick Johns, and I work for the Columbus Police department, and I was hoping to speak with Mrs. Diane Smith, if I may."

Tony invited Officer Johns in as Diane emerged from behind Tony, saying...

"Hello, I'm Diane and we've met before."

Officer Johns was invited to take a seat on the sofa, and Tony Offered him a glass of wine which Officer Johns refused but took a glass of water instead.

Officer Johns looked at Diane and said...

"I appreciate your hospitality, and I know you're wondering why and what I am doing here, and to be honest...I'm a little uncertain myself, but..."

"Here you go."

Tony said, as he handed Officer Johns a glass of water.

Tony sat down next to Diane, as Diane relayed to Tony what Officer Johns was saying while he was in the kitchen.

Officer Johns went on to say...

"In all my years of being a Police Officer, I've come across just about every imaginable thing you can think of and this is no different. "You see, Mr. uh".

Tony interrupted him by saying...

"Just call me Tony."

Officer Johns nodded and said...

"Okay Tony, as I was saying, just about everything that a person experiences has a lot of truth to it, the question is, how we go about seeing the truth.

What I'm saying is this, Tony, when you called today saying that your wife said that I was here at your home earlier today, I said no...well that was the truth and it was also a lie."

Tony waved his hand at Officer Johns saying...

"Okay, you've totally lost me on that one, you said it was and wasn't the truth, but I don't recall you being at our home ever...that is until now...is that what you're talking about?"

Officer Johns said...

"When I woke up this morning, my only memory was being at your home. I recall seeing a Nun, two creepy kids wearing hoodies and a big man wearing a Ballerina's Tutu, and my partner was killed outside, but then I found myself at work this morning, there he was, alive with no memory of last night."

Diane jumped in, saying...

"That's what I was saying this morning honey, I remember Officer Johns, and The Nun and creepy kids, but I don't recall going to sleep or waking up or anything else. The Nun said something and the next thing I know you and I were home, but only you don't remember anything, and I do."

Officer Johns looked directly at Diane, saying...

"Diane...have you see this Nun either before or after last night?"

Diane nodded her head, saying...

"Yes, about a couple hours ago in the shopping mall."

"And did she say anything to you?"

Officer Johns asked Diane, as he drank some of his water.

Diane related the entire day's events to him as he took some notes on a pad he pulled out of his pocket, saying...

"I didn't believe in the spiritual, ghosts, spirits, etc., but recently I've come to respect that they are real and are nothing to be taken lightly. Last night it rained harder that its ever rain in a while, but there is no sign of it.

My partner was dead last night, and yet today, he is alive with no memory. Tony, you and I had several physical fights with this Nun last night, and those creepy kids, and today you know nothing about it…but Diane and I do.

Today while I was at the station attending to a detainee in his cell, the Nun appeared in his place and said that she was coming for you and me, and I just think all of us need to be together in one place, and try to do something, anything."

Diane got up to go into the kitchen and asked, Officer Johns…

"Would you like something stronger than water?"

Officer Johns stood up, saying…

"I'd love anything to mix with this, thanks."

Diane left the room to grab refreshments while Officer Johns explained to Tony the severity of The Nun's threats and what both he and Diane had experienced, when Diane screamed out…

"TONY!"

Tony jumped up and raced towards the kitchen, with Officer Johns following.

When they both reached the kitchen, Diane was standing by the kitchen door with several beers and a bottle of vodka in her hand and the Nun had Diane by the hair.

Tony tried to go to Diane's rescue, but Officer Johns stopped him by grabbing him, saying…

"Hey buddy, No! Just back off and see what she does first."

While Tony was being restrained, the Nun looked at Tony and then to Officer Johns, saying…

"Good Good, now hold the little piggy back, or I'll make him think he's a dog lapping up water on his hands and knees. Better yet, let him go. I feel like a little fun right now."

As Tony was being held back, the Nun, grabbed Diane's face and kissed her on the cheek, saying…

"Mmm, I like your scent, your body odor I may have to have fun with you instead"

Tony stood helpless as Diane wiggled and squirmed trying to break The Nun's grip, when she told Diane...

"Stop it. Stop your struggling, you can't get away unless I want you to."

Crying and moaning, Diane said...
"What do you want...who are you?"
The Nun mocked Diane, saying...

"What do you want, who are you, how many feet are in a mile. Questions, questions, questions. All in due time, all in dur time. My name is Sister Mary Jacalyn. And by the way, your friends aren't coming tonight."

Diane struggled to speak as The Nun slapped her in the face, saying...

"What I want is a little payback. Payback for being convicted and sentenced to a cold dark dungeon without a proper trial."

Diane, Tony and Officer Johns, looked at one another in dismay, before Tony spoke up, saying...
"Look, I don't know who you are, but your beef is not with us, if you got problems with someone in the past, well....I dunno what to tell you."
Sister Mary Jacalyn released Diane and, in an instant, moved over to Tony, and with her long misshapen fingers, started choking him, saying...

"You just don't listen do you, and you have a smart mouth well, let's see how smart you are later tonight, when I come back."

Sister Mary Jacalyn told Tony, Diane and Officer Johns that she was sending them back to a time where their worst dreams becomes their reality. She offered no reason for doing it, or for her appearing to them.

The first to travel back in time was Diane. Her next recollection was prior to meeting and marrying Tony. Diane had recently graduated from high school and was living with her parents.

It was a Saturday and Diane had gone back home to her parents' house to change and get ready to go to work since she had to be there at three p.m.

There were no street lights in the neighborhood because the night before someone crashed their car into the light pole, so Diane decided to use her video cam light on her phone instead of the pocket flashlight because the lighting was much brighter.

When Diane reached her mother and father's house, she could tell that they were already in bed, because she saw their bedroom lamp on and the entire downstairs was dark.

Diane entered the house as quietly as she could and after a trip to the kitchen for a piece of her mother's chocolate cake, headed upstairs to her room. Diane's room was two doors down from her parents', down a dimly lit hallway.

Diane had decided after getting her work clothes off her bed, she would dress on the top steps and then head downstairs and out the door for the fifteen-minute walk to work.

As Diane was standing on the top step pulling up her pants, she heard something fall in her bedroom. Turning, Diane decided to go back into her room, because she remembered that she had a glass of milk sitting on the dresser and didn't want it to ruin her mother's dresser.

Diane very quietly crept into her room and opened the window blinds to get more light because she didn't want to waken her father by turning on the light, and it shinning in the hallway.

Diane checked all around the room, and found that the wind must have knocked over the glass of milk, which was lying in her dresser drawer which contained her clean underwear...

"Damn!"

Diane whispered as she picked up the glass and tried to salvage as many dry pair of her panties as she could. Diane placed her phone facing down on her dresser next to her camcorder and did not notice she hit the record button.

Diane worked at the local hardware center at night stocking shelves and processing orders for the next day's shipment.

At twelve-twenty-five am, Diane gathered her lunch and walked down the hall to one of the empty offices and sat down to eat. Diane packed a light lunch and another piece of Chocolate cake, which she nearly gobbled down. Looking at her watch, Diane noticed that her lunch break was almost up.

"Eleven more minutes...wow!",

Diane whispered to herself, as she decided to lay her head down for a minute. In the employee lounge was a bulletin board, which is where messages are posted for employees.

Diane looked up and saw her name in an envelope and jumped from the table to read it. Diane hoped that it wasn't a notice saying she'd been let go. As Diane carefully read it, it said...

'I'll see you in the morning while you're asleep.'

Initially, it didn't scare Diane, but it did freak her out a little. Over the next four hours on Diane's shift her mind kept drifting to the message and who could have written it. Diane decided once she was not going to let it get to her.

When Diane got home from work around five a.m. her father and mother were outside on the front porch enjoying their morning cup of coffee. Her father and mother often awakened very early in the morning, which was out of her father being a veteran, who was used to early wake up calls, and her mother who grew up on a farm and was used to early morning farm duties.

After greeting her father and mother, Diane thanked her mother for the cake and told them that she was off to get eight sweet hours of sleep. Diane sat on her bed for a few minutes stretching, and then off to get a shower before going to bed.

Diane's shower was interrupted, probably due to one of her parents using the water downstairs. The water would turn real hot and then Luke warm for a few seconds before going back to normal, and Diane didn't want to deal with it, so she stepped out of the shower, after only a few minutes.

No sooner had Diane step out of the shower did she hear her mother's voice calling her name...

"Diane Lee. Diane are you finished?"

Diane didn't hear her mother at first, but then responded...

"Yeah mom, I'm done."

Diane stepped out of the bathroom upstairs, and as she opened the door, there she saw a man. His entire image was pale, as if she had blurry vision.

"Who the heck is this man?"

Diane said, as she ran back into the bathroom.

"Maybe he's a plumber or another kind of worker, maybe that's why mom was asking me if I were done."

Diane said to herself as she cracked the door and called for her mom to come upstairs, which she did.

When Diane's mom got to the top of the steps Diane said...

"Hey mom, who's that man in the hallway?"

Her mother looked around and then said...

"Diane, what on earth is the matter with you, have you been drinking or smoking that wacky weed...you know it'll make you stupid."

Diane stepped out of the bathroom with the towel tightly around her and after looking for the man, said...

"Mom, somebody was there. A few minutes ago, I stepped out of the bathroom and there was a man standing right where you're standing. He had unkempt hair, pale face, a little chunky slightly rounded belly, wearing coveralls."

Diane's mom replied, saying...

"Well as you see, there's no one here, besides, what would someone be doing in our house at this time in the morning?"

"Mom, I swear, I saw someone standing in the hallway."

Diane said as she and her mother walked back down towards Diane's room. Diane's mother told her that maybe she was really exhausted and needed to get some sleep.

Nodding her head yes, Diane went into her room and after shutting the door sat on her bed and began applying lotion to her legs, feet and upper body.

After brushing her hair, Diane put on a tee shirt and her pj bottom and lay back on the bed. She had only laid down for a few seconds and she was asleep, and then as fast as she fell asleep, she awakened.

Diane looked over at the headphones and quickly put them on her head and positioned the record player and plugged in the head phones, put her favorite album on and turned the volume up and lay back in bed.

Immediately her heart started beating very fast. At first there was nothing coming out of the headphones but static and then Diane heard soft voices which grew louder and louder, voices which said...

"Twisted and dread, Twisted and dread somebody's dead, and so will you be too!"

Diane quivered, and she got up and ran to the kitchen where her Mom was making breakfast for her husband. Seeing Diane run into the kitchen, she said...

"If I recall, I left you about to go to sleep, what did you do, change your mind about breakfast?"

Diane shook her head no, and said...

"I just wanted to grab something to drink, maybe a glass of ice cold milk."

Diane hung around the kitchen for a couple minutes more after pouring her milk, when she said...

"I guess it's time to go to bed."

As Diane left the kitchen, she petted her father's head and said...

"Nite all."

Diane reached her bedroom, and immediately saw the album going around and around, and the headphones lying on the bed, and said to herself...

"I'm not going to listen to anything, I'm going straight to sleep, and with that Diane crawled into bed and fell asleep."

Just then, Diane was awakened by noises. As she opened her eyes, saw a glimpse of a white image. This person, or whatever it was passed right in front of her face. He didn't bother Diane, he just walked passed her. Diane's heart beat was very fast, and she could hear her own pulse... and then he vanished in a blink of an eye.

Diane's eyes frantically scanned the room, but there was nobody there. As Diane's eyes began to welcome sleep, she heard a scraping noise against her window.

She thought to ignore it, but it continued scrapping and scratching the glass, irritating and annoying Diane until, she opened the drapes and when she did, she saw the most hideous face staring back at her.

Diane let go of the drapes and turned over on her stomach, pulled the blankets up around her neck and closed her eyes tight.

Diane began hearing inside her head...

"Twisted and Dread, Twisted and Dread, somebody's dead and soon you will be too."

Just then, four pairs of hands emerged from inside the mattress and grabbed Diane and pulled her in and closed up again.

In the blinking of an eye, Tony, Officer Johns and Diane were all sitting at the kitchen table as Sister Mary Jacalyn said...

"Well, how did you like that one? Tony and Patrick got to watch as Diane was tormented. You see, each one of you are going to experience one of your bad nightmares like Diane did. I'm going to make you relive nightmares until we find one that scares the shit out of you, and then you'll relieve that one over and over, but only it will be real.

Officer Patrick Johns Patrick your next, you little gun-toting queen, batter . up!"

Once more everything went dark and while Tony, Officer Johns and Diane could hear one another, they could neither touch or see one another. Then Tony, Officer Johns and Diane heard the Nun saying...

"Fasten your seatbelt Patty, it gets a little bumpier from here out."

Sunday morning 6 am

Patrick Johns woke up suddenly out of a sound sleep, he saw the time on his cell, it was six am. He never ever got up at six am even during the week days! Patrick sat up in bed wondering to himself what made him awake at six am, and on a Sunday too...!

Patrick looked at his mobile to confirm that it was the real time, it said "*Battery down*", and then he glanced over at his partner, Raymond, who had just turned over, snoring.

Patrick got up from his bed to charge his cell. He was still half asleep, and the room was dark yet...! Patrick had to be careful not to bump into anything, because of the marks it'll leave on his fair skin.

Patrick's family and friends didn't care much for Raymond because they thought he was physically abusing Patrick.

Patrick and Raymond swore there was no abuse going on, even though Patrick continues to awaken with bruises, swollen eyes, and busted lips.

As Patrick plugged in the charger, he turned his face to the left and saw into the long mirror, on the other side of the room someone standing behind him...! Patrick could see the blurred image of someone in white clothes and long hair. Seems like a beautiful figure, winking and blowing kisses at him...!

Patrick was thrilled to the point of getting goosebumps...he believed, that if you dream about someone and it arouses you, even if it's a ghost or spirit, there's always the chance of an amazing sex life when you awake.

To make certain that what he was seeing was real...Patrick turned behind himself and looked, No one was there behind him...! No one!

Patrick looked into the mirror again. This time he saw the same image! Same figure standing behind him, touching him, having sex with him, locking his fingers under Patrick's chin and riding him fast and hard, making Patrick scream with passion, only something was different!

Patrick's heart beat increased, the figure who was pleasuring Patrick started, beating and punching him in the face and head, and then suddenly, revealed a set of jagged, sharp teeth, and bent down and sank them into Patrick's back.

Patrick screamed and awakened, sitting up in his bed. Patrick looked all around the room, but he was alone, save his partner Raymond, who was stirring from his sleep, saying...

"Hey, baby, you alright?"

"Was that real? Is it possible? Should I go to the mirror and check? I don't have the guts to look into the mirror for a third time this morning, too many people think that Ray's abusing me, but he's not.... It's my dreams, the figure in my dreams is responsible for it, but no one would believe me, not even Ray."

Patrick thought to himself, as he walked over to the bathroom mirror to check himself out for bruises and bite marks.

Just then the figure that Patrick saw behind him in the mirror was now standing in front of him. He stood five-feet-ten inches tall, light olive pigmentation. Long flowing curly, white hair and the bluest eyes. It was the most handsome looking figure that Patrick had ever seen.

Everything was beautiful, perfect about this figure. The closer he got to Patrick, the more uncomfortable Patrick was becoming. His heart raced, he began hyperventilating and became increasingly fidgety.

The figure stopped right in front of Patrick as he dropped to his knees, then it reached out its hand and caressed Patrick's face and then helped Patrick to his feet. Then Patrick stood, weak in the knees, willing to do anything, everything just to be there for one more moment in front of this figure.

Then the atmosphere in the room changed and Patrick saw the figure move behind him, and he sank his teeth into Patrick's neck as he mounted him again.

When Patrick looked up at the mirror, the image of the beautiful figure had changed into an ugly, grotesque figure with a distorted face. Whatever it was, Patrick was totally terrified.

All Patrick could feel was his heart pounding in his chest and was frozen. Patrick couldn't move because he was so scared. After a few minutes, whoever it was, was gone.

It didn't last too long because after a few minutes it came back. First it was the pretty white-haired figure and then the dark figure, and that's when the loud tutting sound started to happen. It was coming from, in front of Patrick, and then the ceiling and it was really loud and fast, like nothing Patrick had ever heard.

Usually Patrick and his partner would hear sounds from time to time, like a popping noise when the heat comes on, and then sounds like a loud and fast ticking clock. But this sound was very different. This sound went on for a full thirty minutes, and that's why Patrick felt very uneasy and uncomfortable being in the house at night alone, which is why he began asking his partner to spend the night with him.

Patrick had to get ready for bed because he had to get up early for work, so he finally managed to gather up the courage to sleep. Even with Raymond there, Patrick felt uneasy but managed to close his eyes, but he was terrified that he was going to be attacked in the middle of the night.

Patrick tried to go to sleep but he was so scared, that he scooched up close to Raymond and eventually fell asleep.

Just at the time when Patrick was getting his sleep on, the urge to use the bathroom hit him and he got up and walked sleepily to the guest bathroom because he didn't want to awaken Raymond.

On his way back into his bedroom, and while Patrick was walking back, a voice behind him shouted...

"BOO!"

Really loud. Patrick jumped nearly out of his skin and was so scared, because he thought the dark figure was back to hurt him. Patrick turned his head and was expecting someone to be standing behind him, but when he turned around no one was there.

The bathroom window was open, so he looked out the curtain, and in the field across from his house to where some cows were, when one of the cows in particular, looked directly at Patrick and instead of the usual sound that a cow makes, this one said...

"BOO."

Patrick closed the window in the bathroom and hurried down the hallway, back to bed. He was lying in bed trying to fall asleep, when all of a sudden it felt like someone else was in his bedroom other than him and Raymond; and that it was watching him.

It took Patrick ages to fall asleep that night. Patrick recalled seeing a black Smokey figure hovering above him on several occasions when he opened his eyes. Patrick thought that it grabbed his shoulders and pushed him into the mattress. He started swinging to fight it off and grabbed his necklace of the crucifix off the bedside table and started stabbing the Smokey black figure.

After that the black Smokey figure disappeared. Patrick woke up with the necklace in his hand, but also with cuts and bruises on his face. It freaked Patrick out and he quickly jumped up awakening Raymond, who said as he turned the bed side light on...

"Pat, what's wrong—OMG, your face."

Patrick realized that it wasn't a dream at all and said...

"I don't wanna stay here anymore Ray, I wanna leave right now."

Holding Patrick's shoulders, Raymond said...

"What happened to your face, damn, if your family sees you like this they're going to be all up in my ass accusing me, so what happened?"

Patrick told Raymond all about the dreams, and the black figure that's been hurting him, and even showed Raymond his shoulder and the bite marks.

Without any hesitation, Raymond and Patrick gathered up clothes and went over to Raymond's apartment.

A few weeks later, Patrick was sick with the flu, so Capt. Monroe, the department commander, sent him home. Patrick was sick at home for the entire week. Luckily, by the fourth day, Patrick was nearly one hundred percent better, but wasn't sleeping very well at night because of the dreams and the flu.

Raymond was at work, and Patrick lay on the sofa instead of getting into bed and eventually fell asleep watching a western.

After hours of tossing and turning, Patrick started to have a vivid dream that the black Smokey figure and he were at a coffee shop talking, only in his dream, Patrick was bold enough to ask the Black figure what it wanted, and it said something that Patrick would never forget.

The Black figure said that it visits many while they sleep, and if they have a sweet body odor...he bites, or kicks, or beats them, while he torments them. The Dark Smokey figure said that he enters people's dreams, steals the good portions which is why it's so hard to remember all your dreams.

The Black figure said when it enters your dreams, it leaves a trail inside your dreams, almost like the smoke trail that a jet airliner leaves in the air, so that it is easy to find you while you sleep.

The Black Smokey figure said, that no matter where he is or how far apart he is from you, he looks for the trail and follows it right into your dreams.

The Black Smokey figure told Patrick that, when he was alive hundreds of years ago, he had a real mean and nasty family who owned a perfume shop who he worked for, who enjoyed hurting and torturing him for no reason.

He told Patrick that he was so full of rage and hate that, he now hunts those he can smell. He said, the sweet body odor draws him, and that he is attracted to the scent.

The Black Smokey figure told Patrick, that initially, he could only enter dreams, but now, he was able to visit people while they're awake and for Patrick to watch for him, when the door opened.

Patrick's partner Raymond entered carrying a large sack full of food from Patrick's favorite restaurant.

Patrick spent the rest of the day watching TV with his partner and gorging on Chinese food when he decided that he would leave some food for later and go brush his teeth and get himself ready for bed.

Patrick was in the bathroom looking into the medicine cabinet for a dental pic and brushing his teeth, leaving the bathroom door open as he was only going to be in there a short while. While Patrick was brushing his teeth, he could see the hall out the right side of his peripheral vision.

Before you get to the bathroom from the main bedroom you have to walk down a set of three wooden stairs, so you can hear whenever anyone walks down them as they are a bit noisy and the floor boards creak because they are very old.

Anyway, Patrick was standing there brushing his teeth when he heard footsteps walk down the stairs and thought it was his partner coming down to check on him, as he sometimes did.

Patrick looked, and no one was there! He heard no footsteps before the stairs or after and heard no lock on any door click as it opened or any doors close. His partner had the TV going on, loud, and while Patrick could hear it in the hallway, he could barely hear it from inside the bathroom.

Patrick went back to the living room after he had brushed his teeth and asked his partner if he had heard the footsteps and Raymond said he did but thought that it was Patrick coming back from the bathroom. Patrick and his partner were both freaked out a bit, but Patrick told him that it was probably just the heat making the wooden floors creak.

While Patrick and Raymond were sitting and watching TV, Raymond noticed fresh blood stains on Patrick's tee shirt and said...

"Hey babe, what's with the blood on your shirt, did you cut yourself?"
Trying to twist to see if he could spot the blood that his partner

was talking about, Raymond took one of the napkins and after wetting it, dubbed it on the bloody part of Patrick's back and showed it to him.

Patrick looked at the blood stain on the napkin and replied...

"Oh my...that looks nasty as hell."

Raymond lightly touched one of the claw marks, saying...

"I'm going to get some peroxide, anti-bacteria ointment and then you're going to tell me what is going on. I know that you are causing these wounds to yourself, so don't tell me that. Are you sleep walking and falling down or something?"

Patrick removed his tee shirt, saying...

"Ok, but I'll only tell you under the condition that you will hear me out and not laugh at me."

Raymond returned back to the living room and sat down facing Patrick's back and began cleaning and dressing Patrick's wounds, saying...

"Gosh! These are deep, it's like someone used one of those three-pronged hand garden rakes on you or something."

Trying to remain calm, Patrick took a deep breath and said...

"Ray, what I'm about to say is weird, but it's the truth. At night when I am asleep and in dreamland, I have these weird dreams that ghosts, or spirits or demons are attacking me, and then when I wake up, I see all these scars and cuts on me."

Raymond placed the left side of his face against Patrick's face saying...

"I mean if that's all, well I can understand that...damnit honey, I wanna believe you and all that, but do you hear yourself, you're saying, ghost and spirits are beating the shit out of you and stuff."

Patrick pushed Raymond away from him a little, saying...

"Now if it were you Ray, I'd believe you or I'd least try to."

Raymond sat closer to Patrick saying...

"I'm trying to, and I want to believe you...I'm just being honest, it's not the easiest thing in the world to hear, but if that's what you say happened, then, I believe you."

Patrick then said...

"So, what do we do? Do any of the cops in your precinct know about this?

Patrick held and kissed Raymond's hands, saying...

"No! If they knew about this, I'd be on desk duty or some dumb shit like that."

Patrick then got up and went up to take a bath and get dressed, while Raymond went out to the store for another bottle of wine and sandwiches.

Patrick checked on the water and seeing that his bath water was almost as full as he liked it, he cut it off and went into the bedroom and took out a pair of clean underwear, a tee shirt and his bathrobe and returned to the bathroom.

When Patrick returned to the bathroom, he did not waste any time getting in...he wanted to have himself all clean and fresh for Raymond when he came home.

Patrick generally soaked in the tub for a while before washing, but today Patrick was going to wash and then get out of the tub, all of a sudden, the bathroom door flew open.

Standing there in the hallway was an old woman dressed in a Nun's habit, which was dirty and worn. A cold wind started blowing upstairs and suddenly, Patrick's water was ice cold.

Patrick searched for the bath towel, and seeing where it was he jumped out of the tub and placed it around himself, saying...

"What the fuck! Look, I don't know what you want, but leave me alone, will you."

The Nun covered up over her eyes, saying...

"I won't peek, little cock loving girl."

Patrick stood, shivering and shaking, and saying...
"What the hell do you want?"

From downstairs, there came a stomp-stomp-stomping noise as the wind whistled and climbed the stairs. From downstairs, a hollow voice said:

"Nine-one-one. Officer Dead! Officer Dead!"

Upstairs, the Nun shuddered and turned back to Patrick saying...

You tries, and you tries, but nobody ever pays attention. What I want with you, you'll see very soon. I'm here to drive you insane with your dreams because I can!"

A stomp, stomp, stomping sound continued from downstairs, when Patrick yelled...

"Raymond is that you!"

The Nun snapped her fingers and said to Patrick...

"No, it's not your girlfriend, it's somebody waiting to snap his neck as he comes in the front door, and there's nothing a sissy gun toting bitch like you can do about it."

Patrick stood, shivering and coughing, yelling...

"Damnit, what in the hell do you want!"

The Nun shouted back!

"I told you, I am going to change your reality and then make you relive your worst nightmares until I find the one that breaks you, and then you will relive that nightmare for the rest of your life."

Patrick cried...

"Why me, what did I ever do?"

The Nun stuck her crooked index finger in Patrick's chest, poking it, saying...

"You got up this morning, didn't you?"

Patrick's whole body shook with fright as he listened to The Nun talk about what she was going to do to him.

Suddenly, the front door of the apartment burst open with a bang, and then Raymond hollered...

"Hey, I'm back!"

As Patrick turned to look at The Nun, she had disappeared, and Patrick, ran down stairs, to Raymond who was hanging his coat up, saying...

"Am I glad that you're back. The Nun I was telling you about...well, she was just here."

Raymond hugged Patrick, saying...

"Well don't worry I'm here, she won't show her ugly ass when I'm here, will she?"

Suddenly, there was a large popping sound and when Patrick and Raymond looked up, standing in front of them at the top of the steps, was the Nun, Sister Mary Jacalyn, saying...

"Hello boys and girls...here I am showing my face, now what are you going to do about it Raymond?"

For one of the first times in his life, Raymond was experiencing real fear on a completely different level.

Sister Mary Jacalyn then said with a wicked grin...

"Raymond, you are going nowhere. You will neither be here nor there. You will watch and when I bring you back, you will have no memory of where you've been.

All that you'll remember is me. Now for you Officer Patrick Johns, one of the dreams I've pick out for you to relieve is animals chasing you, and finally catching you so buckle your seatbelts, cause this is gonna be one kick ass ride."

As quick as a moment is, Raymond and Patrick were no longer in Raymond's apartment.

Suddenly, there was a darkness and then a growling dog coming towards Patrick. Patrick started running through what looked like a dense forest, and then he came to a fence and he tried climbing it.

When Patrick got over the fence and jumped down to the ground, the next thing he knew he was sitting up in a large room.

He saw the glowing figure of a beautiful Native American woman standing in the distance. He blinked in amazement, and felt chills run all over his body.

She raised her arms and with a gesture transformed herself into a beautiful snow-white hare. The glowing snow-white hare hopped slowly ahead of Patrick, who followed it until they came to an open field.

Patrick followed it closely, for several hours, until the snow-white hare came to a lake and changed herself back into the beautiful Native American woman, with long dark brown windblown hair.

Patrick had a feeling that there was something evil about this woman and kept his distance, even though the woman continued to beckon him to come closer.

Just then, from over the horizon, there were a pack of wild dogs, growling and viciously coming towards Patrick.

Patrick had no choice but to go into the teepee with the Beautiful Native American woman. When Patrick entered the teepee with her, the growling dogs seem to fade out in the distance.

Inside the teepee, were hundreds of fur skins lining the floor and a roaring fire lit and food on an open pit. The Beautiful Native American woman handed Patrick a large wooden cup, which was full of wine.

As she seductively danced in front of Patrick, something in the cup which he drunk from made him unable to move, when she opened the flap of the tent and called for the wild dogs. Patrick screamed in terror as the growling dogs slowly made their way into the tent, with saliva and foam dripping from their mouths.

The next thing Patrick knew he was sitting in the living room with Diane, Tony and the Nun, Sister Mary Jacalyn, who said...

"Welcome back Officer Johns, how was your day? Do you wanna relieve what you just went through, that over and over, or shall I find another nightmare to send you through?"

Officer Patrick Johns sat, with his head down, not so confident, not so self-assured, as the Nun looked over at Tony, saying...

"Oh, Tony, no one has forgotten you, lover boy, you're next. I've picked out a perfect nightmare for you. I'll see you when you get back if you get back."

With a wave of her hand everything went dark. Tony awoke in a dark house, hearing screams and voices.

Calling out to see if his wife Diane, was watching television, Tony listened intently, as he sat shaking and wondering if it everything was simply a dream. Suddenly, there was a tap on the door. Gathering his courage, Tony turned on the lamp on the end table and opened the door only to see that there was no one there.

Bewildered, Tony shut the door and walked back in the living room, he checked his cell phone to see if there was a missed call from Diane or a message, but there was nothing.

Earlier that day, Tony had fallen asleep on the sofa watching a movie and remembered that Diane had kissed his forehead, saying she was going shopping.

Just then, Tony's cell phone began ringing and vibrating, looking down Tony saw that it was Diane calling. Answering the phone as quickly as he could, Tony said...

"Hello, Diane? Baby where are you?"

Diane did not answer, so Tony called her several times more, but all Tony got was a busy signal.

Tony tried dialing Diane's number several times until at last Diane answered, saying...

"Hey, you, I'm glad you answered. Say listen, the car's acting up again, I'm off of exit four-fifty, on the side of the road, you got time to rescue a girl?"

Tony replied, saying...

"Yes baby, I'll come get you...you do know that we have triple A, have you tried called them?"

Diane responded by saying...

"Remember we canceled that, because we never used them, besides, I haven't seen but one car pass me the whole time I've been out here."

Tony stood up and placed his feet into his sneakers, saying...

"Alright you're off exit four-fifty, right? Honey why'd you get off there, there isn't anything out there but an old farm house, you should have stayed on the interstate."

Irritated, Diane said...

"Would've, could've, heck I'm tired, and a little pissed and besides, I gotta pee, so you coming to get me or not?"

"Sorry honey just hang tight. I'm on my way and I should be there in about forty-five minutes."

Tony apologetically said as he left the house.

When Tony arrived at exit four-fifty, he saw Diane's car but no sign of her in the car, except for a note under the driver's side wiper blade, saying…I had to p & p…ran up behind the old farm house - D

Tony made it through the thick grass, to the old farm house and figured from Diane's note that she would be behind it or on the side of the house away from view of the interstate.

Tony called out for Diane several times but did not get an answer. He walked all around the outside of the old farm house, but no sign of Diane.

Tony noticed that there was a door completely open and figured perhaps Diane went inside to do her business, so Tony entered calling Diane's name over and over, but, no response.

Finally, Tony heard a faint grunt and then moans coming from behind the only door in the downstairs and tried the knob.

Unable to open it, Tony called for Diane and pounded on the door. He heard more moans and muffled sounds from inside and decided to bust the door down.

Tony flung himself against and through the door, as his legs propelled him through the room and into the small hallway on the other side. The moans and muffled sounds were coming from behind an old shower curtain.

With Tony's fear heightened, and images flooded his mind as he pulled back the shower curtain and found Diane.

Tony couldn't even vomit as the sickeningly sight baffled him. When Tony pulled back the shower curtain, there was Diane covered in feces and feeding on the remains of a dead rat.

Tony backed into the doorway of the bathroom, shocked at what he was seeing. Diane chased after him until he fell on his back. On top of him he could smell and see the rotten flesh falling from Diane's mouth as she tried talking to him.

Tony could feel the vomit rising in his throat and threw Diane off him, and as he did, he found himself back in his own living room with Officer Johns, Diane and the Nun, who said…

"Well, how did we like that Tony? How would you like to visit that one over and Over again huh?"

Tony sat looking mostly at Diane who looked at Tony with a puzzling expression on her face, as Sister Mary Jacalyn said...

"Well, you folks think it over and when I come back, I expect an answer."

As Sister Mary Jacalyn stood up to leave, Tony asked...
Do you really expect us to choose any of those?"
Stopping and turning, Sister Mary Jacalyn said...

"Well lover boy, if you don't choose, I'll pick one out for you myself, and believe me, you don't want me to do that."

Tony, Officer Johns and Diane sat and watched Sister Mary Jacalyn, as she vanished in the wall.

3
Hard Days Night

Clara and Bill tried to settle in for a stormy night but what they both experienced caused Bill to say...

"Clara, we could always pack the dogs up and make a road trip to Port Clinton if you're still weirded out about staying here tonight, I'm sure Dave and Deanne wouldn't mind."

Walking away from the curtain and sitting next to Bill Clara said...

"Really Bill...now think for a minute how stupid that sounds we don't know where the farm is, and I don't know about driving blind in all this weather, plus Deanne and Dave could be on their way back here while we'd be heading there."

Bill sat back in the recliner and said...

"Well it was just a suggestion."

Clara looked over at Bill saying...

"Did you really just say that...I think you're the one who's afraid to stay in the house tonight, besides when was the last time you wanted to drive at night and in a storm... you hate driving in shit like this."

Bill turned his head pretending not to hear Clara as she nudged him in the side over and over saying...

"I don't feel any feathers...."

Bill kept brushing Clara's hand away, saying...

"I was only thinking of you."

Turning her head to one side Clara sarcastically said...

"Bill, you are so full of it."

Central Ohio is no stranger to intense rainfall and flooding and the weather which Clara and Bill were experiencing that evening was no exception.

With the occasional crackle of thunder and flash of lightning, at least Bill didn't have to worry about the dogs.

Shone was so skittish that both her and Charlie lay on the floor behind the sofa... looking, not moving.

Bill watched Clara walk up the steps as he made a round going through each room checking each window and each door before heading upstairs.

Bill was in the bathroom washing his face when the water in the bathroom commode started gurgling.

At first Bill paid no mind to it thinking it had something to do with all the rain they were getting and turned the light off and went to bed.

Bill laid next to Clara trying to get comfortable knowing in a few hours he'd be getting up to take the dogs out for their morning business.

Laying there in the darkness Bill tried to get his mind off what had happened earlier that day, but for some reason his mind drifted to the back yard and what he knew he had seen.

Clara's light snoring caught Bill's attention and at first, he thought that her snoring would keep him awake, but his eyes were heavy from the events of the day and fell sleep.

Clara awakened an hour later, tugging on Bill's shoulder saying...

"Hey, you, did you forgot to turn the television off."

Bill woke up and turned over to Clara saying...

"What are you talking about, I didn't have the television on."

Clara threw the blankets off her and headed over to the night stand on Bill's side saying...

"Okay, where's the remote?"

Clara turned on the bed side lamp and looked around the table and bed for the remote but did not see it.

Thinking that it had falling on the floor, Clara got down on her knees and lifted the bedspread and begin feeling around for it.

Lying flat on the floor Clara put her head to the floor to get a better look when she screamed.

Clara's high-pitched scream was so loud that it startled Bill, who tried sitting up on the side of the bed.

Clara attempted to get up, when Bill threw his legs over the side of the bed connecting with Clara's head.

Something had frightened Clara so much that she started swinging and hitting Bill's legs with her hands, yelling...

"Get the hell out of the way!"

Not knowing what was going on Bill lifted his legs and threw them back on the bed saying...

"What's going on Clara...whatcha doing on the floor?"

Clara stood over near the mirror and turned the main bedroom light saying...

"Bill... don't move, there's something under the bed."

When Clara had said that, Bill jumped up and scrambled off the bed saying...

"WHAT!"

Clara was looking around the room for something, anything she could use as a weapon, saying...

"I-I was looking under the bed for the remote control to turn the television off when I saw this-this ugly face and these creepy hands trying to get me."

Bill looked over at the television which was off, saying...

"Baby cakes are you sure...I mean the television isn't on, you sure you weren't having a dream?"

Clara glanced over at the television and then back to Bill saying...

"It wasn't a damn dream or nightmare...shit, I saw it with my own two eyes right under the bed."

Bill walked over to the side of the bed to where Clara was pointing and got down on his knees and said as he looked under the bed...

"I'll be damned."

Trying to clear her throat, Clara nervously said...

"OMG...What is it?"

Bill stood up with the remote in one hand and a snickers bar in the other hand saying...

"I got the remote and look, I was hunting for this last week, must've fallen out of my pocket."

Clara stood in amazement, saying...

"I don't care about the remote or the snickers candy bar...what about the face and the creepy hands I saw!"

Bill walked over to Clara and laid the remote on the dresser saying...

"I don't know what to tell you, maybe the light hit the snickers wrapper at the right angle and you thought you saw something, I mean why would you be up looking under the bed at this hour in the morning anyway?"

Clara grabbed Bill's arm and walked over to the bed and dropped down on her knees. After seeing there was nothing under the bed Bill and Clara stood up.

Clara walked over to the dresser and begin pulling bras and panties out and laying them on the top of the dressing saying...

"Hell no...I am not sleeping in this house tonight."

Bill walked over to stop Clara and as she put her face in Bill's chest, Bill said...

"Clara, think for a minute. Its storming like crazy outside, plus where do you think you're going at three-thirty in the morning. C'mon let's go on down stairs and get some hot coffee in us and I'll make breakfast...that'll make you feel better."

Clara threw on her bathrobe and headed downstairs with Bill saying...

"You mean it'll make you feel better...Bill you know you can't cook."

Bill kissed Clara on the back of the neck as they both left the bedroom not seeing a small figure no larger than three feet tall emerged from under the bed and slowly and quietly following them.

Clara was an excellent cook, coming from a large family of seven brothers and three Sisters in the south.

To keep her mind from racing, Clara made Bill and herself a breakfast of cheesy scrambled eggs, fried ham, grits with red eye gravy, biscuits and coffee.

They were enjoying their breakfast way too much to see that they were being watched by something from the staircase.

After breakfast Bill and Clara sat on the sofa to watch the remains of an old movie when Shone and Charlie emerged from behind the sofa and laid near the front door, signaling soon they'd be ready to go out.

Bill turned to Clara saying...

"In a little I'll feed them and let them out in the back yard, that's if it's not

too muddy, if it is I guess I'll have to get a poop bag and walk them. By the way, have you heard anything from Deanne and Dave?"

Clara stretched her legs across Bill's saying...

"Nope, not a word, I'll be glad when they do get back."

Sipping on his coffee Bill nodded his head and said...

"Yeah, I know what you mean, taking care of two dogs and everything."

Clara pinched Bill on the leg saying...

"That's not what I was talking about...didn't you say Dave was part Cherokee?"

Bill rubbed his thigh and grabbed Clara as she attempted to pinch him again saying...

"Yeah, but what does Dave being Cherokee have to do with you pinching me."

Clara lifted her legs off Bill and said...

"Well don't Native Americans have medicine bags and things that ward off spirits?"

Bill saw the serious expression on Clara's face as she got up to go to the bathroom; and said...

"You're a real trip Clara...I tell you and Russell about some hands holding onto to Charlie's legs in the yard, and it's my imagination, but when you see weird ass shit under our bed, you're ready to have an Indian exorcism."

Bill let out a sigh as he lay back in bed repositioning his pillows, and watching Clara walk into the bathroom. It didn't take Bill anytime to fall asleep. Clara came out of the bathroom to the sound of Bill's snoring saying to herself...

"Dang...with all of this racket, I guess I'll be sitting up in bed reading instead of getting any sleep."

Clara tried to ignore the thought of reading instead of trying to get some sleep, but as she lay on her side, thoughts and images raced in her mind.

Clara turned off the lamp and quickly fell asleep, when she was awakened by what she felt as hands going from her feet up her legs resting on her panties.

Clara moved her hips as her panties became wet with moisture while she was fingered, thinking Bill was wanting her.

Clara thought that Bill was thinking that he was exciting her, when she said in a low voice...

"Bill, Bill if you're trying to get me all hot and bothered…. it's working… but your hands are ice cold and you're scratching me."

Just then Clara heard a sniffing sound and felt breathe on her panties near her virginal area underneath the sheet as her panties slowly were being pulled off, Clara again said with her voice raised a little louder…

"Bill, you're screwing up the mood…it feels so good, but I'm really not feeling it tonight!"

Suddenly her panties were yanked off. Clara felt something cold and mushy on her thighs as she reached under the sheet to pull up her panties, but it was too late, her panties were down around her ankles.

Clara jumped up in bed and turned on the bed side lamp and screamed as she saw Bill asleep and snoring, and the Nun with her face in between Clara's legs.

Clara tried to scream for Bill to wake up but as she opened her mouth, The Nun had one hand over her mouth preventing her from calling out.

Clara tried to grab The Nun's Scapular or anything else she could grab but as she did she fell back in bed staring at this Nun who was supposed to be dead.

Clara started kicking and frantically flailing her arms at The Nun, and then fell onto the floor as she reached for Bill. The loud thud from Clara crashing on the floor awakened Bill who yawned and sluggishly shouted…

"CLARA…damn baby…shit, what are you doing on the floor?"

Clara was sitting on her ass with the heels of her feet and her palms face down on the floor in shock and in horror, her panties on the edge of the bed…looking all around as Bill walked over extending his hand to help her up.

Clara took her palms off the floor and covered her eyes and grabbed her panties and started shaking her head from side to side, in a soft tone crying and then saying…

"no-no-no-no-no-no-no."

Bill dropped down to one knee and asked Clara as he held her…

"Baby, what the hell is going on…you had a bad dream and fell out of the bed, C'mon get up and get back in bed."

Clara jerked away from Bill saying…

"Don't touch me right now, just don't fuckin touch me Bill."

Getting to his feet Bill stepped back and began pacing the room saying...

"I don't get it...what in the hell is wrong now...what did I do!"

Clara sat on the floor crying and mumbling about wanting to the leave the house and said...

"How can this be happening. I just saw Sister Mary Jacalyn an Nun from my childhood...but it can't be...she-s-s dead."

Clara got up off the floor and walked into the closet and began pulling clothes off the hangers and laying them on the bed saying...

"No! Look, I just saw a Nun who's supposed to be dead, fingering me... oh hell no, I'm going to my Sister's."

Bill sat down on the bed and said...

"Your Sister's...baby she lives four hours away, I can't drive you tonight...if I drop you off tonight how am I supposed to get to work on time in the morning?"

Clara didn't say anything to Bill she just gave him a look that told him she was going alone.

Ever since they were married, Clara and Bill have never been apart, and this was a little difficult for Bill to handle, but he knew he'd only make things worse if he tried to stop Clara.

Running the risks of pissing Clara off even more, Bill said ...

"Look baby, I'm not going to stop you if you wanna go, but at least let me drive you there tomorrow...and when you're ready to come home I'll come and get you."

Clara walked off into the bathroom with her travel case and started packing make up and her medication bottles when Bill walked in saying...

"Okay?"

Clara stopped packing and placed the case on the vanity saying...

"Okay? What are you talking about Bill"?

Bill reached out and gently took Clara's hand and said...

"I asked you if I could drive you to Renee's and come get you when you ready to come home, tomorrow after work."

Clara turned and faced Bill saying...

"Bill, it's not about you or anything...somethings not right here, there's something creepy in this house and I just need some time away before I lose it."

Bill again tried to down play the situation by saying...

"Baby, what's not right is you leaving. Look we're both tired, not to mentioned

it's been storming like hell all day and all night...I think our imaginations are going in all directions...won't you at least tell me what's got you all upset?"

Clara closed the lid of the commode and sat down and said...

"I was sitting in bed reading when I heard a noise and when I looked up I saw an old woman sitting in a rocking chair in our bedroom."

Bill backed up against the bathroom wall saying...

"Baby, it was obviously a dream...there's no rocking chair in our bedroom."

Clara stood up grabbed her travel case and took a couple of steps and stopped and turned and said...

"It was not a 'dream' Bill, you see I knew you'd say it was a dream and that I'm crazy...I knew it."

With his back still against the wall, Bill removed his glasses and wiped his eyes saying...

"Baby, I do not think you're crazy...I didn't say that, all I said was there's no rocking chair in our bedroom."

Clara continued packing as Bill left the bathroom and went into the bedroom and carried Clara's suitcase downstairs.

Bill could faintly hear Clara crying and sniffling as he went down the steps and then he heard the bathroom down slam.

Bill sat the suitcase down by the sofa and walked into the kitchen to get coffee started when he noticed Shone and Charlie asleep on the same dog bed.

While the coffee maker was filling the kitchen with the smell of the sweet aroma of morning java, Bill was inspecting the dog food bag which was extremely low.

Bill had not anticipated dog sitting for David and Deanne's dog all weekend, and knew he'd be making a trip to the store sooner than expected if David and Deanne were not back today.

Just then all the lights in the house flickered and then went out. Bill knew he was going to have to make his way out in the car port where the circuit breaker was and hollered upstairs to Clara so that she wouldn't be freaked out any more than she already was.

When Bill didn't hear Clara, or see Clara coming downstairs as he continued on to the carport garage area, he thought about hunting for the flashlight but knew it would be much easier to just go to the circuit breaker in the dark.

Bill took a couple of steps when something brushed against his legs causing him to jump and curse...

"Damnit"

Looking around in the darkness, Bill of course saw nothing, but when he felt it brush up against his leg again, he realized that it was either Charlie or Shone, but something wasn't right.

Whatever it was brushing up against his legs was close to his ankles.

Finally, Bill's hands reached the carport door knob and he opened it and stepped into the carport, stumbling into the recyclable can sitting near the freezer.

Kicking the can away from him, Bill reached out with his right hand feeling for his car. Bill thought that if he could get to his car he could turn the car lights on so that he'd be able to see the circuit breaker clearly.

Bill's hand reached the car passenger door handle which was locked, Bill held onto the car as he walked around to the driver's side.

Bill felt a little relief as he felt the driver's door handle and tried to open it, when he realized that it too was locked, saying...

"Fuck!"

Groping the sides of the carport wall, Bill's hands first felt the rake and then the shovel, which were hanging on the wall brackets, knowing that the circuit breaker was only a few feet away.

In a few seconds, Bill will have wished he'd gone for the flashlight or better than that...wished he'd never came out of the house.

Bill couldn't see the dark eerie figured which loomed in the corner next to the circuit breaker, watching and waiting for Bill to approach.

Clara let out a scream as she smelled the foul breath of something or someone standing right in front of her, several times Clara yelled for Bill who did not answer her cries for help.

Clara, shaking and trembling, reached both of her hands out in front of her trying to feel who it was in front of her.

Just then Clara felt an icy blast of air down on her legs as she reached down to wipe her legs, falling into the bath tub.

Clara had fallen into the tub in an awkward position hitting her head against the back wall of the tub and yelling...

"Goddamnit...I hate this damn shit...Bill!"

Clara struggled to swing her legs out of the tub, so that she could stand up when all sudden the bath tub as well as the shower begin spraying hot water.

Clara screamed as she grabbed hold of the shower curtain jumping out and nearly falling on the floor.

Just then the bathroom door slammed shut and Clara heard the door lock button being pushed in.

Clara begin screaming and hollering...

"Who's there...what do you want!"

There was no response to Clara's frantic cries. Clara was about to let out another scream when she heard someone breathing heavily, as she shouted...

"Damnit...who the hell are you and what do you want!"

Having said that, the commode began making a gurgling sound, and the vanity cabinet doors started opening and slamming shut, and Clara felt something scratching at her legs causing her to jump and scream, when she heard...

"All we wanna do is have a little fun."

Suddenly the lights surrounding the mirror, dimly started to glow and the bathroom door knob began rattling.

Something or someone was still clawing and scratching at Clara's legs as she made her way to the bathroom door and began pounding on it and hollering for Bill.

Just then, the lights surrounding the mirror shone bright, the gurgling noise stopped, and the water shut off.

Crying and sniffling, Clara looked all around the bathroom which was full of steam from the running hot water, and down at her legs which were bloody and covered with scratch and claw marks.

The bathroom door slowly opened and although Clara was scared to death, she cautiously and carefully checked the hallway before leaving, when it happened again, Clara started smelling the foul odor and felt cold, icy breath on the back of her neck.

Clara slowly turned and as she did, she saw the face of a Nun behind her and that's when Clara ran out of the bathroom, down the stairs to the front door.

Something was wrong...the door wouldn't open. Clara hollered for Bill when Charlie and Shone came running up to her barking and scratching at the door.

Clara turned the deadbolt lock but instead of opening the door, the door was still locked.

Clara reached down to calm Charlie and Shone when the lightening flashed, and the thunder cracked, sending Shone and Charlie running and taking refuge behind the sofa.

As the two dogs raced for cover, Shone struggled to get her grip as her nails caused her to slide on the hard wood flooring.

When the lightening flashed, for a moment a reflection of the lightening shone through the living room drapes and that's when Clara saw a dark figure, over beside the fireplace.

Clara gasped and right as she did, the lightening flashed again and that's when she saw it was Sister Mary Jacalyn.

The same Nun who was so mean to her when she attended Saint Francis Xavier; but there was just one thing wrong…Sister Mary Jacalyn died twenty-five years earlier.

While Shone was afraid of loud noises, Charlie was the opposite; as he raced and stood beside Clara barking like crazy and showing warning teeth.

Clara hollered to Charlie…

"Get her Charlie…get her!"

Clara started breathing heavy and started screaming as she dimly saw Charlie moving back and forth in the darkness as if he was chasing something.

Clara screamed for Bill and then ran in the direction of the back door, crashing hard into the edge of the curio cabinet and knocking herself unconscious.

Bill's hands found its way to the circuit breaker panel and he opened the panel and all the lights came on as he reset the circuits.

Bill was about to head back into the house when a noise from behind him like people running made him stop and turn around.

As Bill turned, he could hear the footsteps, but no one was there, then suddenly two small kids wearing hoodies appeared at the bottom of the steps.

Bill could not believe his eyes and as he squinted his eyes to get a clearer look he noticed something else unusual, as if the whole day couldn't get any weirder.

The two kids looked up at Bill and gave him a half-crooked smile and then put one of their scrawny fingers to their lips and quickly came straight at Bill in a stop and start-jerky motion.

Bill fell back against the wall when he noticed the kids had large shiny baldheads and black hollow holes, where there should be eyes.

Bill grab a shovel which was hanging on the wall and realizing he didn't have a lot of room to swing the shovel, but that he was ready to defend himself in whatever way he could.

Bill held the shovel in front of him as the two kids approached and that's when something grabbed Bill from behind pinning him to the garage wall.

Bill tried to see who or what had him, but the only thing he could see was a pair of hands protruding from the outside wall.

Bill was either too scared or too mad to yell, but when he focused ahead of him, the face of an old Catholic Nun appeared through the wall saying...

"Twisted and Dread, blood in your bed
And here comes a chopper
To chop off your head!
Chip chop, chip chop
The last one is dead!"

This scary looking Nun came from out of nowhere, straight out of the wall and was now standing within inches from Bill's face, revealing a crooked set of gray and rotten teeth, not to mention the foulish-smelling breath he had ever smelled.

Just as The Nun opened her mouth wide, she turned her head towards the door which led to the kitchen.

Bill also turned his head in that direction as he heard the continuous barking of Charlie and Shone and Clara screaming for him.

Suddenly The Nun disappeared as she passed through the door as Bill hollered to Clara...

"Run Clara, get out of there...run!"

Clara heard Bill yelling but couldn't make out exactly what Bill was saying. The hands which held Bill against the wall, still maintained their tight grip as Bill yelled...

"Baby...I can't get to you, something's got me pinned down, you have to..."

Before Bill could finish his statement, he felt the hands which held him, loosening their grip as he broke free and began violently shaking the door knob and pounding on the door, saying...

"The doors jammed I can't get it open...Clara!"

Unable to open the door, Bill picked up the shovel which was lying on the floor and tried wedging the shovel's blade in between the door jam and the door.

Suddenly Bill looked over to his right at the garage door opener and said...

"Damn...why didn't I try this earlier."

Bill pushed the opener button and felt a sigh of relief as he heard the sound of the garage door motor.

Turning towards the door, Bill noticed that something was wrong... something wasn't right, the garage door had only opened a few inches and then it stopped.

Bill ran over to pull the red manual release cord, but it would not budge, so Bill got down on his knees near the garage door to see if he could get enough of his hands under it to push it up, so he could get out.

It was useless, Bill squatted and tried several times to manually lift the garage door, when suddenly it slammed shut pinning his fingers of both hands underneath it.

Bill could hear Clara screaming and both dogs barking as he tried pulling his hands from underneath the garage door.

Pain shot up Bills arms as he struggled to pull his hands free from the garage door which tore the skin from his knuckles with each pull.

Bill tried kicking and pushing against the door as he tried to pull his hands free, gasping for air and resting from the pain of his skin being ripped from his fingers.

Bill took a deep breath and counted to five before violently kicking the door and yanking his fingers free.

It was no use, the skin on Bill's fingers were coming off against the concrete as he pulled, and his fingers were now wet with blood, making it harder to maintain a good grip.

Clara heard Bill scream in agony as he pulled his fingers from the garage door, skinless and bleeding.

Clara stood at the door pounding and yelling for Bill, while the dogs were growling and barking as Clara tried feverously to open the kitchen door.

Bill stood on the opposite side of the door pounding with the palms of his hand and yelling for Clara to unlock the door.

Just then, the door knob began turning and Clara saw Bill standing there, sweaty, hands all bloody and with a look of complete panic and fright upon his face.

Clara grabbed Bill and hugged him and after locking the kitchen door, rushed Bill over to the sink to wash off the blood and wrap his hands in two kitchen towels, saying...

"Oh my gosh Bill...what the hell is going on, look at your hands, what happened?"

Bill reached underneath the sink and took out the large bottle of peroxide and after taking a deep breath, and putting one of the dish cloths between his teeth, emptied the entire bottle over his hands, yelling and then saying...

"Baby are you alright, I should've listened to you...we gotta get out of here!"

Clara started crying saying...

"Bill, I don't understand it...I don't understand any of this shit!"

Clara took hold of Bill's hands and after pouring olive oil over his hands, wrapped them in one of the kitchen towels.

Bill headed towards the steps and said to Clara...

"Don't you think we're going to need some extra clothes?"

Clara grabbed both leashes and after hooking up both dogs snapped...

"Bill...I am not going back up there...let's just go out the front door and hop in your jeep and put some distance between us and this place."

Just then the cushions flew off the sofa landing on the floor in between Clara and the front door, making Clara scream and the dogs backed up as they barked.

Bill turned and ran ahead of Clara and when he reached down to move the cushions out of Clara's way, something took hold of Bill and tossed him into the sofa.

Suddenly, the recliner began rocking back and forth and Clara saw the impression in the cushion, as if someone were sitting in the recliner.

Bill got to his knees, and as he started to shake off being flung into the sofa, someone began pounding hard on the front door.

Charlie and Shone took off running up the steps with their leashes trailing behind them. Bill backed away from the front door, turning to see the dogs bolting upstairs, when Clara let out an eerie scream.

Bill turned to see Clara slowly rising in the air a foot or two off the floor and just as Bill yelled to Clara, Clara's mouth opened wide and in a raspy demonic voice, she said...

"No one's going anywhere!"

After that was said, the whole house began to shake, and Clara started slowly descending to the floor, as Bill rushed over to her.

Looking at both the front and back door, Bill realized that they were trapped and there was no way out of the house and nowhere to run.

The last thing on Bill's mind was running upstairs, where he knew they'd be sitting ducks, but where else could he and Clara escape to?"

Just then, Bill heard a squeaky sound and as he turned around, he saw a large white Siamese cat sitting in an old small red wagon with uneven wheels which squeaked and hobbled as it rolled across the floor.

Seeing a stray cat was nothing unusual to Bill, but for starters, this cat was in his house and this cat had red spooky eyes.

Bill's eyes followed the wagon to the handle which was extended in the air, and as the wagon rolled across the floor Bill noticed there was no one pulling the wagon.

Just then something grabbed a hold of Bill's arm causing him to jump....it was Clara crying and saying...

"Oh, my God Bill...what's going on, what are we going to do!"

The sudden grabbing of Bill's arm caused him to jump and as he turned to Clara he took hold of her arm saying...

"Honey I don't know what the hell is going on, but all I know is...we got to get out of here."

Bill located his car keys hanging on the wall rack by the door and as he grabbed Clara's hand, he said...

"Hold it together baby, we're going out the door and straight to the car... don't stop for anything."

Clara looked up at Bill, barely able to see his face against the dim lighting, said...

"We got to get Shone and Charlie...we can't leave them."

Bill squeezed Clara's hand saying...

"Look I'll call the dogs, but our number one priority is to get the hell out of here, if they come, they come...and if not.... well I'm not about to end up dead all because of the dogs."

Bill grabbed Clara's hand as he ran to get the car keys, calling for Charlie and Shone and then ran to the door.

Bill and Clara could hear the moans and eerie cries behind them and approaching footsteps as Bill frantically search for the front door key.

At last, Bill had the right key in the key hole, and as he turned the key and hearing the lock click, Bill reached for the door knob with his bloody hands, as Clara yelled...

"Hurry-hurry up Bill they're getting closer!"

As the door opened and Bill reached to unlock the storm door, the hideous face of Sister Mary Jacalyn sitting in a rocking chair, appeared on the other side of the door screaming...

"BOO! You can't leave! he-he-he-he."

Bill knew that there was no turning around, he unlocked the storm door and tried to open it, but The Nun was on the other side of the door holding it shut.

In a desperate attempt to get out, Bill hurled his two hundred and twenty-pound frame against the storm door, which felt as if the door was made from steel.

Bill and Clara were going nowhere, and they knew it. Kicking against the door and pounding on it, Bill took Clara's hand knowing that upstairs was not an option, so they ran towards the carport as fast as they knew how.

Once in the carport Bill opened the car door so that Clara could get in and then he rushed to driver's side door.

Patting his pockets Bill did not have the keys but remembered there was a spare key under the driver's side floor mat and started the engine.

Just then the door locks of the jeep popped in the unlock position as Bill tried several times to lock the doors.

The lights in the carport suddenly went out as Clara screamed pointing in the direction of a pair of black eyes coming towards them.

Bill threw the gear selector switch in reverse and reached up to open the garage door, forgetting it wouldn't open.

Clara was screaming and hollering for Bill to get them out of there, when Bill decided if the garage door won't open he was going to crash through it.

If crashing through the door wouldn't get them completely out of the garage at least enough noise would be made to alert the neighbors that something was wrong.

Bill put the gear selector in reverse and as he was about to gun the engine suddenly there was a loud pounding on Clara's jeep and the entire jeep shook violently.

Clara started screaming as the windshield wipers came on and the head lights began flashing on and off.

Bill was trying to remain calm, but Clara was screaming at the top of her lungs, when Bill yelled...

"Damnit Clara, will you stop all this damn screaming...I can't think for shit!"

Clara stopped screaming and as soon as she did, the front windshield came crashing in on them.

Bill started the car and put the car in reverse and mashed his foot on the accelerator pedal...but all that happened was, the tires spun making an awful high-pitched screeching and producing a gaging thick smell of burning rubber.

With all the noise from the horn and the flashing of the lights, Bill and Clara were sure neighbors, somebody would hear all the commotion and come to investigate, but no one came over.

Suddenly everything became extremely quiet and Clara said...

"Bill, Bill, quiet!"

Clara pointed to the front of the car where the eyes once were and said...

"they're gone!"

Looking directly ahead Bill did not see the eyes and said...

"Good. We got rid of whatever or whoever it was, now maybe we can get out of here, whew!"

Just then, Clara began yelling and pointing. Bill looked over at Clara and noticed that The Nun, Sister Mary Jacalyn, was behind Clara in the back seat and had her Rosary Beads chocking Clara.

Bill threw the car in park and got out of the car saying...

"Who the hell are you! Get your hands off her."

The Nun, Sister Mary Jacalyn was pulling on the Rosary beads, while Clara was clutching them and gasping for air, Sister Mary Jacalyn said...

"Die you fucking cunt...die!"

Bill struggled with the passenger car door handle, but could not get it open, then he climbed back in the car on the driver's side, attempting to free the Rosary Beads from around Clara's neck.

Unable to do so, Bill started punching and beating the wrists of the Nun, who was laughing and saying...

"Is that all you got lover boy, you despicable fat slob, you can't stop me?"

Just then, Clara lost consciousness and Sister Mary Jacalyn, removed the Rosary Beads from around Clara's neck, and said to Bill...

"You want some too, lover boy c'mon, the doors open?"

Bill climbed out of the front seat, and opened the back door, with intentions of strangling the Nun, when she vanished.

Just at that time a Police patrol car arrived, and the two Officers exited the car and ran over to Bill and Clara's garage.

Using a crow bar, they pried the door, and as the door raised, they got to Bill and Clara. They found Bill in the back seat alone, with fishing line wrapped around both of his hands and around Clara's neck.

One Police Officer drew his gun and ordered Bill to put his hands on his head and get out of the car, as his partner, checked for vital signs from Clara.

Panic stricken, Bill complied and placed both his hands on his head, while the Police Officer handed Bill his hand cuffs, saying...

"Alright mister, here's what you're going do, you're going to handcuff yourself, and slowly get out of the car, and onto the ground...NOW!"

Bill cuffed himself and slowly got out of the back seat and onto the ground, saying...

"Officer, this is not what it looks like, there was this Nun..."

The Police Officer yelled at Bill, saying...

"All I see is you, chocking this woman with fishing wire...I don't see no Nun. Just shut your mouth and lay there."

The Officer turned to his partner who was on his radio calling EMS to the scene, when his partner who was with Bill shouted...

"How's she doing, Mike...is she?

The Police Officer in front with Clara, place his index and middle fingers, to the side of Clara's windpipe, checking for a pulse from Clara's carotid artery, when Clara's head slumped back against the head rest.

As Bill lay there on the ground, the Officer took Bill's wallet from his back pocket and told Bill as he kicked him in the side of his stomach...

"You just shut up you piece of shit."

Both Officers, were trained in CPR, but Clara had a slow heart beat and her pulse was faint, the decision was made to stand by the side of the car and wait for EMS services to arrive.

Officer James Peeks, a five-year veteran with the Columbus Police department stayed by the side of Clara, while his partner, Officer William Hooton, a rookie, returned to Bill to ask him questions.

Officer Hooton stood over Bill saying...

"Now, I'm going to help you stand, and then you are going to have a seat in the back of our squad car...you got it?"

As Bill was nodding his head yes, he caught a glimpse of something, off to his right side. It was the Nun, leaning against the garage wall, smiling, laughing and pointing at Bill.

Bill turned to his left side where Officer Hooton was standing, saying...

"There she is Officer, right over there. That crazy ass Nun standing by the wall, strangled my wife."

Officer Hooton looked over to where Bill said, and saw nothing or no one, and said...

"You're trying to cop a crazy plea already, but it is not going to help your monkey ass, now I'm going to help you on your feet, but first I'm going to help you to your knees, and then you stand up."

Officer Hooton got Bill to his knees and then to his feet, as Bill cried out...

"How's my wife, is she going to be alright?"

Officer Hooton slammed Bill against the car, as he closed the back door, saying...

"She's barley alive, no thanks to you, asshole."

As Officer Hooton questioned Bill in the back seat of the squad car, EMS services and several patrol cars arrived on the scene, as Officer Hooton got out of the squad car, following Officer Peeks to the supervisor's and detective's car.

While EMS services loaded the lifeless body of Clara from the stretcher to the inside of the emergency vehicle, Detective Michael Horton, turned to the two patrol Officers, saying...

"Ok, tell me what you got here?"

Officer Peeks, responded...

"We were on routine patrol and I saw from a distance a man running towards us. As he approached us, he said there was trouble over here, glass and a lot of commotion, and a woman screaming, so I told Officer Hooton to swing by there."

Detective Horton continued asking...

"You do know that this is not your assigned patrol area, right?"

Officer Hooton interrupted, saying...

"Yeah, but we were following a car containing occupants who were acting a little suspicious, and they turned several streets back and into a garage. We were on a dead-end street, so when I turned around, that's when Officer Peeks noticed this guy running towards us, so we came to see what was what."

Detective Horton looked at Officer Peeks, and replied...

"Go one."

Officer Peeks said...

"Once we were out of the patrol car, we, or I could hear a woman screaming and a car running. We identified ourselves as officers and asked if they were alright and that's when I heard the woman scream again, so we pried open the garage door.

As soon as we got the door open, that's when we noticed the suspect in the back seat and the woman in the front seat with her head in a backwards stretched position, so we drew our weapons and ordered the scumbag to halt."

Detective Horton, pulled a handkerchief from his coat and after sneezing, said...

"Could you see if he was choking her or helping her?"

Officer Peeks, replied...

"I was closest to the car, and as we came up behind it I could see that the suspect was directly behind her, with his hands up in the air, even with the head rest, it was clear the suspect was attempting to unwrap something from his hands.

So, I drew my gun and ordered the suspect to freeze, and then I told my partner to cuff him while I went to check on the female in the front seat and that's when I noticed, as I shone, my light on her that she had just been strangled."

Officer Hooton stepped beside Officer Peeks saying...

"It's clear that she was being strangled...I mean, Ray Charles could've seen that."

Detective Horton pointed his ink pen in Officer Hooton's face saying...

"First of all, I'm talking to this Officer, and you'll know when I'm talking to you because I'll be looking at you, and secondly, you didn't see shit...your partner did."

Officer Hooton didn't like being verbally upbraided, but being a rookie, knew it was best to shut up, especially since he had already gotten on Detective Horton's bad side several weeks earlier.

Officer Peeks placed his hand on his partner's arm, and nodded, then continued, saying...

"As I stated, I saw the fishing wire wrapped around his hands and my partner had placed the suspect in cuffs, and that's when I noticed the woman's eyes were blood shot, and there were several red pressure marks behind both ears."

Looking over to Officer Hooton, Detective Horton said...

"Now, let's hear what you got to say if anything, beginning with what the suspect told you."

Officer Hooton replied...

"When Officer Peeks told me to cuff him, the suspect said: 'this isn't what it looks like', and that some Nun strangled his wife."

Detective Horton asked him if he saw anybody else out there and Officer Hooton told him that he did not.

The EMS emergency vehicle, supervisor's patrol car and Officer's Peeks and Hooton left the area, leaving Detective Horton alone at the scene.

Detective Horton had processed enough scenes like this one to know, no matter how open and shut it may seem, if the fat lady hasn't hit that high note, then it's not over.

There was very little evidence to collect at the scene, when Detective Horton noticed Rosary Beads on the back-seat floor mat.

Upon closer inspection, there were strands of hair and some type of fluid, so Detective Horton went to the trunk of his car and retrieved a small swab box and collected the hair and fluid separately.

Detective Horton, got into his car and headed for the precinct, not knowing that someone emerged from the shadows, as his car turned the corner.

It was the Nun, Sister Mary Jacalyn, who was dancing and singing in the rain…

> "There was an old lady who swallowed a fly,
> I don't know why she swallowed a fly,
> Perhaps she'll die."

4
The Build Up

The case file on the Nun, Sister Mary Jacalyn, born in the late winter of eighteen hundred, Sister Mary Jacalyn was the only Nun accepted into the Catholic Order having children and two failed marriages.

What was even more unusual about Sister Mary Jacalyn other than her acceptance as a Nun was the mysterious death of both of her husbands and the mysterious disappearances of her children following the deaths.

Outside of her marriages and children, very little is known about her in the Catholic circle other than her acceptance into the order of Saint Francis Xavier and the death of Arch Bishop Geovanni Trapaga, who presided over Saint Francis's.

Whether it was out of respect or out of fear, everyone stayed out of Sister Mary Jacalyn's way at Saint Francis, except for Mr. Jeni Willispe, the grounds keeper, who came from Hungary.

To see the two of them interact with one another, you'd get the impression that the bell announcing a fight bigger than Joe Frazier vs Ali was about to begin.

There was plenty of speculation and controversy surrounding Sister Mary Jacalyn, and where she came from, as she stated initially when applying for the Rectory in Columbus that she was last in a convent in Rome, which turned out to be inaccurate.

In the summer of eighteen-eighty-nine the Franklin County prosecutor's office filed a petition with the Franklin County Grand

Jury and an indictment was summarily handed down to Sister Mary Jacalyn for the suspicious deaths of her husbands and the disappearance of her children.

The other unexplainable thing was, there were a series of senseless murders in the county that year.

From seemingly out of nowhere, wives and husbands and friends were killing one another, with no sensible motives.

A total of sixty-nine deaths occurred in Franklin county, the same week Sister Mary Jacalyn was indicted, no one made a connection, but maybe they should've.

Sister Mary Jacalyn because of her status was placed on house arrest until the beginning of her trial' and along with her Attorney gave a press conference on the courthouse steps, after leaving the courthouse.

While her attorney gave an arduous accounting of Sister Mary Jacalyn's character, Sister Mary Jacalyn made no statement except...

"Not every miraculous touching is by the hand of God; some are by the power of man...stop asking me about my two husbands and my children...why don't you tend to your doings."

As the horse-drawn carriage carrying Sister Mary Jacalyn and her attorney left the courthouse, several reporters released photos showing a sinister and diabolical image of Sister Mary Jacalyn as she headed for the rectory.

Three weeks before the trail was to begin Sister Mary Jacalyn's attorney reported to the DA's office that he received a letter from Sister Mary Jacalyn stating that she no longer needed his services and that she would not stand trial at the hands of man.

The DA's office immediately issued the immediate arrest of the infamous Nun and the Sheriff's office was sent out to arrest Sister Mary Jacalyn, but when they arrived at Saint Francis Xavier, Sister Mary Jacalyn was nowhere to be found.

Law enforcement searched intensely for Sister Mary Jacalyn, who remained at large, until her arrest some years later in a small town in Pennsylvania.

Sister Mary Jacalyn was driven from Pennsylvania to Columbus, which was a week's travel in the freezing cold, chained in a wagon.

The first trial of Sister Mary Jacalyn for the disappearance of her children and the deaths of her two husbands, lasted six months, with the verdict to be decided after the second trial.

Evidence and eyewitness accounts proved that Sister Mary Jacalyn in fact was married twice and did have three children.

When asked about her husbands and their whereabouts, Sister Mary Jacalyn at initially said...

"They went looking for work and never came back, and secondly, changed her answer by saying...I'm a Sister, and its forbidden for me to marry."

Relatives of both of Sister Mary Jacalyn's husbands, testifies that their loved ones were married to Sister Mary Jacalyn, and that they had written notes and letters saying that they were afraid of her.

The bodies of both men were recovered in shallow earthen graves, but decomposition had made it impossible to identify both men, even though the bodies of both men were uncovered in the basement of the church in German Village.

When Sister Mary Jacalyn was asked about the whereabouts of her children, Sister Mary Jacalyn repeated over and over again...

"Kinder Getan", meaning children gone.

One of Sister Mary Jacalyn's husbands, Otto Frielhich's sister appeared in court to testify that her brother told her that, he found mysterious burns on the children's buttocks, and was afraid that Sister Mary Jacalyn was torturing the children.

The DA's office presented evidence that an old wooden bucket found in the church's basement, in a secret passage was discovered, and inside were three different locks of hair and fifty-two small baby teeth.

When asked about this, Sister Mary Jacalyn replied...

"Kinder Suppe, Kinder Suppe, Kinder Suppe, Kinder Suppe.

Once again, there was no physical evidence that anything had happened to them, but the court did decide that Sister Mary Jacalyn did something ungodly at the church involving her two husbands, and perhaps to the children as well.

The court punished her by placing her in the basement of the church in the tiny room, in which the baby teeth and locks of hair were found for the remainder of her life, and that she was to receive no outside privileges.

Sister Mary Jacalyn remained locked in the tiny room, void of visitors for twenty years, until one day, the keeper in charge of feeding her opened her cell and discovered that she was missing.

No one possessed a key to the room except the keeper, and a guard was always posted in the hallway on that side of the church.

It was not known how she escaped, but when the room was examined, it was discovered that in the farthest corner of the dimly lit room was a pile of uneaten food, which was rotting.

One of the other things discovered by the new order of Nuns staying in the rectory was, there were secret passages all over the church which led to doors, which led to the courtyard, garden, and a host of other places in the old church.

No one was allowed in the lower parts of the church, for fear of disease, so none of The Nuns spoke about the hidden passageways.

Through the years it was rumored that in the winter, Sister Mary Jacalyn could be seen roaming outside the church property and some even say, they've seen candles or a lantern in one of the windows in the garden at night.

The case of Sister Mary Jacalyn became a forgotten topic by those living in German village, until the spring of nineteen-fifteen.

The reputation and past association of the church to the community had long been forgotten by the town of Columbus, and the new church leaders, who abandoned The Nun allocation program, had a growing and vibrant connection with the growth of the city.

That spring, several young girls, of poor families were reported missing by relatives. It came as no surprise to authorities to entertain anything other than that they were runaways.

A common occurrence in Columbus at that time, because, families barely had enough food to make a meal, and often children were found at the homes of relatives and strangers who had more than plenty to eat.

Young children and young teens would work in gardens and all sort of odd jobs for a hot meal and a warm place to sleep.

The early homes in German village were fashioned after the actual homes in Europe, which were small and compact, with room enough for a family of four, and no more.

In early nineteen hundred, Columbus was a growing bustling site. Hundreds, even thousands of people could be seen in and around the city and outskirts, where fish, meats, and all kinds of fruit and vegetable stands were set up for sell or trade.

It was a great opportunity for small children and the young to be seen in the wee hours of the mornings, in line for one of the few odd jobs.

Like other cities in the Mid-West, Columbus bankers and financiers, focused their attention of growth and development on the downtown area and the Ohio State University areas.

During the warmer months children and the young could be seen sleeping in the nearby vacant lots, to get first crack at any job, since the vendors would often set up their stands at dawn, some would even allow young children to sleep in and around their stands, just to keep their places, and to cut down on thief.

When the wagon loads of fish, fruits and vegetables, and meat arrived in the early hours in downtown Columbus, frequent sights, were catching produce or meats which were dropped on the ground by those unloading the wagons, so it was not common for a young child up to fifteen years in age to be gone from homes several days at a time.

In the wee hours of March twenty-fifth, after the last frost disappeared, a young couple named Boris Yeats and his wife Alga, were walking from their one-story home in German village, to look for a day's work in the downtown area, when they made a gruesome discovery.

Just as the couple passed Saint Francis Xavier Roman Catholic Church they heard a small groan over in the bushes by the fence which surrounded the property. Thinking that maybe it was a small animal, a cat or dog or something, they continued walking until they heard a voice saying...

"Help me! Help me please."

Alga remained at the corner, while Boris walked to the bushes to see what it was. Boris parted the bushes, and there on the other side of the fence was a young boy, no more than ten or eleven.

He then began telling Boris about all the young children being brought there in the middle of the night, and the terrible things which were being done to them.

Just as the boy was in the middle of explaining things to Boris, Boris heard the squealing of a door being opened and an old woman's voice talking to the boy, saying...

"Haven't you buried that already?"

Boris stood up, saying...

"Hello, who are you. What are you doing?"

The little boy tried telling Boris to hush, but Boris insisted on questioning the old woman, who clearly did not want to talk to him.

When Boris again told the woman that the little boy wanted help, he heard the sound as if someone was being slapped upside the head, and then he heard a whispered voice saying...

"Get in here before I do something to you."

Boris walked back over to his wife and they proceeded onto the search of work for the day.

Around three in the afternoon, while Boris and Alga were walking home, Boris decided that he was going to stop by the church and find out what happened to the little boy, and what was going on.

The church had a bell attached to a rope beside the door knob, and Boris rang it several times until the heavy black door slowly opened.

Answering the door was an old man looking to be about sixty or seventy years of age, wearing an apron and shabby clothes.

Boris said...

"Good Afternoon sir, I was wondering if I could have a word with whomever is in charge?"

The old man said nothing, he just looked at Boris until Boris again asked...

"I'd like to have a word with whomever is in charge, if you don't mind?"

The old man lowered his head, opened the door and led Alga and Boris down a long hall to an opened door, saying...

"In here, wait in here."

After several minutes a priest entered the room. He looked to be about fiftyish, silver hair, small bead, with a cigarette between his fingers which had burned clear down to his skin.

The priest dropped the ashes and cigarette butt on the floor, stamping it out, said...

"Come in, come in, how am I to help you, I am Father Lussie?"

Boris began telling him all that happened earlier in the morning, after introducing himself and Alga.

The priest walked over to the large desk in the center of the room, searching through the drawers until he located a half empty pack of cigarettes.

Returning to his seat in front of Alga and Boris, the Priest placed a cigarette in his mouth and offered one to Boris, who almost accepted, saying...

"I can assure you, no one is up moving about at that hour, and definitely not a child."

The Priest was unconvincing, as Boris looked at his wife and then back at the Priest, saying...

"I tell you Father, there was a young boy and an old woman. I didn't see her, I just heard her voice, but the boy talked with me for a while telling me all kind of wild tales."

Father Lussie took the cigarette from his mouth and answered them, saying...

"I tell you, there is no one here except myself, the servant whom you saw and the gardener and his wife, but they leave for home at five o'clock each evening and return in the early morning...perhaps it was them that you saw."

Boris took his hand and began fanning it to remove some of the cigarette smoke which Father Lussie, intentionally blew in his face, before saying...

"Well perhaps the Constable's office would be happy to hear my story, since there are some children missing in the city."

The Priest then crossed his legs, took a puff of his cigarette and in a feminine tone said softly...

"That wouldn't do, that wouldn't do at all, perhaps, you and your wife, if you are not pressed by other matters, would be my guest for dinner tonight, that way we can talk further, and you can look around all you desire, huh?"

Boris was at the point of declining, when the Priest insisted...

"Aww sure you can, it's not like you have dinner at home waiting for you,

besides, dinner here is almost ready, how does...Wellington, potatoes, carrots, fresh bread and strudel sound?"

Putting his arm around Alga and Boris, the Priest led them out the door and into the dining room, as the old man wearing the apron and shabby clothes, closed the door behind them.

Boris and Alga were never seen nor heard of again, and neither was there any mention of the events surrounding the church or any connections with the missing children.

Almost a hundred years have passed since there has been any mentioning of Sister Mary Jacalyn or any of the events have come to light until now.

Messages

It was Monday March sixteen and Kathleen Morris had just arrived at work in the twenty-first precinct in Columbus, Ohio.

Kathleen Morris was forty-six years old the mother of three; two boys, Adam nine and Mark fourteen, and a daughter Melissa sixteen.

Kathleen and her husband Kenneth had divorced just six months earlier that year, and while Kenneth was living his life and happy since the breakup, Kathleen was anything but happy.

Since the divorce, Mark and Melissa were adjusting very well to their new living situation while Adam was finding it more difficult to believe his dad was no longer living with them.

Several times a month Adam would secretly call his father Kenneth, informing him of how miserable they were and the company of a man that his mother was keeping which was making him feel uncomfortable.

Kathleen and Kenneth's relationship had been strained for over several years prior to their divorce, but the added confusion caused by Adam was making their lives even more difficult to deal with.

Kathleen entered the Police precinct at her usual time of six-forty-five, and as she always does when she arrives at work, she placed her bag and personal items in her desk, made a pot of coffee and proceeded to check the messages from the call center for the Detectives and Officers who would be arriving for their morning shift.

Thirty-three calls were made to the precinct overnight, addressed to Officers and detectives, but three of the calls were a bit unusual.

As Kathleen began writing the messages down for the appropriate Officers and Detectives Kathleen came across the first of the three unusual messages, the first one said...

"Are you still searching for the wicked Nun; you don't have a clue do you Magoo?"

Kathleen paid no attention to the message as it made little sense and because it was not addressed to any person in the precinct until she listened to another message saying...

"Four children dead and two husbands cold...shame-shame-shame, somebody needs to find out who could be so bold."

Kathleen saved the message and proceeded to listen to the third message...

"The wicked Nun is far from dead...in the bell tower, the clues, no one checked."

As the Officers and detectives filed into the conference room for morning report, greeting Kathleen and picking up their messages as they walked by, Kathleen tapped Lead Detective Maria Lopez on the shoulder saying...

"When you get a sec, I need you to listen to something for me."

Lead Detective Maria Lopez smiled, sipped her coffee and replied...

"Sure, thing Kathy."

Detective Maria Lopez had been with the Columbus Police department for over eight years, and a detective in the homicide department for five.

Detective Lopez was promoted to lead detective four years earlier when several of the more seasoned detectives accepted early retirement.

Detective Lopez stood a comfortable five feet ten and maintained an athletic build with a strong personality. Her role within the force was to assign cases and rarely accept cases, except for high profile cases.

Detective Lopez walked over to Kathleen Morris's desk and said...

"Okay Kathy, I got a few minutes...what's up?"

Kathleen grabbed her note pad and signaled to Detective Lopez that she wanted to speak with her in private, and so they walked into Detective Lopez's office.

Detective Lopez closed the door, and took a seat behind her desk saying...

"Okay, you explain what all the mystery is about?"

Kathleen grabbed the chair and placed it next to Detective Lopez who sat down as she handed her note pad to Detective Lopez saying...

"What do you think of that, wasn't there some big stink going on around here about a cold case involving a Nun?"

Detective Lopez stared at the messages on the note pad and looked at Kathleen and said...

"Okay Kathy, you wanna back up a little bit and tell me what this is all about...who wrote this?"

Kathleen took the note pad from Detective Lopez and said...

"You know every morning when I get in, I retrieve all the messages from the call center?"

Detective Lopez nodded her head yes, as Kathleen continued...

"Well, these were three of the messages left on the machine."

Detective Lopez picked up her phone and said...

"Kathy bring me the tape from your machine and ask Don to step in here."

Kathleen closed the door behind her and five minutes later Officer Don Willis knocked on the door and opened it saying...

"You want to see me Detective?"

Detective Lopez stood up and asked Officer Willis to close the door and said...

"What I need from you is to go down into the basement where all the cold case files are kept and bring up every case, note, everything on a Nun named Sister Mary Jacalyn...and Don you don't need to broadcast it all over station, okay?"

Officer Willis proceeded out the door as Detective Mark Ridley was entering Detective Lopez's office saying...

"Officer Willis."

Officer Willis looked up at Detective Ridley and nodded his head and continued toward the stairs at the end of the hallway.

Detective Lopez held open her office door and after inviting Detective Ridley in stated...

"Detective Ridley, I asked you in here because I need you to tell me everything you know about the case about a Nun named Sister Mary Jacalyn."

Detective Ridley has been a part of the Columbus homicide unit for the past eighteen years and was one of the original investigators who worked the Sister Mary Jacalyn case, during his rookie years.

Detective Ridley paced the floor of Detective Lopez several times before sitting down saying...

"What's so important about that case...is there some new evidence or something?"

Detective Lopez took a sip of her coffee, not understanding Detective Ridley's reluctance to her question, said...

"I don't know if it is or isn't, I ran across something in one of the files I was working on, and remembered that you worked on the case...it's not a problem, is it?"

Detective Ridley sat back in his chair with a look of disbelief on his face that he was being asked about that case after so many years.

The case of Sister Mary Jacalyn was one of the strangest cases that Detective Ridley worked on in which there was mounds of evidence which led nowhere, and one of the cases that his superiors told him to back off.

Detective Ridley again asked Detective Lopez...

"I'm curious...what case are you working on that mentioned Sister Mary Jacalyn?"

"Look Mark, I just asked you about the case, so why can't you just answer my question?"

Detective Lopez said as she rifled through a case folder on her desk.

Detective Ridley stood up and walked to the door and turned to Detective Lopez saying...

"I don't remember a lot about that case, but I'll look through my old notes and see what I got."

Detective Lopez laid the case folder down on her desk and said...

"Mark, you're taking this where it doesn't need to go, all I asked was that you tell me what you know about the case.

I didn't ask for notes or files...are you standing here trying to tell me that you don't remember anything about a case that you spent years on?"

Walking and stopping at Detective Lopez's desk, Detective Ridley said...

"I can tell you right now, that the Sister Maru Jacalyn case was the strangest

case I worked on and I'm telling you the same thing I was told...'let it go,' some things people shouldn't mess in."

Detective Lopez stood up and in a surprised and irritating tone said...

"Damn Mark, if I didn't know better I'd say that sounded like a threat!"

Detective Ridley opened the door and said as he exited...

"No threat intended Detective...nobody wants to deal with that sick weird shit again, you weren't here when we were dealing with it years ago, you don't know all the crazy shit that happened..."

Detective Lopez interrupted Detective Ridley before he finished his statement saying...

"That's why I'm asking you about it and what is it about this case that has you going Casper on me, I thought you were the all brass balls...no bullshit Ridley."

Detective Ridley stopped in his tracks and closed the door and said...

"This has nothing to do with the size of my balls or my gun or anything else...all I'm saying is, there are some things that people shouldn't be fucking around with....and this is one of them."

Detective Ridley reached for the door knob to leave Detective Lopez's office when she jumped in front of Detective Ridley slamming the door, saying...

"Damn...what is your problem, do I need to go over your head to get you to help me?"

Detective Ridley took one step back, loosened his tie and said...

"I don't give a shit what you do...now do you wanna step aside, I have better things to do than to stand here and listen to this shit."

Detective Lopez opened her suit jacket revealing her badge saying...

"My badge says Detective just like yours, or is it that you have a problem with me being a Hispanic woman who just happens to be lead Detective over you?"

Detective Ridley push the door open and walked down the hallway but not before giving Detective Lopez that '*fuck-off*' look.

Detective Lopez didn't realize it, but she was only half correct. Detective Ridley did have a problem with Detective Lopez, but not because she was Hispanic but rather because he knew this type of case was too soon for her to take on.

Detective Ridley has been a detective with the Columbus Police department for over twenty-two years and has been on every case imaginable.

Knowing that Detective Lopez was going to the Captain's office to pressure him in to helping her, Detective Ridley hoped that his fifteen-year long friendship with Capt. Jones would make her back off.

Captain Lucas Jones motioned for Detective Ridley to sit down as he was busy on the phone when Detective Ridley walked into his office.

Detective Ridley sat quietly glancing around at the photographs of countless Officers when his eye caught the photo of himself being congratulated by Capt. Jones when he was made Detective.

Capt. Jones finished his call and then looked over at Detective Ridley saying...

"So, Mark what brings you up here...slumming'?"

Detective Ridley pulled a pack of chewing gum from his pocket and after offering a piece to Capt. Jones who declined, stuck a piece in his mouth and said...

"Lou, we've known each other a long time...right?"

"Oh, shit here we go...who lit a bug under your ass this time, every time you start off with that 'ain't we've known each other', there's always something piss ass bad brewing?"

Capt. Jones said as he walked over and closed his door. Detective Ridley got up and followed Capt. Jones to his desk and leaning on it said...

"When did we re-open the Sister Mary Jacalyn case...I just had a conversation with Detective Lopez who has some crazy ideal about digging into that case, I mean if anyone is going to re-open it, that should be me."

Capt. Jones sat tapping a pencil on his desk and said...

"First, of all Mark, I asked her to investigate it, and secondly she's a fellow Officer and the lead Detective in this division and if she asked for your help it's your job to help her."

Detective Ridley picked up one of the files Capt. Jones had laying on his desk saying...

"Okay...for starters she's too inexperienced to handle a case like that and where does she get off thinking that she can order me around, hell there's plenty of fresh meat in this department that she can play 'Police woman' with."

Capt. Jones snatched the file from Detective Ridley and replied...

"For starters get the fuck off my desk, and if you're a part of this department

you'll do whatever and help whomever I say...is that clear, now get the fuck out...I mean you can get back to work!"

As Detective Ridley was leaving Capt. Jones's office Detective Lopez was standing there ready to knock when Detective Ridley said...

"I'll be at my desk if you need to know something about the case, but I still think you're making a big mistake re-opening it, all that old weird shit is going to start all over."

Detective Lopez stood looking at Detective Ridley as he rudely walked past her and down the steps before she entered Capt. Jones's office.

Detective Ridley walked into his office and after unlocking the drawer, took a large file from inside the drawer and stepped out the back door of the Police station to light a cigarette, when he said to himself...

"Detective 'Taco' has no clue what she's in for...this case was the freakiest and weirdest case I've ever worked on...well fine if she wants to be driven out of her mind, then let her."

Detective Lopez approached Detective Ridley's office just as he was coming down the hallway, when he noticed Detective Lopez standing there with two cups of coffee saying...

"Mark, I hope we don't spend all day kicking each other in the balls... can't we set our differences aside?"

Detective Ridley reached out and opened the door to his office and said as Detective Lopez entered...

"You never seem to amaze me Detective."

Detective Lopez entered Detective Ridley's office and sat one cup of coffee down on the desk and said as she sat down...

"What...are you amazed at me going to the Captain, because I went to see him for something else?"

Detective Ridley slightly closed the door behind him and as he took his seat behind his desk said...

"Naw...I wasn't talking' about that, I was talking about the fact that you admit to having a pair to kick."

Sipping her coffee, Detective Lopez snapped...

"Medefore...it was a medefore."

Detective Ridley repositioned himself at his desk shaking his head saying...

"I think it's pronounced 'metaphor' detective, and thanks for the coffee."

Detective Lopez sat her coffee down and said...

"Look Mark why is this case such a flat tire for you, I mean I've seen the cases you've worked on and a lot of them involved some sick and twisted perps...right?"

Detective Ridley continued opening the case files and rifling through them said...

"Now I'm going to show you some things that you may find a little hard to believe but trust me there were others who witnessed the same things that I did."

Detective Lopez raised up in her seat saying...

"About the only thing I'll find hard to believe is if I see Smoky the Bear smoking a pipe full of marijuana and setting fires."

Detective Ridley slammed the files shut and snapped...

"Smart ass, do you wanna see the files or not...you're the one who asked me, remember!"

Detective Lopez sat on the edge of her seat and said...

"Okay, so what's the mystery about, we're talking about a Nun who skipped out on her trial and was found dead...but that was over forty-five years ago."

Detective Ridley handed her a thin file saying...

"What you're reading there happened almost thirty years ago. Sister Mary Jacalyn listed her birth as May one, eighteen twenty-two. There were some mysterious infant deaths registered at the county hospital and long with..."

Before Detective Ridley could finish his sentence, Detective Lopez interrupted him saying...

"What does infant deaths have to do with a Nun?"

Flipping through a case file, Detective Ridley pointed to an old newspaper article and said...

"Here look at this; December fifth, nineteen forty-three...Lyn Caaj, thirty years old, accepts position in Neonatal unit at Sypris Memorial Hospital."

"Here's another...January fourteen, nineteen-forty-four, sixteen unexplained infant deaths at Sypris Memorial. Neonatal staff questioned."

Looking intently at the clippings Detective Lopez said...

"Okay, I'm looking but I don't see anything, what does this have to do with Sister Mary Jacalyn?"

Detective Ridley slid his chair close to Detective Lopez and grabbing a pen and piece of paper said...

"Look closely at the name of the nurse who oversaw the Neonatal unit... Lyn Caaj, and if you rearrange the letters Lyn Caaj spells 'Jacalyn'."

Turning slowly to look at Detective Ridley, Detective Lopez said...

"Whoa, you're making one hell of a leap here...you can rearrange anyone's name and come up with a dozen or more different names, what are you getting at?"

Going through another file, Detective Ridley said...

"Here is a wedding clipping from the same newspaper forty-three years ago, announcing the wedding of Mr. Michael James Morse, sixty years old of Ohio to a Ms. Lyn Ranee Caaj, fifty years old from Venezuela."

Handing the newspaper clipping back to Detective Ridley, Detective Lopez said...

"Okay, so this Lyn person married some guy from Ohio...I still don't a connection."

Pulling several photos out of a file and handing them to her Detective Ridley stated...

"I had these pictures enhanced years ago and I found something interesting... the photo of Lyn Caaj and Sister Mary Jacalyn are a spot-on match even down to the scar on the left side of her cheek."

Looking at the photos Detective Lopez said...

"Okay, so they're both from Venezuela and they both have a scar."

Handing Detective Lopez another set of photos, Detective Ridley said...

"This same woman's husband died mysteriously and five years later married another man and had a total of four children which no one has seen neither hide nor hair of them.

Also, her age doesn't make sense...she listed her date of birth as, May 1, eighteen-twenty-two."

Detective Lopez gawked saying...

"I was following you at the beginning, but now you're losing me."

Detective Ridley stretched to look at his pager which was vibrating and said...

"Let me ask you a personal.... aren't you Catholic?"

Standing up and looking irritated, Detective Lopez said...

"Now you're stereo-typing me Papi. Just because I'm Hispanic...then I must be Catholic, I might be a Lutheran or a Baptist!"

Not wanting to get into a pissing contest with Detective Lopez, Detective Ridley walked back over to his desk saying...

"Hey, I didn't mean to pour beer in your corn flakes all I meant was..."

Detective Lopez turned around saying...
"Why you all jacked up...yes, I'm Catholic, actually Roman Catholic."
"More formal, huh?"
Detective Ridley sarcastically snapped back at Detective Lopez.
Looking puzzled, Detective Lopez said...
"More what?"
Detective Ridley ignored her question and went to the file cabinet, pulling out another file said...
"Aren't Nuns supposed to be under vows of poverty, chastity, and obedience and all of that?"
Detective Lopez responded to Detective Ridley as she stood with her back against the wall saying...
"Yes, Nuns or Sisters model their lives after the example of the Holy Mother Mary, so this Sister Mary Jacalyn can't be this Lyn person, this Lyn person had two not one husbands and children... Nuns are forbidden to marry or have children."
Detective Ridley handed Detective Lopez the file and said...
"Go ahead look inside."
Detective Lopez opened the file and began reading...

"August six, nineteen seventy-eight Detective Mark Ridley interview with Santiago Ruiz-Consuela.

M.R. Sir will you look at this photograph of Sister Mary Jacalyn and tell me if you recognize her?

S.R-C. Si, that is my Sister Jacinta Carlita Consuela.

M.R. Sir when you say that she is your Sister, in what sense are you saying that?

S.R-C. What I saying is...she is my mother's child, my Sister.

M.R. Sir, when was the last time you saw your Sister?

S.R-C. I see her last after we bury her, over forty years...but how can all of this be?

M.R. Can you be sure that the woman we saw at the Saint Francis Xavier Roman Catholic Church is your Sister?

S.R-C. When you grow up with someone, you don't make mistake like this...how can she be alive?

M.R. Can you tell me why you came to the Police station?

S.R-C. Si, I mean yes, our family, we see this picture on the newspaper cover and we can't believe what we are seeing, so I come to Ohio to see for myself, and how this could be.

M.R. Other than your words...do you have any proof that this is really your Sister?

S.R-C. Si, Jacinta was a cutting sugar cane with me, because our papa was too sick to work and one day we were cutting in the field and Jacinta was laughing and not concentrating and cut off her finger next to her thumb on her left hand.

M.R. Here is a picture of her hugging little kids, show me.

S.R-C. Si, if you look, she is a wearing a glove on her left hand.... look, I know this because I was the one who wrapped her finger and I still have all that is left of her finger in this box.

M.R. May I see the box?

S.R-C. Here, all that's left is bone, I tell you I know that it is Jacinta Carlita.

M.R. We could prove that one way or the other but, they won't allow us or anyone to get inside.

End of interview of Santiago Ruiz-Consuela......

Detective Lopez handed Detective Ridley the file and said...
"All of this looks interesting, but what happened to her brother and did you ever investigate it any further?"
Detective Ridley handed her another photo saying...
"Here...I got in and was able to take this picture of her."
Detective Lopez took the photo and immediately said sarcastically...
"I see...wow, a missing finger...so what happened, what did you do?"

Detective Ridley stood up and took a sip of his coffee saying...
"Child protection services contacted us because the mother of her second husband stated she tried to visit her grandchildren and was told that the children were ill and in bed.
Myself, Captain Jones, who was a Lt. then and the lady from child protection services went to talk to Sister Mary Jacalyn and the next thing I know, Lt. gets a phone call and I'm told to back off the case, and on top of that the priest in charge of Saint Francis Xavier Roman Catholic Church Father.... what's his name, falls down a flight of stairs and dies."
Detective Lopez and Detective Ridley were interrupted by a knock on the door by Captain Jones, who stuck his head in the door saying...
"Don't mean to disturb you two, but I wanted to see if you two were fighting fair."
Detective Lopez was about to ask the Captain about his involvement in the case when Detective Ridley interrupted saying...
"I'm cooperating, we were just going over some information."
As Captain Jones was closing the door, Detective Lopez looked at Detective Ridley with a surprise look on her face saying...
"Okay, you wanna tell me what that was about...I was about to ask..."
Interrupting Detective Lopez, Detective Ridley grabbed his coat and headed towards the door saying...
"Keep your voice down, too many ears, if you know what I mean."

After stepping out in the parking lot, Detective Lopez asked Detective Ridley for the meaning of coming out in the cold to talk when Detective Ridley replied...

"*Did you see that. The Captain just conveniently stopped in to check on us...he asked you to look into this case, but he didn't tell you he had first-hand knowledge about it, did he?*"

Not giving Detective Lopez a chance to respond and nervously looking around said...

"*There's some weird shit going on, the Captain acts like he doesn't know shit about this case, and I overheard there are two patrol Officers who went missing after their shift ended last night.*"

Detective Lopez turned in the direction that Detective Ripley was looking, saying...

"*Yea, the Captain's acting as if he knows nothing about does bother me, but I'm trying to connect the dots and who's missing?*"

Detective Ridley pulled a small note pad from his back-pocket reading...

"*Huh, they're two Officers who responded to a disturbance up north off Africa near Alum Creek State Park, we're supposed to go up there and have a look see.*"

Leaning in to Detective Ridley, Detective Lopez said...

Isn't that where a woman was murdered a couple months ago at some old fishing boat area?"

Placing his note bad back into his pocket, Detective Ridley said...

"*That's the place, you remember all the murders we had in the city a couple months ago, hey, weren't you apart of that investigation?*"

Shaking her head Detective Lopez said...

"*No, I didn't get in on any of the heavy shit...I just came back off maternity leave and Captain put me on investigating a couple of kids wearing hoodies bothering people...but I still can't connect the dots, what's this have to do with The Nun?*"

Detective Ridley placed his hand on the door to prevent Detective Lopez from going inside saying...

"*That's how it all started twenty-five years ago, first two patrol Officers missing, and then it was all the weird murders and missing people all over the city, and the good Sister Mary Jacalyn... her name kept coming up in all of it...I'm telling you, it's starting all over again.*"

Detective Lopez and Ridley walked back into the station and prepared to head out to the northeast side of Columbus to investigate the disappearance of the two patrol Officers when Captain Jones turned the corner and said...

"Hey, you two, I thought you were supposed to be out at the Alum Creek State Park investigating the missing Officers...well holdup before you go, I just got word that their patrol car was found."

Detective Lopez grabbed her bag and said as Detective Ridley headed for the steps...

"Do you know if there was any evidence of foul play?"

Captain Jones said as he handed Detective Lopez a file...

"That's what detectives do detect, so I expect to be copied on what you find."

Looking at the file as she headed towards the door, Detective Lopez sarcastically said under her breath...

"Yeah, I wish everybody here knew how to share information."

Captain Jones took three steps towards Detective Lopez and shouted...

"What was that...you don't have to talk to me sideways detective, don't forget I make out the assignments and your ass can be warming any chair in this office, including down in the basement."

Detective Lopez was known for having a short fiery temper, so it was no surprise to Captain Jones when she stopped and turned...when Detective Ridley separated the two saying...

"Hold on there, detective...we've got work out there to do, real Police Officers out there need us not this bullshit in here."

Both detectives were heading down the steps as Captain Jones shouted...

"I'd have no problem seating your ass too Mark...why don't you just retire and do us all a big ass favor."

Detectives Ridley and Lopez exited out of the station and headed towards the car as Detective Lopez said...

"What the hell was all of that about, one minute he's Captain Cool and the next minute he's Barney Fife on steroids."

Detective Ridley started the car, and shaking his head said...

"You're joking right? In any case, captain Jones has not always been like

that…I think working on the Sister Mary Jacalyn case did something to him, as a matter of fact truth be told…it did something to all of us."

Detective Lopez sat pretending not to be bothered by Captain Jones' outburst when she looked over at Detective Ridley who said to her…

"Okay, what's the address we're looking for?"

Shuffling through the file that Captain Jones handed her, Detective Lopez said…

"Huh…we are going to thirteen-twenty-five Carpenter Lane. We have to go seventy-one north and then take twenty-three north."

Detective Ridley interrupted Detective Lopez saying…

"Yeah, like we're going to Lewis Center, right?"

Detective Lopez was about to confirm his directions when the tires screeched, as Detective Ridley slammed on brakes and hollered at the driver in another car…

"YOU FUCKING ASSHOLE…WATCH WHERE YOU'RE GOING!"

Regaining control of the car Detective Ridley took his hand away from Detective Lopez's shoulder saying…

"Before Mr. Asshole almost hit me back there, I was going to tell you about the bad vibes I'm getting from Captain Jones and this case…I mean he knows a heck of a lot more about this than I did.

For example, he was allowed to talk with Sister Mary Jacalyn when no one else could, and that's because of the people upstairs."

"Are you shitting me?"

Detective Lopez said with a look of disbelief on her face.

Detective Ridley took a pack of chewing gum from the console of the car and after offering Detective Lopez a stick said…

"Hell, what did he tell you about this case?

Detective Lopez unwrapped the gum and after folding the stick of gum and putting it in her mouth said…

"He didn't tell me nothing…all he said was, a call came in from a hysterical woman and she mentioned Sister Mary Jacalyn and then he asked me to get with you and find out what I could."

Detective Ridley turned onto interstate seventy-one and handed Detective Lopez his note book saying...

"After he took over the case of the missing kids from me, he took a vacation for three weeks and when he returned, he went to command school for a couple of months and then the case was dropped."

"What do you mean the case was dropped?"

Detective Lopez said, as she fumbled through the pages of the note book, when Detective Ridley said...

"All I'm saying is...the case was never investigated and when I asked about the kids and where were we in that part of the investigation, what I was told was, there are no missing kids and then I was reassigned to another division."

Detective Lopez closed the note pad saying...

"That's messed up, so just what am I supposed to be looking at?"

Detective Ridley pointed with his finger to the last few pages telling Detective Lopez how he followed Sister Mary Jacalyn one night and saw the most unusual thing...

Detective Ridley picked up his radio and after a short conversation hung it up saying...

"You see there, right there...I went to Cheezie's bar on Mt. Vernon Ave to have a few drinks after work and while I was sitting there I turned and there was Sister Mary Jacalyn standing outside looking at me through the window."

"You got to be shitting me...but she's dead?"

Detective Lopez said as she scanned the area looking at the Police cars which dotted the area.

Detective Ridley slowed the car down looking for a place to park, and said...

"I left the bar and followed her, for an old woman she was moving extremely fast until I turned the corner and she was gone...'poof' like a fart in the wind.

"I stood looking and decided to turn back and head for my car when suddenly there she was standing right behind me, and when I looked at her face I noticed one of her eyes was solid white and the other one was normal.

I thought my heart was going to jump out of my chest when she said...

"...those who follow in the dark should be careful about where they step."

Detective Ridley placed the car in park and stopped for a minute, then he continued saying...

"Then she grabbed me by the collar and as I reached for my gun, with the

*other hand, she grabbed my hand stopping me from pulling it out of my holster
and said, 'beware of the thing you just found.'*

Detective Lopez took her gun from her purse and stuck it in her
shoulder holster saying...

"So, what happened, did you arrest her, shoot her or what?"

Showing Detective Lopez his right hand he said...

"Do you see this?"

"Damn Papi, what happened to you?"

Detective Lopez said with a look of disgust on her face.

While Detective Ridley was turning the engine off he said...

*"That Catholic bitch is what happened...oh, excuse my French, but what
is this 'Papi' shit?"*

Detective Lopez reached out to touch Detective Ridley's withered
hand saying...

*"Papi is like macho daddy...kind of like that, and it's not good to call a Nun
a bitch you know, anyway, how did she do this to your hand?"*

Detective Ridley pulled his coat sleeve back down over his wrist
saying...

*"I dunno, when she grabbed me, my wrist and hand started burning and
I passed out, I guess from the pain, and when I came to, most of my skin was
burned or melted off."*

*"Damn.... that's some nasty looking shit, you mean to tell me that she did
this when she touched you?"*

Detective Ridley opened his car door saying...

"I told you, this bitc—I mean Nun, is messed up or something."

Detectives Ridley and Lopez exited the squad car and walked past
the school reporters towards the members of law enforcement just
behind the yellow marking tape.

Looking at Detective Ridley, Detective Lopez said...

*"Nobody said anything about this being a crime scene, I thought we were
going to investigate two missing Police Officers."*

*"You should know procedure; the tape has to go up in the event it becomes
a crime scene."*

Detective Ridley said as he ducked under the yellow crime scene tape, as Detective Lopez followed saying...

"Screw procedures...you see how everyone is trampling all over everywhere, shit if it does pan out to be something, all were going have is a bunch of cops' foot prints everywhere."

Detectives Lopez and Ridley approached a group of four Officers standing at the end of the street and approaching them Detective Lopez said...

"Okay, what do we have here?"

The first Officer to respond was Officer Daniels, who said...

"Detective, what we got here is all messed up, I mean, we're looking for their squad car, we uncovered Officer Willis's body with a single gunshot to the back of the head, and no sign of his partner Officer Johns."

Detective Ridley walked over and examined the body saying...

"Okay, we got a missing Police Officer and a dead cop...did anyone talk to witnesses or people who say they saw them. What were they doing up here?"

Police Officer Daniels pointed up to a row of houses saying...

"The third house there with the lamp in the yard belongs to two dykes who said they spoke with the Officers last night."

Detective Lopez immediately replied...

Thanks Officer, but in the future please do not refer to them as dykes... they are women who wear a different shoe size and most of all, they're people."

The Officer nodded and began walking towards the house until they were stopped by another Police Officer who motioned for them to come his way, which was several hundred feet.

Detectives Lopez and Ridley approached the Officer who said...

"Hey Dicks, you might wanna see this."

Detectives Lopez and Ridley immediately caught glimpse of the rear end of one of the Police department squad cars whose rear end was barely visible in the brush.

As they approached the car Detective Ridley turned to Police Officer Rodney Smith and said...

"Okay, tell me what you know about this, just the nuts and bolts...not the whole friggin alphabet."

Police Officer Smith showed Detectives Lopez and Ridley traces of blood on the outside driver's door and what seemed like a struggle on the inside.

Officer Smith then turned and said...

"The only thing I found when I got here was the body of Officer Willis, he wouldn't have just let anybody walk up on him like that."

Detective Lopez reached out for the note pad and then she said...

"That's good Officer let's put out an all-points on Officer Johns, I need to talk to him."

Detective Ridley carefully closed the door of the patrol car and joined Detective Lopez who was walking towards one-fourteen-ten Pecan Drive, the home of Bill and Clara Scott, the last people who reportedly saw the Officers.

As they walked and scanned the area Detective Ridley pointed ahead and to the left saying...

"I'll be damn would you look at that, looks like someone's pet monkey has gotten out of its cage."

The little monkey caught Detective Lopez's eyes as it stopped in the middle of the street watching every movement of the two detectives, as Detective Lopez said..."*That little fellows probably lost, it's just sitting there staring at us."*

Detective Lopez was right and wrong, the monkey was staring at them, but it was not lost.

As they arrived in front of the house of Bill and Clara Scott, Bill emerged from the house and stood on the porch saying...

"Morning...what's all the commotion about, is there something wrong?"

The detectives showed their badges and told Bill that they were investigating the disappearance of two patrol Officers who spoke with them the previous day and asked if they could come inside, and Bill stated yes.

Once inside, the detectives were met by Clara who was standing by the counter finishing a bowl of cereal when Bill said...

"Clara, you remember the two Police Officers we spoke with yesterday.... well, their missing."

Clara sat her bowl in the sink saying...

Really I can't remember much of anything?"

Detective Lopez approached Clara saying...

"*Mrs. Scott, we have a report that says both Officer Willis and Johns were out here speaking with you and your husband, can you tell me what time that was and what you talked about?*"

Before Clara could answer, the monkey which the detectives saw, jumped from the counter and onto Clara's shoulder, as Detective Lopez responded with...

"*We were wondering whose monkey had gotten out, we saw it in the street a few minutes ago.*"

Clara started petting the monkey, saying...

"*Mommas little munchkin's been out again...bad munchkin, bad munchkin.*"

Detective Ridley hoping to stay on track said...

"*So, Mr. and Mrs. Scott, getting back to the two Officers, what time were they out here?*"

Still petting the monkey, Clara said...

"*No Police have been out here...good Lord, why would the Police be out here talking to us, we haven't seen the Police, isn't that right honey?*"

Bill motioned for the two detectives to have a seat and said...

"*Gosh yea, we are law abiding citizens why would the Police come and talk to us?*"

Detective Lopez declined to sit saying...

"*You're not in any trouble were just trying to find out the whereabouts of the two Officers who according to our last report shows that they were coming out here to talk to you...this is one-fourteen-ten Pecan Drive, is it not?*"

Clara interrupted saying...

"*Yes, this is one-fourteen-ten Pecan road, but like we said we haven't talked with any Police yesterday or any other day.*"

Detective Lopez took the note pad out of her pocket and said...

"*Mrs. Scott, why do I get the impression that you're lying to us, we know the Officers came here and they spoke with you?*"

Just then Bill Scott got in between Detective Lopez and Clara saying...

"*What have you got there...we told you we haven't seen or talked to any Police.*"

Detective Ridley walked over and stood alongside of Detective Lopez saying...

"It's a note pad which belongs to Officer Willis who wrote that they were here and did in fact talk with you two about some kind of disturbance."

Just then with an odd sounding laugh and chuckle Clara said…

"Oh-oh, honey don't you remember the two Police who spoke with the couple down the street, you know Mrs. and Mrs. uh what's their names, the ones with the dog?"

Bill stood there for a moment with an irritating and angry look on his face saying…

"Oh yeah, they stopped us, but they were looking for the couple down the street…so if you don't mind…"

Detectives Ridley and Lopez looked at one another and then back over to Clara and Bill when Detective Lopez said…

"Look we want you two to come down to the station with us and give us a statement, because we feel you're deliberately lying to us."

Clara walked into the living room shouting…

"Hey, we got rights and we haven't done anything wrong, we don't have to go anywhere!"

Detective Lopez was walking after Clara and about to respond when Detective Ridley grabbed her arm saying…

"Okay partner slow your roll…they don't have to come downtown, but Mr. Scott if we have any more questions can we come and talk with you again?"

Detective Lopez looked at Detective Ridley saying…

"Slow your roll? Did you spend Sunday afternoon in the hood or something?"

Bill was following Clara and Detective Lopez when he stopped and turned to Detective Ridley and said…

"Yeah…sure you can, we don't mind but it's like I said we don't know anything about who you're looking for."

Outside, Detective Lopez said…

"Damn Ridley, they were lying, and you know it, it's all down here in Officer Willi's notes…they interviewed them for over an hour!"

Detective Ridley walked down the steps and into the street saying…

"Sure, I know it and so do you, but were going to have to find some witnesses who can confirm that they were having a conversation with the Officers…which means door to door."

Detectives Lopez and Ridley combed the entire twenty-two houses in the upscale neighborhood, but many were out for the morning as it was a mild mid-March morning.

Of the residents that they could talk to, many had stated they hadn't heard nor seen anything because of the storm that night, so, they left their business cards and continued looking for evidence.

As they returned to where the patrol car was parked, it was being loaded onto the Police crime lab tow truck and that's when Detective Ridley said...

"Did you notice something odd about the fourth house, the one with the busted front window?"

Detective Lopez said...

"The only thing odd I noticed was you, not wanting to talk to the people that we know spoke with the missing Officers...that's the only odd thing I see."

Detective Ridley walked over to their car and as he unlocked the door, turned and said...

Let's go grab some coffee and breakfast and then we'll come right back out here and do it again."

Detective Lopez opened her side of the car and as she got inside, said...

"I'm starting with Mrs. Scott too, so get that through your head."

Detective Ridley started laughing to himself when he said...

"Did you see that monkey...that was one ugly S.O.B., it looked as if it had a yeast infection."

Both detective Lopez and Ridley began laughing and drove off to get breakfast.

Detectives Lopez and Ridley returned from breakfast to question the neighbors, and while they caught many more residents at home, they provided no additional information.

Detective Lopez however, was extremely pissed over the fact that the Scotts were not at home.

Detective Ridley look over to Detective Lopez as they sat in the car assessing the day's lack of progress, saying...

"Hey, let's call it a day, I'm suddenly not feeling so hot, I think something I ate went down the wrong way."

Detective Lopez looking disappointed simply nodded okay, but when she looked at Detective Ridley she noticed he was sweating profusely with sweltering pools of perspiration on his forehead, which began to run down his face.

"Seriously Papi, you look like shit... do you need to go to the hospital or something, because I can get you there?"

Detective Lopez said as she reached in her purse for a Kleenex.

Detective Ridley's voice was a higher pitched than usual, saying...

"Oh shit...my insides feel like they're on fire...I think I better pull over and let you drive!"

Detective Ridley pulled the unmarked car over, saying...

"I feel like I'm coming down with something bad."

The two exchanged positions and after several miles of driving Detective Ridley shouted in a weak and anxious voice...

"Oh shit...pull over, I'm going to puke!"

The road they were traveling on barely had enough room to pull over safely, when up ahead Detective Lopez saw a driveway and turned off onto it saying...

"Okay, hold on Papi..."

Detective Lopez pulled into the drive way and stopped, as Detective Ridley opened the door, up-chucking.

Little to no attention was paid to anything else except Detective Ridley's condition, which would prove to be costly.

Detective Lopez exited the car and went to the trunk to look for a rag and anything else to help Detective Ridley...and saw nothing but your standard jack, spare tire and first aid kit.

As Detective Ridley was outside the car bent over at the waist puking his guts, Detective Lopez spotted two small kids wearing hoodies walking down the driveway approaching them.

Believing that they lived in the house which was at the end of the drive way, she turned her attention back to Detective Ridley who was now on the ground on his hands and knees puking.

With lightening type speed, the two kids who were only moments ago, seventy feet away, were standing right beside the two detectives.

Suddenly Detective Lopez began moaning and screaming out in pain as the two children pointed skinny elongated fingers at her.

Detective Ridley lifted his head and saw what was happening but was powerless to do anything about it as his own condition grew worse.

On the ground, twisting and writhing in agonizing pain, Detective Lopez snatched at her blazer, ripped it open revealing her stomach which looked as if something was underneath her skin moving.

The two detectives could see and hear everything around them, but for some unknown reason, they could physically do nothing to help themselves.

It was then that another figure appeared standing over top of them… it was Sister Mary Jacalyn.

She stood above them dressed in her habit, clutching her fists and making swirling motions with her hand as the pain the two detectives felt grew worse.

Sister Mary Jacalyn had a sinister and devilish look on her face, her smile was sinister looking, and both of her eyes were completely white. Her teeth were extremely crooked and grey and looked as if they did not belong in her mouth.

Sister Mary Jacalyn then violently shook her head and began speaking to the detectives saying…

"You come after things you don't know,
You seek something you don't understand
If you continue to come after me, I'll come after you,
And trust me, you don't want that."

Detective Lopez was on the verge of blacking out from the pain when she noticed out of her right eye, Detective Ridley reaching for his gun.

Detective Lopez struggled as hard as she could to reach for hers as well when Sister Mary Jacalyn held out her hand and Detective Lopez slowly ascended in the air, meeting her face as she said…

"It would be so easy to swat you like a fly but, we're going to play a little game, you and I you and I you and I."

Suddenly, Detective Lopez fell to the ground and along with Detective Ridley who was no longer experiencing pain.

Detective Ridley stood up and removed his coat jacket shaking the vomit from it when Detective Lopez said…

"Tell me that just didn't happen?"

"Now you see what I was talking about…I don't think I can go through this shit again."

Detective Ridley said, wiping his mouth with the Kleenex…

"…and this is only going to get worse."

The two detectives gathered themselves and stood alone by their car when the sound of a horn honking grabbed their attention.

It was the home owners wanting to get into their drive way. Detective Ridley walked up to their car and explained he felt sick and they pulled onto their drive way until he felt better.

The drive to Columbus was usually a thirty-five-minute serene trip with a promising view full of luscious scenery, but for Detectives Ridley and Lopez, it would be a long and dark drive.

Ten minutes into the drive Detective Lopez looked over at Detective Ridley saying…

"Tell me what we just experienced, were the two kids and that creepy Nun, who was she…tell me we imagined it."

"This is why I begged you not to open this case. That was Sister Mary Jacalyn…now do you see what I was talking about. It took several years before I could get a good night's sleep."

Detective Ridley said as he reached into the glove compartment and pulled out a pack of cigarettes, lighting one as Detective Lopez said…

"When did you start smoking, I didn't know you smoked?"

Rolling the driver's side window down a little to let the smoke out, Detective Ridley said…

"Back in the seventy's when this mess all started I used to smoke, and after this case was closed I stopped…I guess I'm starting up again."

Detective Lopez sat shaking her head and saying…

"I can't believe this Papi, I'm a good catholic… I go to confession and I try to do the right thing, why couldn't I see an angel or the Mother Mary instead of this crap…I can't believe it."

Detective Ridley chuckled and said...

"I'm not laughing because of what you said...it's just that I said the same thing years ago, all except the part of being a Catholic and all, and can you stop calling me Papi."

Detective Lopez pulled a stick of gum from the console and asked...

"So, what is your religion Papi, oops sorry about that, it's a habit?"

Detective Ridley replied...

"Religion...mmm, I don't have one, I think that religions are a made-up word to keep people from facing the reality of what's really going on all around them in the world.

I believe there is more than what we think we see, so you tell me...after what we just saw, how does that fit into your Catholic sense of confession and rosary beads, and right and wrong?"

Detective Lopez didn't respond, she just sat there as quiet as a roach at an exterminator's convention.

5
Hide & Seek

Clara and Bill sat at the kitchen table discussing what they were going to do with their day when Clara said to Bill...

"Say, I feel like I'm not supposed to be here..."

Bill shook his head saying...

"Of course, you are.

Bill headed downstairs as Clara disappeared up the steps into the bathroom. Bill decided to feed both dogs and placed Shone's remaining dogfood by the front door, so they would not forget to give it to Deanne and David when they dropped by to pick up Shone.

Wondering what was taking Clara so long, bill went upstairs to check on Clara. Bill put his ear to the bathroom door and heard splashing water, and knew Clara was still bathing, so he laid across the bed waiting on Clara.

Clara came into the bedroom and sat on the edge of the bed, towel drying her hair when something out of the corner of her eye grabbed her attention. Turning slightly to the left Clara saw the comforter move, so she placed her hand on top of the comforter but there was nothing there.

To the right of Clara, a dark figure emerged from the walk-in closet and stood behind Clara. Again, Clara noticed something moving under the comforter.

This time Clara slowly raised the comforter and when she did, laying there was a six-foot Copperhead snake.

Jumping off the bed and screaming and jumping up and down,

Clara scanned the bedroom and saw Bill's baseball bat and glove in the corner and raced for it.

Grabbing the bat Cara quickly turned back to the bed and could still see the movement and the snake's head emerging from the comforter.

Clara took the towel which was draped over her right shoulder and tossed it over the snake and then begin striking the snake over and over until the towel was a bloody mess.

Clara took the end of the bat and nudged the towel and when she did it moved again, but not as much as before, so Clara furiously struck the towel harder and harder over and over until it lay still.

Almost out of breath and shaking, Clara placed the end of the bat under it and slowly lifted it and when she did, she screamed and fainted.

Clara rose to her feet still feeling a little dizzy and foggy-headed, slowly lifting the towel, then screamed hysterically.

Her husband, lover and best friend for twelve years lay on the bed, face unrecognizable by the extensive blows from the baseball bat, which was now at Clara's feet.

Clara's ear-piercing screams suddenly were replaced by shock and an eerie silence. Clara's hands were shaking uncontrollably not to mention the shock which came over her like an extension of Niagara Falls.

Clara knelt beside Bill crying uncontrollably, as her hands slightly touched Bill's face. Shaking uncontrollably, Clara cried...

"OMG.... Bill, Bill baby, what have I done, OMG Bill, get up, get up."

Bill lay bleeding profusely from the blows from the baseball bat, as Clara sat holding his head in her lap crying...

"OMG Bill...what have I done, I didn't know it was you I was trying to get the snake...oh Bill............HELP ME.... somebody HELP ME!"

Clara softly laid Bill's head on the bed and stood on her feet and slowly walked out of the bedroom to the bathroom with an aimless, blank look about herself.

A minute later Clara returned with wet towels and began wiping the blood from Bill's face and then called the Police.

Clara was sitting out on the front steps as the Police and ambulance arrived, not seeing the dark figure exiting out the back door.

The first Police Officer on the scene approached Clara asking if there was anyone else in the house and where the victim was.

Clara sat in a daze, responding to the Officers with a lethargic demeanor. Just then another Police car pulled up and exiting the car was Detective Lopez and Detective Ridley.

Detectives Lopez and Ridley emerged from the bedroom, walking the entire crime scene and then headed downstairs as Bill's body was bought out on a stretcher.

Clara, upon seeing Bill's body being loaded into the back of the emergency vehicle, became hysterical and uncontrollably emotional, racing to the stretcher as Detective Ridley stopped her, as Clara said...

"OMG...I killed Bill, I killed Bill!"

Many of Bill and Clara's neighbors stood in shock and horror over the tragic and brutal murder of Bill.

Just then Clara, turned to the Police Officers and emergency personnel and in a soft, and trembling tone said...

"I did it, I killed Bill...OMG, what have I done?"

Bill and Clara's neighbor, Russell, was standing near the scene and hollered to Clara, as the Police taped off Clara's front door with yellow crime scene tape and escorted Clara to the back of an unmarked car...

"I'll call our attorney Clara, don't say a word till he gets there."

News of the murder of Bill Scott spread through the small Alum Creek community like wild fire as Deanne motioned to David and Wendi to look at the news.

Wendi turned to Deanne and asked...

"Did you guys know them, the news said this is the third murder in your neighborhood?"

Deanne looked over at David and then back at Wendi saying...

"Yes, we knew them, they live just three houses down at the end of the Cul De Sac, they dog sit for us whenever we can't take Shone with us, but I didn't know anything about any other murders...what's going on in our neighborhood?"

David walked over to Deanne saying...

"Wow, can you believe that...we left Shone with them, I don't get it, Clara killing Bill, we got to get back there."

Wendi pulled out her cell phone as it started vibrating and said...

"It's sad when couples can't walk away and resort to murdering one another, it's just..."

Looking down at her cell phone, Wendi was interrupted by what she was saying by a text message she received, saying...

"Hey everybody, that was Steve, he said he's stuck in traffic down at the entrance, some kind of car accident."

David looked at Wendi saying...

"Steve must have been flying...it hasn't been that long since he left the Wild Life Center?"

Wendi responded...

"Oh no, Steve said he was on his way home, I mean here, he didn't say exactly where he was when he called me."

Deanne walked over to the window and as she looked out she turned towards David and Wendi saying...

"Steve just pulled in to the driveway."

Wendi jumped up off the sofa running to the door and opening it, said...

"Steve...oh baby, it's so damn good seeing you."

As Wendi stood on the porch hugging and kissing Steve, David and Deanne came to the door and David said...

"You guys need to get a room."

Wendi, with her arms still wrapped around Steve turned to David and Deanne as Steve said...

"Hey Dave, hey Dee...it's good seeing you guys, bad accident on the road?"

Wendi and Steve entered the house as David began telling Steve all about the murder as he closed the door.

Sitting around the kitchen table Deanne stood up saying...

"Hey everybody, how about bacon, eggs, grits and pancakes?"

Almost in unison, Wendi, Steve and David said...

"ALRIGHT."

Wendi jumped up saying...

"I'll give you a hand Deanne."

"Thanks Wendi."

Deanne said as they both headed in the kitchen, leaving David and Steve to talk.

David started telling Steve the thoughts that Deanne, Wendi and he were having and their conversations about what they thought was transpiring, when Deanne yelled from the kitchen...

"Don't forget, Tim and Mary and Kristin will be here soon."

"That's right, I almost forgot."

David responded, as Steve said with a look of confusion, saying...

"Tim, Mary and Kristin...they're driving all the way from Wisconsin.... why?"

Wendi bought two cups of coffee and handed them to David who said...

Thanks Wendi...no Steve, Tim and Mary called us saying they picked up Kristin and were on the road, but we'll know when they get here."

As the two of them sat and drank their coffee Steve said...

"Dave, I don't know how to put this, but one minute I'm hunting and then the next minute I'm on my way here to the farm."

David nodded and said...

"Let me ask you this, was there a creepy ass Nun, a big guy in a Ballerinas' tutu and a crazy old man involved in any of this?"

Steve sat back shaking his head saying...

"Yeah, all of them, and I killed two of my buddies back there at the lodge. I remember, you were hurt, Wendi was dead, and there were a lot of other people there, Police detectives.... oh, wow man, we were all there, and now we're here.

I just killed my two friends and I was trying to drive to the lodge office to report it, and the next thing I know, I'm on my way here...what the hell is going on?"

David poured Steve a double shot of vodka and handed him a beer to chase it with, saying...

"Steve, that's the question the rest of us were tripping over, was that a dream, or is this the dream, we remember The Nun, talking with us and messing with us, but I dunno?"

Just then, Deanne and Wendi came into the room bringing food and setting it on the table when the doorbell rang.

David got up and headed to the door saying...

"Now what."

Standing on the front porch was Tim and Mary as David greeted them...

"Hey, you two, what the hell are you doing here in Port Clinton, and where's Kristin?"

Tim and Mary entered as Tim shook hands with both David and Steve saying...

"That's a good question...one minute we were helping Kristin out in Madison and the next we're here in Port Clinton...feels like some twilight zone shit."

Tim, David and Steve set at the table as they heard the women in the kitchen whispering, normally they'd be doing their... *'girl I haven't seen you in a while bit'*, but what they have been through in past week gave little reason to laugh let alone celebrate.

Tim asked David for a shot of vodka and while David was pouring his drink, he said...

"Tim, I thought you'd light up a joint or something, it's not like you to get your drink on."

Tim downed the shot of vodka and went to refill his glass, saying...

"Dave, after dealing with all that shit, I couldn't smoke anything, I need some hard liquor to get me there in a hurry, if you know what I mean."

Deanne, Mary and Wendi entered the dining room where the men were sitting, when Deanne said...

"Can we just eat first and then discuss all this afterwards?"

While the women were in the kitchen cleaning up, Steve, Tim and David were enjoying another round of drinks before Mary and Wendi entered saying...

"Hey, you guys, you're going to be plastered in a bit, don't you think somebody needs to have a clear head?"

Placing his shot glass on the table David said...

"Wendi's right, we need to talk about last weekend everybody."

Tim swallowed his drink and sarcastically said...

"Talk about it, um...Mary and I are in Madison Wisconsin, four states away and suddenly we're in Port Clinton in mere seconds, what is there to talk about?"

Steve stood up and pointed at Tim angrily saying...

"Tim, you need to chill on that attitude. You're right, we were all in different places and suddenly we're here at the farm in Port Clinton, but what we need to talk about is, how all of our experiences are connected so we can find some way to prevent this from continuing to happen again and again and come up with some way to deal with this."

Suddenly Mary said...

"Let me get this straight...there's a demonic creepy ass Nun all jacked up-on steroids, who can just snatch us from one place and put us in another, who can make us see what she wants us to...so, how in the fuck are we going to prevent that?"

Steve stood up and clanged a fork against his glass saying...

"People take it down a notch, I think what we're saying is that each of us experienced something different from one another and sharing our story might help us, because if it happened once it can happen again, and why do all of us need to be here in Port Clinton?"

David sat at the table saying...

"Deanne and I were in Columbus and kept seeing Mary being tortured here at the farm, so we headed to Port Clinton, which is where we found all of you.

Steve took another sip from his glass and said...

"So, you see, that's what we're talking about, one of the things we now know is, this Nun, this thing or whoever she is, wants all of us together, in one place."

Just then Deanne let out a scream and said...

"OMG.... we-we're re-living it all over again, now."

David looked at Deanne and said...

"Doing what...baby?"

Deanne grabbed hold of David's arm as she turned to Steve and said...

"You just said this thing wants us all together in one place...well Kristin called and left a text, saying she was passing Bellefontaine, Ohio and should be here in two and a half hours."

David walked over to the table and after everyone came and joined him, said...

"Look people, this thing or whatever it is, has planned to have us all here and it seems like there is little we can do to stop it. I suggest we wait on Kristin and when she gets here we can plan on what to do."

Nobody was in a mood to argue with David, because right or wrong everyone knew that what was happening to them was real and unexplainable, and something, anything needed to be done.

Just then the doorbell rang, and everyone knew that it couldn't be Kristin, because she has over two hours left to drive, but Deanne hollered and said...

"Come on in Kris, the door is unlocked."

At that moment, the door burst open and a strong gust of wind blew in causing the women to scream and the men to jump.

David and Steve got up and walked over to the door, but no one was there. They returned to their seat after closing the door when the doorbell rang again.

This time David and Steve walked to the door as David yelled...

"Yeah, who is it?"

Hearing no response, David reached and grabbed the door knob and opened it and standing there on the porch was Kristin with her cell phone to her ear.

As Kristin entered, Deanne jumped up and ran to the door, while Wendi and Mary walked to greet Kristin.

David closed the door and put the dead-bolt on and returned to the table, as Deanne said...

"Damn girl, you must have been doing some driving, you said you'd be here in two hours and that was minutes ago."

Kristin walked straight over to the fridge and grabbed a bottle of wine and poured a large drink, saying...

"Yeah, I just left Bellefontaine, and then all of a sudden, I'm standing on your front porch...but what's got me is, I live in Madison Wisconsin, so why would I be near Bellefontaine, Ohio, when the direct route is South Bend Indiana to Port Clinton."

Port Clinton, Ohio

The light in Harmon's Country store was barely visible through all the dense fog as Mark Hennessey was restocking the cooler when he heard a loud thump against the back door.

He had worked there after school when he was a teenager, so sounds and noises never bothered him when he worked late nights in the store.

There was nothing but woods across the street and no neighboring houses in sight. Harmon's Country Store was the last stop until you reached Port Clinton, about ten to fifteen minutes.

The temperature was probably in the mid-seventies, as Mark Hennessey stretched and yawned with thoughts of getting home for the night.

Mark Hennessey lived five miles to the east of the store and knew the path to his small unadorned house in the dark better than most would in the light of day.

His house was built in nineteen-o-four, a single-family home, wood frame setting on a concrete block foundation.

Mark had been living there since nineteen-forty-five, and paid little attention to updating the house, even to the old wall dial phone which sat on the wall in his kitchen.

Mark walked to the front door of the store and looked out in the darkness, waiting for ten more minutes until ten o'clock...closing time.

Mark was old fashioned, unchanging, always closing at the same time every night even though he had no customers...it was always the same time...ten on the nose when out of the corner of his eye in the darkness he sees it.

It is a shadowy figure, right at his peripheral vision. A feeling of dread and uneasiness washed over him. Although Mark wasn't scared of much, he just didn't like being messed with, he didn't care for games.

The dark figure tapped and scratched on all the windows of the store, gaining Mr. Hennessey's attention, when Suddenly, an eerie laughter filled the night air as Mark walked away from the door yelling...

"Hey, fuck you, I don't have time for this shit".

The dark figure watched as Mr. Hennessey removed the night's cash from the register and place it inside the safe.

While Mr. Hennessey was on his knees locking the safe door, he was unaware that someone had snuck up behind him.

As Mr. Hennessey stood up, he was grabbed from behind and heard in a loud voice...

"I gotcha now, you old bucket of gizzards."

Struggling and then finally breaking free, Mr. Hennessey yelled...

"Damn you Melvin, what in Sally's milk wagon are you doing out at this time of night scaring folks!"

Melvin was Mr. Hennessey's twin brother who lived on the adjacent farm next to David Blue and Deanne Byrd. Melvin spun Mr. Hennessey around laughing and said...

"You thought somebody wanted your old measly five dollars...whew, you better check your drawers, I think somebody has the shit scared out of them for real."

Mr. Hennessey punched his brother on the arm saying...

"I just came to walk home with you, The Nun wants to see you tonight."

"You mean to tell me that you walked all the way down here just to tell me that...hell, I'll be along shortly."

Mr. Hennessey replied, as he dug in his nose and ate what was on his finger. Melvin turned his head away in disgust saying...

"You are one old nasty fart... I don't know why Sister Mary Jacalyn wanted you to help us in the first place, you bugger eating fart."

The Hennessey's are the oldest and oddest family in the area. It was said that their grandparents were practicing witches and devil worshipers and were responsible for a dozen or more missing teens over the last fifty years.

They walked carefully through the brush until they reached Melvin's farm. While they made their way through the cool damp grass, they heard the sounds of crickets and frogs which led to the sounds of dogs barking.

The full moon gave the men dim lighting which soon turned to a light fog. One could tell Melvin lived in the area, as he effortlessly made his way as if it were daylight, to the basement cellar door.

Melvin's farm looked as if it had abandoned for years...there was a massive tree on the side whose branches and leaves helped to camouflage the farm even further.

The main house looked as if it were at least a hundred years old, empty for years, weather-worn and in need of demolishing.

Upon arriving, Melvin lifted the storm cellar door and headed down the steps into the basement, brushing to the side, the buckets, rope, and several large knives which were suspended from the ceiling.

As they entered through the storm cellar, screams and moans could be heard coming through the basement walls...screams of people wanting out, people in agony.

At first glance the basement of Melvin's farm house looked like an ordinary dusty, dark, basement, but the reality of it is anything but.

Unless, of course, if your idea of an ordinary basement includes the gruesome torturing of people chained and locked in cages, and the violent ghosts of people burned alive.

Built in the early eighteen hundreds, Melvin's farm was originally intended to be a refuge and escape route for the Colonist and slaves, but since the seventeen fifties the infamous farms has been owned by the same continuous bloodline, the Hennesseys.

The design included three farms which were connected by underground tunnels which led to what is now known as Catawba Island, where ships could deliver supplies to the members of the thirteen colonists seeking their independence from Great Britain and provided an escape route for runaway slaves.

It was the distinguished Hennessey family, and not all of them were very nice. They scooped up the surrounding land during Columbus's second visit to America.

For a time, the farm's underground tunnels were the first line of defense against invading Great Britain making their way across the border on the King orders. That's where the dungeons came in.

Quite often, the British were sealed up in the deepest darkest holes of the tunnels and were subjected to terrible tortures. Men would have their arms and legs broken before being carried up and tossed into Lake Erie, and they'd drown, because they couldn't swim.

During the height of slavery and most recently, during the civil war, runaway slaves found refuge in the tunnels and the farms, often working the farms by day and hiding out in the tunnels at night.

There were two clans of the Hennessey's who controlled the land at that time. Cambridge Hennessey and his two brothers Asther and Miles, who was the more sympathetic of the clan, and cousins Calderon Hennessey and his two sons Winston and Shefler along with their cousin Melos Hennessey.

One night, Calderon, Winston, Shefler and Melos Hennessey captured and tortured to death Cambridge and his two brothers Asther and Miles and took total control of the land.

Over the years, there were many stories and reports of people who went missing and stories about people who visit the farms, only never to be seen alive again.

Over the years, the farms were passed down to their great grandsons, Mark, Melvin and Cambridge Hennessey's Great Grandson Harry, who mysteriously went missing in nineteen sixty-nine.

Mark and Melvin Hennessey were never charged nor even questioned in the disappearance of their cousin Harry, due to their influence in the town and their reputations, but many in the town of Port Clinton knew of the brother's mysterious past.

In nineteen seventy-two, a young eighteen-year-old runaway from Iowa showed up at the farm seeking refuge and work went missing, according to her parents.

It was reported that Melvin Hennessey was the last to see her alive and the young eighteen-year-old worked for his brother and were intimate, and often seen in very compromising positions.

Rumor has it that the young lady was pregnant and was growing tired of living with the brothers on the farm and had called into town to check on a Greyhound bus to Iowa...the young lady checked her bags in, but never picked up her ticket, nor ever caught the bus, nor has she ever been seen again.

The Hennessey's and the goings on up on their farms have always had a shroud of mystery associated with it.

There have been no relatives, friends nor people from town who have ever visited the Hennessey's farm until early September two thousand and six, when a young couple from Columbus moved to the middle farm, and though there is a cloak of uncertainty about what really happened up there.

Melvin closed the door the storm cellar after Mark and the two men disappeared in the darkness.

As they walked from the basement to the tunnel opening, they could hear people's voices crying out for help...people who sounded lost. All through the tunnel as they walked, they could hear the moans and cries, but could not see them.

Room after room revealed empty mattresses on the floor with small wooden empty bowls and collars attached to chains.

The walk through the tunnel from Melvin's farm to that of his neighbors David Blue and Deanne Byrd was over two acres and every five feet there were small rooms on every side.

The rooms were nothing more than a five-by-five-by five hewn spaces out of dirt. The spaces were cold, damp and musty. All along one side of the dirt walls, rusty old rings with worn out ropes running through them lined the path.

Ahead of the two men was an opening dimly lit, sat a figure dressed in a Nun's habit in a chair. The long hallway was lit by several candles, and the dirt walls loose and crumbling.

Melvin and Mark reached the end of the tunnel directly under the farm house of David Blue and Deanna Byrd, though neither David nor Deanne had any knowledge of the tunnels.

Sitting in a lone chair wearing a dusty, dirty habit was Sister Mary Jacalyn. The portion of the habit which was normally white was old, worn and dirty.

Sister Mary Jacalyn sat quiet in the chair, her gaze fixed upon the dirt ceiling above her. When she finally lowered her head as Melvin and Mark entered, she seemed to cause fright in the two old men momentarily, and then as if nothing was wrong the two brothers stood before Sister Mary Jacalyn saying nothing.

The room was filled with a strange, strong vanilla scent, and there was a strange feeling of evil in the room, as Sister Mary Jacalyn's malevolent gaze filled the small room.

Sister Mary Jacalyn sat with an old crooked wooden walking stick across her lap, clutching it with her elongated, crooked and knotted fingers.

Sister Mary Jacalyn's face was wrinkled and badly careworn. Her eyes were another story, they revealed a dark blue eye while her entire left eye was opal-looking, almost solid white.

The sun was coming up as Mark and Melvin headed towards their farms, and as they walked Melvin turned around to see Sister Mary Jacalyn just sitting in the wooden chair when Melvin leaned into Mark saying...

"So, what the hell was that all about...we go there to meet her, and she says nothing?"

Mark softly replied...

"I heard every word she said, didn't you?"

Mark and Melvin walked in the same direction leaving Sister Mary Jacalyn alone, when Melvin said as he picked in his nose...

"Hell no, I didn't hear anything."

After five-to-six hundred feet the tunnel veered to the left to Melvin's farm and to the right to, Mark's farm...the two men went to the right and climbed a flight of stairs leading to small door as Mark said...

"Be prepared for company at the farm...she's arranging for a lot of souls to be bought here...but don't worry, they are going home to their lives, after she steals their realities."

Melvin interrupted saying...

"Yeah but, they'll call the cops and we'll have to deal with everyone trampling all over the place...what are we going to do?"

Mark pulled Melvin's arm saying...

"Look all those people are back to their normal lives, they just have a different reality. The Nun is going to make them think that they're living in nightmares and they'll never know anything, and there's nothing they can do about it."

The two men climbed the stairs to Mark's farm house laughing and giggling.

Witham Ct SE

Diane and Tony turned to see Officer Johns knocking on the window and yelling at the Police cruisers which were now beginning to leave, saying...

"Hey! Hey over here...we're over here, Hey!"

Tony and Diane raced over to the window just in time to see the Police Officers turn in the direction of Tony and Diane's house.

Tony, Diane and Officer Johns watched as the Police Officers acted as if they heard something, but then turned and got into their cruisers and left the area.

"Did you see that...OMG!"

Diane anxiously said.

Turning away from the window, Tony responded...

"Yeah I saw a bunch of chicken-livered-no heart-doughnut eating pussies running away."

Officer Johns was about to interrupt in defense of the Officers when Diane said...

"No...something is wrong here,"

Officer Johns said...

"Give the woman a prize for getting a clue."

Tony walked over and got in Officer Johns face shouting...

"Don't you ever say anything against my wife, you are a fucking guest in our house….and besides all of this shit happened when your punk ass showed up."

Running in between Officer Johns and Tony, Diane said…

"Fellas…. Whoa, c'mon will you. Don't we have enough to deal with, we still got those stupid ass creepy kids and whatever that is outside to deal with."

Diane pulled Tony's arm as he said to Officer Johns…

"I didn't mean to be all up in your front seat, you can say what you want about me but man, my wife is off limits…okay?"

Officer Johns reached out to shake Tony's hand saying…

"No disrespect intended, with all this shit, well you know."

Tony accepted and shook his hand saying…

"Damn, that's a sorry ass excuse for an apology, dude."

Just at that moment, loud banging started on the walls of the house. They were so loud that there were several photos on the wall that fell, hitting the floor.

Just then Diane felt something cold on her shoulder and jumped and turned screaming…

"AWWWW"

No one was there, as Tony yelled….

"Holy shit look!"

The two kids in hoodies were standing on the front porch and there was a big fella with them.

Diane, Tony and Officer Johns stood looking out the window as Tony pulled his gun from his coat pocket and grabbed Diane's car keys off the rack in the kitchen saying…

"Man, this shit is all jacked up, I don't know 'bout anybody else, but staying here all locked up, is stupid, Diane you with me baby?"

Diane nodded her head when Officer Johns said…

"What are we going to do push your car or something?"

Tony loaded and put two extra magazines in his pocket and handed Diane a knife from the kitchen saying…

"Diane's car is parked on the street in front of the house…on three we run out of the carport and to Diane's car."

Officer Johns' attention went to the window as he heard that big fella had just removed the screen from the window, when Officer Johns said...

"*Whatever you're thinking we better move fast, cause this big fucker is about to come through the window.*"

Tony went to the living room window and clicked the cars' remote to open the doors when Diane screamed.

Turning around, Officer Johns and Tony saw the two kids in hoodies coming in the *back* door, as Tony pointed and raised the gun at them, and fired twice, saying...

"*I've had enough of this shit!*"

One of the bullets went through the back-door window, while the second bullet struck the tallest of the two kids.

Grabbing his head and sounding like Yosemite Sam, the kid said as he dropped to his knees...

"*Yep, I think ya done got me real good...I'm melting.*"

The kid stood up immediately, and they both pointed their fingers at the three of them and in a spooky voice uttered...

"*ooooooohh*"

Diane did exactly what you shouldn't do and that was, to run upstairs. Officer Johns tried stopping her, but she was on the first step before he knew it.

Meanwhile, Tony fired several more times before Officer Johns shouted...

"*Save your bullets Tony, they're passing right through them!*"

Tony wasn't about to run upstairs but Diane had, so Tony started yelling for Diane while backing up to Officer Johns who was standing near the door...

"*Diane, get your fucking ass down here now...Diane!*"

Diane came running down the steps just as the two kids with the hoodies came closer and closer, but Tony decided to rush them and over power them.

Officer Johns took a few steps closer to Tony when he stopped in his tracks.

Officer Johns saw Tony being pinned against the wall unable to move, all with a slight hand motion by one of the kids.

As Officer Johns backed up, Diane screamed…

"Look out!"

Officer Johns wanted to move but it was too late, the window broke and Officer Johns was being held by the neck by an enormously large man.

The man stood almost seven feet tall and weighing up to three hundred pounds, wearing a Ballerina's Tutu and dingy white stockings with a pair of old black and white sneakers, and wearing a clown's mask.

Officer Johns fought as hard as he could, but the grip of the big man was more than Officer Johns had ever encountered.

Diane came running and screaming towards the two kids with a large knife to help Tony, when Diane was also stopped dead in her tracks.

The kids started opening and closing their hands, making a fist and uttering unusual sounds as Diane screamed in pain.

The man in the Ballerina's tutu began slamming Officer Johns' head and back against the wall over and over until his head slumped down, then the big man let his body drop to the floor.

With Tony and Diane helpless to come to Officer Johns' rescue, the kids grabbed him by the ankles and drug him out the back door.

Finally, the two kids returned without Officer Johns and freed Tony from the wall and took him outside as well.

Diane knew that she was next, and she began to holler and cry hysterically.

The two kids were in front of her, and just like that, The Nun, Sister Mary Jacalyn was there.

Diane continued screaming hysterically as Sister Mary Jacalyn grabbed a handful of her hair and drug her out the door, as Diane screamed…

"Let me go you bitch!"

12 20 p.m.

Marcia emerged from the shower with a towel wrapped around her as Denise stood with a small brush and the blow dryer saying...

"Hey babe, you want me to do you?"

Marcia had her eyes closed drying her hair and didn't see that Denise had the blow dryer in her hand as she said...

"Denise is sex the only thing on your mind, you said we were going to the market."

Marcia looked up and saw what was in Denise's hands and said...

"Oh honey, I'm so sorry.... I didn't mean to..."

Denise walked over to Marcia and hugged her and kissed her saying...

"Denise don't worry, okay?"'

The two woman spent all day at the mall and farmer's market looking for things that they really wanted.

Times were not always so kind to Denise and Marcia, especially when they revealed that they were a married couple.

As a matter of fact, there was a period of a year where they had to down play their relationship, and not because people treated them mean, but because of the lack of state and local benefits.

Denise and Marcia didn't flaunt their relationship in public. About the only public display seen by them was and occasional hand-holding or, one day when Marcia reserved a room for them at a restaurant, Marcia said it was for Mr. and Mrs. Wesson.

When Denise and Marcia arrived at the restaurant, they were told that a mistake had been made and that there was no reservation with that name.

Needless to say, Marcia lost it and made such a big scene until they were escorted from the premises.

A combination of time and education or maybe plain old waiting for people to accept them, made it possible for Marcia and Denise to live a somewhat normal life together.

Leaving the Easton Mall in Columbus was anything but life in the fast lane. It seemed as if it took Marcia more time just sitting in traffic than the actual drive home.

Marcia and Denise were no more than a mile from home when they were pulled over by the Police, for speeding.

Denise looked at Marcia and said...

"Honey promise me that you're not going to get into with the Officer, let's just get the ticket and leave...besides we bought wine and you can always vent then."

Marcia nodded her head as the Police Officer was tapping on her window saying...

"License and registration please."

Marcia rolled her window down and handed him her license and registration and said...

"Hi there, sorry..... for speeding I lost my concentration back there."

Not showing any concern for what Marcia had just said, the Officer took the items and walked back to his patrol car.

The Officer spent no more than a couple minutes at his patrol car when he returned to Denise saying...

"Miss, I pulled you over because you were speeding, and your license plate cover is too dark, I'm afraid you're going to have to remove it and if you want a cover, get one that has a might lighter tint."

Denise leaned forward and thanked the Officer meanwhile Marcia snatched the ticket and said...

"I'll change it when I get home...thanks."

The Police Officer stated...

I appreciate that Miss, but I'm afraid you are going to have to change it now."

Marcia looked over at Denise and then back to the patrol Officer saying...

"Can you believe this shit; look Officer, we don't have any tools in the car, can't we do it once we get home we're only a mile away?"

The patrol Officer shook his head no and then said...

"First, I appreciate you watching your language and secondly I have a screw driver you can use if you'll wait right here."

The Officer came back to the rear of the car and Marcia got out and accompanied him to the rear of her car as the patrol Officer said...

"Here you are."

Marcia removed the license plate cover and put it in her trunk and handed the patrol Officer his screw driver when the Officer said...

"Have a good day Miss, and don't forget to lock up your home really good and tight tonight."

Denise noticed the Officer walking back to his car and Marcia beginning to follow him when she exited the car yelling…

"Marcia…Marcia!"

Marcia stopped in her tracks as the patrol Officer pulled off. Marcia walked back to where Denise was standing as they both got back in the car, Denise asked…

"What was that all about?"

You didn't hear what that Barney Fife wanna be said to me?"

Marcia said as she started the car.

Denise put her seat belt on and said…

"I will as soon as you tell me."

Marcia backed out of the parking space saying…

"He told me to have a nice day and make sure to lock all of our doors and windows tonight…son of a bitch".

Denise sat back in her seat saying…

"I don't know why you're getting so jacked up, that's the kinda things the Police say."

"It's not so much what he said, but how he said it…you know?"

Marcia said as she turned on to her street.

After putting up all the things that they had bought, Marcia said…

What do you think about a glass of wine and just chillin and watching a movie?"

Denise looked at Marcia and touched her hand saying…

"That sounds really good, but can we listen to music instead?"

Marcia and Denise settled back as Marcia put in a Sade CD, singing…

"…You give me you give me the sweetest taboo You give me you give me the sweetest taboo too good for me."

Marcia and Denise sat snuggling and listen to CDs when they heard scratching from somewhere.

They looked around the room, and that's when they heard it again.

Denise got up and turned the music down, saying…

"Did you hear that?"

Denise and Marcia sat down on the bed and out of nowhere, the CD player, slid to the side of the dresser and fell to the floor all by itself.

Denise screamed and called for Marcia, she saw her standing up against the wall.

Marcia started yelling about something, but Denise couldn't hear her, because she was too busy screaming and crying.

It was like something out of a horror movie. Then the door flung open and shut, open and shut. Denise was on the floor, with her back against the side of the bed crying repeatedly, saying...

"What the hell is going on?"

Yelling at Denise, Marcia screamed...

"What the hell is happening here, Denise?"

Then suddenly, the room turned ice cold and the lights began to flicker, then the lights suddenly stopped flickering, and the room was back to normal again.

Shaking, both women slowly walked to the door and as Marcia walked past the bedroom mirror, she turned around and looked at Denice's back. There where scratches all over her, six or seven big scratches that looked like fresh claw marks.

Marcia, then using one of her hands covered part of her mouth, she then told Denise to get dressed while she grabbed her clothes off the chair.

Denise only grabbed a few things from the bed post, and then opened the front door, and as she did, Denise let out a scream and slammed the door shut.

It was very quiet while Marcia and Denise were shaking when suddenly, they heard the sound of footsteps, running on the floor in the attic. Both women looked at each other and then slowly walked to the door.

"There was no way someone could be walking up there let alone running in that space, its crammed with stuff."

Marcia said as she held onto Denise' arm. The women cautiously looked out the door to the left and then to the right, and then closed the door again.

Then Marcia turned to Denise and said...

"Shhh...listen, do you hear that?"

As clear as day, Marcia and Denise heard a little girl giggling right next to them.

Denise whispered in Marcia's ear saying...

"Let's get the hell out of here."

Marcia turned the knob and opened the door carefully and then they both left the bedroom towards the stairwell when they heard something behind them.

There at the bathroom door stood a woman who had a janitor's mop and bucket in her hand. She was wearing a Nun's habit, all gray, including her stringy gray hair extending well beneath her veil, Marcia and Denise screamed and ran down the steps.

No matter how fast Marcia and Denise ran they could feel The Nun breathing down their necks.

Just then Marcia and Denise heard chanting...

"You shameful dirty girls you should both be punished,
You disgusting smelly girls, who should die horribly!"

Denise did it right, before she ran out of the bedroom she remembered to grab her keys because she just purchased a new car with the push button keyless ignition.

The two women raced down the stairs and around the corner of the living room when Marcia crashed into the glass table top splitting her right thigh open on the table's end.

Denise reached the carport door and when she turned she did not see Marcia and went back into the living room where Marcia was leaning against the wall with a deep gash to her leg.

Denise screamed...

"OMG honey...oh shit your leg is bleeding bad, baby."

Denise took a kitchen towel off the handle of the oven and wrapped it around Marcia' leg, when Marcia said...

"Oh, baby get me out of here...get me out of..."

Before Marcia had a chance to finish her statement, Denise replied...

"Don't worry baby, I got you and we're going".

Just then the two creepy kids in the hoodies were in front of them and the face of The Nun appeared in the window in front of them, saying...

"Nobody leaves here, ever he-he-he-he, ah-ha-ha-ha-ha!"

Denise grabbed onto Marcia's arm and looking at the front door, said…
"This way!"

Within a flash, one of the kids was standing in front of the door blocking their exit, as Marcia said…

"What the hell do you want…. Leave us alone!"

Just then Denise noticed that she could see Marcia's breath as she spoke, signaling how cold it had suddenly become.

When Marcia had turned her head back in the direction where the other kid was standing, she felt the cold icy breath of Sister Mary Jacalyn on her neck saying…

"You are a smelly nasty girl, and I'm going to enjoy watching your corpse rot."

Denise tightened her grip on Marcia as they bolted past the creepy kid in the hoodie and out the front door, into the pre-dawn hours and the rain.

There was a large section of woods just across the street from where Marcia and Denise lived, and that's the direction they ran, anyplace was better than where they were.

Without thinking, Marcia and Denise found themselves deep in the wooded area near a creek, a mile or so from the interstate.

All the while they were running, they could hear the voice of the creepy Nun behind them, getting closer and closer.

Just when Marcia and Denise thought that they eluded The Nun and the two creepy kids, Denise noticed standing by a tree that Marcia was against, there The Nun was.

Wearing a dirty ragged habit, was Sister Mary Jacalyn, standing there asking Marcia for a hug.

Sister Mary Jacalyn reached her hands towards Marcia in the motion of someone waiting for a hug, and that's when both Denise and Marica ran off as fast as they could.

Denise and Marcia ran in the direction of the interstate hoping to flag down a motorist, and as they ran they could hear The Nun laughing real loud with a low, manly tone.

Marcia was finding it harder and harder to keep up the pace and a sound rang out in their ears...the sound of multiple car horns, but Denise and Marcia would have to make it up a steep embankment to get to the top of the interstate.

For fear of being caught, Marcia and Denise stopped and hid in the thick brush before climbing the hill, and that's when they saw it.

A large man appeared out of nowhere, wearing a Ballerina's Tutu, dirty white tights and a clown's mask. This man was well over six feet tall, maybe seven...Denise and Marcia couldn't be for sure because he was hunched over in the brush.

At first, Marcia started to call to the man for help, when Denise put her hand over her mouth saying...

"Be quiet...we don't know what this guy's up to and why is he out here in the brush anyway...let's let him leave then we'll sneak around and up the hill."

The only problem was, the man was not moving, he just stood there by the tree as if he were waiting on someone.

Marcia and Denise were right, he was waiting on someone because a minute after thinking that, they saw and heard Sister Mary Jacalyn coming up behind them again saying...

"There you are you smelly nasty girls time's up!"

Just then the big man in the Ballerina's tutu came towards Marcia and Denise and grabbed Denise and Marcia in a headlock and drug them back into the thick brush, as they screamed...

"Help...helllllp!"

Marcia and Denise's screams were silenced by the choke hold that the big man had on them.

Marcia and Denise thought that they were going to be choked to death, when suddenly, the big man released his hold on them and walked off into the woods.

Marcia hugged Denise, as Denise jumped up and pointed, screaming...
"Look!"
Standing behind Marcia was Sister Mary Jacalyn. Sister Mary

Jacalyn grabbed Marcia by the hair as Denise scrambled to hold on to her until her grip slipped.

Denise yelled at Sister Mary Jacalyn...

"Let go of her you perverted bitch...let go!"

Still clutching Marcia's hair, Sister Mary Jacalyn pointed a finger at Denise saying...

"Perversion and sense Tattered and worn,
Into your mind the burning comes!"

With that, Denise placed her hands up besides both sides of her head and began screaming in pain.

Denise was rolling on the ground, first to the left and then to the right with her legs kicking violently.

Suddenly, Sister Mary Jacalyn raised her left hand with a handful of Marcia's hair in her right.

With her long-crooked fingers made movements as of someone running.

Just then, Denise got up on her feet and began running through the wooded area, faster and faster, up the hill towards the interstate traffic and in the path of an oncoming semi-tractor trailer truck.

The impact of the collision of the semi hitting Denise was so intense until Denise's body was thrown up over the trucks' cab and landed on the other side of the interstate and was hit, by another tractor trailer's eight massive wheels.

Marcia scrambled up the hill and down the side of the road where Denise's mangled body lay.

Moments later, several Police cars arrived on the scene, while several cars parked on the side of the highway.

Emergency services arrived, and an emergency team was providing aid to Marcia's leg while the Police secured and closed the lane of the highway where Denise's body lay on the shoulder.

Meanwhile several Police Officers were questioning potential, witnesses while emergency services loaded Marcia on a stretcher and into the back of the ambulance.

Before the ambulance took off one of the Officers went in back of the vehicles where Marcia lay and placed handcuffs on her securing them to the stretcher.

As the ambulance doors closed, Marcia was crying and asking...

"What are you doing, why did you handcuff me...what are you doing?"

As the ambulance sped down the interstate, Marcia asked again and again...

"Why are you handcuffing me."

The Police Officer finally said...

"Witnesses stated that you were chasing the young lady and that you pushed her into traffic...you're being held for vehicular homicide."

Marcia turned her head to the left and to the right crying...

"She was my love, my life, you guys are making a mistake, I didn't, I couldn't.... DENISE!"

As Marcia lay crying and confused, she could only see flashes of lights and colors, and then she passed out.

Marcia came to before reaching the hospital, and instead of seeing an EMS attendant, she saw the Nun, Sister Mary Jacalyn, sitting next to her, saying...

"You're mine now, and I've only just started with you."

6
Bad Dreams

Tuesday, 5:45 p.m.

Detective Lopez sat down on her bed removing her jeans, shirt, shoes, gun and badge and put on her jogging outfit for her evenings work out at the gym, when the phone rang...

"Hello."

She said, recognizing Detective Ridley's voice.

Detective Ridley's voice sounded a little anxious and nervous...

"Hey Detective, have you recover from today?"

"Yes, I have...I was trying not to think about it, but how can you forget something like that, so what's on your mind this evening?"

Detective Lopez replied as she laced up her sneakers, when Detective Ridley said...

"Look Maria, I got something to show you, are you going to be home in the next half an hour?"

Detective Lopez stood up and placed her gun and badge in her gym bag saying...

"I was about to go to the gym, is this something that can wait until tomorrow?"

His voice sounding more nervous, Detective Ridley replied...

"Uh...no it can't, thirty minutes is all I need, can I meet you somewhere?"

Walking to the door and fishing her keys from her bag, Detective Lopez said...

"Like I said, I'm on my way to the gym, but if it's that important I can meet you, let's say at seven-thirty, in the parking lot of Sweat Less gym...over on West Mound street."

Detective Ridley responded in a more excitable tone...

"Damn, that's way across town..."

Detective Lopez butted in before Detective Ridley finished his statement...

"Look Papi, you either meet me or show whatever you have to show me tomorrow at the station."

Detective Ridley agreed to meet Detective Lopez at the gym and then hung up as Detective Lopez exited her apartment building for her car.

The drive from her apartment to the gym was a straight shot down East Broad street to Mound street, which normally took five miles.

On any other given night, Detective Lopez would have jogged to the gym, but there was a chilly light mist in the air and Detective Lopez feared it would rain while she was jogging.

As Detective Lopez was two miles from the gym the light mist turned into a heavy rain. Detective Lopez thought that perhaps she ought to turn around and go home but she was so close to the gym.

As she put her wipers on full and turned the window defogger up she caught a glimpse of something in the rear-view mirror.

It was the face of Sister Mary Jacalyn dressed in her habit, smiling at her.

Detective Lopez slowed down the car and suddenly realized what an idiotic thought it was, thinking she was seeing someone in her back seat.

Suddenly, she heard a loud BANG! BANG! From the driver's side window.

She screamed and looked over. A man in a clown's mask was pounding on her window and jiggling the handle of her car door.

Had it not been for the heavy down pour Detective Lopez would have sped up, but all she could do was drive slowly and keep her door locked.

Detective Lopez remembered her gun was in her gym bag in the back seat, and she fought with all her might to keep from looking in the mirror, for fear of seeing Sister Mary Jacalyn's face.

Fear gave way to sheer panic as she looked in the rearview mirror and saw that there was no man or Nun in the back seat, only her gym bag when BAM!

Detective Lopez slammed into something which threw her head violently backwards and forth.

Detective Lopez's right front bumper hit one of the streets' trash cans, and then a street sign.

Remembering her training and feeding into her instincts, she grabbed her cell phone from the passenger seat and dialed nine-one-one.

The operator's voice was weak and crackling as Detective Lopez yelled out for help, looking around to see if she could back up, when the operator's voice said...

"This is one night you should've stayed inside Maria...hee-hee."

Still on the phone with operator, Detective Lopez screamed...

"Officer needing assistance...send medical, shots fired."

Detective Lopez quickly told him who she was and what had happened and even though she was close to the gym, the operator told her to keep driving.

After a few minutes, Detective Lopez had calmed down and pulled over down the side-road from the gym and stayed in the car.

As Detective Lopez gathered up her things, she saw a very large man talking to someone on the side walk,

Whether it was the weather or the faces she'd seen earlier, Detective Lopez hunched way down in her car when she heard a voice coming over her radio in Spanish saying...

"Mama, por favor venga y me llego, es frío y húmedo y estoy asustada."

Detective Lopez thought to herself...

"Mommy, please come get me, it's cold and wet and I'm scared...what the fuck."

Just then the door handles on the car started shaking as if someone was attempting to open the door. Detective Lopez scrambled to get to her bag in the back seat for her gun.

WHAM...WHAM...WHAM!

The front windshield was being pounded on as Detective Lopez took aim with her gun ready to shoot.

As the windshield came crashing through, Detective Lopez fired five shots.

When the ringing in her ears settled, Detective Lopez saw her husband Richard laying at the foot of her bed with several shots through the chest and face.

Screaming and shaking her head and looking around, Detective Lopez saw that she was not in her car, but in her bedroom, dressed in her bed clothes, as she screamed...

"NO...NO...NO!"

Detective Lopez dropped her gun and walked over to her husband in disbelief of what just happened.

Sitting at the dining room table, Detective Lopez called nine-one-one to report a shooting and then she called Detective Ridley.

Detective Lopez knew how things worked, so she got immediately dressed and then left a message for her attorney explaining she needed him.

She knew that getting legal counsel immediately, could either be a smart move or an act of guilt, but to say she was in trouble, was an understatement.

Detective Lopez sat at the kitchen table drinking her coffee when the Police and emergency personnel arrived.

Detective Lopez opened the door and stood aside after telling EMS that the body was in the bedroom.

Officers and detectives from her own precinct arrived, as well as Detective Ridley.

A uniformed Officer stood in the kitchen with Detective Lopez while the detectives went over the particulars with the first two Officers on the scene.

Detective Ridley walked over to Detective Lopez saying...

"How you holding up"?

Detective Lopez looked up in the ceiling and then to the floor, shaking her head in disbelief saying...

"I don't understand it...I was like aiming at the car window and...

Detective Ridley quickly cut her off saying...

"It's good you called your attorney, because he can't testify against you... you know what I mean?"

Detective Lopez shook her head not understanding but at the same time knowing what Detective Ridley had just said was in code.

Just then the uniformed Officer and Detective Robert Butler approached Detective Lopez with a pair of handcuffs saying...

"I'm afraid we're going to have to take you downtown Detective, if you don't mind, we're going to have to put these on you."

Detective Lopez turned and placed her hands behind her back saying...

"I'm telling you I-I didn't do it, I mean I couldn't have done this, you got to believe me."

Detective Lopez watched as the body of her husband was carried out of the house and she and Detective Butler followed, leaving Detective Ridley and the crime scene lab personnel behind.

As Detective Ridley was preparing to leave he took one last look around when he noticed over in the far corner next to the window a dark figure standing there.

Detective Ridley squinted his eyes and took a step in that direction when he heard...

"Hey Detective, we're about to lock this up, are you coming?"

Detective Ridley turned around to Detective Jim Martin, Detective Butler's partner and co-investigator standing by the door.

Detective Ridley turned back to the window where the dark figure was standing, but no one was there.

Walking out to their cars, Detective Martin looked over at Detective Ridley saying...

"Looks like pinned up rage over another woman, or some one's dirty."

Detective Ridley turned back at Detective Martin saying...

"Now you've only been on this case what...thirty minutes, how do you know what went down?"

Standing next to his car, Detective Martin said...

"It's all there for the seeing, five shots at point blank range, no struggle or signs of spousal abuse."

Detective Ridley stood staring at Detective Martin for a few seconds and then said...

"If you guys need help with this one, let me know okay?"

Detective Martin got in his car, started it up and rolled the window down saying...

"Naw...we got this one, O & C...open and closed."

As Detective Ridley watched Detective Martin drive off, he stood there for a few minutes thinking to himself when he felt someone behind him.

Turning, Detective Ridley saw a sight he thought he'd never see again...standing there plain as day was Sister Mary Jacalyn, who smiled at him and said...

"What a waste what a waste. She started chasing something she didn't understand and now look. What about you detective you going to chase me too?"

Detective Ridley place his hand on his gun, but he could not move his hand, nor could he speak as Sister Mary Jacalyn slowly walked away saying...

"Be careful the things you do don't come back on you bad!"

Detective Ridley stood there looking all around for what seemed like an eternity, watching Sister Mary Jacalyn slowly fade out of view.

At last Detective Ridley was able to move and speak, as he said to himself...

"Dammit, I'm too old for this shit, three weeks more and I'm all the way gone, but something tells me that with Detective Lopez is in this jam...I'm going to be asked to play quarterback a little longer."

Columbus South Side Precinct

Detective Ridley entered the precinct a changed man and not for the better. While he did not know Detective Lopez all that well, he respected her for being a stand-up kind of person.

From the front desk to his small office, Detective Ridley could feel the eyes of sympathy following his every step, and for a moment found himself close to guilt.

Sitting at his desk he thought over and over how Detective Lopez could go to the extreme like that, and so sudden.

Having a secondary degree in Psychology, coupled with his ability to read people, it bothered him as to why he could not sense anything troubling in Detective Lopez.

Detective Lopez appeared so certain, so confident, so happy. Detective Ridley wondered what was it that could have made her turn, make her snap?

Standing at the window thinking about the events and Detective Lopez, Detective Ridley's phone rang, it was Capt. Jones, he wanted to see Detective Ridley in his office.

Detective Martin and Capt. Jones were talking when Detective Ridley entered saying...

"Whoa, I didn't know that this was going to be a 'menage a trois'"

Captain Jones replied...

"C'mon in Mark, and close the door, now we have two cases tonight and I'm making a change in assignments,

Jim is going to take Detective Lopez and Mark I need you to take the baseball bat murderer in number six."

Detective Ridley said...

"Capt., I can handle Detective Lopez's, besides..."

Captain Jones stood up and interrupted Detective Ridley saying...

"Before you get going on this, you're too close to Detective Lopez and..."

"Too close, hell we had our first conversation yesterday...what do you mean?"

"Snapped Detective Ridley.

Captain Jones angrily replied...

"We don't get to pick and choose our assignments, I say what the fuck goes, and you do the assignment I give you."

Detective Ridley took a clip board and pad of paper from the cabinet and headed down to interrogation room six to interview Clara Scott, accused of killing her husband with a baseball bat, while Detective Martin headed to interrogation room four to interview Detective Lopez.

Detective Ridley entered interrogation room six, and sitting in the corner crying was Mrs. Clara Scott, fifty-six.

Detective Ridley introduced himself...

"Hello Mrs. Clara Scott, my name is Detective Mark Ridley, may I call you Clara?"

Clara Scott was still in a state of shock and Captain Jones wanted to take advantage of this, seeing that Clara had not requested an attorney.

Detective Ridley sat a hot cup of coffee in front of Clara Scott saying...

"*Clara, I'm here to find out what happened to Bill, your husband, can you tell me anything about that?*

Clara looked at Detective Ridley saying...

"*I'm not sure...I don't know, I was sitting on the bed...*

Just then the door burst open and there stood Capt. Jones and Jeremy Stands, Attorney saying...

"*Hold on Clara don't say another word...Capt. I'd like a word with my client please.*"

Detective Ridley stood up from the table and said...

"*Of course, counselor, but I do need to complete my interview...you understand.*"

Thirty minutes later Mr. Stands signaled for Detective Ridley to continue his interview with Clara Scott.

Detective Ridley began by saying...

"*Clara are you warm? Would you like a cigarette? Is there anything I can get you?*"

Clara leaned forward and responded...

"*No, I'm fine.*

"*You and your husband Bill went to bed and when you awakened you found him dead. Could you please describe what happened from the time you awakened until you found him?*"

Fidgeting with her hair and playing with a stick of chewing gum, Clara said...

"*It was the usual night, I got in late, Bill fixed dinner, we ate, then I showered, and we went to bed.*"

Detective Ridley flipped the pages on his pad back and forth and said...

I am Detective Mark Ridley deposing Mrs. Clara Scott about the death of her husband William C. Scott.

"*For the record will you state your full name?*"

C: "*Clarice C Scott*"

R: *"When you got home up till the time you awakened, did you two have an argument or did you have a fight or anything like that?"*

Clara sat back in her chair and said...

C: *"Fight...no Bill and I never had fights, he loved me, and I loved him."*

R: *"Do you take any medication for nightmares or have you ever sleep walked?"*

C: *"No I'm not on any kind of medications...except vitamin A at night."*

R: *"Which one of you normally awakened first you or Bill?"*

C: *"Bill always gets up first, it's an Army thing...he's up sometimes at four in the morning."*

R: *"What do you remember about this morning, when you got up, what do you remember doing...did you bathe or take a shower?"*

C: *"After I got up I huh, showered and washed my hair and sat on the bed to dry it."*

R: *"Did you see your husband in bed or in the room with you?"*

C: *"Yes he was...I mean I didn't see him, but I know he was in bed asleep."*

R: *"Was your husband in bed asleep the whole time you were drying your hair?"*

C: *"Yes, I guess, I didn't look at him, I mean I know he was there because of his body shape and his snoring."*

R: *"The autographed baseball bat found in your bedroom, who's bat was that?"*

C: *"The bat belonged to my husband Bill.*

R: *"During your daily chores, do you ever move the bat to clean?*

C: *"No, Bill only bought it upstairs yesterday...he was going to give it to his son who's starting college next week."*

R: *"What time did you go to bed?"*

C: *"I-I can't remember."*

R: *"You can't remember?"*

C: *"I just came out of the shower."*

R: *"And where was Bill?"*

Mr. Stands stood up immediately saying...

"Detective, my client has already answered that question, you need to move on."

R: *"Just a couple more questions...if you didn't touch the bat, how do your finger prints come to be on it?"*

C: *"I-I was killing a snake."*

R: *"Mrs. Scott, your story is that you were killing a snake...was the snake on top of the bed, under the sheets...where?"*

C: *"No, but I tell you, there was a snake in the bed and I was trying to kill it."*

Mr. Stands stood up shouting...

"Okay detective, this interview is over, if you're going to continue to badger my client!"

Detective Ridley apologetically said...

"Your client is talking about she killed a snake, but no snake was found, only her dead husband, I'm just pursuing this."

Jeremy Stands nodded his head to continue as Detective Ridley said...

R: "Just one more question Mrs. Scott...was this so-called snake under the bed or on top of the bed before you threw the towel over it?"

Clara looked up and to the left and then said...

"It was on top of the sheet."

Detective Ridley gather up his note pad, and pen, and stood up and before he left the interrogation room, said...

"I asked that Mrs. Scott, because the only thing we found on top of the sheet was your husbands battered and bloody head."

Detective Ridley was met outside the interrogation room by Captain Jones who said...

"So, what do you think, the cunts ABC's are mixed up with her numbers... snake! How many people find a snake in central Ohio this time of year, in their bed, let alone beat it with a baseball bat?"

Detective Ridley leaned his back against the wall saying...

"All the evidence points to her but,"

Captain Jones placed his hand on Detective Ridley's shoulder saying...

"But what, we got her prints on the bat, her DNA on the towel used to cover the victims face, no forced entry...yes according to circumstantial evidence there's enough to wrap this case up."

Detective Ridley looked over at the hand on his shoulder and said...

"I don't know, I got a sneaky feeling in my gut that there's more here than what we see.?"

Captain Jones looked down at his pager which had just gone off when Detective Martin came up to him and Detective Ridley holding out his tablet saying...

"Captain, you are not going to believe this, look read this...

October fifteen two thousand nine, interview of Detective Maria Lopez Re: shooting/murder.

M: *"Now Detective Lopez for the sake of identity can you tell me your full name and your birthday?"*

L: *"My name is Maria Santiago Lopez and I was born January fourth nineteen fifty-nine."*

M: *"Where do you work and what do you do?"*

L: *"I work for the Columbus Police department as lead detective in the homicide division."*

M: *"Can you tell me when the last time was, when you saw your husband?"*

L: *"I saw Richard this morning getting dressed, before I left for work."*

M: *"Have you spoken with him all day?"*

L: *"No, I had not spoken with Richard, we had a long day."*

M: *"You mean you went all day without talking to your husband?"*

L: *"It's like I said.... We were busy today, lots of couples go all day without talking to one another until they get home."*

M: *"Can you tell me what time you got home this evening?"*

L: *"Sure, I got home at four-forty-five."*

M: *"Was Richard home?"*

L: *"No, he doesn't get home until five-thirty."*

M: *"Tell me everything you did when you got home."*

L: *"Let's see, I got the mail, changed into my exercise outfit and headed to the gym."*

M: *"And how long were you there?"*

L: *"Uh...it started raining so hard and I never made it."*

M: *"Raining detective... Columbus did not receive any weather today, are you sure you're not talking about another day?"*

L: *"It was raining hard and I wrecked my car, and then somebody was trying to break into my car and I shot at him, you can check with central dispatch, I called it in."*

M: *"Central did get a call from you."*

L: *"You see, so once I got home..."*

M: *"detective... the call central received was the call where you say that you just killed your husband, Richard."*

L: *"I did not make that call, and I didn't kill Richard."*

M: *"Well detective, your husband is lying up on your bed with five bullet holes in him, not signs of forced entry, and your gun clip is missing five bullets... can you explain that?"*

L: *"All I'm saying is, I didn't shoot Richard...I was shooting at this man that was trying to break into my car."*

M: *"Well tell me detective, how come there is no signs of any type of tampering with your vehicle, not bullet holes, as a matter of fact your car's engine is as cold as ice."*

L: "I'm telling you the truth…I didn't not shoot my husband, why would I shoot him huh, you tell me that."

M: "At this time I need to advise you to stop answering questions and to get an attorney, because as of this time I will be charging you with the murder of your husband Richard Lopez.

End of interview

"Well Captain what do you think…she actually believes that she was somewhere else and just magically woke up in her house."

Captain looked over at Detective Ridley and then to Detective Martin saying…

"The reports gentlemen, I want them on my desk by the end of the day."

As Captain Jones walked away talking on his cell phone and looking at his pager, detectives Ridley and Martin stood there in shock looking at each other and wondering what just happened when Detective Ridley said…

"I think we need to get together and share notes, looks like both our cases have a little too many similarities…what do you think?"

Detective Martin began walking to his office and said…

"Yeah, let me grab a few things and I'll be down."

While Detective Ridley was waiting on Detective Martin to arrive he poured a cup of coffee and put a shot of whiskey in it and sat down at his desk.

Detective Ridley took a sip when there was a tap on his office door, Detective Martin walked in saying…

"I know this isn't an invite for coffee and a round of kumbaya, so what do you want Mark?"

Detective Ridley handed a cup of coffee to Detective Martin and then offered Detective Martin the small flask of whiskey to him, which he willingly accepted, saying…

"So, this is the secret to how you get a jump on cases?"

"No, this is how I have my coffee when I'm stumped by a case….and this case has me stumped from jump street."

Detective Ridley said as he sipped more of his coffee.

Detective Martin said...

"I'm really surprised that you want to share information with me, I seem to recall the last three times we worked a case together, you ended up pulling rank and taking the cases from me."

Sitting his cup on his desk, Detective Ridley said...

"This is not the same, I heard what you read to Captain Jones and my interview sounds a lot like yours...an outrageous story, a witness that believes that she was one place when she was in a totally different other place."

Detective Ridley handed a file to Detective Martin saying...

"Do we sit here and see who can piss the farthest or we can work together because this thing is only going to get messy."

Without looking at the file Detective Martin said...

"What thing...all we got is a couple of cases, and from what I can see they are a one and done."

Trying to remain calm to solicit his help, Detective Ridley said...

"All I'm asking is for you to look at the files I collected over the years, what I'm saying is, there are going to be more murders and that Nun, Sister Mary Jacalyn is going to walk away Scott free."

Tossing the files back on Detective Ridley's desk, Detective Martin replied...

"I'm not trying to get caught up in your fantasy, number one, you're talking about a case that's thirty years old and number two.... The Nun you're talking about has been dead, missing or whatever ever since you joined the force."

With his emotions beginning to show Detective Ridley again handed him the files saying...

"Just take one look, one look is all I'm asking and if you don't see anything... fine I'll drop it, but please just look."

Detective Martin picked up the files from the desk saying...

"Alright, but I can't look at them now, I'm off duty in a bit and I'm meeting my wife so..."

Without finishing his statement, Detective Ridley said...

"Take it home with you and look it over tonight...don't worry, I made a copy."

Detective Martin exited the office saying...

"So, Rip, the word is you've only got two weeks before retirement, I don't see why you want to get all caught up into something when you're not even gonna be here."

Detective Martin walked down the hallway shaking his head in confusion as Detective Ridley answered his phone and closed his door.

Six Thirty P.M.

Detective Martin was glad to finally be spending time with his wife, of ten years Melissa. Detective Martin and his wife Melissa were entering their eleventh year of marriage on a sour note and the night's dinner, was to be a new start for them.

Detective Martin met Melissa who was waitressing at a local coffee shop in Columbus and was immediately infatuated with her.

Detective Martin would purposely stop by and have coffee just to see Melissa, and over the next several months they were inseparable.

Many of Detective Martin's colleagues opposed to him dating her based upon past association with her and what they knew about her, but Detective Martin was so love struck that he was blind to anything and everything people were saying about Melissa.

Several years before they met, Melissa was a frequent visitor on Mt. Vernon Ave, on Columbus' east side known for drug dealers and prostitutes.

As to whether Melissa was into drugs or prostitution Detective Martin's partners would not say, they just knew she was a regular to the area.

Over the past six months or so, Detective Martin discovered by accident large amounts of money underneath a throw rug in their bedroom.

Detective Martin never questioned Melissa about it but whenever the subject of finances came up, instead of arguing as many couples do, Detective Martin would become withdrawn and when pressed, insinuate that Melissa should contribute to the household more money herself.

The night's dinner was the best time that Detective Martin and Melissa have had in all the time that they've been married.

Detective Martin did all the right things, he ordered Melissa's favorite things to eat, kept the conversation all about her and genuinely displayed the affection that he showed Melissa when they first met.

Melissa responded to Detective Martin's public display of affection in a very adolescence manner by rubbing her feet up Detective Martin's legs under the table and watching Detective Martin squirm as the couples sitting next to them watched.

Detective Martin and Melissa decided to take their new-found affection to their north-side home.

The ride home was as steamy in the car as it was in the restaurant, as Melissa unzipped Detective Martin's pants as he drove the twenty minutes to their home.

As Detective Martin pulled into their driveway, the darkness shielded the fact that his zipper was down and his shirt half out of his pants.

Giggling up the steps, Melissa began undressing Detective Martin as soon as the key found the front door lock.

The evening's love making was the best that either one of them could remember as they lay in bed and fell asleep sweaty with each other's scent.

Several hours as they lay in bed, Melissa awakened Detective Martin saying...

"Honey...wake up, I just heard something...I think someone's in the house."

Gathering his clothes which lay on the side of the bed, Detective Martin grabbed his service revolver and quietly headed out the bedroom.

Standing at the top of the stairs Detective Martin heard the creaking sound coming from the area of the kitchen and turned on the lights saying...

"I'm Detective Martin with the Columbus Police, and you have broken into my home...I have a gun and I advise you to come out with your hands raised."

Detective Martin took several steps down when a shadowy figure coming from the kitchen to the living room startled Detective Martin as he fired four shots in the darkness.

In the faint light provided by the gun's muzzle flash, Detective Martin saw the silhouette of someone falling to the floor.

Walking over to the sofa, Detective Martin picked up the phone and called nine-one-one saying...

"This is Detective Martin of the tenth precinct and I'd like to report that I just shot someone who has broken into my house."

Curious to see whom it was who he had shot Detective Martin walked over towards where the body fell, and cutting on the light yelled...

"Oh, my fucking God!"

Lying there in a pool of blood was Tina, his daughter...not a burglar. Surprisingly, his wife did not hear any of the noise as she was showering.

Detective Martin kneeled in horror yelling and crying as the sound of sirens loomed in the distance.

Forgetting all his training, Detective Martin held in his arms the lifeless body of his dead daughter Tina, when his phone rang, and someone began pounding on his front door.

Slowly and dazed Detective Martin lay his daughter's head on the floor as he got up from the floor and in a weak voice answered his phone...

"Hello."

In his confused and dazed state Detective Martin didn't see the dark figure standing against the wall, but he recognized the voice of Detective Ridley on the other end of the phone saying...

"Jim...Jim, this is Detective Ridley, look the call just went out and some of the guys are on their way to bring you in, I think it's best that you make a mad dash out the back door and I'll pick you up on Broad street and Livingston, behind the Chinese restaurant."

Wiping the blood from his cell phone onto his pants Detective Martin replied...

"Rip, what the hell is going on...I-I- just shot my daughter, I just shot my daughter!"

The dark figure which stood against the wall drew close to Detective Martin as he ended the call and headed towards the back door.

No sooner had Detective Martin exited the back yard and into the alley behind his house he began running as he heard the sirens and cars stopping in front of his house.

Detective Martin made his way towards Broad street, staying in the alleys with dogs barking and the sounds of Police sirens in the distance, he wondered if he would make it to Broad and Livingston, and wondering about his wife finding their daughter.

Detective Martin emerged from the alley a half a block from Livingston Ave when a patrol car slowly passed in front of him.

Ducking behind a trash dumpster, Detective Martin noticed Detective Ridley's car pulling into the front entrance of the restaurant and slowly coming around the back.

Detective Martin saw his chance to make it to Detective Ridley's car and started his move, he checked twice and after making sure the coast was clear stood and started towards Detective Ridley's car when another patrol car pulled up alongside Detective Ridley's car.

Dropping down, Detective Martin watched as the Officers and Detective Ridley talked, not knowing if Detective Ridley was setting him up or not.

After what seemed like an eternity, the patrol car slowly pulled away and Detective Martin saw Detective Ridley waving at him and saying...

"C'mon...get in here!"

Detective Martin scrambled to his feet and hopped in Detective Ridley's car as it slowly pulled away without attracting too much attention.

Roughing up his hair, Detective Martin said...

"I just don't fucking get it...what in the hell is going on, shit I just shot my daughter, man!"

Slowly going through the little sleepy area of Bexley, Detective Ridley pulled on to Eastmoor Blvd and into his driveway at six-twelve, saying...

"Wait until we're inside, okay?"

Entering through the back-door Detective Ridley and Detective Martin did not see the dark figure standing in the front yard.

Detective Ridley took a bottle of vodka and two beers and poured two drinks handing one to Detective Martin saying...

"It's not going to be long before the Captain sends someone over here looking for you, so..."

Interrupting Detective Ridley, Detective Martin said...

"What did you do tell them you were helping me or something?"

Throwing back the vodka and taking several gulps of beer Detective Ridley said...

"Hell no, what do you think, I am some kind of damn fool...it's her don't you get it, the damn Nun is responsible for all of this crazy shit and she knows that you are here, and somehow she'll put the ideal into the Captain's head that they better search here."

Detective Martin took the final sip of his drink and said...

"I don't get any of this, and what the hell has a dead Nun got to do with me shooting me daughter?"

Detective Ridley walked over to the window and peeked out and just as he did his cell phone started ringing.

Looking down at his phone, Detective Ridley turned to Detective Martin putting one finger to his lips saying...

"Shhh...it's the Captain."

Pretending that he was awakened by the phone call, Detective Ripley said in a sleeping tone...

"Hello, hey Capt. Jones, what's going on?"

Putting the phone on speaker, Detective Martin heard...

"Ridley, you wouldn't by chance be standing there with Detective Martin, would you?"

Shaking his head in disbelief, Detective Ridley replied...

"No...as a matter of fact I was trying to get some sleep, what do want Jim for?"

With the phone still on speaker Capt. Jones said...

"It looks like Detective Martin just shot his daughter, and since both of their cars are in the garage, it appears someone is helping him avoid us."

Detective Martin and Ridley both looked at each other as Detective Ridley said...

"Capt. give me about thirty minutes and I'll come on down to the station, but tell me, is she alright?"

Detective Ridley took the phone off speaker and was about to end the call when Capt. Jones said...

"No, she took a nasty hit, but she'll be okay.... I just sent a car over to your place, it should be there any minute."

Detective Ridley hung up saying...

"Damn...they're on their way here, you gotta go Jim."

Detective Martin began pacing the floor looking first to the front door and then the back door and then placing his hand on the door knob, saying...

"Man...this whole thing is messed up, what I need to do is turn myself in, I mean, I didn't mean to shoot her, and running is only going to make things worse for me."

Grabbing his hand, Detective Ridley said...

"Worse...this is as worse as it gets, you shot your daughter for no damn reason and if you turn yourself in right now with that story about a burglar... I'm telling you, they're going to bury your ass under the prison."

Snatching his hand from Detective Ridley's grip, Detective Martin said...

"I'm not a common criminal, she was in school and wasn't supposed to be there."

Cutting Detective Martin off from finishing his sentence, Detective Ridley said...

"I see, that they'll uncover that there was no one else in the house but you and your wife and that you two were having problems and they'll charge you and that'll be all she wrote."

Just then Detective Ridley walked over to the window and upon seeing the unmarked car pulling into his drive way turned and said...

"In about thirty seconds you can test that theory of yours if you like or you can climb up into the attic and wait for us to leave...your choice."

Detective Martin pulled up a chair and aligned it under the attic access panel and climbed up, as Detective Ridley opened the front door allowing both Officers to enter.

Detective Ridley recognized Detective Fisher but was unaware who his partner was saying...

"Hey gentlemen, Capt. Jones said you were coming to get me, but I'll follow you, I got some personal business to do later, by the way what's going on?"

Detective Fisher shook his hand while his partner Detective Kuhn nodded and scanned the living room area saying...

"You'll have to take that up with the Captain....we were told to come get you."

While Detective Ridley was slipping into his shoes he said...

"Come get me for what?"

Detective Fisher walked over and leaned on the counter not noticing the little pieces of drywall falling on the counter, from Detective Martin easing the attic panel open to listen in on their conversation.

"We just want to talk to Detective Martin about what happened at his home."

Tucking his shirt into his pants Detective Ridley replied...

"What things is he a suspect?"

Detective Ridley and Detective Fisher walked towards the door while Detective Kuhn inspected first the closet and then the two bedrooms saying...

We found Detective Martin's daughter lying on the living room floor with four bullet holes in her chest, no forcible entry, the back door was open, both cars in the driveway alas, no Detective Martin...is that enough for you?"

Detective Ridley led the Detectives out the front door and went to his car, meanwhile Detective Martin had quietly climbed down from the attic access and peeked out the window, watching them as they drove away.

Detective Martin walked into the kitchen saying to himself...

"I'm going to have to find somewhere to lay low for a while until the dust settles, but this is my life I can't trust it to someone I hardly know, besides what is Ridley being so chummy about...we hardly know each other."

Detective Martin removed the cell phone from his pocket and placed a call to his brother Mark who lives in New Jersey saying...

"Hey Mark, I'm in a real mess of shit here, I need you to pick me up in Columbus, okay?"

Mark replied...

"Okay, well I get off work tomorrow at seven, I can come then."

Detective Martin responded anxiously...

"No, I need you to come get me right now and I'll send you directions on where to meet me, okay?"

Detective Martin hung up the phone and slipped out the back door.

7
Something Rotten

Friday Morning 8 a.m.

Reggie stood quietly at his station staring over at Amy, while she was assisting a guest with directions.

As soon as Amy was through, she walked over to Reggie and asked...

"Hey coach, you're staring at me as if you're surprised to see me today, last night at dinner I told you I'd be in, so what's up?"

Reggie was stunned and could not believe his eyes that Amy was alive, he had witnessed her mutilated corpse, but she was standing in the lobby of the Ohio Atlantic Power company, acting as if nothing happened.

What was more incredible and disturbing to Reggie was the fact that he also was at his station. Reggie had no recollection of driving to work, let alone how he'd gotten out of the basement in Port Clinton.

Everything was a blur, a nightmare actually, but Reggie knew that he and his wife as well as five others were held in a basement and tortured, it was real...but how did they end up back on their jobs, and how was it that Amy was alive.

Amy stood looking at Reggie and said...

"Hey coach, you didn't go home last night and hit the juice bottle, did you?"

Trying to collect his thoughts, Reggie responded...

"No way, if I had done that, a hang-over is all I'd have instead of what's going on in my mind."

Amy walked over and stood next to Reggie saying...

"Alright partner I can see something has been on your mind all morning, so what's up?"

Reggie just looked at Amy and hesitantly said...

"First, you got to promise me that what I say to you, you'll listen and keep an open mind."

Amy placed her hand in the air signaling to Reggie to hold on as her cell phone started ringing, and then after her call she placed her cell phone in its holder and said...

"Really partner, do we have to go back to kindergarten...don't I always keep an open mind, just say what you got to say?"

Reggie walked Amy over to the side of the lobby where his desk was and said...

"You need to have a seat because what I'm about to tell you, you're going to find it kind of hard to believe."

While Amy was sitting down, Reggie glanced around the lobby making sure no one was in sight before saying...

"Like I hinted to earlier this morning, it's as if yesterday never happened...me and Perry were being held captive in some kook's basement in Port Clinton, and..."

Amy interrupted Reggie saying...

"You were being held – what? Perry, you, me and Jerry left the restaurant at eleven-thirty last night...how could you have been held captive in Port Clinton...this is not making sense coach, do you know how far Port Clinton is from Columbus?"

Reggie walked over and leaned against the counter in front of Amy and said...

"I know it sounds like a bunch of bull but I'm telling you after me and Perry left you guys we went home, and then that next morning we drove to Port Clinton."

Tapping Reggie on the hand and pointing at the desk calendar on the counter, Amy said...

"Coach, first we were with you at dinner last night, so how can you say you and Perry went to Port Clinton the next morning...this is the next morning, and secondly why would you drive up to Port Clinton on a work day anyway?"

Nodding his head up and down and looking irritated, Reggie said...

"I know-I know- I know…but I'm saying, Perry and I woke up in our house the next day and drove to Port Clinton looking for…"

"You went to Port Clinton looking for what?"

Amy said sarcastically.

Reggie turned his head in the opposite direction of Amy and said…

"I went up there looking for clues that would lead me to the killer."

Amy leaned back in her chair and said…

"What killer case are you working on that I don't know about?"

Trying hard not to get too loud Reggie said softly…

"I was looking for clues as to who murdered you."

Amy stood up and got in Reggie's face, lowering her voice and said…

"Who murdered me… who murdered me… coach are you serious…damn, you need to start taking your psyche meds, or have your doctor increase them, you can't go around talking shit like this, they'll say that you're unfit for duty and then bounce your happy ass home."

Signaling for Amy to sit down and lowering his tall frame down, Reggie replied…

"Look, I know what this sounds like, but I'm telling you exactly what me and Perry went through the last few days and what's even more weird is, Perry and I were tied up with some other folks and the next thing I know is, I'm standing right here with you."

Scooting in closer to the counter Amy said…

"Look coach you know the drill, dreams can seem more real than reality, it's a dream and your mind is trying to make you think that it really happened.?"

Reggie threw his hand up and waved and said to Amy as the mail carrier entered the building…

"We'll continue this later."

Amy got up out of Reggie's chair and said as she walked back over to her station…

"What's there to continue…this conversation's a wrap."

Amy sat at her desk greeting employees and customers as they exited the building for lunch, when Reggie walked up to Amy saying…

"Do you wanna take lunch first while I hold down the fort?"

Amy nodded her head and picked up her bag saying…

"Yes, do you want me to pick you up something?"

"Where are you going?"

Reggie said as he locked one side of the lobby doors behind Amy.

Amy handed her radio to Reggie saying…

"I was thinking about going to that new Thai restaurant on Broad and Cleveland."

Shaking his head, Reggie said…

"Aw never mind, you know if I eat that stuff I'll be smelling up the lobby all afternoon, what about that rib place over on third street…they're pretty good."

Amy turned to Reggie saying…

"You men are all alike, no imagination…why does it have to be ribs, steaks or burgers?"

Reggie flexed the muscles on his six-foot-four, two hundred-and sixty-pound frame saying…

"You don't maintain all of this eating bean sprouts, water chestnuts and seaweed."

Amy walked past Reggie heading for the employee exit saying…

"Okay, I'll get you the rib plate…what do you want the half or whole plate?"

Reggie extended both arms out to the sides of his body saying…

"The whole plate, I can always take some to Perry."

Shaking her head and mumbling under her breath, Amy said as she exited through the door…

"Perry won't see any parts of those ribs."

The lobby in the Ohio and Atlantic Power Company is usually a boring assignment for Police Officers who have witnessed their share of traumatic events, but as usual when you don't expect it, surprises have a way of sneaking up on you.

Reggie had just sat down when he heard a commotion coming from the area near the elevators, and he got up and walked towards them.

Upon arriving at the elevators Reggie saw two men engaged in a heated conversation over the elevator.

Reggie approached the two men saying…

"Whoa…you gentlemen want to take this down a notch… what's going on here?"

Both men were employees who worked on the tenth floor, as one of the men shouted…

"I have a very important meeting that I'm late for and this ass here, is standing in the door of the elevator not allowing it to close."

As Reggie stood in between the two men he asked the other one why was he holding up the elevator, which he replied...

"I told this guy that my partner ran to the car to get a really important presentation and he'll be back in a minute, but no...he thinks he owns this building."

Not known for his diplomatic approached to situations Reggie stated...

"Look Mr. huh..."

The man holding the elevator said...

"Gaines, my name is Mark Gaines."

Reggie continued...

"Okay look Mr. Gaines let the elevator go and when your partner comes in I'll use my pass key for the service elevator to let you go up...now how's that?"

Mr. Gaines nodded and stepped out of the doorway of the elevator, allowing it to continue.

Reggie walked back over to the lobby entrance area when Amy asked...

"So, what was that all about, somebody punch all of the buttons in the elevator again?"

"No, some idiot was holding the elevator not letting it go up waiting on his partner, I convinced him to let it go and when he comes in I'll use the service elevator to take them up."

Reggie said as he turned to look for Mr. Gaines' partner saying...

"Okay, now back to what I was saying earlier."

Amy sat uninterested at her counter, eating and saying...

"Aw c'mon coach, are we going to revisit that conversation...it doesn't make any kind of sense, to me it sounds like a dream or a nightmare...here, I got baked beans and slaw."

Reggie repositioned his belt and pants saying...

"Amy, I can tell the difference between a dream and a nightmare and this was neither. I'm telling you we all met and had dinner the night before, and then we all got the call from the station saying that you and Jerry had just been murdered."

Amy walked over and stood directly in front of Reggie saying...

"You see, that's what I'm talking about...Jerry's at work and I'm standing right here."

Reggie began pacing the lobby eating a rib and searching for something to say when he said...

"Alright...you have a small note pad in your purse, right?"

Amy nodded her head and said...

"First of all, get that sauce off from around your mouth...and secondly, yeah, what does that prove, you've seen me writing in it a million times."

Reggie placed one hand on her shoulder saying...

Yes, I've seen it but, has anyone including me ever read what is written inside?"

Amy walked back to her counter and after pulling the small note pad from her purse said...

"No, no one has read it because some of the things in here are personal...so are you going to tell me you know what I've written?"

Reggie replied...

"I can't tell you what every page says, but I can tell you what the last note you wrote says."

Amy flipped through the note pad to the last page saying...

"Alright Houdini go for it."

Reggie leaned against the counter and after taking a deep breath said...

"It says that you were planning to go to Port Clinton to check on some clues you got regarding some murders and you were going to let me in on it."

Amy read the last entry to herself and then looking at Reggie said...

"Well, you don't win what's behind door number one, and you don't win the new car either...you want me to read the last thing I wrote?"

Standing with a look of complete shock on his face Reggie said...

"C'mon stop screwing around, you know it says that or something pretty close to it."

Shaking her head, Amy began reading...

"Thursday...talk to coach, about my decision. Pick up clothes from cleaners."

Reggie's jaw dropped as he said...

"Wait a minute are you trying to tell me that you didn't write that you found some clues and were going to Port Clinton to check it out?"

Amy closed her note pad and looking at Reggie said...

"I admit Port Clinton is a nice place to visit and they have some awesome seafood, but why in the fuck would I want to go there, we don't have any jurisdiction there."

Reggie began pacing the lobby floor again and then started talking out loud saying...

"Wait a minute, I read what you wrote in there Amy and I know it said

that you were going to Port Clinton to check out some clues, that's how I knew to go to Port Clinton."

Amy put the note pad back in her purse saying...

"I appreciate that in the near future, if you wouldn't go through my purse, by the way, my purse is always with me so when did you have time to go through it?"

Still in shock Reggie said...

"I told you...when I found out that you were murdered, your purse and everything was in the car, I know what I read, there's no way all of that could've been a dream."

Amy walked back over to Reggie from placing her note pad in her purse saying...

"Sorry kiddo, but no cigar...I didn't mention Port Clinton, and as a matter of fact I haven't thought about Port Clinton in at least two years when Jerry and I vacationed there."

Slowing his pacing down, Reggie began mumbling...

"I know I read where you were going to Port Clinton to check some clues out and that you were curious about the skeleton key you found, I know it."

Amy grabbed Reggie's arm saying in a surprised tone...

"What did you just say?"

Reggie looked Amy in the eyes and said...

"I said that I read about you going to Port Clinton...why?"

Walking back over to her purse and getting out the note pad, Amy came back over to Reggie saying...

"No, you said something else, what did you say?"

Reggie replied...

"Oh, that you were curious about where and what the skeleton key with the red ribbon goes to...why?"

Amy opened to the last two pages in her note pad and handed it to Reggie saying...

"There's nothing in here about a skeleton key, but I did find one tied to my front door knob yesterday...what is this, are you messing with my head coach?"

Reggie stood there shaking his head no, saying...

"I'm not messing with your head or any other part of you smiles, all I was doing was telling you about what I read in your note pad yesterday...look how else could I have known about the skeleton key, did you tell me or anybody else about it?"

Looking puzzled, Amy replied...

Okay, so you know about the key.... but you couldn't have heard me mention it, because I just discovered it early this morning."

Reggie grabbed Amy's arm and walked her over to the counter and whispered...

"What that has do with is...you found the key before we went out to dinner, and the message you wrote on your note pad about Port Clinton, well, it's obvious that you wrote it after you and Jerry left, the point is you and Jerry were murdered and...

Amy interrupted Reggie saying...

"I'm alive and Jerry is alive and so are you, and this is nothing but a dream, coach and I don't know how you know about the red ribbon and the key."

Reggie began walking towards his side of the lobby when he turned back to Amy and said...

"Okay, we'll bury this conversation for the time being."

All day Reggie had one thing on his mind as he continued to eye Amy and that was, he knew that Amy and Jerry were murdered, and he knew he was held in Port Clinton with Perry.

Finally, a thought came to Reggie's mind... he hadn't spoken to Perry since they were held in Port Clinton.

As a matter of fact, Reggie had no recollection of getting up this morning or even going to bed last night.

One minute they were in Port Clinton and the next thing he knew, he was standing in the lobby at work.

Reggie began patting his pockets for his keys and they were not in his pockets either...

"How the Fuck did I get to work?"

Just then Reggie walked over to Amy and said...

"Can you hold my side down for a minute I need to make a call home?"

Amy nodded as Reggie walked out the front door and stood there making a call to Perry.

Reggie let the phone ring several times and was about to hang up when Perry answered...

"Hey there babe, how's work going?"

Reggie let out a sigh of relief as he replied...

"Oh babe, I'm alright now, all I needed was to hear your voice."

Reggie's calm suddenly turned to shock as Perry said...

"Aw that's sweet babe, but we just talked a couple hours ago, you sure everything is alright?"

Just then as Reggie leaned against one of the pillars in front of the building, he looked around and for a second, he was back in Port Clinton tied to the chair along with Perry and as he looked again he was standing in front of the O.A.P. building.

Reggie was no stranger when it came to dealing with all types of situations, but what was happening to him at that moment was something not even he was prepared to deal with.

Perry was still on the phone calling Reggie's name as Reggie continued to find himself back in Port Clinton one second and then in Columbus the next, suddenly Reggie collected himself and said...

"I'm sorry babe, one of the clients was talking to me, I think I'd better let you go and we'll talk later.

Perry called out Reggie's name again until he answered saying...

"Yeah babe, I thought you hung up the phone."

Perry said...

"I was going to ask you what time you want me to pick you up?"

Just that quickly Reggie had forgotten what he called Perry for as he said...

"Sorry babe, it's been one of those mornings...come get me at about four-forty-five...okay?"

As Perry was about to end the call she said...

"Okay sexy man, I'll see you then...bye."

With a look of bewilderment on his face, Reggie walked back inside the lobby and as he leaned on his counter top Amy came up to him saying...

"Gosh coach...you look as if you just found out that Santa is not real."

Scratching his head Reggie replied...

"Nope, what's not real, is the way my day is starting out..."

Before Reggie completed his sentence one of the executives approached Amy, saying...

"Can I have the keys to one of the exec cars, got to pick up a client from the airport."

While Amy was attending to him one of the elevator doors opened and Reggie turned sharply towards it as he heard a squeaky high-pitched sound.

Coming down the hall towards the front of the lobby Reggie saw an old rusty red wheel barrel and behind it was a six feet eight-inch man wearing an old dirty Ballerina's Tutu, in black and white sneakers approaching him.

Reggie turned in Amy's direction, who was attending to the executive and then back to the approaching man.

Looking at the man and recognizing him as one of the people from the farm at Port Clinton, Reggie readied himself when the man began talking to Reggie, but not with his mouth, saying...

"Part of you is here and the other part of you is back at the farm you can't escape us. What you see is not what it seems beware The Nun."

Reggie reached down at the gun which was in his holster, preparing himself all the time glancing over at Amy, who had finished dealing with the executive and who was now sitting down at her counter.

Reggie turned his attention back to the man who was skipping behind the wheel barrel and out the lobby doors.

Reggie slowly walked over to Amy as he continued to watch the man skip out the door, saying...

"Do you believe that...no way I imagined that?"

Amy looked at Reggie and then stood up looking all around the lobby saying...

"Imagined what...Oh don't tell me you're back to that shit again, what the fuck are you tripping on coach, there's no one here but us?"

Reggie stood looking at Amy as the elevators opened and crowds of employees began filing out and heading towards Amy and Reggie.

As Reggie and Amy continued checking employees out for the day, he could not shake the feeling that something wasn't right...that he wasn't right, that the whole day, Amy and everything else wasn't right.

The last of the employees inserted their badges into the check-in check-out meter while Amy was gathering her purse and personal belongings and looking in Reggie's direction, saying...

"Are you going home or are you going to stay here and watch for the invisible people?"

Reggie smiled and chuckled lightly saying...

"I got to wait on Perry, she's picking me up."

With a concerned look on her face Amy replied...

"Earth to Reggie...unless I missed something here, but you drove, you picked me up this morning, have you forgotten that you're driving me home?"

Reggie cocked his head and said...

"Yeah okay, you got jokes, c'mon...Perry's picking me up."

Amy laid her bag and purse on the counter saying...

"You think I'm bull-shitting you don't you, don't you remember picking me up this morning?"

Reggie grabbed his uneaten ribs and took the keys from his pocket saying...

"Look Amy, I don't remember picking you up or driving to work my own damn self, it's like I've been trying to tell you all day...one minute me and Perry were in Port Clinton and the next minute I'm here at work."

Removing her cell phone from her purse, Amy said...

"Look, don't worry about it, I'll call Jerry and have him come get me."

Still looking puzzled and confused Reggie replied...

"You don't have to call Jerry, if I drove, I'll take you home...I gotta call Perry first, it's that I just don't remember anything it's as if I lost twelve hours."

Reggie hung the phone up after talking to Perry saying to Perry...

"Damn, I could've sworn Perry told me she was picking me up, but like you say...I drove."

As the two of them left the building and crossed the street towards the employee parking lot Reggie noticed something unusual on the passenger front seat, and as he opened the door he reached to remove the coat when Amy caught his hand saying...

"That's mine, I brought it with me this morning in case it rained...see I told you I rode with you this morning."

Shrugging his shoulders, Reggie got inside the car and backed out of the parking lot and headed towards interstate seventy east

Reggie did not say anything to Amy for the whole twenty minutes it took to get to her house, when Amy said...

"Look coach, all this stuff about being in one place and then not knowing how you got from one place to another is kinda jacked up.

It's that I don't know how to respond to that, I think that sometimes our mind plays tricks on us when we're tired or stressed out, you know?"

Reggie reached and turned the volume on the radio to low saying...

"Partner, I wished that I could say that you're right and yeah I'm tired or stressed and all that shit but, being in Port Clinton and you and Jerry being murdered was not some fucking figure of my imagination?".

Amy started laughing when Reggie asked...

"Now what's so damn funny?"

Amy tried composing herself when she let out a big laugh and said...

"You said...fucking figure of my imagination."

Very lightly Reggie pushed Amy with his right hand saying...

"Dingle Berry, you know what I meant to say and thanks for trying to cheer me up, but the point still stands...I know what I know, and I saw what I saw."

The two continued on, not being far from Amy's house as Amy laughed saying...

"Dingle Berry?"

With that, Reggie joined her in laughing as Reggie turned up in her driveway, as Amy said...

"I will not eat it in a car, I will not drink it in a bar...see ya tomorrow Dr. Seuss."

Amy headed up the drive way and Jerry came out to meet her when Reggie honked his horn and rolled the window down saying...

"You going to drive tomorrow, or do you need a lift?"

Jerry stood next to Amy waved at Reggie and hugged her as Amy replied...

"No, that's okay, Jerry's off tomorrow so I'll take our car, thanks anyway."

Reggie waved okay and backed out of the driveway and headed home on the east side of Columbus.

While Reggie drove, he happened to look over at the passenger seat where Amy's jacket was draped over the back of the seat saying to himself...

"Aw look at this."

Reggie glanced out the passenger side window at the rain clouds approaching dark and ominous thinking...

"That dust bunny has the nerve to call my happy ass forgetful…I'll have something to pick on her with tomorrow."

Just then, Reggie's cell phone started ringing as Reggie scrambled in the car's console for it and answered it as the rain began pouring down…

"Hello."

It was Perry, who said…

"Hey babe, where you at?"

Slowing his speed down as the rain began intensifying, Reggie said…

"Hi babe, I'm at Broad and Champion, why what's up?"

"I was wondering if you could stop at the store and pick up a few things." Perry said as the thunder cracked, making Reggie jump who said…

"Whoa…yeah I can stop, what do you need?"

Perry told Reggie that once they were off the phone she would text him the things she needed as she said…

"I heard you saying whoa…you sure you're alright?"

Reggie dropped the cell phone, and finding it on the passenger seat said…

"Yeah, I'm good babe, the thunder cracked."

Just then, Reggie lost signal with Perry when suddenly as the lightening flashed Reggie saw through the rear-view mirror someone sitting in the back seat.

Turning his head and seeing nothing, the lightening flashed again, and Reggie looked back in the mirror and saw a woman dressed in a Nun's black Habit who said…

"Reality is what you perceive you see or think, and just wait until I am through with you, but for now, you'd better buckle up your seat belt because it's gonna be one hell of a ride."

Again, the lightening flashed, only this time there was no one in the car with Reggie as he pulled into the 'Save Moor' parking lot.

Reggie placed the car in park and turned on the interior lights which revealed an empty set of rear seats.

Sitting still for a moment, Reggie tried to make sense out of what he had just seen when his cell phone buzzed and vibrated, causing him to jump a little.

Grabbing his cell phone, Reggie noticed the text message from Perry as he ran through the parking lot and into the store which was packed full of shoppers.

It was not unusual to see that many shoppers at night, but what was unusual was that when Reggie headed for a checkout lane there was no one in line.

Reggie pulled his collar up around his neck and grabbed the three grocery bags and headed out the door and just as he did, he was surprised by several things.

The first thing which caught Reggie's attention was the fact that it was not raining, as a matter of fact, the more Reggie looked, he did not notice any wetness on the ground nor on his car.

The second thing that Reggie noticed was, there were no cars in the parking lot except his car, and as he turned back to the store, there was no one inside nor were there any lights on in the store.

Reggie stood out in the parking lot for a few minutes trying to make sense out of what had just happened when the biggest surprise of all became clear as Reggie looked in his bags and said to himself...

"What the Fuck...how in the hell can this shit be!"

Inside the bags that Reggie held on the seat were empty rusted cans, an empty bread sack, and two empty boxes.

Reggie walked up to the store and put the grocery bags in the dumpster and when he lifted his eyes he saw that the store was all boarded up with brown sheets of paper covering the windows.

Being a Police Officer, Reggie dealt with facts, so he examined all three bags for a receipt, which he did not find one, then he checked his wallet because he paid for the groceries using the last thirty dollars he had, which was still in his wallet.

Very quickly Reggie ran to his car and once inside looked back at the store as he fled out of the parking lot.

In fifteen minutes, he would be home and there wasn't another grocery store near his house, he'd have to go another twenty minutes in the opposite direction, and after what had just happened Reggie was not thinking about going anywhere except home.

On his way home Reggie thought about what he'd say to Perry when she asked him about the list she texted him.

Reggie's first thought was that he'd tell Perry that he lost signal because of the storm, but the only thing wrong with that was, there really had not been a storm.

So, Reggie thought he'd tell Perry, the store was so crowded, and he was so tired that he just came home, because there was no way she'd believe him if he told her the truth.

Reggie turned onto his street and noticed the outside lights on when over the radio he heard...

"I told you reality is what you think you see, and I hope you got your seat belt buckled good and tight, because this is gonna be one kick ass ride."

Reggie reached up and cut off the radio, parked the car and made a hasty retreat for the house.

Reggie entered the house and was met by Perry who hugged and kissed him.

Reggie hung up his coat and removed his shoes and figured he'd best apology for not getting the groceries, said...

"I'm really sorry babe, I got inside the store and they had two lanes open and both of the lines were from the register all the way to the end of the isle, and all I could think about was getting home and putting my feet up."

Perry stood looking at Reggie saying...

"I didn't need anything from the store...what are you talking about?"

Reggie sat down in the living room, handed Perry the bag containing ribs, saying...

"I got a grocery list in a text message asking me to pick up some stuff."

Perry pulled several frozen bags of veggies from the freezer saying...

"Umm ribs...but, I didn't send you a text."

Reggie grabbed a bottle of wine from the bar and as he poured a glass, and started to show Perry the text message, saying...

"Babe, what the hell do you mean?"

Perry looked at an empty text message, saying... "Must have been from one of your other ladies, I don't see anything."

Taking a large sip of wine, Reggie replied...

"Oh shit...this has been one weird day, I could have sworn..."

Perry walked back into the kitchen saying...

"Slow down there, big guy, you're not getting drunk...you owe me from last night remember?"

While Perry was eating, she looked at Reggie and said...

"You sure you're not hungry?"

Reggie said...

"Oh no hun, I ate a huge late lunch"

Eating the last bite of her food, Perry got up from the table grabbing the take-out box and saying...

"I just remembered that I was going to put the new set of teal sheets on the bed, but I'll change the bed before we go to sleep."

Perry placed the take-out box in the trash when Reggie came up behind her saying...

"With that look on your face, I thought something was wrong, can't the sheets wait until tomorrow."

Walking into the living room and sitting on the sofa, Perry replied...

"The sheets have been on the bed for two days and you know how I am about sleeping on clean fresh sheets, that's where you get your best sleep."

Reggie sat back in his recliner and grabbing the remote control and began changing the television channels, as Perry went upstairs to change the bed linen.

While Perry was upstairs, Reggie wondered to himself how much if any he was going to bring up to Perry about Port Clinton and all the things that he had been experiencing all day.

Bed time approached, and Perry came downstairs saying...

"Hey baby, you ready for bed?"

Reggie had fallen asleep and didn't hear Perry the first time she spoke to him, but awaken saying...

"What did you say?"

Perry repeated herself saying...

"I asked if you were ready for bed, but I guess since you were snoring...you are."

Both Perry and Reggie walked up to the bed room as Perry said...

"You're going to love these new sheets, they are double-ply Egyptian sheets, guaranteed to make you feel like you want to stay in bed all day."

After a quick shower Reggie climbed into bed saying...

"Egyptian sheets don't know why they call them Egyptian sheets, Pharaoh didn't sleep on sheets?"

Perry climbed in bed next to Reggie saying...

"I don't know about the Pharaoh, but I'll be your Cleopatra or anything else you want me to be."

Reggie and Perry lay and talked awhile when Reggie decided that he would attempt to talk about Port Clinton and what if anything, Perry remembered when he looked over and discovered that Perry had fallen fast asleep.

Perry awoke the next morning to find that not only were the bedsheets a different color than what she put on the bed, but they were also cheap and worn out. She was confused and disturbed by this fact.

Not being able to come up with a rational explanation, Perry decided to waken Reggie and ask him about the sheets, so that they could get ready for work.

While Reggie and Perry were preparing for work, Perry said...

"Reg, didn't I change the sheets last night to the new teal set?"

Reggie looked at the bed saying...

"I thought you did, but these are yellow and besides they smell."

Perry stood there for a few more minutes and then said...

"Well I don't have time to waste trying to figure this shit out I'll..."

Reggie cut Perry off by holding up the unopened package of sheets, as Perry said...

"Hold on a minute, those are the ones I put on, I know I put those sheets on the bed last night you saw me."

Laying the package of sheets on the dresser, Reggie said...

"I didn't see you actually change them, but I do remember that they were a bluish-green color, besides I don't recall us ever owning a yellow set of sheets, do you?"

Looking at Reggie and shaking her head in disbelief, Perry said...

"Somethings not right here."

Reggie laced his shoes saying...

"Babe, you're going to have to drive yourself this morning, because I won't have time to drop you off and make it down town."

Nodding her head Perry headed into the bathroom as Reggie kissed her on the back of her neck saying...

"Love you babe, hey, we'll talk about this tonight, okay?"

Reggie was sure that he would talk with Perry after work especially after what had just happened with the sheets.

Reggie noticed the new sheets on the bed when he came in the bedroom and was going to comment on how good they felt, but the sheets they woke up to were different, Reggie played down the whole thing because they were both running late for work.

Reggie was certain that Perry would remember being in Port Clinton, but for whatever reason didn't bring the subject up with her.

Perry walked out to the driveway and notice her car was in the same spot she had left it the night prior. She got in and drove off, taking the same path, she had grown accustomed to since moving into their new house seven years ago.

Besides the bed sheets, everything else seemed normal to Perry. That is until she arrived at her job.

Inside the office building there were a few people she had not met before but that didn't raise any red flags, because they were always hiring temps and interns.

Perry walked towards her own office only to discover that there was a different name tag on her office door... it wasn't her name.

She then thought that maybe she had gotten off on the wrong floor of the building, however a quick look revealed that she was on the right one. She had gone to the right office, it was just that her name had been replaced.

Perry opened the door slightly and there was someone else sitting at her desk...

"Who in the hell could this be?"

Perry thought, and then eased the door shut and walked back down to the lobby and sat at one of the empty desk wondering and thinking.

Perry then took out her laptop and connected to the company's wireless network. There she found that she was still on the company's roster however it showed that she was under a different manager, in a totally different department... now her head was hurting.

Perry worked hard for the company and was just recently promoted to manager, and the day prior she left her office and now someone else has been moved into her office.

Perry immediately checked her credit cards, driver's license, and work ID. They all reflected the right information as far as she knew. Same name, same picture, same numbers, and same home address.

Not knowing what to think, she called upstairs to her job and left a message saying, she was taking a sick day. The inconsistencies that morning made her think that something was wrong mentally with her.

She took the rest of the day off and headed straight to her psychiatrist's office. Her psychiatrist ordered blood work, checking for signs of any illicit drugs in her system. The tests came back negative. She had no alcohol or drugs in her system.

Perry went back home and began going through her personal files. Bank statements, personal checks, bills...she double checked them all. They all showed the right information.

Then a thought popped into her head...

"What if this is amnesia? What if something happened to me and I can't remember certain parts of my life?"

Perry called her manager, and after speaking with her, discovered that nothing had changed, and her office was still her office.

Immediately she logged online and began scouring the internet. She saw that the news and top stories were the same as the previous night, so there were no missing events. As far as Perry knew, she had woken up living a slightly different life.

Perry didn't drink on the week days, but she was feeling a drink was in order. She picked up her phone and decided that she was going to call Reggie, and then a scary thought came across her mind...*'what if Reggie is Reggie but not married to me?'*

Reggie's phone began ringing and on the fifth ring as Perry was about to hang up, Reggie's voice came over the line...

"Hello, Hello."

Perry hesitated not knowing what to say, but she had to say something, she had to find out if that part of her life was unchanged or not, so Perry answered...

"Hey Reg, it's me."

Reggie responded...

"Me who...I can barely hear you, who is this?"

Perry's entire life was suspended in time for a few seconds, thinking that Reggie didn't know her until he responded...

Is this you babe...Perry, is that you?"

Sweet relief rushed in and gave Perry a joyous calm as she answered...

"Oh yes babe, this is me...just wanted to hear your voice, having one of those days, so I took a sick day.

Reggie replied...

I love you babe and it'll be alright, what time is your meeting?"

Perry paused for a moment thinking...

"Meeting, what kind of a meeting am I having?"

Reggie asked again saying...

"Did you hear me Perry, what time is your meeting this morning?"

Perry nervously responded...

"What meeting, I don't have a meeting this morning."

Perry's heart suddenly began pounding as Reggie said...

"I thought that you told me when you left that you'd be in meetings all morning."

Just then Perry's uneasiness turned to panic as Reggie continued...

"Babe, you told me that you were going to be in meetings all morning, so you might not be able to call me...is everything alright?"

Pausing for a moment Perry said...

"Hun, I hope that we're not on two different planets, because I'm here at the house I didn't go anywhere except to work, then back home."

By now Reggie realized that Perry was experiencing the same thing that he had been going through and said...

"Babe, tell me something, do you know anything about Port Clinton?"

Perry let out a sigh and said...

"Oh my God Reg, what is going on...what are we doing here...we're supposed to be in Port Clinton all tied up!"

Reggie gathered his things and said...

"Honey, don't leave the house, just stay right there I'm on my way home."

All the way home, Reggie's thoughts were consumed with adulation that he was not alone in what was happening and what he was remembering, and relieved that Perry remembered Port Clinton and the grisly things which had occurred.

Only four more blocks and Reggie would home, when just then, up ahead as Reggie reached his street, there underneath the corner street light stood the old man from Port Clinton and the big man wearing the Ballerina's Tutu.

Reggie blinked twice and as he was even with them he noticed that they were standing there smiling and waving with their thumbs stuck out as though they were trying to hitch a ride.

Reggie glanced in the rear-view mirror as he drew closer to his driveway noticing that the old man and the big man wearing the tutu's was no longer standing on the corner. There was a bone chilling feeling that Reggie would see the old man and the big guy in the Ballerina's Tutu again.

Hurrying up the walkway, Reggie fumbled with his keys until he found the right one which opened the front door. Reggie walked inside calling Perry's name as he went from the front room to the living room and then upstairs.

Climbing the stairs, Reggie went into the bedroom and then in the bathroom which was empty. Just as Reggie turned to leave the bathroom and calling out Perry's name, he heard a soft whimper coming from behind the door.

Reggie opened the door wider and that's when he found Perry standing and looking as if she were in some kind of 'catatonic' state. Perry would later tell Reggie that she had no idea where or who she was, let alone why she was standing there.

Softly yet firmly, Reggie took hold of Perry's arms and gently shook her and asked…

"Perry, baby are you alright?"

For a few seconds there was no response from Perry. Reggie shook her several more times and with each time he shook her, he shook her harder and harder until finally Perry came to her senses saying…

"Reg, oh Reggie I'm glad you're home."

Hugging and kissing Perry on the forehead Reggie asked…

"Perry, I thought something was wrong, I mean I came into the house and yelled out your name and when you didn't answer I freaked out, baby you look like you've seen a ghost."

Reggie and Perry walked into their bedroom and Reggie removed his jacket as they sat on the bed when Perry said…

"Oh my God, Reggie you wouldn't believe what just happened to me."

Sitting close to Perry and looking intently in her eyes, Reggie said...

"Babe, after what I been seeing all day, I can believe anything, so what's going on babe?"

Perry took Reggie's hand and Reggie could tell by the way Perry's hands were shaking that something or someone really frightened Perry.

Perry hugged Reggie saying...

"Right after we ended our conversation on the phone, my plan was to take a quick shower before you got home, when I heard strange sounds coming from upstairs.

Perry shook her head as Reggie said...

"What kind of sounds were they?"

Perry was looking downward towards the floor and then lifted her head slowly, and staring at Reggie, and saying...

"The sounds I heard were weird, for maybe thirty minutes or so, it sounded like two people having a conversation, and their voices sounded like they were in a bubble because their voices echoed.

I pushed open the bathroom door and there stood a big man wearing a Ballerina's Tutu and a creepy looking old man."

Perry suddenly began to cry softly and then she continued...

"Oh Reg, they were standing in the bathroom talking. I don't know about what, all they were saying, all I know is, when I pushed open the bathroom door they both turned and just looked at me, as if I were interrupting them.

While I stood there, the little old man walked up to me and pointed with his finger and touched me, and the sound stopped, just like that. It just ended, I-I don't remember anything else after that until you came home."

Reggie again kissed Perry's forehead saying...

"Perry, how long ago was this and where did they go?"

Perry took a deep breath before saying...

"It was about ten minutes ago, they were standing there in the tub in all their clothes and then something pushed me out of the way, and they both walked past me and out the door, the creepy part was...I couldn't even move or make a sound...oh Reggie, you do believe me, don't you?"

Reggie took a hold of Perry's hand saying...

"Baby I believe you, of course, I believe you. On my way home, I saw the same old man and the big huge guy on the street corner, just standing there waving at me."

Perry looked all around her and then back at Reggie saying…

"Reg, I'm scared to death, I keep having these images of being tied up in an old farm house and then the next minute I'm here…am I losing my mind or something?"

Looking at Perry, Reggie said…

"Perry I'm here and I am not going to let anything happen to you. I'm going to tell you something and I don't want you to think that I'm one 'cheerio' away from a full bowl, ok?"

Perry jumped and then got up saying…

"What was that…did you hear that?"

Reggie pulled Perry back down on the bed saying…

"Baby, that was my foot tapping on the floor, why don't you sit down and try relaxing a little okay."

Perry resisted sitting down on the bed saying…

"Reg, you got to be kidding, I'm hearing creepy ass noises, people or ghost or whoever the hell they are, are popping in and out of our house like it's a 'comfort inn' hotel and you want me to relax…no way Jose.

Reggie stood up saying…

"Perry, will you just listen to me, like I said yesterday, you and I went to Port Clinton to look for clues as to who killed Amy…"

Perry interrupted Reggie saying…

"Amy's dead?"

Reggie rifled through his hair and said…

"Yes, I mean no, not now. I got word that Amy was killed yesterday, and she left clues mentioning Port Clinton.

You and I drove there and were held hostage and tied up in a basement at a farm off of fifty-three somewhere, but anyway, you, me, and some other people who were tied up by a sick old man and a big guy wearing some damn Ballerina's Tutu, got away."

Amy walked over to Reggie saying…

"I don't remember going to Port Clinton, as a matter of fact I've never been to Port Clinton, I just keep seeing images, about it."

Reggie said…

Will you just shut up baby and let me finish!"

Perry sat back down on the bed and said…

"Amy's dead…I talked to you today and you said that you and Amy were

about to leave, Reg what's going on, I'm serious, I love God and all that, but the church never told us about any of this shit?"

Reggie moved back over and sat next to Perry saying...

"Look, I know, there are a lot of things the church never tells people. The reality is, somehow we were in Port Clinton, tied up by some whackos, and they erased our memory or something."

Perry laid her head in her hands saying...

"Do you know how ridiculous that sounds..."

"Wow...I mean I don't remember going anywhere yesterday, let alone Port Clinton. Reg, we're here and how can a person be in two places at one time?"

Reggie grabbed Perry's hand saying...

"I know how this sounds...one-minute Amy's dead and we are in Port Clinton and the next thing everything is back to normal. Perry, don't you think I know how this sounds."

Suddenly the telephone rang, and Perry answered it...after a few seconds Perry laid the phone down and turned to Reggie saying...

"That was Amy, guess what, she's not dead?"

Reggie walked over to the refrigerator and grabbed a cold beer and said...

"Very funny Perry, I would laugh if this shit wasn't so serious."

Perry sat next to Reggie saying...

"Look babe, I'm not trying to make a joke out of this and I know it's serious because I'm scared down to my 'Victoria Secrets' but we can't add imaginary shit to it. I mean this is two-thousand- and six, creepy ass shit like this just don't happen.

Looking at Perry and shaking his head, Reggie said...

"Wont, can't, shouldn't are words that we were taught, but the stuff that's happening right now... the stuff that we are witnessing...there isn't any school or teacher that can educate us on this."

Perry leaned into Reggie and asked...

"Do you really believe what's going on, what are we supposed to do?"

Reggie sat down and drank his beer saying...

"I really don't know Perry, I talked with Pastor Dearborn about praying, but that has not done any good, maybe I don't know how to pray right or something...I don't know."

Perry held Reggie's hand saying...

"Honey this is serious we got to do something, you're not crazy and I know I'm not either, but we can't just sit and do nothing and end up dead or going crazy."

Reggie walked over to the fridge for another beer and coming back to Perry said...

"Perry. We see movies about this kind of stuff all the time, maybe we're going to have to stand up to whatever it is and make it leave us alone, I mean what else are we going to do, huh?"

Perry gave Reggie a look of disbelief saying...

"Reg, what if this thing or whatever wants to hurt us or threatens us, then what do we do...get garlic and wooden stakes or lumps of silver shit and throw it at 'em?"

Perry looked at Reggie expecting some kind of reaction and instead Reggie sat on the sofa laughing, when Perry kicked him saying...

"What is so damn funny?"

Reggie grabbed his leg where Perry kicked him saying...

"Ouch...what did you do that for?"

Just then Perry and Reggie looked at one another and snickered as Reggie said...

"Damn baby, lumps of silver shit my ass...where'd you come up with that?"

Perry walked over to Reggie and punched him on the arm and then they both began laughing as hard as they could.

Then as Reggie lay across the bed flipping through the channels with the remote, they heard a knock at the front door. It was just two loud knocks. Perry asked Reggie to go see what it was, since it was dark out.

Reggie went to the front door after looking out the window first, but there was no one there. Reggie opened the door and stepped out on the porch and looked around and there wasn't anyone there.

Reggie locked the door and went back and laid down with Perry and told Perry...

"Babe there's no one there."

Perry and Reggie were both kind of tired and just shrugged it off and forgot about it. The house Reggie and Perry lived in was old, and it had been Reggie's grandmothers house and like any old house, made noises whenever the weather changed, from hot to cold, to windy or rainy.

After a minute or two, Perry heard this loud crashing noise coming from the living room. It sounded like glass breaking. Reggie had fallen asleep with his head in Perry's lap and didn't hear the noise.

Perry was scared because of their conversation earlier and got up and laid Reggie's head on the pillow and went to see what it was.

There on the floor by the side of the dining table, was the vase and the flowers that Reggie had gotten for her. The vase was shattered, and the water and flowers were spilled all over the floor.

The terrifying thing was, the table were the vase was sitting on was about four feet away from where it had fallen, and the vase was a very heavy old handblown vase.

How it got from the center of the table, all the way across the room, was baffling. There weren't any animals in the house.

Really scared by then, Perry started hearing footsteps and scratching noises and smelled a nasty foul odor coming from the hallway, which sounded like it was getting closer to the living room.

Perry screamed, waking Reggie up, saying…

"Reg, Reggie, get up there's something in the house…I swear I felt something brush up against my hair and look at the vase and flowers over there."

Perry and Reggie had lived in the house for five years and knew there was always something weird about it because sometimes they could feel something, as if there was someone there.

They always just sort of played it off, but after all that has happened they knew there had to be something there and weren't taking any more chances. This isn't the first time that they heard noises and heard weird things.

Reggie helped Perry clean up the mess and after looking all over the house, confirming that no one was in house except Perry and Reggie they sat down on the sofa to watch television.

Reggie and Perry moved into their home five years ago. A four-bedroom colonial designed house in a family-oriented subdivision that was built in the early thirties. There are a handful of original owners living in houses surrounding Reggie and Perry, mostly people with teenagers and empty nesters.

Their house was left as an inheritance by Reggie's grandmother who originally bought it sixty years earlier for two hundred-thousand dollars and a promise that no violent souls were to enter or occupy the property.

Reggie had heard that the house was haunted years before they moved in and while Reggie couldn't say for sure that it was, there have been many incidents which have occurred, without little to no explanation.

Reggie sat and told Perry he could recall showing up to meet the home inspector when the first incident happened. They were standing in the kitchen, Reggie was entering some information onto his laptop which he had set on the counter while he was standing on the other side of the kitchen by his phone.

Suddenly Reggie and the inspector heard what they thought was a door slamming hard behind them and jumped about a mile and whipped around to see what it was. They didn't know if either of the two doors had been open in the first place, and they were both hollow doors, then the inspector said…

"What was that!?"

He looked up from his laptop, which was now closed, and again said…

"What was what?"

"You didn't hear that, maybe the wind caught it and made the door slam?"

The house inspector suggested to Reggie that when he slammed his laptop that the sound echoed in the empty house.

Before going to bed, Perry went into the kitchen to do the dishes, over the running water, Perry heard another sound, a motorized noise. She turned off the water and listened and realized it was coming from the garage.

Perry called Reggie to check it out, and when Reggie walked outside he saw the garage door up. Finding that odd, Reggie checked the garage out, and after assuring it was empty, pushed the button and closed and opened it and then closed it and went back inside.

A minute later Perry heard the noise again and sure enough, the garage door was open. This went on for about fifteen minutes. Reggie got up once more to close it, and a few minutes later it would open, then he said to Perry…

"Baby, either you're messing with me, which isn't funny, or someone else's remote is crossing with our unit?"

Perry said…

"Now how can I do anything while I'm up to my knees with all of these dirty pots."

Finally, it ended, and it never happened again, and the garage door has functioned normally since.

Reggie told Perry as he went to sit back down...

"Twice you had me go shut the garage door, no one was outside, and I never heard of a garage opening and closing by itself unless someone was pressing the remote."

Perry hung her apron across the oven's door and came in to sit down with Reggie saying...

"Do you think that someone else's garage door opener somehow interfered with ours or the signals got mixed up like you said?"

Grabbing the TV remote control Reggie selected a movie station and said...

"I don't know, but when it comes to electrical things anything is possible."

Perry got up, poured a glass of wine and said to Reggie...

"Baby, can I ask you something?"

Reggie sat up straight saying...

"Sure babe, you know you can ask me anything, what?"

Perry got on her knees and crawled over to Reggie saying...

"Tonight, when we go to bed, can you prop up chairs by the front and back doors...please?"

Reggie held Perry's hands in his hands, saying...

"Of course, babe if that is going to make you feel secure, also I'll get the Christmas bells from the attic and string them up on our bedroom door if you want me to, okay?"

Reggie knew that placing chairs against the doors was going to do very little because if what he suspected was right, they were dealing with things which were not human, but for Perry's sake he tried to comfort her."

After Reggie had set the chairs by both doors and tied up the Christmas bells, he grabbed his glass of wine and he and Perry went to bed.

Reggie was awakened out of his sleep by a noise he heard, he could see the time on the clock next to his bed, it was early, and Reggie often slept with the drapes open and the window slightly raised.

Reggie wiped his eyes and looked out onto the open fields but there was nothing moving, nothing in sight. Reggie lay in bed a few minutes listening for sounds and when he was satisfied, he laid back down.

Reggie didn't recall precisely when, but after a while - maybe a minute, maybe a bit longer, he started to hear another strange sound. He didn't give it much thought at first, but then the sound grew louder and more pronounced because after a while it became unsettling.

Trying to calm himself down, Reggie couldn't shake the sounds he heard of someone breathing. The wheezing sounds were easy to place, they appeared to be coming from the opposite corner of the room, near the door and, near the light switch.

Reggie stayed in bed for a while longer, thinking about his options, but now that he was aware of the wheezing sounds and knew where it was coming from, it became or seemed to become louder and, although this sounded stupid, the wheezing seemed as if there were words in each sound.

Reggie didn't move out of the bed, but he did search with his hands in the night stand for his service revolver. Reggie was more scared than he'd ever been in his life to the point where his fear kept him in bed, or maybe it was the hope that if he could just hold out till morning the wheezing would stop and everything would be alright.

Moment by moment Reggie heard the wheezing sounds growing louder and louder, and in between the wheezing Reggie could hear the ticking of the clock on his bed night stand.

All through the night, Reggie had thoughts about getting get up and turning on the light switch, but that would only take him near the wheezing sounds and who were making them.

Reggie thought to himself how much longer he could endure the situation; he was not a coward and he had located his gun, but his gun didn't make him gather any courage.

Reggie laid there listening to the wheezing sound for what seemed like hours and hours. The raspy wheezing had more than gotten on Reggie's nerves, rather it was pissing him off.

Finally, Reggie got up talking to himself and resolutely, moved towards the other end of the room with his gun in his hands as if he were ready to physically attack someone if necessary and found the light switch without fumbling or showing signs of nervousness.

The split-second before Reggie turned on the lights, he could hear that he was very, very close to what was making the noise and that it definitely was coming from inside the bedroom, but it never moved.

The moment the lights came on, it was gone, and the wheezing stopped. Reggie held his breath, and listened, but nothing.

He stood at the bedroom door for what seem like a long time, not afraid to move but afraid to see what the light would reveal. Reggie placed his hand on the door and turned the knob slowly until it opened.

Reggie moved all through the house, room after room but there was nothing. Reggie looked in the last room which was the kitchen, and upon seeing nothing, turned slowly, and as he was about to, he felt something cold on the back of his neck and jumped, crashing against the wall.

Reggie looked up and realized that it was Perry who had awakened and came down stairs to make coffee and breakfast saying...

"Aw baby, did I make you jump...I'm sorry, did you sleep good?"

Reggie thought about sharing with Perry about his night and the wheezing sound which kept him up all night, but decided the less Perry knew, the smoother his day would go.

Perry turned to Reggie saying...

"Babe, I'm going to make some breakfast, do you want me to make you some too?"

Reggie quickly hid his gun from Perry and followed her in the kitchen, turning on every light as he went saying...

"Yes, that sounds good."

Perry pulled out and loaded on the table, eggs, bacon and the waffle maker from under the cabinet saying...

"Maybe we're going to be okay, since we sleep all night without being bothered by anything, or seeing anything...what do you think?"

Again, Reggie kept his silence about the things which he saw, and said...

"Perhaps baby, perhaps."

After breakfast, Perry began walking towards the stairs with Reggie behind her when suddenly there were a series of loud banging on the doors and the sides of the house as Perry screamed out...

"Oh no... not again!"

Reggie turned all directions holding Perry, when from out

of nowhere like in a science fiction movie, Reggie and Perry saw themselves and everything around them moving in slow motion.

They saw glimpses of figures and scenes moving in a rapid pace. They saw trees and water, and the sign for route fifty-three north, and the lift bridge to their left and the wild life park.

Suddenly Perry and Reggie found themselves in the basement in Port Clinton.

As Reggie and Perry looked around, there were others tied up as well and standing in front of them was old man Mr. Thomas, and the big man in the Ballerina's Tutu and a Nun dressed in a raggedy habit.

At first Reggie and Perry were unable to make a sound and then as if someone removed their hand from Perry's mouth, she let out a scream.

The Nun positioned herself in front of Perry and Reggie, with a set of pom poms and a megaphone in her hand, saying...

"Good even and welcome it's such a pleasure seeing you here again, before you take another breath let me explain something..You two are in another reality. Whenever I choose, I can fling you into this reality or the one you just left or create another one of my choosing."

Struggling, Reggie tried opening his mouth to speak when The Nun said...

"One hundred years ago, I was accused of murdering children, but no one saw me, there was no evidence, but still I had to endure years of life in a dungeon the descendants of the men and women who sentenced me will see what that's like.
Starting with you, all of their ancestors, will suffer the same fate as I did through you."

As The Nun backed away from them, Perry let out a scream and then the entire basement went dark.

8
Revelations

Marcia awakened and held Denise with all her might. The attention of caressing and kissing Denise awakened her, and in a quiet tone she said...

"Mmm honey, why weren't you like this last night, you just rolled over and fell asleep."

At first Marcia didn't answer Denise she continued hugging and kissing her, holding her tight, and then she said...

"Oh my God...I can't believe it, I thought that I lost you for good."

Thinking that Marcia had just had a bad dream, Denise said...

"Hey baby, you're on me as if I'm not a cheeseburger, I'm not going anywhere, are you okay?"

Marcia began stroking Denise's back and running her fingers through her hair saying...

"Dee, you're probably going to say that I was dreaming or off my meds or something, but there was some old woman dressed like a Nun who chased us outside the house and pushed you onto the freeway where you were struck and killed by a truck."

Sitting up in the bed and wiping the crusties from the corners of her eyes, Denise replied...

"Yepper, I think you are off your meds when you say shit like that, as you can see...I'm right here."

Marcia scooted right in front of Denise saying...

"No, I'm serious, there was this Nun sitting over there in the rocking chair

and we woke up and ran out of the house and ended up in the woods near I-seventy, where she chased you and then pushed you onto the freeway."

Denise took a finger and began poking Marcia saying...

"Do you feel that...I'm not dead, I'm here, besides why did you say that like that?"

Marcia got up out of bed turning the light on and saying...

"Say what like what?"

Denise sat on the bed next to Marcia saying... *"Well for starters you said...'when we woke up this morning', well we just woke up and no one's chasing us or any of that whacked shit, Marcia."*

Marcia looked at Denise saying...

"Look, I've never lied to you right, I'm telling you we were in our house and then all this banging on the door and on the side of the house made us go outside and that's when we saw this creepy looking Nun and this big man."

Denise took Marcia by the hand saying...

"Honey, what you're telling me sounds like a dream, first you said this nun was in the rocking chair....you know how real dreams can seem."

Marcia again tried explaining what had happened...

"I remembered searching for my cell, and you found it, wedged in between the cushions on the sofa, and that's when the garage doorknob started wiggling and someone was banging on the windows in the living room.

"Through the window this woman wearing a Nun's habit, who was watching our every move, so we shot upstairs at first and then we decided to go outside to get in the car."

Denise then said...

"Well if I were there, how come I don't remember any of this?"

Marcia replied...

"Well, maybe when the truck hit you, you lost your memory or something...I don't know.

Denise got up and began pacing the room saying...

"Marcia this doesn't make any sense, you said it happened yesterday morning, well how come I don't have any scratches or anything?"

Walking over to Denise, Marcia said...

"Honey please believe me, I'm telling you, this really happened."

Just then someone started pounding on the front door. The pounding was so hard it seemed as if the door was going to burst wide open, when Marcia screamed…

"Oh my God…. it's happening again."

Denise quickly grabbed Marcia saying…

"Calm the hell down Marcia, it's probably a dumbass teenager that is always teasing and playing with us, just because we are married to one another."

Denise turned and peeked out the window saying…

"Hold on, I see two people pacing on the front porch. I'm freaking going to call the Police, and if it's that kid I'll put his Vienna sausage in a meat grinder."

While Marcia was on the phone, one of the people on the front porch broke the main window glass. Marcia ran upstairs, with Denise following fast behind her, scared to death.

Suddenly, everything went silent. Marcia and Denise were in the bedroom shaking and breathing heavily in the pitch-black room for what seemed like an eternity, then, they both heard the sirens.

Denise with her hands, felt Marcia in the darkness saying…

"The Police are here, let's go on down stairs and let them in."

Holding tight to Denise's arm, Marcia said…

"Go down stairs my ass, let's just wait right here until the Police call for us."

Denise replied to Marcia…

"Honey use your head, how the fuck are the Police going to get inside the house unless we open the door?"

The two women eased out of the bedroom and headed downstairs when Marcia said…

"Wait a minute…I don't hear the sirens anymore, wait Denise!"

Denise was already halfway down the stairs when Marcia came up behind her whispering…

"Dee, we need to get the hell out of the house, we can meet the Police outside."

As soon as Denise got to the bottom of the steps she realized the sirens she had heard a few seconds ago had passed their house and headed down the street, when she turned and said to Marcia…

"Marcia, we can go outside and walk down the street to the Police…see, they're just at the corner."

Marica nervously replied…

"Don't you see, this is the way it happens…pretty soon all that banging on the doors and sides of the house is going to start and then we'll be chased outside."

Denise stood looking all around the house when she said...

"We have two choices, one, we can hop in the car and drive to the corner and bring the Police back or we can stay inside and be trapped for whoever breaks in...which do you wanna do?"

Marcia grabbed onto Denise's arm, nodded her head and started patting her pants pocket for the car keys when the banging on the front door sounded, scaring the two women out the back door and into the wooded area.

Denise turned to Marcia saying...

"C'mon this way, we can make it to the car."

Marcia slowly followed Denise, and as Denise grew closer to the corner of the house a very big man wearing a Ballerina's Tutu appeared, causing Denise and Marcia to turn around and run towards the woods near the back of the house.

The two women screamed as they tried cutting over to the left which would have taken them to where the Police were, but whoever it was who was chasing them, was chasing them from that direction, cutting off any possibility of them getting near the Police.

Denise was wearing jeans, while Marcia had on cut offs and a tank top and began complaining as the thorns from the brush started to cut into her exposed legs and thighs.

Denise yelled back to Marcia...

"This way, we're close to the interstate."

Marcia slowed down and eventually stopped and leaned against a tree as Denise ran back to her saying...

"No...baby we can't stop now."

Marcia knew that they were repeating what had occurred earlier, when she said...

"Not this way Dee, this is how it happened, how they killed you, we gotta find another way, any way but this way."

Suddenly the two women turned behind them and noticed a very large figure emerging from out of the brush...it was the man wearing the Ballerina's Tutu, when both Marcia and Denise screamed.

Then Denise and Marcia looked to their right as someone or something was coming from their immediate left.

Coming out of the brush and into the clearing stood two teenagers wearing hoodies saying...

"She's coming to get you!"

Marcia grabbed onto Denise's arm, and then both women began holding one another, shaking and screaming...

"What do you want, leave us alone."

The two teenagers wearing the hoodies and the man in the tutu drew closer and closer when a voice cried out from the brush, in another direction saying...

"She's going to do things but leaving you alone NEVER!"

Marcia and Denise frantically scanned the entire area looking for the voice which had just spoke, when suddenly the wind began to howl, and the rain started pouring down.

Through the pouring rain Marcia tapped Denise on the shoulder, pointing and saying...

"Look over there Denise."

The two stared out in front of them and feeling as if something or someone was staring back. It was a very uneasy feeling, not to mention the man and the creepy kids behind them.

Denise tried to shake off the fear that she was feeling, when a bloodcurdling sound erupted to the left of them which froze Marcia and Denise in their tracks.

This sound was unlike any other that they had heard, and it made every hair on their bodies vibrate and tingle. The only way to describe it is, it sounded like a wild person with no language skills being gutted alive or something.

There were no words, just this high-pitched bloodcurdling scream. Neither Marcia nor Denise moved or said a word. They just stood there fixed in their stare, when suddenly a second scream was let loose with even more force than the first.

By this time, Marcia and Denise had taken off sprinting through the woods, not knowing which direction they were running in, only that they had to get away as fast as they could.

Denise and Marcia came to a small clearing when Denise stopped and said...

"*Whew, I got to catch my breath.*"

Marcia rested her back against a tree, when she looked over at Denise saying...

"*I don't recognize where we are, we can't be too far from where the Police are, and why don't they hear us?*"

Denise got that feeling like they were being watched by something that didn't want them there and had some intent on harming them. Denise looked around and walked up to Marcia and put her hand over Marcia's mouth whispering...

"*When I tell you to, run, we have to run, something is looking at us from over there behind that tree.*"

The moon was very bright that night and Denise could clearly see all the way to the tree lines, probably fifty yards on both sides of them.

As they were about to run, they suddenly heard this whoosh-whoosh-whoosh sound, flying from behind them. It was like the sound that a stick makes if you're swinging it.

Whatever it was, dove straight down at them causing Marcia and Denise to dive down on the cold wet ground. After laying there for a few minutes, Marcia said...

"*I'm not trying to freak you out or anything, but I'm headed towards the interstate. I don't know which direction the Police are in, but I can hear the cars on the interstate...this shit isn't supposed to be happening.*"

Neither Marcia nor Denise had an idea what the hell was going on at this point. Denise replied...

"*Be careful, we gotta climb up the hill in all this rain and shit...*"

Denise barely finished her statement when she noticed Marcia climbing the wet slippery slope towards the interstate.

Denise looked down at her shoes wondering if she should try climbing the hill barefoot, because she had on clogs and was afraid they would prevent her from making the climb. Removing her shoes, Denise heard that whoosh sound and started hauling ass up the hill trying to catch Marcia.

Denise said she had the feeling to stop and look around and as she did, she felt something behinds her, barely crunching twigs and sloshing on the wet ground.

When Denise stopped, all the sounds of movement stopped, and she froze in that spot to listen for more sounds. Then she yelled to Marcia...

"Marcia, I feel 'hot breath' hitting the back of my neck."

Marcia at that time had stopped and turned around saying...

"Get the fuck up here."

As Denise picked up her pace, she still had that feeling of being followed and watched but she was too afraid to turn around and look. Denise had never had that kind of feeling before.

Denise had finally caught up with Marcia and they slowly were making their way up the hill, when they saw something slithering down out of the tree to their left.

Denise and Marcia saw something out of the corner of their eye about the same time which crashed to the ground and followed parallel to them.

Initially it looked like a huge, brown dog. Honestly, at first, Marcia's mind was playing tricks on her and she thought it was a bear. It crashed through the thicket and awkwardly slithered along the ground, as if it were an injured animal.

As it grew closer, Marcia and Denise begin getting nervous. Marcia and Denise were almost up the hill when a hand reached down to pull Marcia up. Marcia could barely make out who it was when she noticed an elongated misshapen hand with knotty fingers stretching out to her.

Upon seeing this, Marcia screamed and lost her grip, sliding down into Denise who was directly behind her. When Marcia slid into Denise, Denise grabbed hold of her leg and the two women went crashing down the hill.

The creature that was slithering up behind them, which came out of the tree, was directly behind Denise, clawing at her leg.

Marcia slipped and fell on top of Denise, and when Marcia saw what was happening to Denise, she began screaming and trying to claw her way back up the hill. Marcia attempted to get up the hill by pulling on a large branch which was sticking out of the ground beside her, but the branch was not connected to anything, and she slid down the hill in the mud.

Marcia grabbed the limb which was in her hand and began blindly swinging it. Marcia must have hit whatever she was swinging at several times, because it let loose of her and Denise and let out a high-pitched scream. Marcia helped Denise to her feet, when they heard someone in the darkness cry out...

"Is somebody out there...is there anybody there?"

Marcia and Denise began screaming and running in the direction of the voice they heard when there was a weird deafening 'WOMP' sound. The sound was so loud that every time they heard it, they could feel pressure building in their ears.

Immediately they looked about twenty feet away and saw a faint outline of someone coming towards them.

Whoever it was, was not walking in a straight line, but moving from side-to-side in a staggering motion.

Thinking perhaps it was the Police, they ran as fast as they could in the rain, darkness and the night until they were several feet away from the outline when suddenly, they saw it...it was not the Police but, a man, a man with a face which terrified them, which was as white as a sheet, staring at them.

Standing there, Marcia and Denise heard the sound again, 'WOMP, WOMP!' Again, Marcia and Denise grabbed their ears from the eerie pressure building in their heads and fell to the ground.

Sprawling on the ground in the mud with every hair standing on its ends, Marcia and Denise saw the figure bending down and revealing its face in front them.

Marcia and Denise saw a bright bluish glowing figure in front of them. It was emitting a shimmery aura, and Marcia and Denise both grew more and more frightened and panic stricken.

For some unknown reason, they could not move nor make a sound, they wanted to scream but were unable to. All they could do, was stand there and stare as it motioned for them to follow him as he walked through the woods and out of their sight.

Suddenly Marcia and Denise's hair was grabbed from behind and they would've been dragged backwards through the woods had not they both slipped and fallen in the mud.

Denise screamed at Marcia saying...

"Run God damnit...C'mon!"

Not knowing in which direction to run, Marcia began running in what she thought was the direction to their house when she started noticing odd things.

Sticks carved like spears stuck in the ground with doll heads on them, weird carvings in the trees, a child's stuffed animal, and dead birds and bones hanging from nooses up in the trees.

This place was nowhere near their house, nor did it seem to fit anything that belonged in their neighborhood, but still Denise was behind Marcia urging her to run.

The further they ran the more familiar things began to look. Suddenly and without any warning Marcia and Denise found themselves back in their back yard, and without any warning, their bedroom.

Marcia looked around the bedroom and then at Denise saying...

"What in the hell just happened Dee?"

Denise sat down on the bed next to Marcia with a puzzled look on her face saying...

"Honey we were sitting here and you were about to tell me something about me being killed, and the next thing I know, you just blanked out on me...as if your mind were somewhere else...so, go on, finish your story."

Marcia looked at Denise with a frustrated look on her face saying...

"Now, don't you dare tell me that we just weren't outside running from creepy things a few seconds ago?"

Denise turned over and lay on her stomach with her feet in the air and her legs crossed saying...

"C'mon girlfriend, all I know is that, I've been sitting here for the past five minutes waiting on you to finish telling me about this dream or whatever you had about me being killed, when suddenly you blanked out on me."

Marcia got down on her knees in front of Denise saying...

"Baby, you don't remember anything, don't you remember that we were just outside in the woods, and something was chasing us?"

Denise started running her fingers through Marcia's hair saying...

"Marcia, I mean get a grip, you're not going to go fruit loops on me, I'm telling you that I don't remember going or wanting to go outside since I got home today, especially in all this rain."

No sooner did Denise say that, when there came a pounding on the front door. Denise walked over to the front window and peeked outside. There standing in the rain, in front of their yard was an old woman and two small kids wearing hoodies.

Marcia motioned for Denise to come over to the window to see for herself, when the door started rattling and the two kids were scratching at the windows trying to get in.

Denise and Marcia propped furniture up against the doors and windows and then Marcia took out her cell phone and called for the Police, saying...

"Hello, I need the Police."

The operator told Marcia...

"Hello Marcia now, why don't you just open the door and let them in, they're going to get in anyway do you think that you and your LOVER are going to get away?"

Marcia motioned for Denise to hurry up and come over and listen to what was being said on the phone, saying...

"Dee, come over here now, listen...I tried telling you that all this was real."

Denise bent down to listen while Marcia said to the person talking to her over the phone...

"What do you want, I didn't tell you my name. I'm calling the Police to report suspicious people are on my front porch trying to break in our house."

The voice on the other end of the receiver said...

"Oh, Marcia that's so nice of you to let your LOVER listen in. Hi Denise, we were telling little Ms. nasty panties, that you are helpless to resist us, now, watch this and scream! just love a good scream, don't you he-he-he-he-he."

The sinister laughing faded as Marcia pulled the phone away from their ears and just as she was about to hang up the phone, Marcia and Denise found themselves outside again in the rain in the woods.

Marcia was holding onto Denise looking around, scared and shaking saying…

"W-where are we? I wanna go home… how'd we get outside!"

Just then the voice that they heard over the phone in the house came echoing through the woods and the rain and the night saying…

"Scared, are we? Oh, you ain't seen nothing yet."

Denise was also equally scared as she replied…

"Oh my God, we're not even in the city anymore…look."

Marcia looked all round and saw no street lights, nothing but trees. The night suddenly appeared darker and blacker as she said…"

"Denise look, there is a path over there, see it?"

Denise looked ahead and down and below her to her right, she saw a dirt covered path, saying…"

"Okay Marcia let's go."

Marcia drew closer to Denise and said."

"Wait a minute, did you just say let's go…are you out of your fucking mind…I vote that we just stay here?"

Marcia and Denise began following the path when they heard the sounds of people talking and car horns honking, when Denise said…"

"I don't know where this is going to take us, but at least I can hear other people talking and cars, so what other choice do we have…huh?"

Marcia nodded and continued following Denise down the path as it led them from an opening to a wooded area when Marcia screamed saying…

"W-What are we gonna do. Now I'm really starting to freak out, we left the woods, and came to an opening now we're back in the woods again. Somebody or something is playing with us."

Denise stopped dead in her tracks and pointed in the distance saying…

"Look! there's a house over there, maybe whoever lives there will let us call the Police, get home or something."

Marcia looked past Denise trying to see the house more clearly saying…

"I don't know about you, but I'm in favor of being in our bed and in our house…I'm not too crazy about all of this, whoever lives there might be one of these things or something."

Denise turned to Marcia saying…

Oh please, you actually don't believe in those things, do you? C'mon let's go, we're just a couple feet away."

Holding onto Denise tighter, Marcia said shaking...

"I don't like this. I don't like this at all, where do you think all of this shit is coming from?"

Denise jerked her arm lose from Marcia's grip saying...

"Oh, shut up, nothing's going to happen."

Denise and Marcia reached the house, when Denise knocked on the door, the door slowly opened. Marcia grew more frightened as she said...

"Somethings gonna get us, somethings gonna jump out and get us, I just know it."

Denise put her hand over Marcia's mouth saying...

Hello, is there anyone home? Is anyone here? We need help, we're lost, and we need help."

Denise and Marcia could clearly see that the lights in the kitchen were on, when suddenly the door slammed shut behind them and Marcia screamed saying...

"H-How did the friggin door close all by itself?"

Denise tried keeping her cool by pretending that she wasn't as scared as Marcia was, saying...

"Oh, that was the wind, that's all it was."

"OW! Denise. What was that on my foot? Something stepped on my foot."

Denise said ...

"Sorry."

Denise could not have stepped on Marcia's foot because Denise was ahead of Marcia, but because Marcia was so frightened she would've believed anything.

Suddenly Marcia screamed out...

AHH! Dee, did you feel that?"

Denise stopped and turned and said...

"Feel wha-AAHHT?"

Marcia begun stretching her hands out in front of her, yet feeling only empty space when she cried out...

"Dee? Dee? Where did ya go"... AAAAAHHHHH?"

When Marcia came to, she was laying across her bed. She looked all around the room, still in a daze over the events which took place a few seconds ago.

Clearing her head, Marcia turned and looked around and said...

"Where is Denise." More importantly, how did I get back in my bed, I don't remember walking here. The last thing I remember Denise and I were in someone's house."

Marcia said to herself as she slowly made her way through the house. After an exhausted search of the entire house and the garage, Marcia picked up her cell phone and tried calling Denise's number, but the call went directly to her voice mail saying...

"The person you're looking for is no longer available, if you stay on the line, someone you know will respond."

Marcia stood in the living room with a *'what the fuck'* look on her face, not knowing what to do or where to go or what to think; outside of looking for Denise.

The only other important thing pressing on Marcia's mind was that she had to pee bad.

Marcia knew that Denise would not have left her alone under any circumstances nor would she have left without telling her or leaving a note.

Denise's car was in the garage, her keys were on the kitchen table and her purse was beside the love seat, so where could she be?

The two did not have any friends in the neighborhood due in part because the residents didn't approve of their relationship as man and wife, so there was really no one nearby that Marcia felt comfortable going to.

All that Marcia could do was notify the Police that she was missing, but she had to be careful not to mention the woods or the voices. Marcia waited an hour more before calling the Police just in case Denise came walking through the door, but somehow, she knew that was not going to happen.

An hour passed, and Marcia picked up her cell and dialed nine-one-one...

Operator: 911, what's your emergency?

Marcia: *Uh, (relieved that it was a human voice this time, Marcia said...) I want to report a missing person; my husband is missing. I believe she was abducted from our house.*

Operator 911: Ok stay on the line for Columbus Police.

Marcia: *I will.*

Columbus Police: Columbus Police Department, Sgt Jamison.

Marcia: *Hello, I need to report a missing person, she was abducted from our house.*

Columbus Police Sgt Jamison: Ok, how old?

Marcia: *44 years old*

Columbus Police: Ok, I believe this is your husband, is that correct?

Marcia: *Yes*

Columbus Police: Why do you think he was abducted?

Marcia: *First, it's not a he, but a she… and I have no idea, we woke up this morning, I went to go get her up for coffee and she's gone, I looked everywhere in the house.*

Columbus Police: I thought you said your husband was missing?

Marcia: *I did, my name is Marcia, and my husband's name is Denise, can we skip this shit and get on with it?*

Columbus Police: (interrupted Marcia) Ok, hang on.

   Marcia could hear the Officer laughing in the background and saying…"
Hey bill a 'Dykes on the phone, apparently she misplaced the other Dyke'.

Columbus Police: Sorry for that miss, my screen just went black, but it's ok, so, where were we?

Marcia: *By the way I heard that smart-ass shit you said too, and If I wasn't so pissed off I'd come there so all your buddies could watch this Dyke beat your ass down!*

A few embarrassing moments passed and then the Officer said...

Columbus Police: What's your address Miss, uh?

Marcia: *Thirty-Two-Thirty-Two Africa*

Columbus Police: What's your name Miss?

Marcia: *My name is Marcia, M-a-r-c-i-a, middle initial D, last name is Mims, M-i-m-s.*

Columbus Police: M- as in Mary?

Marcia: *Yes*

Columbus Police: Ok, what's his-I-I mean her name?

Marcia: *Isabel, D-e-n-i-s-e, Denise, M-as in Monday is the middle initial.*

Columbus Police: Ok, same last name?

Marcia: *Yes, I said that we are married.*

Columbus Police: Ok, what's her actual birth date?

Marcia: *June 28, 1962*

Columbus Police: Ok, is there anyone else there with you?

Marcia*: Uh, no. It would only be Denise and she's missing.*

Columbus Police: Ok,

Marcia: *And her purse, car keys and cell phone, are here at the house.*

Columbus Police: What kind of vehicle is she going to be in?

Marcia: *I just told you, her car keys and her car is here, at the house*

Columbus Police: Ok, how tall is she?

Marcia: *She is 5'8"*

Columbus Police: Ok, is she black, white, Hispanic?

Marcia: *She's, uh, fair-skinned, with, uh, clear eyes and light brown hair*

Columbus Police: And what do you mean by fair skinned clear eyes?

Marcia: *Uh, she's white and her eyes are a little bit green with grey in them...*

Columbus Police: Isn't that the same as Hazel?

Marcia: *I don't know...just, say hazel or grey, whatever.*

Columbus Police: Hazel, ok, you said she's about 5'-8", do you know how much she weighs?

Marcia: *Uh, probably I believe she is 155-ish...yes, she is about 155 pounds, she's probably right about 155 pounds.*

Columbus Police: Right, okay, I got that about 155 pounds, ok, do you remember what she was wearing last night when you last saw her?

Marcia: *Uh, before she went to bed I believe she was wearing navy blue shorts and-and a pink, ah, a pink like, uh, tank top.*

Columbus Police: Pink tank top, ok, navy blue shorts. Has she ever tried to sneak out of the house before, uh?

Marcia: *Oh no, what are you implying?*

Columbus Police: Oh, just that, do you think perhaps someone doesn't want you to know they came by and picked her up or something....

Marcia: *No, she does not cheat on me.*

Columbus Police: Have you guys been receiving any weird phone calls, anything like that, somebody hanging around outside the house?

Marcia: *No. We got home late from, uh, a baseball game, you know about seven-thirty last night, we took showers and went to bed.*

I was in the living room watching the Indians game, and then half of a movie around midnight and I fell asleep, and I never heard anything, and I was like, just on the other side of the wall from her, in the den.

Columbus Police: Ok, and what's your birth date?

Marcia: *Why do you need that?*

Columbus Police: This is just for the report

Marcia: *July 5th, 1960*

Columbus Police: Ok, so you're not having any family issues anything like that?

Marcia: *No.*

Columbus Police: Ok, and you haven't noticed anybody hanging out in front of your house?

Marcia: *No.*

Columbus Police: Alright, we've got a couple of Officers on the way, I want you to stay there in the house.

Marcia: *I will.*

Columbus Police: Ok

Marcia: *Bye, bye...jerk.*

Marcia wasn't totally truthful with the Police, but she couldn't tell them about the banging and pounding on the doors and walls and what happened in the woods. No one would believe her.

Marcia made certain the porch light was on and then poured herself a drink and then paced the floor rehearsing what she was going to tell the Police when they arrive.

9
Starting All Over

Lancaster, Ohio

Amy heard the shower running and called for Jerry, saying...

"I hope you are going to save me some hot water?"

When Jerry didn't answer Amy went upstairs to talk to Jerry. Amy went to the bathroom, saying...

"Hey Jer, did you hear me, I said save me some hot water."

Still there was no answer from Jerry, as red flags were going off in Amy's head especially when she did not see a silhouette of Jerry in the shower, so Amy opened the shower door, the shower was running, but Jerry was not in there.

Amy felt a cold chill run across her neck as she jumped turning and looking around as the bath room door was slowly closing, Amy assuming it was Jerry messing with her, went into the bed room and then the other rooms upstairs, but Jerry was nowhere to be found.

Amy searched the downstairs and then went to the carport to see if Jerry's truck was there and it was. Amy looked inside the truck and then raised the carport garage door, but still no Jerry.

Amy then walked back into the house calling Jerry's name, but he did not answer, so Amy picked up her cell phone to call Jerry's cell number. Jerry's cell number rang, and Amy heard the voice of someone she did not recognize on the phone saying...

"Startin' All Over, bet you can't find Jerry, Startin' All Over, wait and see, you're next.

Amy stood in her living room dazed and confused as to where Jerry was and the meaning of the message she'd heard, but more over...where was Jerry?

Amy started to call Jerry's sister, Amber, when suddenly a strange feeling came over her and before she knew it, she was sitting in the car with Jerry on their way home from Columbus.

Amy looked over at Jerry and pinched his arm to make sure she wasn't dreaming or in a nutty nightmare.

Jerry put the windshield wipers on the fastest setting and looking at Amy he said...

"Okay, and just what was that for?"

Amy ignored Jerry and glanced over her left shoulder towards the back seat saying...

"Jer, what are we doing?"

Jerry turned up the cars window defrost saying...

"Uh...unless I'm in a cartoon or something, we are headed home, what do you think we're doing?"

Amy reached in the glove compartment and pulled out her service revolver and after checking it, placed it in her lap saying...

"We are not supposed to be doing this Jer...we've done this before."

Not knowing what Amy was talking about Jerry replied...

"Yeah, I know, the next time we meet Reggie and Perry for dinner, they are gonna have to come to Lancaster, so we don't have a long drive in weather like this."

Amy's coat was draped across her, as she began putting on her coat saying...

"Jer, you're not listening to me, we did this yesterday and...t-this can't be happening."

"Yesterday, what are you talking about?"

Jerry said, as he struggled with his right hand to help Amy get her arm through her coat sleeve, when Amy's voice got a little sterner, saying...

"Jer, don't you remember any of this?"

Before Amy's comment was finished Jerry yelled...

"HOLD ON!"

Jerry and Amy's car hit a large puddle of water and hydroplaned, sending their car down a ravine and coming to rest in a field and inches from a tree.

Jerry placed his hands on his head and looked over at Amy said...

"You alright babe?"

Sliding off the road and crashing into the ravine sent Amy's knee into the glove compartment box as Amy held her knee saying...

"OW! Oh, my knee, oh my God...Jer we gotta get out of here now."

Jerry tried turning on the windshield wipers as a small tree branch was lodged between the window and the wipers, saying...

"Well first I gotta get that branch from the wipers so I can see..."

Amy nervously looked around saying...

"No Jerry, that's one thing you're not going to do...fuck the branch, we gotta get out of this car."

Jerry was revving the car's engine and alternating between drive and reverse trying to get the car free, but they were stuck in the mud as Jerry said...

"Okay, that's it, we're stuck for sure; we're going to have to call for a tow truck."

Amy recalled what happened on their first encounter at this spot and pleaded with Jerry...

"Jer, please, if you really love me, for God's sake, please let's get out of this car and walk up to the road."

Jerry placed a hand on Amy's shoulder saying...

"I know we have to, but I'll climb up the hill, so the tow truck can find us? I promise I'll be extremely careful, you just sit tight here."

Jerry placed his hand on the car door lock button, and as soon as he did, the driver side door glass shattered, and Amy screamed.

"AHH"!

Jerry had shielded his face to protect it from flying glass, and as he lowered his hand, a large pair of hands reached in and grabbed Jerry pulling him through the shattered window.

Amy retrieved her gun from her coat pocket and fired five shots out the window, screaming...

"JERRY, JERRY!"

Amy heard the muffled screams of Jerry before hearing a blood-curdling sound and then gaging and then nothing but the rain.

Knowing what was going to take place, Amy struggled to get the door open, but was unable to. Realizing that she only had three shots left,

Amy fired a shot through the passenger-side window, shattering it and then climbed out.

Hearing a large thud hit the ground, Amy knew that it was Jerry, and as she lay down looking under the car she could see someone's shoes approaching from the rear of the car, so Amy jumped up and begin running.

Amy ran through the rain, and the fog until she came to an abandoned house just ahead.

She approached the rear of the house, running as fast as she could because she knew something menacing was behind her.

The bottom two steps were missing so Amy lay on her stomach and pulled herself up and took refuge behind an old table in the corner of the room.

Looking all around, and then with her eyes fixed on the door, Amy could see where she was, which was in a part of the house which had been used as some type of work area.

The strong scent of gasoline, kerosene and car parts, mixed with the cold rain was eerie and unnerving enough until Amy saw the size of the man who was chasing her, through one of the windows coming.

Suddenly, Amy heard the voice of someone saying…

"Come out, come out wherever you are I can smell your scared sweaty skin from over here, you're hiding somewhere in here, aren't you? Mmm, you are going to taste good."

Amy lay motionless, scared of being discovered because she was out of bullets and she knew the man was going to kill her.

The corner where Amy was hiding shielded her pretty well, the table was in a corner where very little light shone. Suddenly, Amy noticed the man approaching in her direction as her level of fright began to rise.

This man was extremely large, Amy knew she'd be no match for him if she had to resort to hand-to-hand fighting. Suddenly he stopped in the middle of the room, cocking his head from side-to-side.

Amy noticed that in one of his hands was an old pipe wrench, which he laid down against the door. To Amy's surprise, the man turned and walked out of the house leaving Amy to think that he was abandoning his search for her.

All the while the man was gone, Amy scanned the room looking for a way out, a place that she could run to. And then her mind shifted to Jerry and what had happened to him.

Amy wondered if the man was going back outside to cause Jerry more harm. Then Amy's mind wondered on why Jerry had no memory of being here in this situation before.

Amy spent about thirty minutes just sitting there, hoping that her heart would calm down, or trying to convince herself that all of what was happening was a dream.

Amy started to talk to herself...

"C'mon Amy slow your breathing down, don't be like those women who are hiding and breathing as hard and as noisily as they can."

Amy tried to put enough temporal distance from what 'was happening' to the edges of what 'should be happening'. The old house that Amy was in, looked as if it should've been condemned or was on the verge of falling by the next light wind.

Every blast of wind that hit the house, made every wall in the room where Amy was hiding, creak and pop. Amy thought that any moment the man would hear the wind hitting the house and think that it was her moving around in the house and find her.

Somehow Amy's suspicions came to life as the door flew open and there in the doorway stood the man, pushing a wheel barrel.

Amy at first had thought that her eyes were the work of a frightened helpless person, playing tricks on her until her eyes noticed something.

The man wasn't moving. He just stood there looking like he was posing for the fall edition of *"creepy & psychotic"* magazine. And so, Amy had no choice but to stay where she was, as long as the psycho stood there.

Amy wasn't sure how long she had been hiding there. Time in situations like that, really hammers home that it is a construction of human imagination that is in control, the imagination that is timeless. That there is no measurement, time is lifetimes pass.

Just then, the man heard a noise and picked up the wheel barrel and pushed it outside. Amy hoped that this would be the break she was looking for, so that she could escape.

She slowly and carefully got up and inched her way towards the window to see where the man pushing the wheel barrel had gone to, when she heard something growl. At first, Amy thought it must have been coming from outside, but the growl came again, and it was coming from somewhere much closer, and off to her right.

Amy looked out the window again and then turned and saw a dark shape crouching in the hallway. Amy had just enough time to wonder if a stray dog had somehow gotten inside when the thing *stood up* and rushed at her, snarling.

Amy freaked out and bolted towards the front door when she caught glimpse of something in the hallway. Over a dozen people shuffling up and down the hallway, and they're all emaciated and silent, moving and staring straight ahead in the dark, none of them looking at Amy or in her direction.

The man with the wheel barrel stood there a few feet from Amy, grunting, standing in between Amy and freedom.

Even though Amy was a Police Officer, she had a history of being paranoid, so Amy closed her eyes, and that's when the feeling of absolute horror and fear seized her.

It was unlike anything she had ever felt before. Amy couldn't even describe it, she was terrified, and couldn't move.

It was like Amy was paralyzed. A part of Amy wanted to open her eyes, even though a part of her didn't want to, there he was, standing there next to the door, watching her. Amy stood there in complete horror, unable to move, and he stood there too, stock still, but kind of shadow-y.

He shifted his feet, pushed the wheel barrel away. He was breathing hard. Amy wanted to scream or do something, but she couldn't. It felt like it lasted forever.

Finally, Amy just closed her eyes again, unable to pray she was so scared. Then there in the doorway where Amy stood creaked under her. Side-by-side, the man stood swaying and then Amy opened her eyes and the man and wheel barrel was gone.

Amy tried to convince herself that it was just a terrible hallucination, but she knew she was awake, she knew that Jerry had been killed there earlier and that she woke up with Jerry at the house. Amy knew that the whole nightmare was never going to end.

About the only thing that Amy was uncertain about, which was real, and that was...'was yesterday real or is now real?'

Amy quietly made her way back in the woods looking for Jerry. As she walked through the woods, she noticed, wheel barrel tracks leading from the house to the woods.

Stopping several hundred feet from their car, until she came across Jerry's lifeless, bloody body, laying slump against the tree.

Amy wanted to scream out loud, but she muffled her screams with her hands, and also, she knew that the man with the wheel barrel was somewhere nearby.

Amy stood over Jerry's body softly crying, when she heard her cell phone's ring tone coming from the woods not far from Jerry's body. As Amy walked about twenty feet from where Jerry's body lay, she discovered her cell phone smashed lying at the base of a tree.

Amy bent over and picked it up and while it was ringing she could barely see the caller ID because the screen was all smashed to hell.

"How could it still be working?"

Amy thought as she picked it up saying...

"Hello?"

Amy listened in astonishment as the voice said...

"Well hello Amy, hope you aren't finding all of this a little too unsettling, are you? We've got plenty in store for you so beware, oh by the way don't turn around."

Unable to see the screen because it was busted, so she asked...

"Who is this?"

The voice on the other end remained quiet, so Amy repeated herself...

"Hello, who is this?"

Amy was not the bravest soul walking the earth but asking who was calling gave her some measure of certainty, some degree of strength, even if it was short lived. Suddenly the voice softly stated...

"Turn and see Amy."

Amy turned to see but could vaguely make out her appearance. She was a tall woman, around five feet ten, wearing a dirty 'Nun's habit.' When Amy focused her eyes to look directly at her, what she saw was terrifying.

The woman levitated a few inches in the air off the ground, then she threw her head backwards and Amy heard what seemed like bones cracking and breaking as she stretched backwards. Her torso was up in the air and only her feet and hair were touching the ground.

The woman then began speaking to Amy in and old Italian dialect, which Amy should not have understood, but she was able to understand clearly the voice saying....

"La realtà che si vive, non è la realtà potrai soggiornare in" = The reality that you live in, is not the reality you will stay in."

The sight of this woman and the way she stretched her body backwards was so terrifying that Amy turned and started to run, forgetting all about Jerry, but the woman's body came back to its normal shape and as she stretched her hand towards Amy, Amy froze in her tracks, unable to move as the woman said...

"All is not as it seems, and I control what you both see and do. Your worst moments, your worst fears, I'll make you revisit them over and over and over again."

With that Amy looked around and found herself back in her house with Jerry sitting on the sofa saying...

"Hey honey, I'm going upstairs to hop in the shower."

Amy jumped from the sofa saying...

"No! No baby, you can't take a shower right now, just sit with me, hold me."
Jerry got up saying...

"What do you mean I can't take a shower, what is it, do you wanna take yours first?"
Jerry sat next to Amy saying...

"Amy, what is it, I have never seen you looking so anxious?"
Amy reached and grabbed ahold of Jerry's hands, saying as her voice broke...

"Honey, something's not right. I'm so scared, I think I'm, losing it...and, before you say this is a dream or nightmare or whatever, let me tell you that I'm completely awake and I'm not hysterical...yesterday you and I left to meet Reggie and Perry, right?"
Jerry nodded his head and said...

"Then we left, came home, and went to bed...why?"
Amy shook her head no, saying...

"Babe, yesterday we never made it home, we ran off the side of the road and into a ditch and then...
Jerry tilted his head to the right saying...

"Hold it babe, how could we have not made it home...well, tell me where the hell are we then?"
Under any other circumstances Amy was a strong woman and rarely let her emotions run rampant but the events that she was trying to get across to Jerry scared Amy down to the very core of her being.

Getting up and walking towards Jerry, he held Amy in his arms saying...

"Honey honestly, tell me what's got you so upset, I mean, how can you expect me to believe what you're saying...that can't be, I mean we are here...gosh babe, I don't know what to say."
Amy pushed Jerry away saying...

"I should've known better than to say anything, now you're looking at me like I'm 'miss losing it, two-thousand-and six'...just forget it, I'm going up for a shower, then I'm going to go to my Mother's for a while."
Jerry followed Amy as she started upstairs saying...

"Babe let's not fight, all I'm saying is..."
Amy turned cutting Jerry off saying..."

"Jerry, just save it! I mean really, I come to you with something serious and

you treat me like I'm a fucking nut-bag. All I got to say is, I would never treat you like that.

And with that, Amy marched upstairs and closed the bathroom door behind her. Jerry walked into the kitchen and removed a glass from the cabinet and then poured himself a large shot of vodka and grabbed a beer from the fridge and went and sat on the sofa, saying to himself...

"Damn...how does she expect me to react to something like that...damn!"

Jerry sat on the sofa drinking his vodka with a beer chaser and watching the Cleveland Cavilers game when Amy came downstairs and sat a bag by the front door and then walked in the kitchen.

Jerry sat quietly and then thought to himself...

"I see we got to play this game...she has her bags packed and at the front door, then she walks into the kitchen.... I mean, what is she doing taking a bottle of mustard with her. I know, I know, I'm supposed to get up and go into the kitchen and apologize to her, all I can do I guess is just listen."

Jerry got up and walked towards the kitchen when Amy met him at the doorway and said...

"Jerry, I don't wanna fight with you anymore, but you could have showed a little understanding. I know I asked you to believe something that sounds incredible, but I'm telling you the truth Jerry."

Amy walked out of the kitchen to the front door and picked up her bags and then handed them to Jerry, who instead of taking them out to the car, took them upstairs.

As Jerry climbed the last step and disappeared down the hall, Amy heard something that sounded like a lid to a pot hitting the floor and went into the kitchen to investigate.

Amy was not prepared for what she would see. Standing by the fridge eating a turkey leg, with chunks of turkey falling from her mouth, was The Nun, Sister Mary Jacalyn in an old dirty 'habit'.

Amy started to scream but The Nun was too fast for Amy and covered her mouth before Amy could make a sound.

The Nun removed her hand from Amy, and when she did, it looked as if Amy's mouth was glued shut, as Sister Mary Jacalyn said...

"That's a good girl, you try to scream and I'm gonna have to shove something

in your mouth to shut you up, or better yet, I may sew it up. Now listen, we're about to have some fun.

Poor Jerry doesn't have a clue, but I'll tell you what...by the time I'm through with him, he'll more than believe...hell, he might even subscribe to our monthly magazine."

Amy stood shaking, as urine ran down her leg as she looked at the Sister Mary Jacalyn, struggling to talk, Sister Mary Jacalyn said...

"Aww, what's a matter, care for a bite?"

The Nun got real close to Amy and after taking a bite of the turkey leg which was covered with maggots, pushed it up to Amy's mouth saying...

"Care for a bite you'd be surprised what people will throw away, I had to dig way down in the bottom of the dumpster for this."

Not hearing what had just transpired, Jerry called downstairs saying...

"Hey babe, do you mind bringing me something to eat on your way out?"

Jerry waited a few moments and when he heard no response came downstairs and walked towards the kitchen, when Sister Mary Jacalyn said...

"I think I better go now remember what I said, get ready because we're going to have some funnnn."

Jerry entered the kitchen and was surprised to see Amy standing in the middle of the room with a turkey, lettuce and tomato sandwich, hanging from her mouth, saying...

"Hey you okay? Didn't you hear me, I wanted something to eat, anyway, I hope that isn't my sandwich in your mouth?"

Amy took the sandwich from her mouth and laid it on the kitchen counter saying...

"That's it! I can't take this creepy ass shit anymore."

Jerry thought a minute and walked over and blocked Amy saying...

"Whoa babe, I thought we had all of this worked out...what's going on now?"

Amy stood there with her hands on her hips saying...

"You don't have to be so fucking sarcastic, it isn't going to matter and you're not going to believe me anyways."

Jerry followed Amy into the living room saying...

"I'm sorry if I sounded that way, but I don't know what to say...talk to me Amy.""

Amy sat down on the sofa crying, and after a few minutes said...

"Jer, there are some kind of ghosts or spirits in this house and you don't believe me...I got to get out of here."

Jerry got up to get another beer from the fridge saying...

"Okay my badd...tell me what happened, and why didn't you call out for me when whatever it was, was here?"

Amy started biting her nails, saying...

"That creepy Nun said if I said anything, she was going to do something to shut me up, and then she said you and I were going to experience things far beyond our imagination, and then she disappeared."

Amy walked over to Jerry crying and then sat next to him saying...

"Jer, I'm really scared. The only way that you're going to believe me is for you to see her, and that means that I will have to see her again, and I don't want to anything to do with her."

Jerry took all the sarcasm out of his tone saying...

"If you're telling me the truth, then we'd better keep all the lights on and you said that reading scriptures and praying and stuff keeps all that shit away...right?"

Amy got up and paced the floor and then sat back down and said...

"I used to think that- that kept away evil and ghosts and stuff like that... but I guess I grew up.

Once when I was around eight or ten, I can't remember which, but I was with my mother at her grandmother's house while she was helping granny because she had fallen and broke her hip, I saw something spooky.

I didn't believe in ghosts or ghouls and things like that, but what I saw that night changed my whole thinking about it. I was exploring my great grandmothers house, while my mother was getting her ready for bed when I saw something strange, 'there was a hole in the ceiling and I swear someone was peeking through it at me.'

Through that hole I could see an eyeball moving every time I moved, I was frozen stiff with fear, and then I thought that, 'someone is up there'.

"I ran and told my mother and grandmother that someone is upstairs in the attic. My grandmother grabbed my hand and said...leave them be, you're not supposed to be up there messing around anyways."

I had so many goose bumps, and suddenly I felt so cold. Anyways, we put her to bed and then after eating supper my mom and I watched television and then we went to bed. I wanted to sleep in my mom's bed, but I knew she'd tell me that I was too old for ghosts and goblins and that's not what a good Catholic girl thinks about.

About an hour after getting into bed everything was silent, but then I heard this sound coming from above my bed. I closed my eyes and then pulled the blanket over my head, but I could still hear the sound.

It was a dragging sound, like someone pulling something really heavy across the floor.

After waiting awhile, I had to go pee, but by then I managed to work up the courage to get out of bed and turn on the light and walk to the bathroom.

My grandmother was asleep downstairs, and I started hearing this noise again coming from up in the attic. As I sat on the toilet, I heard something ripping like paper being torn, and so I looked up and there in the ceiling was a hole and someone peeking at me, as clear as day.

Then I heard voices saying...Shhh, be quiet, she might see us."

Jerry appeared to be really interested in what Amy was saying, and so he asked...

"Did you guys find out what was making the noise, and who was in the attic?"

Placing a pillow on her lap after crossing her legs, Amy said...

"No! I crept into my mama's room, but she was snoring loud, so I went downstairs to see if grandma was awake and when I got down there she was not on the sofa at all.

All that night we wondered where could that old lady have gone to with a broken hip, and if she somehow crawled up to the attic."

Several years later, my grandmother died and then Mom passed away last year, and a realtor recently called. She said that the couple who bought the house had begged to speak with me about some of the stuff that's been going on there. Forget it, I said...their house...their worries."

Jerry sat close to Amy and said...

"Wow babe, this is the first I've heard of this, no wonder you are freaked

*out over this, but you were little then, besides you don't think that has anything
to do with right now, do you?".*"

Jerry hugged Amy as the house began shaking, and then there was
an eerie wind which filled the house and Amy screamed as glass from
the kitchen began bursting and smashing out of the cabinets against
the walls.

Amy grabbed onto Jerry's arm, while Jerry jumped up and pulled
Amy and then without warning or anything Jerry began pulling Amy
towards the garage and into the car.

Amy resisted because she knew once they were in the car the
nightmare would start, but it was too late, they were back in the car
and driving down thirty-three south, away from Columbus heading
for Lancaster.

Whether or not Jerry knew, but Amy did. She knew that the route
that they were on was taking them to certain death, a death which
would go on and on and on. Amy looked in every direction and then
screamed as Jerry's car slid off the highway and down into a ditch.

Dazed and crying, Amy knew that a big man wearing a tutu and a
mask would pull Jerry from the car, kill him and then come after her.

Amy knew she and Jerry were going to die just as they did twenty-
four hours ago, but something inside of her said…

"I-I gotta change something, anything, so that we make it out of here alive."

Before Amy could do anything else, they were off the road and
down in a ditch and in a lot of dense brush.

The vapors from the radiator and the wind which blew the rains
sideways, made Amy so scared till she began screaming. Jerry sat holding
his head and Amy was nursing her knee which had banged into the
glove compartment box.

Amy snapped saying…

"Jerry, Jerry we got to get out of here, Jerry can you hear me!"

Dazed and confused Jerry looked at Amy saying…

"Oh…babe, are you okay?"

Amy began pulling on Jerry's arm and struggling to get her side of
the car door open saying…

"I'm okay, but we gotta get out of here now Jer."

Jerry started jerking away from Amy saying…

"Hey, calm down... we're not going anywhere, let me catch my breath, will ya?"

Amy again grabbed Jerry's arm saying...

"If we don't go now Jer, we're not going to be breathing because we won't have any fucking breath left."

Jerry made a move to come to Amy's side of the car when something smashed the driver's side window, shattering it.

Amy screamed and as she did she quickly said to herself...

"I can't believe I'm screaming at this stupid ass window...I knew it was going to get smashed and I'm still screaming, boy, I need some medication."

That thought had no longer left Amy's head when the glass burst again, and Amy saw Jerry being dragged through the window.

Amy knew what was coming and managed to get her window down and climbed out of the window and out onto the muddy ground.

Just then Amy screamed as someone had its hands around her neck. Amy broke loose of the persons hand and tried running, when she slipped and fell on top of Jerry's lifeless body.

Amy tried looking down at Jerry's body, but the rain and the darkness made it literally impossible to do so.

Amy screamed again and that's when someone or something caught Amy by the hair and began pulling upwards off the ground.

Amy tried twisting and struggling and that's when she saw who it was that held her. It was the very large man in a Ballerina's Tutu and a doll's mask.

Amy's two hands were free, and she tried with all her might to scratch and beat on the man's arm when he reached down and grabbed Amy's throat with his other hand and slammed Amy hard onto the ground.

It was obvious that by the way the man was dressed he had some sort of mental issue, not to mention that he was out in the middle of the night in a storm hurting people.

The man in the Ballerina's Tutu, picked up Amy's body and slammed her against the ground repeatedly...laughing as her body made contact the muddy ground.

Amy barely regained her senses after what seemed like an eternity of being smashed to the ground and that's when she found herself inside a wheel barrel, aching from every part of her body as well as suffering what seemed like a broken back.

Grabbing her head Amy knew she would never walk or get away from this man without any help, so she started screaming again, until the man bent down to the ground and scooped up a large handful of mud, leaves and god knows what, and began shoving it down Amy's throat.

Amy's screams were muffled as the big man in Ballerina's tutu, massaged her throat forcing the pile of mud, leaves and bugs down her throat, making Amy gag.

Even though Amy knew what was going to happen to her, she was powerless to stop the big man. One minute she was there in the wheel barrel assured of certain death and the next second, she was back at work at her counter.

Somehow, she was going in and out from one place to another, from one reality to another.

Sheer panic, frustration and fright, which began to show on Amy's face as she laid her head on the counter, hoping that Reggie would come over inquiring.

Every time Reggie took a step in Amy's direction, Amy would find herself back in the car with Jerry or tied up in the wheel barrel, going through some unimaginable horror at the hands of the big man in the Ballerina's Tutu.

The big man in the Ballerina's Tutu told Amy that she would continue to bounce in and out of different realities as long as Sister Mary Jacalyn willed it.

Polaris

Tim sat next to Mary, rubbing the back of her neck, and saying to David…

"Dave, you know this is some messed up stuff, I mean look at this shit, this is two thousand and six, stuff like this isn't supposed to be happening…this is television movie shit.

Tim, David, Mary, Deanne, Kristin, Wendi and Steve each appeared at David and Deanne's condo in Columbus. Each had no recollection of driving there, they just suddenly appeared.

David walked into the living room asking...

"Deanne, you wanna help me with the drinks and food in the kitchen?"

Deanne stood up and walked into the kitchen saying...

"Okay babe, we've got plenty to make sandwiches, but I can make something else."

While Deanne was making sandwiches, David walked back into the living room with a six pack of sodas and water and after sitting it on the table said...

"Okay people, we are going to have to talk about what just happened."

Steve walked over and grabbed a soda saying...

"Did you just say...'what happened'? Well here's a news flash Dave, demons and spirits are what happened, and I don't think talking with them is a good idea...because people in movies always make that mistake.

Dave, you can't talk or have a conversation with a dead person, they tend to fuck you up on a whole new level."

David backed out of the kitchen saying...

"Well I'm not going to sit here and let them do whatever they want, whenever they want...that's stupid."

Just then Deanne yelled in the living room to David asking...

"Honey what are you talking about, I didn't hear you?"

Raising his hand to signify 'hold on' to Deanne, David said...

"You tell me Steve, what are we supposed to do...huh?"

Steve reached in the cabinet and grabbed the fifth of vodka saying...

"People want to see angels, not demons. When you see an angel, you get to relax and dream and sleep...when you see demons your whole day is messed up.

All I'm saying Dave is, we can pray, hold hands, roast marshmallows and sing Kumbaya and whatever, but talking to a dead person or spirit is out of the question."

At that moment Tim walked over saying...

"All I know is, this conversation is getting way too weird. All the stuff that happened to us, I mean there has to be a rational explanation...right?"

David picked up a glass and held it to Steve, as he poured him a shot of vodka saying...

"*Wake up people, when was the last time creepy ass shit like this happened outside of a movie...you all know this is real?*"

Steve placed his hand on top of David's shoulder saying...

"*C'mon Dave, real or not, fucking around with this kind of shit, opens up a whole new level of 'scared shitless' don't cha think, I mean, what are we supposed to do, invite the spirits or pissed off dead people over for a drink and dinner and then ask them to leave us the fuck alone?*"

Looking back over at Steve, David said...

"*You're laughing, but that is exactly what we have to do...starting with that old creepy looking Nun.*"

Just at that moment, Deanne called for David to come to the kitchen, saying... "*I got your sandwich ready.*"

Walking in the kitchen, David looked at the sandwich sitting on a paper towel on a plate on the table and Deanne sitting.

Taking a sip of water, to wash her sandwich down, Deanne said...

"*Blue, c'mon now, don't start this weird ghost, creepy little people shit up again, I'm really not in the mood.*"

David walked in the living room with Deanne following him saying...

"*Blue, you asked what about who's sandwiches...do you see anyone here?*"

Looking all around the living room, David said...

"*Deanne, I'm not tripping, Tim, Mary, Kristin, Wendi and Steve are here, they're right here, look.*"

David took Deanne's arm and pulling her to the door and said...

"*Now see...who's that then?*"

When Deanne and David looked into the living room, there was no one there, and David said...

"*Aww, c'mon, somebody's playing a sick joke on me...Hey, Tim, Steve... stop fucking around.*"

Deanne sat the rest of her sandwich down and walked up to David saying...

"*Blue what is it, do you need to go to the VA...I can take you to Dayton or Cincinnati?*"

"*No, No! I- OMG, this can't be happening again, Tim, Mary, Kristin, Steve and Wendi were sitting right there.*"

David said shakenly, as Deanne handed David a Seroquel and suggested he go upstairs and lay down.

David went into the bedroom and grabbed fresh underwear, socks, a tee shirt and a pair of jeans from the closet and laid them on the chair in the bathroom and went to sit on the bed until his bath water was ready.

Not long after David sat on the bed Deanne came and sat next to him saying…

"Blue I'm not trying to cause any more stress on you or anything but, Blue, every time you start talking about people disappearing and voices and seeing creepy kids or old ladies, it just makes me wonder if you're really well, if they should've discharged you from the hospital so soon."

David sat quietly, cracking his knuckles and then he slowly lifted his eyes and said…

"Deanne, just yesterday you not only believed in everything that I was saying, but you were there, you were experiencing everything I was and now, you act like nothing happened and that you can't remember any of it, so now, I am the one who's a car missing a tire."

Deanne started to respond but David cut her off saying…

"Hold that thought Deanne, I gotta turn my bath water off."

Whether or not it was a string of coincidences or not, but by the time David got back to the bed room Deanne was on the phone with someone, and David waved and walked in and got in the tub.

David lay in the tub soaking and thinking about what was happening and if there was any way to bring an end to all this madness, when suddenly and without David knowing it, the hot water valve began turning and squeaking.

The bath room was full of steam until David could not see but a few inches in front of him.

David frantically started searching for the handles to turn off the hot water and turn on the cold, because David's body was burning under the heat of the hot water.

David not only was burning under the intense temperature of the scalding hot water, but David started feeling icy cold hands pushing and holding his body down in the tub.

David started kicking his feet wildly, as his shoulders were suddenly pinned against the bottom of the tub and a few more minutes and David would surely drown.

David began calling out for Deanne, hoping that she would hurry and open the bathroom door and let all the steam out and help him.

David was also thinking not only would Deanne save him from drowning, but she would also see that it was not David's mind playing tricks on him, but that there was something...something very evil in their home.

As the water started rising higher and higher, David faintly heard Deanne's voice calling for him, then he tried with all his might and lifted his head and hollered for Deanne.

David could no longer hold his head up and began swallowing bath water through his nose. David finally thought it was all over, his head sank down in the tub and his once strong grip on the side of the bath tub, was now simply resting.

Everything was still and silent. David's eyes were fixed and still. The frantic splashing of David's feet in the water, rested calmly and lifeless against the water knobs.

Just then, small bubbles from around David's mouth, and nose multiplied, and his eyes shut tight, and David came up out of the water, coughing and gasping for air.

Then suddenly as if it were choreographed, the door opened and there was Deanne, with her cell phone, covering it up with it pressed against her ear, saying...

"Blue look at all the water you got on the floor...gosh, make sure you pick up the rugs from the floor and hang them outside please?"

David struggled to catch his breath and once he did, he said to Deanne before she left the bathroom...

"Babe, I was almost killed a few minutes ago."

Deanne ended her call with her cousin and turned to David saying...

"Say what?"

David climbed out of the bathtub, and after drying himself off and putting on under wear, socks, t-shirt and jeans followed Deanne in the bed room saying...

"Deanne, baby, I don't think you understand...I was sitting in the tub just soaking and then suddenly, the hot water handle started turning on and I know it sounds weird, but something held me down and I almost drowned."

Deanne sat on the bed, and looking at David said...

"Or maybe you fell asleep and left the water running. Damn Blue, you just insist on taking me down this funky-ass road, don't you? Well I got news for you Blue, I'm not going there with you, your doctors said if you have any problems to contact them.

Blue, I don't mean to sound cold and heartless baby, but you got a whole lot of issues and you need help."

Slamming his fist hard down on the night stand table, David said...

"This can't be happening again, it can't."

Deanne stood at the top of the stairs shaking her head and watching David as he turned to go to the bedroom.

David sat down on the bed murmuring to himself saying...

"This has got to end, I can't keep going through this shit; Deanne is one second from having me committed back in the hospital, and it's all that creepy ass Nun's fault...bitch!"

David grabbed his watch and necklace from on top of the jewelry box and put them on. Not looking at anything, just doing the kind of thing a person does, his eyes were drawn to the walk-in closet.

Suddenly, his clothes which were hanging in the closet begin moving, as a pair of hands parted his clothes, and out walked Sister Mary Jacalyn, saying...

"Oh, so now I'm a bitch huh? I was going to take it easy on you, but now I'm going to take you on one helluva ride. A person ought to know better than to mess with a Catholic Nun, especially a dead nasty bitch like me."

David looked at the door-way where Deanne was and then back at Sister Mary Jacalyn who had moved closer to him, as he said...

"Who are you, and why are you doing this to me?"

Sister Mary Jacalyn stood in front of David shaking her head from side to side and pointing her finger at David saying...

"I'm doing this because I can, and there's nothing you can do about it, and since you called me a bitch, I got something special in store for you."

Deanne walked up to David and stood looking at him, not saying anything, when David asked...

"What? What did I do?"

Deanne gently pushed past David and stood on her side of the bathroom vanity and began brushing her teeth and washing her face, while Deanne stood preparing herself for bed.

David could not take his eyes off Deanne. He could not stop looking at the pretty shape of her legs and her feet and how her small firm round ass looked so good to him.

Deanne lifted her head slightly and turned, catching David staring at her body when she said...

"I don't know about you, but it's crappy outside, and even though I'm pissed at you, I need you to make love to me all night, but I'm not going to wait on you forever, so no more creepy shit."

David hurried past Deanne forgetting about his encounter with Sister Mary Jacalyn and gathered his bed things and went back in the bathroom where Deanne was just finishing up, and softly tapped Deanne's ass as he went to his side of the basin, saying...

"Hey babe, no problem I'm just going to brush my teeth and use a little mouth rinse and then you'd better have the Police on call, because what I'm going to do to you is going to be a crime."

Deanne turned and walked out of the bathroom into the bedroom with David slowly and closely behind her.

Deanne slowed her sexy walk down allowing David's body to rub up against her from behind, as David leaned over kissing the back of her neck and removing her clothes from behind.

Deanne bent down on the bed pulling back the comforter and sheet, switching and grinding her ass against David's body, until he gently guided her onto the bed and licking her body, starting with her feet and moving upwards.

Deanne stopped as she reached the middle of the bed, pulling David's shirt off and unbuckling his pants.

David climbed on top of Deanne as their bodies molded steamily into one. As their bodies announced the climax soon to come, David and Deanne begin kissing one another with kisses so sensual, Picasso would have a hard time sculpting them.

As David entered inside of Deanne her finger nails found their way into David's back, as both of them let out screams of shared passion, but David screamed even louder as Deanne's nails dug deeper and deeper into his back, causing deep wounds and blood to trickle from the wounds.

Just as David hollered for Deanne to stop, Deanne began laughing and that's when David realized that something was very wrong. Deanne had never been a violent person nor was she prone to outburst of any kind, so when David heard her laughing, he knew it wasn't like Deanne, as a matter of fact it wasn't like Deanne at all.

David pushed back onto the bed and when he glanced into Deanne's eyes, he yelled...

"AWWW!"

With his left hand grasping his forehead, David sat looking in terror at what was lying on the bed next to him, at what he had just passionately kissed, at whom he made love to...

David yelled out loud...

"This-this can't be. What in the world is going on...it can't be happening again, oh my God!"

In frustration, David began kicking the bed with his feet and with balled up fist, swinging in the air, screaming...

"Aaarrrggghhh...fuck!"

With that being uttered, David sat on the edge of the bed with his hands in his face, covering his mouth.

David was so carried away with grief that he did not hear nor see, the bed covers part between his legs and Sister Mary Jacalyn appear from under them.

David was uttering a combination of screams, cursing and cries, when Sister Mary Jacalyn stood against the wall and said...

"There's no sense in carrying on like that your misery is just beginning."

David pulled himself together and turned to look at The Nun who had a smirk on her face as David said...

"Oh my God.... what did I do...oh my God...?"

Sister Mary Jacalyn shrugged her head and said...

"Just think, you're much sicker than I thought, and what do think Deanne's gonna say when she sees those scratch marks on your back?"

David looked at her and tried to make himself speak to The Nun, to get her to leave him alone, saying...

"I mean y-you're a Nun, you're supposed to be good, nuns can't torture and kill people."

Sister Mary Jacalyn walked closer to David saying...

"You got something there but I'm dead, you stupid fuck, but you'd never know by the way you were kissing and making love to me."

David jumped up out of bed and begin wiping his lips and trying to catch his breath, when, the bedroom door opened, and Deanne stood there saying...

"I am not getting up all of that water off the bathroom floor, besides are you in here talking to yourself again?"

David turned around, looking at the place where The Nun was, saying...

"I was getting ready to clean it up when...

Deanne walked out and over to her dresser and came back interrupting David saying...

"Blue, you're standing in the middle of the bedroom talking to yourself, and what the f**ck is that?"

Deanne walked up to David's back pointing to the scratches on his back, as David arched his back and tried to position himself in the mirror to see them, saying...

"Babe, I'm not going to try to explain this, because if I do, all you're going to do is call me a liar and say that I was with someone else."

Deanne got into David's face angrily, saying...

"Oh, hell no, you're going to explain this shit. So, who the hell is she Blue, was it Mary?"

Rarely did David get angry at Deanne, but this time he yelled at Deanne saying...

"Shit Deanne, I've been going through shit all day, and every time I try to *tell you about it, you go… 'it's my meds, or I'm having a dream or nightmare or some bullshit like that…I'm trying to tell you that there is creepy ass Nun in here."*

"You see, you see, why I go there Blue, you keep coming up with ghost and now a Nun…fuck you Blue!"

Deanne snapped, as she picked up a pillow and slapped David with it upside his head."

Grabbing the pillow and snatching it from Deanne, David yelled…

"Deanne, yesterday you, me, Mary, Tim, Steve and Wendi and some other people we don't even know, were at the farm, tied up in the basement and we were being tortured by some big ass man in a Ballerina's Tutu and Mr. Thomas…

"We were at the farm in Port Clinton yesterday? Blue, I was working yesterday."

Deanne shouted back as David drew close to Deanne trying to hug her, as she said…

"No Blue, no, I'm pissed as hell at you, now don't try to get all up in my grill. How the hell can you say that, knowing that I worked yesterday, you knew that before you said it."

David sat down and pleaded with Deanne to listen to him, saying…

"Babe, don't you see how much sense that makes. Yes, I knew you were working, but I also know that you and I went to the farm in Port Clinton to look for Mary."

"To look for Mary, what does Mary have to do with anything, shit Blue, she lives in Madison, Wisconsin?"

David reached out his hand to help Deanne sit, saying…

"Babe, I know this…you don't remember this but, we were watching a movie when suddenly Mary appeared on the screen, crying for our help, and she was at the farm, so we went there to help here."

David grasped Deanne hand as Deanne said…

"Blue, I don't wanna hear about some damn spooks and goblins story, I wanna know why you have fuck scratches on your back. Blue stop trying to change the subject, you have four finger nail scrapes on both sides of your back…. that's what I wanna hear about."

Deanne jerked lose from David and stood up as David said…

"Babe, if you don't believe what I'm saying, then there is no use in us trying to talk about anything…if you don't believe me or at least hear what I'm trying to tell you."

Deanne looked at David intensely, saying…

"Why is it that, when we're about to get into something serious, you come up with this spirit, ghost shit...or there's someone creepy in the house shit.

Damn Blue, everybody has something creepy in their house, but this time, it's you whose acting creepy. So, about those scratches on your back... let's start there.

Its Mary again isn't it?"

David stood for a moment looking at Deanne without saying a word, when Deanne jumped up from the bed and walked out the room heading down stairs. David thought about following Deanne, but he knew it would be better to give her some time to cool off.

David sat on the bed trying to come up with something he could say to make Deanne believe him, when he walked into the bathroom to clean up the water which all over the floor.

Deanne walked into the bathroom as David was wiping up the last bit of water from the floor saying...

"Blue, we've been together for over twelve years and I forgave and forgot about you and Mary cheating on me, but....you're still talking about Mary being in Port Clinton, and you got 'guck scratch marks' on your back!"

David rang out the last towel and placed it in the dirty clothes hamper, saying...

"Aww shit! What do you want me to say...Deanne, all I can say is, I haven't been with anyone but you and there is a spirit in here that made these marks on me."

Deanne turned her head to David, yelling...

"Ooh let me guess...you fucked a spirit thinking it was me, right?"

Thinking Deanne's sarcasm was way out of line, and knowing that it was not worth getting into it, David said...

"I'm not saying another word, if you don't want to listen or believe what I'm saying, then, pack your bags and leave or I'll leave whatever."

Deanne shook her head in disgust and after putting her sweater on, said...

"Oh, fuck no! You don't get off that easy, I've invested twelve and a half years in us...you just don't brush shit off like that, no we're gonna finish this shit if it takes all night."

David stood looking at Deanne, not knowing what to do or say, when he said...

"You're right, twelve and half years is a lot of time to disregard. I will agree to sit and talk with you, but on one condition."

Deanne was about to respond to David when she was interrupted by the sound of footsteps in the hallway and the pounding on the bedroom walls.

David jumped up and went over to Deanne, as she looked all around the room saying...

"Blue...Blue, what the hell is that?"

Just then one of the pictures on the wall fell off, crashing to the floor and breaking as Deanne let out a scream...

"AAAAH!"

Just then the bedroom door slammed shut. Deanne grabbed David and nervously began crying...

"Oh my God-oh my God! Blue, what's happening?"

Putting his arms around Deanne, David walked her over to the bed where they huddled for a moment. David immediately whispered...

"Thank you, God...thank you God."

Looking at David with a puzzled look, Deanne asked...

"What is that all about?"

David looked Deanne in the eye and said...

"Just a few seconds ago you didn't believe me when I said spirits were in here and now you'll see that I was telling the truth."

Deanne laid her head into David's chest crying softly...

"Oh Blue..."

To make sure that he wasn't going to be tricked again, David pushed Deanne away slightly and said to himself...

"If Deanne tries to kiss me or anything like that, I'm not falling for it, it might be that creepy ass Nun again."

Then there was a pounding on the bedroom door, and a voice saying...

""Little Piggies, little Piggies, open up and let me in."

David's eyes scanned the bedroom to where he kept his gun as Deanne screamed...

"What the hell is this Blue!"

Again, there was pounding on the bedroom door, and the voice cried louder...

ittle Piggies, little Piggies, let me in if you don't, then I'll huff, and I'll puff, and I'll knock this damn door off its hinges and get you anyway!"

Locating the gun just under the bed on David's side of the bed, Deanne started stomping both her feet on the floor in a panicking state, and screaming…

"Oh fuck, we're gonna die, we're gonna die, we're gonna die!"

David found his way back over to Deanne, and got in front of her and pointing the gun at the door, said…

"I don't know who you are and what you want, but you can puff your ass through this door all you want, and the only thing you're gonna get is shot the hell up!"

When David had said this, the voice from the other side of the door said…

"David Blue, David Blue you know who I am, and what I want is the both of you!"

Deanne became more hysterical as David, chambered a bullet saying…

"Get the hell out of here and leave us alone…we're tired of your shit."

With that the door knob began jiggling, not opening, just jiggling left and right very quickly. David fired three shots through the bedroom door, and then the door knob stopped jiggling and there was silence.

Whether it was the noise of the gun firing being so close to Deanne or not, but she was quiet as the dead, when David said to her…

"This is what I've been trying to tell you Deanne, there is a spirit, a spooky ass Nun who has been messing with us, only I'm the only one who remembers anything."

Deanne stood shaking her head from left to right hysterically saying…

"No Blue! This can't be for real…what do we do?"

David replied as he slowly pushed away from Deanne saying…

"Baby, we're going to have to open the door and see what's what…we just can't sit here all day locked in the bedroom, if we're going to get out of here…we have to open the door."

As David made a move towards the door, Deanne grabbed tight to David's arm crying...

"We don't have to go anywhere, we can stay in here until someone comes for us."

Looking at Deanne, and keeping the door in sight David said...

"Babe, we got to get out of here. No one's coming for us, because no one knows we're in here...or that we need help."

Deanne began to calm down a little more as David began pulling away from her grip when the bedroom door handle began jiggling again and someone was pounding loudly on it.

Deanne cried out to David...

"Blue! The door's opening!"

Through the door came the Nun in a dirty habit saying...

"You two should know better than to miss confession it's not going to look good on your damn resume hehehe"

Deanne screamed, as her and David began backing up against the wall, all the while David had his gun trained on her saying...

"Now, I'm sick and tired of this shit, take one more step and I'm going to drop your old Mother Inferior ass right where you stand."

Sister Mary Jacalyn continued coming towards David and Deanne with an old large ruler in her hand. David fired his gun at her, hitting her with every bullet, in the head.

The Nun was suddenly in front of David smacking him upside the head with the ruler, saying...

"Don't call me that name, I'm the real deal I'm Sister Mary Jacalyn, ass hole, and you two are vexing the shit out of me and trying my last fucking nerve."

With that, Sister Mary Jacalyn grabbed David by the neck and flung him on the other side of the room, and then went towards Deanne saying...

""'But, grandmother, what large hands you have!'

'All the better to get at you with.'

'Oh! but, grandmother, what a terrible big mouth you have!' ...'All the better to eat you!'

Suddenly, Sister Mary Jacalyn started laughing and said, as Deanne looked on frightfully...

"You know, I've always wanted to say that line to someone hehehe!"

Deanne calmed herself down, and looked over at David who was laying on the floor, still unconscious, saying...

"W-who are you; what do you want with us?"

Sister Mary Jacalyn cocked her head once to the left and said...

"Damn are you deaf, now as to what do I want um, you really don't want to know"

Sister Mary Jacalyn interrupted herself, while looking over at David, who still lay unconscious on the floor saying...

"Well, should I say, poor ole David over there should've figured this out a long time ago, but I always did give more credit to ass holes than they deserve.

Sister Mary Jacalyn took a step in David's direction when Deanne jumped in the middle of them, begging...

"Please don't...if you're going to hurt anyone, hurt me instead...please?"

Sister Mary Jacalyn stopped in her tracks and then waved her arm as furniture overturned, and dishes smashed against the wall, and then with a grim face said...

"You see, that is what pisses me off, just when I'm ready to fuck somebody up, someone has to intervene and play the hero everybody, somewhere has an ass kicking coming, and today happens to be his day and yours."

Deanne slowly sat down next to David, and began caressing his face, saying...

"I-I-don't understand what you mean... Everyone's not bad, I mean I'm not saying that I'm a saint or anything..."

As Deanne was trying to finish her statement, Sister Mary Jacalyn interrupted her saying...

"Good, because if you said that you were, I was about to come over there and slap you silly!"

David started moaning and showing signs of coming around, as Deanne said to Sister Mary Jacalyn...

"Can you tell me what I can do to correct whatever, to make everything right. I'm a good Christian and I'm just trying to live my life the best I can?"

Sister Mary Jacalyn stood near the bed and placed her hands on her head, and began banging her head into the bed post, saying...

"Now what does that have to do with anything! Do you honestly think that by saying you're a Christian, or I go to church and I do good, that it makes everything alright, that it means something?

Deanne felt David attempting to rise to his feet as she helped him stand saying...

"Blue, oh Blue I'm so glad you're alright."

Sister Mary Jacalyn positioned herself in front of David and Deanne, and began mocking Deanne saying...

"OH BLUE, I'M SO GLAD THAT YOU'RE ALRIGHT."

David turned his attention to Sister Mary Jacalyn and then back to Deanne saying...

"Deanne what's going on and where the heck did she come from?"

Sister Mary Jacalyn sashayed over to David saying...

"Oh, come on lover boy don't tell me that you forgot momma, well after tonight you'll never forget me?"

Deanne attempted to interrupt Sister Mary Jacalyn, when she grabbed Deanne by the neck and said...

"Don't you ever interrupt me again!"

And with that, Deanne flew across the sofa backwards and hit hard against the wall.

David started to rush over to Deanne when Sister Mary Jacalyn grabbed David from behind hugging & kissing him saying...

"Aww, come on lover boy, you loved me once, come on all I want is a wet sloppy kiss and some of this chocolate, long hard business in your pants."

David struggled, and resisted Sister Mary Jacalyn, until he broke free, saying...

"Get the hell off me, you damn sick ass fuck!"

Sister Mary Jacalyn stood there sensuously licking her lips and rolling her tongue across her lips, saying...

"Ooh look at who's trying to be Mr. bad ass, you just wait, before the night's over I'm going to have you doing what I say, when I say, and for as long as I say, and there isn't anything you can do about it"

Deanne picked herself up from the floor and with that, she also grabbed the gun which David dropped, and she was now staring at Sister Mary Jacalyn, saying...

"Look bitch, I'm scared, tired and most importantly, I'm fucking pissed off...now get out of our house and leave us the fuck alone or else, I'm fucking your shit up..."

Sister Mary Jacalyn quickly turned from David to Deanne and took a step in her direction when Deanne attempted to shoot her, not realizing the gun was empty.

It was unclear if Deanne intended to run or not, but that became of moot point, when Sister Mary Jacalyn reached out her hand and caught Deanne by the throat.

It seemed as if Sister Mary Jacalyn was toying with Deanne, as she slowly lifted her by the neck until Deanne was several feet off the ground.

David attempted to intervene and help Deanne, but Sister Mary Jacalyn wagged her finger at David, saying....

"Don't try it lover boy I'm not going to kill her just yet, I'm just having a little fun."

Watching as Deanne's leg frantically kicked in dead air, and her flawless white skin turning ashen, David yelled at Sister Mary Jacalyn...
"You're killing her...stop!"
Sister Mary Jacalyn put Deanne's face in her face and then she sniffed at Deanne and let her fall to the floor saying...

"She isn't dead but she'll wish she were in a few minutes."

Caressing Deanne's face, David cried to Deanne...
"Oh baby, Deanne, you okay baby?"
Sister Mary Jacalyn stood above David and Deanne, looking and saying...

"Wake her up lover boy, you two have a long day ahead of you."

Looking up at Sister Mary Jacalyn, David looked puzzled, and said...
"A long day ahead of ourselves...what are you talking about, say, why don't you just go and leave us alone, we haven't done a damn thing to you."
Sister Mary Jacalyn bent her twisted face down near David's face and after her black rotting tongue licked David's face, she said...

"This has nothing to do with what somebody deserves and doesn't deserve the living has run out of grace and last chances. It's a new day and as you say everything is under new management."

Just then Deanne began waking up, saying...

"Oh Blue, what happened, I must have been dreaming, I thought some old nasty ass bitch was trying to kill me."

Deanne couldn't see past David's body, as Sister Mary Jacalyn appeared in front of Deanne saying…

"You ready for a little trip, bitch? The only question I have is, where do I send you to as I told ya before, every day, every minute you two are going to live out one of the scariest times that you experienced. I been waiting a long time to get revenge for the way I was treated I took care of the children and helped feed the mothers and I was arrested and convicted of what?"

Holding David in her arms, Deanne responded under her breath…

"Yeah, you took care of them alright…you and that jacked up priest preyed on all them young girls, for your perverted pleasure."

Sister Mary Jacalyn's head snapped around, letting Deanne know that she heard every word, as she said…

"Well, fasten your seat belt, because you and lover boy here are about to take a little trip, and I don't mean to Gilligan's Island The wonderful thing about it is, you won't have any memory of it. I'm sending you back to the moment you first were visited in Port Clinton by your Doppelganger and here's a bonus, you'll relive this moment over and over again."

David tried screaming no, out to Sister Mary Jacalyn, but it was too late, the next thing David and Deanne knew, they were pulling into the parking lot of the country store on fifty-three, as David said…

Oh my God Deanne, do you smell that…it's like a strong sickening vanilla scent."

Deanne straightened up in her seat and then turned to the rear seat, saying…

"Blue, I don't smell anything, are you alright over there?"

David had opened the front car door, upchucking as Deanne reached for her bottle of water and a handkerchief from her purse, saying...

"Eww...here Blue, wipe your face with this, you want some water? I think I'll go in the store and shop, you stay here with Shone and keep the window down to get some cool air!"

David got out of the car after making Shone jump in the back seat, saying...

"I'll be alright once I get a little fresh air."

As David and Deanne were walking up the steps to the store, Deanne once again asked David if he were feeling better, which he replied he was.

David held the door open as Deanne walked into the store, when David turned to check on Shone to make sure she wasn't jumping from back seat to the front seat as she normally does...when David saw what looked like a little boy sitting in the front seat.

Suddenly, things went crazy...it was as if David and Deanne were watching television and the characters on the screen were being fast forwarded.

David and Deanne suddenly had a loaded basket of groceries and were at the counter ready to pay for them.

They looked at one another in shock, when the store employee, Mr. Hennessey said...

"I think its customary for you to take the groceries out of your cart and place them on the counter and then I ring them up for you."

David looked at the man and then over to Deanne who was looking around the store, as David asked the store clerk...

"These are ours?"

The store clerk Mr. Hennessey replied...

"What the hell are you smoking son...you guys went up and down the aisles, putting things in your cart, and then you pushed it up here....so, I say, they are yours...they sure as hell isn't mine."

David started to tell the clerk that they just got to the store seconds ago. Mr. Hennessey stated...

"I don't know what kind of game you're playing but are you going to pay for the groceries or am I going to have to call the police?"

Deanne whispered to David to not argue and pay for the groceries.

While David was loading the groceries onto the counter, he said…

"Look sir, I'm not trying to be difficult, but we just got here a few seconds ago, and we haven't had time to do any shopping."

Mr. Hennessey replied…

"First of all, you've been here over thirty minutes, and you're right 'we' didn't do all the shopping, the lady you come in here with, helped you until she had to go to the pee."

David replied to Mr. Hennessey, as he turned around to Deanne…

"What are you talking about, she's right…"

As David turned to Deanne, he was in shock to discover that not only was Deanne not standing there beside him, but Mr. Hennessey was holding out his hand for money with an ass-o-holic expression on his face, saying…

"You believe me, don't you… that'll be one-hundred-and thirty- dollars and fourteen cents."

"While David was reaching in his wallet to pay for the groceries, he mumbled to himself…

"Deanne…where did she go?"

Mr. Hennessey put the money in the drawer saying…

"I hope your lady won't be too long in the porta john, I got to be getting on home in a little bit, nasty storm is coming."

David opened the hatch and tail gate and started putting all the groceries in, and as he did his eyes focused on the porta johns at the rear of the store.

David drove over near the restroom and took Shone out of the back and tied her leash on the rear bumper and took his cigarettes from his pocket.

As he stood at the rear of the SUV smoking a cigarette, trying to figure out what was going on. He remembered something from a dream or something, about reliving things, but it was not clear.

After finishing his cigarette, he noticed Deanne had not come out of the restroom and, he walked over to the restroom, knocking on the door saying…

"Hey Deanne, you alright in there, say look, the old man in the store says he's got to close up…Deanne!"

David pounded on the door for a couple more minutes and then he left Shone tied to the SUV bumper and walked back to the store.

As David approached the store steps he could see Mr. Hennessey, as he walked to the door, saying…

"Hey, I'm glad I caught you…look I need the porta john key, my girl's…"

David cut himself short as he saw Deanne standing at the counter. Opening the door, Mr. Hennessey said…

"It's about damn time young man, I was about to lock the doors, me and your lady friend here, have been waiting on you for almost thirty minutes, you're not all locked up, are you? Prunes, you gotta have prunes like I do every morning."

Looking past Mr. Hennessey to Deanne, David shouted…

"What the hell! Babe, I just left from looking for you, did you bring Shone with you?"

David looked down beside Deanne and then all around the store, when it occurred to him…

"Hey, wait a minute…how the hell did Deanne get past me without me seeing, there wasn't a backdoor to the porta johns?"

Deanne interrupted David's thoughts saying…

"Earth to Blue, earth to Blue…you okay?"

David shook his head saying…

"Yeah, I'm good, I was thinking…I mean wondering, how'd you beat me in here from the porta john, me and shone didn't pass you, or anything."

Deanne snapped her fingers at David as she pointed to the full cart of groceries, saying…

"Blue, I don't have a clue about what you're saying…all I know is, we have all these groceries to load in the car and what are you talking about, anyway?"

David grabbed the cart's handle and as he pointed the cart towards the car, he said…

"You're going to have to go get Shone, and drive the SUV around front, I drove it there and…"

Deanne interrupted David as she pinched his arm and stood pointing at the SUV saying…

"Blue, does this look familiar?"

David stood for a moment without moving, looking as if he saw a ghost or something, when he said…

"No! Hey, come on, I know I drove the car around back, how'd it get… okay Deanne, you can quit anytime."

Deanne walked around the back of the SUV and opening the hatch and tailgate, yelled at David saying…

"Let's just get the groceries in and then we can talk about this shit on the way Blue."

David pushed the cart to the back of the SUV, saying to Deanne…

"That's another thing Deanne, I already loaded the car once already with groceries."

Putting both hands on her hips and giving David the 'dead eye', Deanne replied…

"So, where did they go…did they grow little grocery legs and hop out of the car?"

David continued loading the SUV softly, but angerly saying…

"Something is fucking wrong, and instead of hearing me out, you're blowing smoke up my ass."

Deanne turned, looked at David and said…

"When you start tripping like you are, what am I supposed to do…humor you?" All I expected was for you to put the groceries in the SUV and you're up here tripping.

David had just loaded the SUV with groceries and Deanne got in on the passenger side, when Mr. Hennessey opened the door waving for David to come inside.

David had already started the SUV and did not notice Mr. Hennessy signaling to him, so Deanne had David stop in front of the store and told him that Mr. Hennessey wanted him.

David left the SUV running as he reluctantly got out and walked into the store. Seeing Mr. Hennessey, David said…my wife told me that you wanted to see me.

Mr. Hennessy asked David…

"Hey, I don't mean to prod, but, are you going to finish your shopping, I mean you got half a cart full of groceries, and your woman is in the restroom. I'm only saying something because, it's like I said, I'm going to be closing soon and the faster you two can get on your way the quicker I can be home.

David had a look of shock on his face, as his attention went from Mr. Hennessey to the cart next to him.

David placed his hand on the cart, and touched a few of the items in it, saying...

"Oh, now, don't you start. Did Deanne put you up to this?"

Mr. Hennessey walked from around the counter and got up in David's face saying...

"Now wait a minute young man, isn't these your groceries in this cart?"

David looked towards his parked SUV saying...

"For your information, my groceries and my lady are..."

"It's like I said, are you going to finish your shopping, so I can get home or what?"

Mr. Hennessey said as Deanne came up from one of the isles asking Mr. Hennessey...

"Excuse me Mr. Hennessey, where's your restrooms?"

Mr. Hennessey turned and bent down to retrieve a small board with a key attached to it as David grabbed Deanne's coat saying...

"Where did you just come from, I thought you were in the SUV?"

"SUV are you crazy or something, I've been over by the deli meats...where you left me a second ago."

Looking very annoyed and irritated, David replied...

"I don't know what you're talking about, but I left you in the SUV, and what's up with these groceries...we have ours in the SUV, loaded ...we-we were just about to leave when you said Mr. Hennessey wanted to see me."

"There you are miss, we got two porta johns in the back of the store...and I don't wanna rush you or anything, but I am going to be closing up as soon as your man pays for the groceries and you're done.

Mr. Hennessey stated, as he interrupted David and Deanne's conversation.

Deanne kissed David on the cheek, saying...

"I'll be right back babe, you got enough money to pay for all of this?"

David replied as he pulled Deanne close to him...

"More groceries, babe we got all our groceries in the SUV babe, somethings' wrong, we already did this..."

Deanne gave David a real 'irritated look' as she crossed her legs and anxiously said...

"If you don't let go of my arm, so I can go pee, the only thing that'll be wrong is me peeing on this man's floor, I'll be back in a second and we can talk about it then."

Mr. Hennessey came up to David as he stood watching Deanne walk towards the back of the store, saying… *"I guess the old bitch was right huh?"*

David cocked his head to the left and then grabbed Mr. Hennessey's shirt collar, saying…

"What did you say!"

David had a tight grip on Mr. Hennessey, till he was pulled off the floor and on to the counter, when Deanne appeared saying…

"BLUE! Gosh Blue, what are you doing?"

When Deanne got up to the counter, David released his grip on Mr. Hennessey and saying to Deanne…

"No Deanne, I was standing here watching you walk down the aisle and this son of a bitch here said, 'the old bitch was right, wasn't she'?"

Deanne looked at Mr. Hennessey who was looking pale in the face, saying…

"Miss…I promise I wasn't talking about you, I was talking about something else."

Deanne handed Mr. Hennessey the restroom key saying…

"Mr. Hennessey, I'm sorry about all of this…"

Mr. Hennessey placed the key on a hook which was on the wall and turned to David and Deanne laughing and saying…

"Ain't no need to worry, he-he, the Nun has already taken care of everything, you guys ain't never gonna get out of this."

Deanne and David both gave one another concerning looks and then turned to Mr. Hennessey, saying…

"WHAT?"

Mr. Hennessey looked at David and Deanne saying…

"The Nun, Sister Mary Jacalyn says…. you will never leave."

Just then at that moment, David and Deanne looked at one another and then in an instant, they were no longer in the store, but being pulling back into the parking lot.

10
Criss-Cross

Lynne Byrd sit at her desk feeling a little more anxious, a little more excited than normal, because in just three more days she would be marrying the love of her life, Ray Moore.

Lynne and Ray had known each other and been in love for over sixteen years. They met each other while they were both working as nurses at Columbus Memorial hospital, on the far east side.

Falling in love can be an awesome thing, but in their cases, it was less than idyllic...you see, both were coming off of failing marriages, but they managed to keep their love affair secret.

They both worked the third shift, the same schedules, and they were in love. They would meet at a motel, on the same days of the week. Both worked out plans to call one another, using only the phone located at a gas station, next to another motel, on the opposite side of town, to prevent phone bills from giving away their secret.

Lynne and Ray were both fifty years old, and you'd think that the game they were engaged in was a game for the young and foolish of heart, but you know what they say...'when you're in love', common sense takes a back seat to everything else.

After sixteen years, both had been granted divorces from their spouses, and both were looking forward to what seemed like a dream come true...that they'd both be able to be with one another at last.

A great comfort for them was, they'd never have to hide their affair, and that they could move away from Columbus, and settle in a place where they'd be left alone to live out their lives, but there was something, evil lurking, looming over their plans.

Lynne had been receiving phone calls from a mysterious caller, threatening to ruin her wedding plans. At first Lynne thought it was her ex-husband, or maybe even one of her two daughters, who didn't want her wedding to Ray, to go well, but it was more than that.

It was something more sinister, something far eviler than that… it was a darkness from a place that Lynne nor Ray would have ever looked for.

Lynne sat at the nurse's station at four-thirty in the morning, two hours away from the ending of her shift, trying to stay awake until her relief reported, when the phone rang…

"I.C.U., this is Lynne."

Anywhere from thirty minutes to two hours prior to shift change when the phone rings, you can always count on a call in for work, but this call was different.

The caller answered after a few moments of silence…

"Is this Lynne?"

Not recognizing the voice of the caller, Lynne replied…

"This is I.C.U., Lynne speaking, how can I help you?"

It was the raspy voice of what appeared to be a woman with a bad cold saying…

"Hey Lynne, I'm not going to be coming in today, can you let everybody know?"

Putting her left hand over her ear to hear clearer, as the call light in one of the rooms on her unit was going off, Lynne replied…

"I'm sorry, who is this?"

Again, the raspy voice sounded…

"You know the wedding will never happen this Saturday."

Suddenly, Lynne recognized the voice. It was the same voice that had been calling all week, as Lynne responded…

"Excuse me…can I help you?"

The voice on the other end of the line remained silent for a moment, and then said...

"Your wedding"

Lynne looked all around her, thinking perhaps it was a joke being played on her by her friends, and when she saw no one peeping and laughing, she said...

"My wedding...what are you talking about, who is this...Cindy, Rachael?"

Again, the raspy female's voice echoed...

"Maybe you'll have a funeral instead, maybe no one will show."

Lynne's voice grew a little louder as she said...

"Hey! I don't know who this is, but this is way beyond funny."

Lynne was already nervous over her approaching wedding, but to get a strange call like this, heightened her nervousness and magnified her jitters.

Lynne answered the call light from the Nurse's station, but the unusual thing was, no patient was assigned in that room, just then, the call light went off.

Hanging up the phone, Lynne dialed her best friend and Matron of Honor, Cindy Smith. As the phone rang without an answer, Lynne was on the verge of hanging up without leaving a message when Cindy's voice came over the phone...

"Hello Lynne, thank God, I almost missed you, what's up?"

Catching her breath and tapping her pencil on a pad in front of her, Lynne replied...

"Oh nothing, just getting the last-minute jitters, I guess."

Projecting as calm a voice as she could, Cindy said...

"Hey girlfriend, everything alright. Its four forty-five in the a.m.

You got nothing to worry about. Julian said Ray was calm at his bachelor party last night, and that he was staying at Ray's until Saturday...oh, don't forget, I'm picking you up at five-thirty tonight."

Sighing, Lynne said...

"Yeah I knew you'd be getting for work. I told you, a bachelorette party is too infantile, besides..."

Cutting Lynne off from finishing her comment, Cindy stated...

"*Infantile, versatile, blah-blah-blah-blah-blah-blah-blah...whatever, just think of it as a bunch of ladies, getting their drink and their party on.*"

Lynne leaned back in her chair, saying...

"*Thanks girlfriend...oh, before I forget, have you heard anything from Theresa this week. Her cousin is supposed to DJ during the reception.*"

Cindy yawned and said...

"*Nope, haven't heard a thing, but I can give her a shout out to see what's going on, and once I hear from her, I'll let you know...ok?*"

Lynne sat straight up in her chair saying...

Okay look, I gotta go, see you around five-thirty."

The remaining of Lynne's day went pretty much the same as usual... in the mornings, slow and then towards the end of the day the rush from hell is on.

The unit was particularly quiet, with few patients in I.C.U. due to a low census, and Lynne sat thinking it would be her luck if her relief called out for the day or would be late for her shift.

Lynne sat thinking about that, and all the things she had to do that day and the rest of the week to get ready for Saturday, until she felt herself nodding, so she got up to walk around the unit.

In most hospital settings, for a nurse to fall asleep on duty, was considered the worst thing, next to medication errors, you can make, but Lynne's immediate supervisor, the Nurse Shift Coordinator, had a habit of falling asleep and not making her rounds for several hours.

After about an hour, Lynne returned to the nurses station, and looking around, she fixed her hair with her hands and stood up to shake off the sleepiness from her eyes when something over to the right of the nurse's station caught her attention.

Sitting on the edge of the counter of the nurse's station sat a young girl dressed in a bright yellow fedora, with a red bowtie on, singing...

"Hey nurse Are you sleepy? Are you sleepy? Lynne Byrd, Lynne Byrd! You're gonna be in darkness, gonna get your throat cut! Ding, dong, Ding, dong."

Looking at Lynne, the girl walked closer to her saying...

"Aww, don't fret look, I found this knife, and now look at what I've done do you think this is gonna be a good look at your wedding?"

Lynne stood in disbelief, her eyes filled with shock. Lynne stood frozen, she wanted to move, but somehow, she was frozen in that spot, in that space.

The small girl had made several slices along her stomach and sides, bleeding and whimpering with each slice.

Lynne looked all around her, expecting the phone to ring or for someone to check on all the noise made, but there was no one.

Lynne reached up to pick up the phone to call someone, anyone from another floor to witness what she was seeing, and when she put the phone to her ear, she felt blood all over her hand and the phone.

Lynne dropped the phone, as she saw the girl with the knife cutting himself and bleeding all over the nurses' station.

Lynne let out a small scream as the girl wallowed over to where she was saying...

"T'aint no use in screaming bitch, it is, what it is oh, by the way, see you at your wedding this weekend"

Suddenly, Lynne heard her name being called from behind. As she turned, she saw her counterpart, John Miller, RN and Lalyne French, CNA coming from one of the patient's room.

Stopping at the nurse's station to drop off a patient's chart, John and Lalyne looked at Lynne with surprise, saying...

"What the hell are you doing in here?"

Lynne glanced up, to where the girl was and then back to John and Lalyne, who was charting some data into a patient's chart, saying...

"What am I doing here, are you crazy, waiting on my relief, so I can go home."

John grabbed the schedule and handed it to Lynne, who had glanced down at herself, saying...

"Aww, c'mon man, don't tell me that I'm not supposed to even be in tonight...but, I."

John cut Lynne off, saying...

"Besides, how are you supposed to be charge, dressed in flip-flops, jeans and *a sweater. I mean if you really wanted the shift tonight, you should've changed and called me?"*

Lynne didn't know how to answer John, or even what to say, for that matter, but she knew she had to say something, because if there's one thing that Lynne knew, John was going to have to document that she was there.

If something were to happen involving Lynne before she left the hospital, and John didn't document it, then it would put John in a precarious situation at worst.

Lynne again glanced down at how she was dressed and stood in amazement for a few minutes because, no more than an hour ago, when she was making her med pass, she was wearing her teal scrubs.

There was no doubt in Lynne's mind, because she recalled spilling a little bit of Pepto-Bismol on her top scrub as she was pouring one of her patient's, Mr. Dobb's nightly dose.

Lynne knew that she needed to answer John quickly and come up with something that he'd buy, other than her silence.

Lynne knew if it came down to it, John would be asked how she was acting, so with a deep breathe Lynne...

"I needed to recheck the schedule...promise me John, if you're ever invited to Roger and Deb's, that you won't let Roger fix your drinks...ugh, I'm still kinda hung over."

In a surprising move, John replied...

"It's funny you mentioned that, I was over there two weeks ago and got myself wasted, but I didn't mix my drinks...took me all weekend to sober up."

Lynne stood there for a moment shaking her head and then said...

"Oh well, I'll see you in a couple days."

Lynne left the nurses station as John turned from charting saying...

"No, you won't...remember, I'll be on the psyche unit all next week."

Acknowledging him, Lynne nodded her head and got on the elevator.

Lynne stood with her back against the rear wall of the elevator wondering what had just happened...something wasn't right.

Lynne knew she was scheduled to work and she knew she was wearing her scrubs. The thought in her mind was, should she really leave and go home, or should she hang out on another floor in the hospital?

What if she bumped her head and was hallucinating, and she wakes up in a few minutes in her scrubs...every thought stirring inside Lynne's mind was more real and more serious than any she's ever had.

Lynne decided to walk to her car and sit for a little while, to think things over. Lynne thought about dialing her sister Deanne, but wondered what kind of mood Deanne's boyfriend, David would be in, and if they'd have a chance to talk, when a tapping on the driver's side car glass startled Lynne.

It was Lalyne, saying...

"Hey, I'm glad I caught you...I'm going out to get something to eat and John said, if I see you to tell you, he's feeling sick and wanted to know if you'd cover for him, he said he could stay until you went home to change?"

Lynne pushed open her door saying...

"I'll call him, I keep a set of scrubs and shoes in my locker, so I'll see you when you get back, by the way, where are you going?"

Lalyne replied...

"I'm heading to get some breakfast at that new place over on Parsons Ave, why you want something?"

Lynne pulled twenty dollars out of her purse and handed it to Lalyne, while Lalyne pulled a piece of paper from her pocket along with an ink pen, saying...

"I'd like to get an order of, eggs scrambled, bacon and cheesy grits and toast."

Lalyne fished in her purse and then said...

"Here, keep your money until I get back, because all I got is a fifty-dollar bill."

Lynne headed onto the elevator as Lalyne hurried across the street to the parking deck, saying...

"Okay, I'll be back in about fifteen minutes."

Lynne changed into her scrubs and shoes, and then headed to the nurse's station, when she saw John and Lalyne sitting and playing cards.

Thinking that Lalyne picked up the food and made it back fast, Lynne looked at Lalyne and John saying...

"Wow, that was fast...okay, I'm ready for report and then you can get gone."

Startled, John and Lalyne looked at one another and then John said...

"Ready for what? I thought you were out of here and going home."

Lynne sat her purse under the counter saying...

"I was just about to head home until Lalyne stopped me and told me that you were feeling sick and wanted to get out of here."

Lalyne got up from the table and went to answer a call light, when John said…

"Look you really ought to go home, I'm not sick, and Lalyne's been sitting with me all evening, what are you talking about?"

Lynne, looked over, as Lalyne returned from answering a call light, saying to John…

"Wait a minute, Lalyne caught me on her way to pick up food and said that you were sick and wanted me to cover for you."

John stood up and walked Lynne over to the treatment room saying…

"Hey, I'm trying to help you, and I don't want to see you in a world of shit, but what the hell are you talking about?"

Lynne had the most worried expression on her face as John explained that for starters, that he was not feeling ill, and secondly, that his wife made dinner for them and he and Lalyne had already eaten several hours ago.

Lynne's feeling that it was sick joke quickly faded and fear swooped in and engulfed her.

She knew that John was going to have to write it all down in his notes and report it to the off-tour coordinator, if she didn't leave and get out of the hospital.

A question of Lynne's mental stability was going to be called into question, more importantly, the question of Lynne possibly stealing drugs from the hospital for her own personal use, would come into play, and that would mean her license.

Lynne had been a registered nurse for eighteen years, and something like this on her record would be a 'one and done' deal with the nursing board.

Lynne decided that she would tell John that she'd been partying hard over the week, and that she thought some of her friends were merely messing with her, and that she was going home.

Hoping that John was satisfied and that he wouldn't report her, Lynne left the hospital and headed for her car.

While walking to her car, Lynne noticed someone lurking in the shadows, as she took her car keys from her purse and put them in her hand and picked her pace up and made it through the parking garage to her car.

Lynne thought about informing security, but then they would surely have to make a record of it, which would be the first thing her nurse manager would hear about at morning report and wonder why John hadn't reported it and what she was doing on the floor of the hospital.

Glancing around and behind her, Lynne looked for the mysterious stranger who was standing in the darkness, but there was no one to be found.

Lynne took her cell phone from her purse with her other hand, and as she got into her car, locked the doors, started it and then placed a call to her sister, Deanne.

Deanne was also a nurse and would be awake at that time in the morning, so Lynne placed the call.

Lynne placed the phone to her ear when she felt something crawling on her pants leg. Lynne jumped and dropped her phone in the darkness. She could hear Deanne answering...

"Hello, hello Lynne, hello?"

Lynne reached up and pressed the overhead light switch, when she heard something tapping on her car window.

Lynne turned and let out a scream, as it was a security guard asking her...

"Excuse me, are you alright?"

Spotting her phone and rolling down the window, Lynne told the guard that she was okay and had come in to check the schedule and had dropped her phone.

The guard nodded okay as he turned and continued his round of the parking area, while Lynne picked up her phone, only to discover, Deanne had hung up.

Lynne's first thought was to go home, but with the kind of night she had, she decided to drive immediately over to Deanne's house... unaware that things were no less sane there. Deanne had given Lynne a spare key and told her that...anytime she needs to use, to do so.

Deanne lived on the opposite side of town from Lynne, and it was over thirty-five minutes to get there, providing the traffic was smooth.

Lynne decided to take the expressway to cut some time off her driving, so she got on to I-seventy-one-south. The night air should have been damp and cool, but for some odd reason it was unseasonably warm out, so Lynne lowered her window a little to let in some fresh air when suddenly both windows started going up and down by themselves.

Lynne reached down with her left hand and pulled up on both buttons to raise the windows, but every time she got the windows to raise, first one and then the other would fall.

Lynne's thinking was that, there must be a short in the switch or something. Twenty minutes away from Polaris in Westerville, Lynne thought about stopping and getting a hot cup of coffee, since there was a White Castles up ahead.

Lynne slowed down to turn into the White Castles as she thought…

"I know it's been a minute since I've been up here…I wonder when they put in this White Castle?"

Lynne found herself behind a car which seemed as if it was never going to move. Lynne stretched over to the passenger seat to get her purse and when she straightened herself she saw nothing. No car in front of her, no White Castle…no nothing.

Lynne sat there, wide-eyed and then she began to cry. Lynne put her head down in her hands crying and shaking her head in disbelief, when the flashing of the Police car, pulled up beside her grabbed her attention.

When Lynne looked over at the Police car, she didn't see anything out of the ordinary. But then something strange happened. The Police Officer, motioned for her to roll her window down, and then he said…

"Well-well-well, if it's not Lynne, what's the matter…you're not seeing things, are you?"

Lynne sat straight up and with disbelief looked at the Police Officer saying…

"Excuse me, do I know you?"

The Police Officer leaned on Lynne's door saying…

"Oh no, we don't know each other, but we'll all know each other soon enough."

Lynne replied to the Officer in a more definite tone…

"Now, what is that supposed to mean, Officer?"

The Police office walked back to his patrol car laughing and saying…

"Ha-ha-…you have a good night if you can Lynne."

Lynne took a deep breath and slowly blew it out saying to herself…

"Okay, girl get it together, you need to keep it together until you make it to Deanne's…don't sit here looking as dumb as a cucumber."

Finally, Lynne instinctively went to roll up the window and as she was leaving the parking lot, and in the intersection, the window fell down hard, scaring Lynne.

Lynne found herself back on interstate seventy-one heading for the Worthington Rd exit, to take her to Africa Rd.

Lynne began thinking even though Deanne gave her unlimited access to the house, at this time of night she'd better try calling her again.

As Lynne had the phone to her ear, she heard several rings and then Deanne answered the phone saying...

"Girl what's the matter, I got a call from you earlier and then the next thing I know nothing."

Lynne checked her rear-view mirror and then said...

"I'm sorry sis, I'm on my way, I hope it's okay? I just had some weird shit going on tonight and I need to vent."

Before Lynne could get everything out of her mouth, Deanne said...

"Aww shut up girl, we're family, what's more we're friends...don't worry, I'll even leave the door unlocked if you don't have your key, and a pot of coffee ready."

Lynne replied...

"You see, that's what I'm talking about...better be glad you're my cousin."

Laughing, Deanne said...

"Now there you go again, I told you I'm too much woman for you, just get here and be safe, there's a lot of fog around Alum Creek State Park."

Lynne laid her cell phone in the console and continued on Worthington Road when she looked over at the passenger seat and screamed.

Sitting there was a Nun, dressed in an old dirty habit. Instead of the Rosary around her neck, she wore on a necklace the eye of Horus.

Lynne was in shock until she froze in place, suddenly terrified, as someone moaned in terror from the other side of the road. The Nun looked over at Lynne, saying...

"Aww, c'mon bitch, don't go faint or anything on me I'm real, the question is are you real."

The sound of scraping, as the window was raised, made Lynne's nerves raw. Lynne fumbled around in the darkness for the door handle, which was now icy as the Nun shouted...

"Lawdy, bitch, where do you think that you are going? You stupid bitches kill me, you're in a car trapped, going down the street fast, and for some unknown reason, you just wanna jump out.
You could at least wait until the car stops, you see, that's why tormenting you seems like the right thing to do it's like, somebody let the dirty bath water drain out, and your dumb ass slid through the strainer."

Lynne looked straight ahead, saying to herself...
"This is not real, this cannot be happening, oh God, make this go away."
Lynne turned her eyes back to the passenger seat, as The Nun sat there, mocking her saying...

"Dear God, please make this thing go away I'm not going anywhere bitch, and as a matter of fact neither are you."

Suddenly, the turn signal in Lynne's car was activated, indicating a right turn when Lynne said...
"What the hell."
Lynne's car began slowing down all by itself, and when Lynne tried pressing the brake pedal, the pedal was stiff and unmovable, as The Nun laughed and said...

"You might as well sit back and enjoy the ride Lynne this car is under my control, and don't think about trying to jump out of the car, you are going nowhere until we get to where we are going, and to keep your dumb ass occupied here's something to play with."

Lynne looked around in the darkness of the car and saw nothing until she felt something on top of her feet. Lynne cut on the overhead light and screamed when she looked down at her feet.
A few inches from her feet, slithering all around Lynne's feet, under the accelerator pedal was a four-foot copperhead snake. Lynne began crying and squirming, saying...

"Oh, my fucking God…oh my god!"

Lynne didn't know what to do, all she knew was, she had to get out of the car as fast as she could.

Scrambling around trying to keep her eyes on the road and her eyes on the snake which was now, extending its head up toward the front seat, Lynne grabbed and pulled up on the emergency brake hard.

The car swerved, and the tires squealed, and the car spun around, as Lynne held onto the emergency brake. Lynne gasped, her heart hammering.

Frightened out of her mind, Lynne glanced over to the passenger seat and noticed The Nun still sitting there, being bounced around in the front seat, and laughing hysterically.

Suddenly, the car's brakes locked, and Lynne was thrown up against the steering wheel, smashing her right hand and sending the left side of her head against the side window. The car came to a complete stop in the middle of the road, as The Nun said to Lynne…

"You see what happens to stupid ass people, who don't listen, now I told you to sit back and enjoy the ride, but no you gotta try to take control."

Lynne placed her left hand up side her head and feeling blood, said…
"Ow!"

Lynne was unaware, but they were stopped in front of Deanne and David's condo. When Lynne looked up, she thought…

"Oh, I hope Deanne or David comes out…so all of this shit will disappear or stop."

Just then, The Nun turned to Lynne saying…

"I can tell you what's going to disappear the thought that you were even here."

Lynne looked and tried to unlock her door when she found herself inside her apartment having coffee with her fiancé, Ray Moore. Lynne glanced around the apartment, as Ray said…

"Hey honey, so all that's left for me to do before Saturday is, leave my brother Duncan the apartment key, so he can get in. Take two truckloads of your things over to my house and pay 'M. P's for catering.

Lynne stood in the middle of the living room with fright, wonder and bewildered in her eyes, because she knew something wasn't right… she shouldn't be there, even though it was her apartment, she just knew that somehow, she belonged somewhere else.

Lynne looked over at Ray as he kissed her neck and said…

"Did you hear me babe, I was telling you about the things I have left to do before we get married this Saturday."

Lynne looked at Ray wild-eyed, saying…

"How did I get here?

Not knowing exactly what to say, Ray replied…

"Uh…we got up and came downstairs, uh, what do you want me to say Babe?"

Sitting her coffee cup down on the counter, without drinking any, Lynne said…

"No, Ray, something is not right. Don't you remember having breakfast and going to work this morning? How in the world did we get back here, it's like we're repeating our whole day all over?"

Ray walked up and Kissed Lynne on her forehead saying…

"Babe, I really don't have the time this morning, I got to get to work…but if you're still bothered we can talk about it tonight when I get in."

Walking out the side door to the carport, Ray waved so long to Lynne, as she was shouting…

"No, Ray, I'm talking about…"

The garage door extended open as a voice said…

"Don't you just hate that when a person you're talking to leaves you right in the middle of a sentence?"

Lynne's head almost flew off her shoulders as she quickly turned around, only to see the Nun in the dingy habit, standing there. Letting out a small shriek, Lynne said…

"WTF! Who-who are you… where did you come from?"

The Nun stopped and walked up to Lynne laughing, saying…

"Who me? Ooh, this is gonna be fun, well, you are about to experience terror on a whole different level. Every time you awake, you are going to relive the worst day of your life over and over again."

Lynne stood there shaking her head and crying, saying...
"Oh my God...this can't be happening to me, this can't be happening."
The Nun, with her wrinkled deformed right hand, lifted Lynne's chin and said...

"This is only the beginning, you are about to take one shit-ass of a ride buckle up!"

Lynne jerked away from The Nun, and taking a step towards the door, and said...
"I don't know who you think the fuck you are, but I'm not going to stand here and let you do whatever you want, and how do you call yourself a Nun... cussing and threatening people?"
The Nun crossed her hands in front of herself saying...

"You're right, I am a Nun, and I shouldn't be cursing and threatening people but I'm dead and I am cursing and threatening you bitch!"

Next, The Nun touched the Eye of Horus, which hung around her neck and waved her hand at Lynne, and in slow motion, everything in Lynne's apartment began moving in slow motion, and stopping with Ray standing at the bottom steps handing Lynne a cup of coffee, saying...
"Hey honey, all that's left for me to do before Saturday is, leave my brother Duncan with the apartment key, so he can get in and take all of your things over to my house and pay 'M. P's for catering.
Lynne stood in the middle of the living room with fright, wonder and bewilderment in her eyes, because she knew she had just lived those moments.
Lynne looked over at Ray as he kissed her neck and said...
"Did you hear me babe, I was telling you about the things I have left to do before we get married this Saturday."

Lynne looked at Ray wild-eyed, saying...

"*This is messed up.... Ray, I want you to listen to me, we've already said this, this conversation has already happened, don't you remember any of this?*

Not knowing exactly what to say to Lynne, Ray replied...

"*Yeah, that sucks, I know what you're saying?*"

Setting her coffee cup down on the counter and hugging Ray, Lynne said...

"*Oh, thank God baby, so you know what's happening, I thought I was losing it?*"

Ray walked up and kissed Lynne on her forehead saying...

"*Yeah, we wake up every morning, saying and doing the same ole thing, it's like we've done this...*"

Lynne interrupted Ray, saying...

"*No Ray, that's not what I'm talking about, we've already had this conversation this morning, twice.*

Look, I'm not tripping or anything, but it's like the movie ground hog day... Ray, there is a demon, or a witch or a spirit or something that's making us see and relive the same thing, over and over."

Ray walked up and Kissed Lynne on her forehead saying...

"*Babe, it's called a dream, besides I'm running late this morning, I got to get to work...but we can talk about this when I see you at noon, don't forget, I'm picking you up for lunch.*"

Walking out the side door to the carport, Ray waved so long to Lynne, as she shouted...

"*Oh fuck, Ray...Ray!*"

As the door closed and Lynne heard the sound of the garage door opening, she started after Ray, when the creepy Nun appeared in front her, pushing her into the wall, blocking Lynne from opening the door, saying...

"You just don't get it do you you are not leaving here today, you're all mine bitch!"

Lynne turned and raced to the window in the front room, after jerking away from The Nun, only to see the rear end of Ray's car as it drove away from the apartment. Scared and panicking, Lynne began stomping her foot and screaming and crying, saying...

"Oh my God.... you are not real...this bull shit *CANNOT BE HAPPENING!*"

The Nun walked up behind Lynne, pulled her hair, saying...

"Get your panties unscrambled and listen up! told Deanne she was not getting out of this, and since you are her family well, you're in this too.
You think a little prayer and shutting your eyes and wishing and acting crazy is gonna help you, well, I got a surprise for you, 'it ain't gonna work'."

The Nun dragged Lynne by her hair and threw her on the sofa and began mumbling something in her ear, when the phone rang.

The answering machine automatically took the call as Lynne heard Ray's voice on the machine, saying...

"Hey honey, sorry for rushing out, almost at work...remember I'll pick you up for lunch and we can handle the marriage license down at the courthouse afterwards, okay, see you later."

Lynne lay on the sofa struggling to get free, kicking her feet, and trying to push The Nun out of the way when The Nun said...

"Ooh look at you, you're gonna need to practice a little hygiene you smell nasty."

Lynne screamed louder at The Nun...

"Get the fuck off me, let me up!"

The Nun straddled Lynne and with her old black rotting tongue, licked Lynne from her lips up to her forehead, saying...

"In a little while, you're going on a trip, and when you're back, if you get back, we'll see how much sanity you have left."

Before Lynne could say another word, her doorbell rang. Running to the door, Lynne peeked out the window and noticed it was her mother Katherine. Scrambling to unlock the lock, she was about to open the door when, the Nun touched her forehead saying...

"FORGET"

Lynne stood there for a few seconds shaking her head, before she finally opened the door, letting her mother in. The relationship that Lynne and her mother shared was a lot closer then Deanne.

Even though Lynne and Deanne were only several years apart, Katherine always favored Lynne over Deanne. Lynne opened the door and happily kissed and hugged her mother saying...

"Baby girl tell me how you and Ray are holding up, only one week before the wedding...nevertheless, I do wish you two would think about a nice church wedding?"

Lynne walked into the kitchen and picked up a coffee pack and showing it to her mother, dropped it in the brewer, saying...

"Mom, why do we have to keep on having the same conversation...it's not like anything is going to change?"

Katherine followed Lynne into the kitchen saying...

"Baby girl, I didn't come over here to fight with you this morning, I merely wanted to check and see if there was anything that I could do, I mean it's not every day your daughter gets married.

I just wish your sister would consider it, I mean she's been living with David for twelve years."

Lynne poured her mother a cup of coffee and then took the creamer from the fridge and placed it on the counter saying...

"You just had to throw that in, didn't you?"

Katherine took a seat at the kitchen table and sipped her coffee saying...

"Your right honey, I need to back down and let you and Deanne handle your own lives."

Lynne sat down next to mother and pulled the mint coffee creamer from the fridge saying...

"So, is this you talking, or the caffeine which is heading straight to your brain?"

Lynne and her mother sat for a few moments sipping their coffee without saying much.

Lynne noticed her mother looking around the kitchen, when she said...

"No mom, I haven't taken down most of the things in here, because the couple moving in wants most of the things, and besides, me and Ray won't need them."

Throwing her hands up in the air and sipping her coffee, Katherine replied...

"I didn't say anything, but I was thinking...."

Lynne grabbed a Danish from the plate in front of them and said...

"You were thinking what Mom...I know that look?"

Joining her, Katherine picked up a Danish and began tearing small pieces of it with her fingers and eating it and saying...

"Nothing, it's just that, I gave you some of this when you first got this apartment."

Dunking her Danish into her coffee, Lynne said...

"Yeah Mom, that's because you said you were giving it to Good Will."

Katherine looked at Lynne and asked her...

"What's crawled up your butt and made you wiggle?"

"Nothing's crawled up my butt, it's just that with the wedding and all, I'm a little edgy."

Lynne said as she got up to get a paper towel.

Katherine took one of the paper towels from Lynne and said...

"You're a wonderful nurse, and a great daughter...but you've always been a terrible liar.

I mean hell, this is not your first or your second trip to the altar...what's there to be edgy about."

Lynne motioned to her mother to walk to the living room, and as they sat on the sofa, Katherine asked...

"So, are you going to say what's, what?"

Lynne did not hear her mother as she was remembering some of the things which occurred with the Nun before her mother showed up.

Again, Katherine tried getting Lynne's attention, saying...

"Hello, earth to Lynne."

Lynne appeared a little startled and jumped as Katherine touched her shoulder. saying...

"Mom, I can't remember everything, but I think someone, or something was in here, in the apartment with me that I can't explain."

Katherine looked up over the top of her eye glasses, and with a pseudo motherly voice, said...

"Please tell me, that he was six-foot- three and two hundred pounds, and goes by the name of Brad?"

Lynne shook her head, saying...

"No Mom, it wasn't somebody named Brad, and for the last time, just because Brad and I are getting along, it doesn't mean I want to marry him. I mean, Ray and I have always shared something special, Mom, I just can't...

"Katherine placed her hand on Lynne's knees, saying, you can't wait forever baby girl.

I know you think you love Ray, but Brad's a fine catch"

Lynne, put her hands in her hair and pulled it back out of frustration and said...

"I know you're going to think that a pissy ass slug has more sense than I do when I tell you what's on my mind, but I'm not dreaming or tripping.

Katherine eased herself to the edge of the sofa, looking at Lynne, and said...

"Okay, now I'm getting concerned. Whatever are you talking about."

Lynne took a deep breath, exhaled and said...

"There's a Nun who I've been seeing in the apartment, in the morning and at night."

Katherine interrupted...

"A Nun, baby girl you're not even Catholic, you're Evangelical, what's a Nun doing coming to see you?"

Twirling her hair, Lynne replied...

"I know, I know Mom, but you and Dad are Evangelicals...not me, you guys just dragged me and Deanne to church every Sunday...but it's not like this Nun is coming to see me or anything, but more like...she's haunting me."

Katherine stood up, saying...

"Okay baby girl, you're losing me on this one, are you saying that you're seeing ghost or some dumb shit like that...that's crazy...I think it's nothing more than wedding jitters!"

Lynne shouted back.

"Mom don't call me crazy, I'm serious."

Walking from the living room to the kitchen and peeking out the window, Katherine replied...

"I'm not saying that you're crazy, I'm saying...you're working too hard, you're having nightmares, or too damn stressed over the wedding, is all.

Once this Saturday is over, you'll be back to normal."

Lynne walked up to her mom, saying...

"What I'm saying is, I think. The operative word is 'think' Mom...I think that an old creepy ass Nun's been in here and left these Rosary Beads on the head board of my bed."

Katherine took a pack of cigarettes from her coat pocket, and offered Lynne one, who shook her head no, saying...

"You see that's what I'm talking about, a person sees or believes that they've seen something...but baby girl, you're saying, 'you think' that you've seen something.

After this weekend, after the wedding, when the pressures off, you and Ray will go on a nice week-long rest and you'll see that it was nothing more than, stress and being under a lot of pressure."

A part of Lynne heard what her mother was saying, and wanted to believe her, while another part of her knew that there was something more to what she was feeling, and what she had just seen.

Lynne knew that there was something or someone intent on doing her harm, but her mind was still a little unclear, a little too foggy about everything.

Katherine conveniently changed the subject and was about to leave when she said..."

"Oh, I know what I wanted to ask you, on Friday, and I know you have a lot going on, but do you think that I can drop Olin off over here for a few hours?"

Looking at her mother cock-eyed, and mumbling under her breath, Lynne said...

"Of all the times Mom...geez, only for a couple hours, we do have a party going on here on Friday, in case you forgot."

Katherine kissed Lynne on the cheek, saying...

"Oh, thanks baby girl, I'll bring him by after school, and pick him up and we'll be out of your hair long before your party...okay?"

Katherine unlocked the door and headed for her car as Lynne waved and watched her back out into the street. Closing the door, Lynne began feeling a cold, blast of air on her neck and as she turned there was the Nun, Sister Mary Jacalyn.

Standing in her dingy old habit smiling. Lynne wanted to scream, she wanted to attract someone's attention, but as soon as she opened her mouth, The Nun placed her finger to Lynne's lips and immediately Lynne was unable to make a sound.

The Nun held Lynne against the wall in between the front door and the window, and with one finger, prevented her from moving or making a sound.

Lynne didn't know what to think or how to feel. She had watched horror films and scary movies before, but this wasn't supposed to be happening in real life.

Lynne knew she wasn't dreaming, because there was too much detail, besides, you know when your awake...you know when you wake up from sleep, and Lynne knew she was awake.

As Lynne stood wondering what to do, she could smell the musky, rotten order coming from The Nun's skin.

Lynne felt that as soon as The Nun releases her, she was going to run...but where to run to. The way this Nun keeps appearing and disappearing, and coming in and out of thin air like this, Lynne thought...

"Could she really run from her, and would it make any sense to try?"

Many things ran through Lynne's mind as she stood there, she had even thought about...what if her friends from church came by, there might be a chance that everyone praying...night be enough to defeat this Nun.

Instantly, The Nun grabbed Lynne by the hair saying...

"Don't even try it prayer and all that churchy shit won't help you, you might as well get used to it, there's a new Sheriff in town bitch!"

There are simple rules for governing most paranormal phenomena, and they love finding ways around them. As Lynne will find out, there is one basic rule that will keep ghosts, spirits, entities away from her and that is..." they can only go and visit people and places that they are familiar with, but that's if they play by the rules."

Before Lynne knew it, she heard the sound of a horn honking, and as Lynne looked out the window she saw Ray's car in the driveway.

Frantic to move, Lynne was still being held by the Nun, and was still unable to talk or to make a noise.

All Lynne could do was to hope that Ray would get out of the car and come inside to check and see what was keeping her, and as fate would allow...Ray shut off the car and began up the driveway. Lynne felt a sigh of relief as she noticed Ray getting closer to the door, and said to herself...

"Now, this stinky-smelly old Bitch, is out of here."

Lynne looked at the Nun who had a wicked looking grin on her face, as she too noticed Ray at the door.

The Nun whispered to Lynne...

"Now, I'm going to remove my hand from your lips, and let's see what you do."

The Nun released her hand from Lynne's lips as the door came flying open. Ray looked around and cried out...

"Lynne! Lynne, where are you baby?"

Lynne was three feet from Ray and was moving towards him as Lynne tried touching him, but her hand passed right through Ray's body.

Lynne stood looking at her hand, and crying, saying...

"Ray, baby, I'm right here..."

Ray headed upstairs as Lynne turned to see the Nun laughing hysterically, falling into the wall, saying...

"Oh, my badness, I can't take it this is too damn easy ha-ha-ha-ha-ha."

Lynne turned back to Ray as he was coming down the stairs and dialing a number on his cell phone, saying...

"Hello Lynne, hey baby, where are you at, I thought we were going to meet each for lunch and take care of some errands today?"

While Ray was carrying on a conversation with Lynne's voice mail, Lynne was trying to get his attention, hollering...

"I'm right here in the apartment, look, I'm right here...!"

Unable to finish her sentence, because the Nun was rolling on the floor in laughter, said...

"Oh, this is so good, the stupid mule's ass has not one clue what is happening."

Suddenly, Ray put his cell back in his pocket and bolted out the front door, into his car and drove off.

Lynne meanwhile, stood at the window watching, unable to follow him or to leave the apartment, as the Nun said...

"Are you getting a clue yet? As long as I'm in the room, the rules in my world apply. No one will be able to see, or hear you, and I can do anything I want, but enough of that...you got a little trip to make in a few moments."

Lynne, tried to distract The Nun by talking about one of the lessons she learned in Sunday school, and by also singing...

"Jesus loves me this I know, for the Bible tells me so, little ones to Him belong, they are weak, but He is strong...Yes Jesus loves me...

The Nun cocked her head to the right and drew a disgusting look on her face as Lynne continued singing, and then the Nun started dancing and singing...

"Sister Mary has a bitch, she doesn't know how to quit, she thinks that she is so smart, but I'll show her ass, today her nightmares start."

Instantly, Lynne was no longer in her apartment, but she was at work in the hospital, and dressed in her scrubs, walking from her car.

Lynne could tell something wasn't right but had no recollection of The Nun and the events which occurred and could not think what could be the matter.

Do you ever get the feeling that what you're doing at the moment has already been done, well, Lynne had that feeling, and couldn't shake it?

Lynne kept thinking that she was not scheduled to work, but still made her way towards the hospital. Suddenly her cell phone rang, and Lynne scrambled to retrieve her phone out of her bag, which was sitting on the front passenger seat.

Locating her phone, she noticed it was her sister, Deanne, as she answered it saying...

"Hey Sis, on my way to work, what's up?"

Deanne's voice sounded panicky, as she said...

"I thought you were off tonight?

"I thought so too, but apparently I'm doing a back-to-backer, so what are you up to?"

Deanne said as the phone signal between her and Lynne started breaking up.

Just then, the call between Lynne and Deanne was completely dropped as Deanne turned to Kristin and said...

"I'll wait ten or fifteen minutes and try her again, hopefully, she'll be in a better area."

Deanne and Kristin were on their way to an appointment they had with a spiritualist, who claimed that she could get rid of unwanted ghost and spirits.

Deanne tried again to reach Lynne, but got a message saying...

"We're sorry, but the number you've reached is not working at this time, perhaps you shouldn't call it, Deanne...oh tell Kristin, we'll be seeing her again soon."

A look of shock came over Deanne's face when she heard the message, but particularly her name and the message for Kristin, as she thought...

"How'd our names get on a recorded message?"

Pulling into the Goodale address, Kristin said to Deanne...

"What! What did you just say?"

Deanne redialed the number and handed the phone to Kristin and when Kristin heard the message, she yelled...

"What in the hell is this! Is this a joke or some kind of game?"

Deanne lit a cigarette and said...

"Game! Kristin, did you hear what the fuck it said?"

Kristin redialed the number to hear it again, and when the number rang, there was no message only the sound of sinister laughter.

Kristin shoved the phone in Deanne's face saying...

"Girlfriend, this is messed up, let's go inside and get this over with."

Deanne and Kristin took the elevator to the third floor and continued down a long hallway. As the two of them passed under a ceiling lamp, it flickered and then the intensity of the light grew exceedingly bright and then returned to normal.

They were told to get off on the third floor and come to the last room at the end of the hallway, but when they arrived the numbers on the doors read…

"Two O' Four."

Glancing around at the next two doors, the numbers all read correctly, three O' six, three O' eight.

Standing there in surprise, Kristin said to Deanne…

"Tell me we're not seeing this, will you?"

Deanne was on the verge of nodding her head in agreement when the door opened and young lady in her early thirties said…

"Hello, I'm Christine, Dr. Olme asked me to bring you in before you get yourselves into trouble…you wanna follow me?"

Deanne and Kristin followed the young lady passed a crowed reception area into a large office.

Kristin asked…

"Wow, that was strange."

Taking a seat, Deanne said…

"What's strange Kris?"

Looking at Christine and pointing in the direction of the reception area, Kristin said…

"I mean all those people, they stared at us like, we were jumping in front of them or something."

Christine closed the door and replied to Kristin…

"I'll inform Dr. Olme, that you're waiting, just a moment please."

Deanne looked at Kristin saying…

Maybe those folks didn't have an appointment, or their appointments are later, who knows."

Deanne took her cell phone out, to call Lynne's number to see if the message was still there, to show Dr. Olme, when the door opened, and a lady emerged through the door saying…

"Hello, I am Dr. Olme."

11
Dr. Olme

Dr. Hema Olme, who pronounces her name...'Hema Ole-mah', one would expect an average to short woman from the Bangladesh or the Pakistani region with such a name as that, but Deanne and Kristin were shocked to discover that she was over six feet tall, and from Cantor, West Des-Moines, Iowa, of all places.

Dr. Olme spoke with a slight British accent. Her hair was dirty blonde and in a pony tail which hung over her right shoulder. Both Kristin and Deanne looked at one another as Dr. Olme shuffled papers around, until Dr. Olme stated...

"Alright now, first, the people in the lobby are not real, and secondly, they have been all around you, you just have not paid attention."

Deanne interrupted, saying...

"Dr. Olme, excuse me...the reason we're here is..."

Dr. Olme, shifted in her chair saying...

"I know why you are here, but if you don't listen to what I am saying, things are only going to get a little harder for you."

Dr. Olme, looked past Deanne to Kristin saying...

"They weren't real?"

Looking over at Deanne, Kristin turned back to Dr. Olme saying...

"What did you say?"

Dr. Olme pointed her finger towards the door saying...

"I sensed that you were wondering about the people you thought you saw when you came in...those were not real people."

Deanne, with a look of amazement replied...

"How'd you know what I was thinking?"

With a not so concerned look on her face, Dr. Olme stated...

"Both of your thoughts are easy to read, because they smell bad, you and your friend here, have witnessed a lot of things that you don't understand because you think things only evolve and exist in this present reality...but they don't."

Looking back to Deanne, Dr. Olme, lowered the tone in her voice saying...

"Miss Byrd, my senses tell me that you have been contacted by the Nun, and others too...is that correct?"

Deanne nodded her head, saying...

"I don't know what or even who they are. At first my boyfriend, David, was saying he was seeing things and people, and that people were appearing and disappearing.

Initially, I didn't believe him, until we all, I mean myself, Kristin and a lot of our friends began seeing them."

Dr. Olme offered Kristin and Deanne a stick of gum, before putting a piece in her mouth saying...

"That's because someone opened the door, these spirits really can't enter this world without our permission and now they don't want to leave.

Some of the people that you are acquainted with, have given that permission without realizing they've done it, and it looks to me like you've given that permission where your condo and where the farm is concerned and that's why they are focused on those two places."

Deanne looked over at Kristin, saying...

"Who gave what?"

Dr. Olme folded her fingers and said...

"Someone in your group, or family has given permission, through something they've said or done, permission for these spirits to enter in through the door of this dimension and..."

Dr. Olme paused for a few seconds, before Kristin asked...

"C'mon now, you really can't be serious about this shit, can you?"

Dr. Olme, scribbled something on her pad and said...

"Some shit just stinks worse than others...and you'll believe that before you believe anything else. Yes, I'm serious and so should you be, you called on me, remember?"

Deanne scooted to the edge of her chair saying...

"What about God and prayer, surely that'll work, right?"

Sensing Deanne was more of a believer than Kristin, Dr. Olme said...

"Things of the spirit belong to the things of the spiritual realm. The spirit cannot engage with the earthly realm unless invited and once you invite one spirit, you cannot invite another spirit to cast the other out."

Kristin was sitting and shaking her head in disbelief, and said...

"I don't mean to be rude but, what you're saying sounds like bull shit."

Dr. Olme looked over at Kristin, saying...

"It's this kind of negativity, which these entities feed off of, don't you know that?"

Kristin replied...

"All I know is, we got spooks and spirits and shit jumping out of the wood works and all you can do is, tell us to take an aspirin and call you in the morning."

Seeing that Kristin was becoming too defensive, Deanne grab hold of Kristin's arm and pulled her back into her seat, saying...

"David did say that all this started at the farm last year. He inherited it from his family who came to Port Clinton in the early eighteen hundreds from North Carolina."

Dr. Olme nodded saying...

"What's going on could be left over from the people who owned the farm before you inherited it. It's possible that there were a lot of negative feelings, anger, sadness, maybe even deaths, from the people who lived there before.

These emotions can move with people, from place to place and they can also be imprinted on a place."

Deanne sighed, saying...

"David mention how his mother wanted nothing to do with the farm, because she felt it was cursed or haunted. How one of her Cherokee ancestors went missing, but it was later uncovered that the plantation owner had her hidden in the cellar for his own pleasure and was ultimately murdered."

Trying to be calm, Kristin looked at Deanne and said...

"Why don't you guys just sell the place, get rid of it and these spooks will go too, right?"

Dr. Olme, shook her head and said...

"I'm doubtful if that'll work, these spirits have become connected with you *and your family and friends, and just walking away won't solve things, they'll just follow you, besides, they may stop you from trying to sell it.*

In order to get rid of these beings or spirits, is to change the atmosphere. If the negative atmosphere is removed from a place, then they may go away. They simply can't survive on happy, positive emotions."

Kristin interrupted saying...

"So, we gotta learn the words to Kumbaya, and the recipe for girl scout cookies...huh?"

Dr. Olme stood up and looked at Deanne saying...

"Since you accepted ownership of the farm and probably are quite happy with it, you are going to have to change the atmosphere in it. Which is likely why these spirits are finding themselves at home.

If you keep things positive and upbeat, they shouldn't hang around for long, and then on the other hand...they may feel as though the farm and everything and everyone associated with it, is theirs, and they'll never leave."

Deanne and Kristin stood up, as Deanne said...

"Okay, we need to tell it that it has to leave our property and never come back, right?"

Dr. Olme, opened the door saying...

"I wouldn't be rude or condescending, just firm. Then just keep things positive and see if that gets rid of them...oh, you might also have your friend here, tone it down a little...I can sense they are quite fond of her."

Deanne, Kristin and Dr. Olme walked down the hall to the doorway, when Deanne asked...

"Thanks for your advice, how much do I owe you?"

Dr. Olme raised her hand and shaking it said...

"We'll talk later about what type of payment I'll take."

Deanne and Kristin were almost to the elevator when from seemingly out of nowhere, there stood Dr. Olme who said...

"I'm glad I caught you two before you left. I'm actually calling it a day, but I did want to ask you if I would be able to inspect your condo as well as the farm in Port Clinton?"

Looking surprised, Deanne replied...

"I don't see why not, but I will have to run it across my boyfriend first."

Kristin leaned into Dr. Olme saying...

"Now that, is going to be a whole lot of running, let me tell you."

Deanne turned and snapped at her saying...

"Damn Kris, why do you always have to spell bitch with a capital 'B', can't you give it a rest?"

Reaching into her coat pocket for a cigarette, Kristin replied...

"C'mon, you know I didn't mean nothing by that, besides, Dave can be an asshole when it comes to asking him to do something simple."

Stepping close to Kristin and Deanne, Dr. Olme said...

"Ladies, I didn't mean to cause the balloon to go up, if it's going to be an issue, I don't need to inspect your places."

Deanne depressed the remote and unlocked the car, telling Kristin...

"Just get in Kristin."

As Kristin got in the car, Deanne and Dr. Olme continued their conversation for a few minutes and then Deanne got in the car and drove off.

As Deanne and Kristin headed towards their condo, Deanne was very quiet, so much till Kristin asked...

"Deanne, what in doodle shit made you even think that going to a nut case like that was going to pan out, I mean we could've gotten more useful information from a convention for the mentally challenged."

Deanne continued without acknowledging Kristin until Kristin screamed...

"WATCH OUT!"

Deanne swerved the car to keep from hitting an old man crossing the street pushing a grocery shopping cart.

Deanne's car came to rest inches from a telephone pole. Several cars behind Deanne slammed on brakes to keep from running into them, as one car pulled in front of Deanne and the driver came to check on Deanne and Kristin saying...

"Hey, are you two okay...you almost caused a two or three car wreck back there?"

Shaken but not injured, Deanne rolled the window down and spoke with the man, saying...

"We're so sorry sir, is anyone back there hurt?"

The man placed two hands on Deanne's car, saying...

"No one's hurt, we were concerned about you and your friend here; gosh you gave us a scare."

Kristin nodded that she was okay, meanwhile Deanne did not notice that inches from her face, the man was wearing an unusual ring on his finger. It was the same kind of symbol that the Nun was wearing, A silver eye of hours.

Both Deanne and Kristin got out of the car to inspect not only her car, but also to see if anyone was hurt in the two vehicles behind her.

Kristin noted that Deanne was obviously distracted, as she said…

"Hey Deanne, let me drive."

Without hesitation Deanne gave Kristin the keys and sat on the passenger side, saying…

"Wow that was close, I mean I was concentrating on where I was going and everything, and then all of a sudden…"

"All of a sudden what Deanne?"

Kristin said as she handed Deanne her pack of cigarettes to get one out of the pack for her, so that she could keep her eyes on the road.

Deanne lit Kristin's cigarette and handed it to her and Kristin rolled both front windows down a little to let the smoke out, as Deanne said…

"Back there, while I was driving, I saw Dr. Olme and the Nun standing on the side of the road with their thumbs out, hitch hiking…I'm serious."

Kristin turned the heat up in the car and glanced over to Deanne saying…

"Dee, I don't know about that freaky ass Doctor nor any Nun, but all I saw was an old man you were about to run over…I mean it was like you were aiming for him or something."

Deanne turned back to Kristin saying…

"I don't know anything about an old man…I-I just remember seeing the Nun and Dr. Olme standing by the road and looking dead at me."

Kristin continued onto the freeway ramp and then onto interstate seventy-one south. Just then, the radio came on, with the music blaring.

Deanne reached up to turn the volume down when the voice of Dr. Olme filled the car through the speakers, saying…

"Hello ladies are you two listening to me…I told you that I would let you know what my charge for today's session was gonna be and here it is."

As Deanne and Kristin sat in shock of what they were hearing, when a gust of wind picked up making it hard for Kristin to steer the car.

Without any time to react, a metal trash can lid came crashing into the passenger side of the car, causing Deanne to jump and scream and causing Kristin to jerk the steering wheel hard to the right, sending the car onto the shoulder, barely hitting a road sign and then back onto the interstate.

Kristin hollered to get Deanne to stop screaming, saying...

"Damnit Dee, will you shut the fuck up please!

Kristin took the first exit she saw, saying to Deanne...

"Dee, I'm so sorry for yelling but you were weirding me out here. I think we'd better stick to the streets instead of the interstate, that was pretty close back there."

Deanne was sitting back in her seat, trying to calm herself down, when she glanced at Kristin saying...

"Okay Kris, I don't care which way you take as long as we get home soon...I just want out of this car and to be home."

Kristin turned onto state route three-fifteen, which ran alongside of interstate seventy-one. It was a beautiful night with a full moon. At last, Kristin was coming to Westerville, which meant they had at least twenty minutes of driving left.

Deanne and Kristin's mood even changed, they were laughing and discussing Dr. Olme, when the engine started to cough, and the emergency light came on and off.

They had just reached twenty-three north, which leads them to Cornerstone Dr. and then home.

Both Kristin and Deanne saw the emergency light come on and go off, but with all the things which have already happened to them, neither one wanted to think about anything else happening.

Travelling that stretch of road at night was as they say...." *drivers beware.*" That area was the place where a school bus full of children had stalled on the tracks and was hit by a train.

Everyone on the bus was killed by an oncoming eastbound freight train, which did not see the bus through the heavy fog until it was too late.

People who live in the area, as well as fishermen out on the lake say...'they can hear the ghosts of the children haunting that intersection with small screams and cries'.

Before coming to the tracks there is a nice stretch of road, a hundred feet, and then everyone hits their gas pedal, and then a short smooth bump over the tracks.

Deanne and Kristin knew about the tracks and the legend associated with it and was silently hoping the car would make it safely across the tracks before breaking down or dying completely.

Kristin looked over at Deanne saying…

"Almost home…we hit the little bump, glide over the tracks and a couple blocks and I'm going to make a lot of adult beverages disappear."

Kristin started depressing the gas pedal, and wouldn't you know it, several deer were crossing in front of them, so Kristin couldn't maintain her speed, she had to slow down to keep from hitting them.

Kristin felt, that if she could give the car a quick burst of speed, everything would be alright, but the railroad signals started flashing and a bright light appeared a little way down the track, bearing down fast on Kristin and Deanne.

Kristin hit the gas pedal, as Deanne yelled…

"Hurry up, Kris! Oh my God the train's coming," as if Kristin didn't see it.

The car approached the intersection, but not with the speed the average drivers use to clear the tracks.

Right where the car's tires would've slightly left the pavement to send them gliding over the tracks, the car's engine died, and stopped, leaving several inches of the car's rear bumper dangerously close to the tracks.

Knowing that they were in trouble, Kristin struggled with her seat belt, which was not releasing as it should.

Deanne had no problem with her seat belt and seeing the trouble Kristin was having, tried her door to see it if would open, and it did not.

Deanne threw herself across the stick-shift and fought with pulling on Kristin's seat belt which gave no signs of releasing.

The approaching train saw the stalled car and began blowing its whistle sharply. Deanne risked a quick glance over to look at the train even though it was a little ways off, nevertheless a person still wants to have plenty of time in any situation to avoid disaster.

The train came closer and closer, and Kristin and Deanne struggle and struggled and turned back looking at the train barreling down on them, until the women waited too late to exit the car.

The train came fast, horning blowing. Deanne grabbed onto Kristin, as they both screamed and buried their faces into each other, as the train was now upon them.

The sound of the train's horn and the wind and noises from the train filled the car, when suddenly, it felt as if the car was given a sharp shove from behind.

Not the kind of shove you'd expect if something bumped your car, but more, the kind of shove you'd get from something powerful pushing you.

Deanne and Kristin both gasped for air as Deanne fell onto Kristin's shoulder as the car started to roll forward, slowly at first, and then with more speed, down the hill.

The rear end of the car had cleared the tracks with mere inches, just a second before the train roared past.

Deanne's car rolled once more to a stop on the far side of the tracks, and into the curb.

Neither Deanne nor Kristin noticed the engineer sticking his head out the window of the engine and shaking a fist at them; shouting something nasty for scaring him.

"Th-that was close."

Deanne gasped as Kristin sat upright in the driver's seat, saying...

"How did you get the car moving?"

Kristin reached over and grabbed her seat belt with all her might, and went to pull it apart, when it came unfastened all by itself, as she said...

"What the hell."

Deanne looked at Kristin with the *'what'* look, when Kristin said...

"All that struggling to get this damn seat belt loose, when it just comes undone moments after we could've been choo-choo mush."

Deanne and Kristin tried starting the car, which would not start and decided to walk the three blocks to Deanne and David's condo.

The wind had picked up a little, swirling around them in the darkness, patting their hair and their shoulders like the soft touch of a someone's hand. Deanne shivered and interlocked hands with Kristin.

Looking at each other as they walked thinking...

"We almost bought it back there".

As Deanne got closer to home, she pulled out her cell phone, to call David, so that he could be on the lookout for them.

Kristin stopped suddenly, staring at the car, and said...

"Deanne, look!"

They both walked back several feet to the car. Scattered in multiple places all across the back of Deanne's car were glowing handprints. They were handprints, the kind that you'd find of kids who lined the walls of any elementary school.

Deanne and Kristin started shaking as they remembered the story about the school bus full of kids who were killed, when Deanne said...

"You seeing this Kris? It's like my car was pushed off the tracks by the ghosts of those kids who were killed here years ago."

The wind swept around Deanne and Kristin again, when Deanne said...

"I thought I heard an echo in the distance of children's voices, whispering... 'You're welcome'.

Kristin looked at Deanne, then the wind died down and the handprints faded from the back of the car.

Deanne and Kristin clung together for a moment in terror, and then quickly started walking towards David and Deanne's condo.

On any given day, Deanne and David would take a walk in the neighborhood, specifically, the same path that Deanne and Kristin were on, and it would take them, at a slow pace about twenty minutes, but for some reason the walk home seem to take hours.

Deanne and Kristin should have made it home in fifteen minutes, but something was wrong...something was very wrong.

Deanne looked over at Kristin saying...

"Let's go this way, we'll cut across the open field instead of walking all the way around."

Kristin stopped to light a cigarette and to scan the area where Deanne was pointing before she said...

"Oh, hell to the Naw! We start walking through the woods, and then something creepy jumps out and grabs our dumb asses...no way."

Just then, it started sprinkling, and Deanne said...

"We keep walking this way and we're gonna get soaked, I'm telling you, we cut through the open field and...boom, we're home in no time."

Flicking her cigarette butt in the wind, Kristin replied...

"Only if you call Dave and Steve and tell 'em that we're cutting through the field and to meet us halfway, and then I'll do it?"

Deanne took out her cell and called David, saying...

"Hey Blue, Kristin and I are going to cut through the field behind the condo, can you meet us?"

David told Deanne that he and Steve were on their way, and Wendi was staying at the condo.

Deanne put her cell back in her pocket and she and Kristin begin walking through the field when the rain started picking up to a moderate shower.

Deanne remember looking at the time on her phone when she was talking to David, it was ten past midnight on the dot, nothing odd at the time, except it was taking them longer and longer to get home, but Deanne didn't want to alarm Kristin.

As peered through the open area, Kristin screamed. Deanne anxiously whispered...

"What's wrong?"

Kristin said she had just seen a dark figure leaning against one of the bare trees to her right.

Looking intently in the direction Kristin pointed to, Deanne saw nothing and said...

"Aww girl, that's just the fog moving in, there's nothing there."

Just then, a big cat slowly crossed in front of them, making both Deanne and Kristin scream, as Kristin yelled out...

"I told you that going this way was a bad idea...but no, you gotta drag our happy asses through it."

Just as Kirstin and Deanne were ten or fifteen feet into the open field Kristin turned and saw something coming up behind and said...

"LOOK! Did you see that."

Deanne has known Kristin all their adult lives dating back to college at Ohio University, and she knew Kristin well enough to know that she has been and continues to be one of the biggest drama queens ever, so it was no surprise that everything had to be about her.

Deanne turned slightly saying...

"Okay, now what? I don't see anything."

Deanne barely got the words out of her mouth when she noticed several figures about fifty feet behind them, and said...

"What the fuck?"

Deanne told Kristin...

"C'mon girl, let's get the hell out of here."

Deanne and Kristin picked up their pace and were now walking extremely fast through the field, but no matter how fast their pace was, it seemed that the two figures behind them were matching them, step by step.

Deanne turned back several times to monitor how close the figures were to them, when Kristin tugged on her coat, saying...

"Quit that shit! This is how people get caught, it's called horror one 'o one...when something is after you don't become so distracted that you trip and fall over something."

Deanne glanced back again behind her, before responding to Kristin, saying...

"You, that's why I won't look at horror shows, or any of that bullshit you watch...it weirds you out and makes you paranoid."

Just then, Kristin looked over at Deanne saying...

"Dee, I'm not looking back, but it feels like someone is breathing on my neck."

Deanne tapped Kristin on the arm saying...

"Kris, when I tell you to run...run, and keep up with me."

The smell of the midnight air and the rain, had picked up considerably, providing an almost portentous ingredient to the night air. Where there was once silence, was now replaced by what seemed like the laughter of children.

The faster both women ran, the more the night rain began blinding them from seeing clearly, so much till Deanne slipped in the mud as she was turning around a row of bushes. Kristin, slowed down and then stopped to go back to help Deanne to her feet, saying...

"C'mon Dee, you gotta get up."

As Deanne got to her feet, both women looked behind them, and saw that the two figures were still pursuing them, as they started running again.

The rain was now pouring down, as Deanne and Kristin struggled to keep from slipping in the leaves and mud, when Kristin let out a scream.

Both Deanne and Kristin stopped, wet hair down in their faces, and out of breath, Deanne said...

"What? What were you screaming at?"

Kristin, shaking and pointing dead ahead, said...

"Now, don't you say you don't see that?"

Deanne squinted her eyes to see through the rain, as Kristin looked back at the two figures who were getting closer, saying...

"What are we going to do Dee, whoever those creeps are, they are getting close?"

Deanne was concentrating on trying to see who it was, that was coming at them when she said to Kristin...

"That's Blue and Steve, Kristin."

Kristin turned her attention back to Deanne, as she said...

"How do you know Dee, it could be anyone."

Just then, from behind, a hand touched Deanne on her shoulder and said...

"Hello Deanne, I told you we were going to talk about what I would except for my services today."

Deanne recognized that voice as Dr. Olme, whom they met earlier. Deanne looked at Kristin and yelled out to her...

"RUN Kristin, RUN!"

Deanne and Kristin took off, running as fast and as hard as they could. With Deanne and David's condo in sight, Deanne and Kristin had only one obstacle left and that was to navigate a small hill in the rain and mud.

Kristin followed Deanne around the corner as they ran into David and Steve, as Deanne said...

"Oh my God Blue...my heart just stopped!"

Deanne looked behind her, but there was nothing but rain and darkness. David and Steve took Deanne and Kristin by the arm and led them around the side of the unit to the front, when all of a sudden, they stopped.

Looking at their unit, they noticed that the main front door and sliding door (which they never leave open) was wide open, so were the upstairs windows, nothing was merely opened half way or a quarter of the way, they were opened as far as they could go.

Deanne looked at David saying...

"Blue, wow, you didn't have to leave all the doors and windows opened like that."

David, Deanne, Kristin and Steve walked up the steps to the front door, as David and Steve inspected the door and downstairs windows, and closing them said...

"*What's going on, we closed the door before we left, didn't we?*"

Deanne told Kristin to come up stairs so that they could wash up when David turned to Steve saying...

"*Hey, Steve, close the windows and the back door will you, I'm going upstairs to check to make sure everything is alright up there.*"

David was upstairs a total of fifteen minutes when he backed out of the bedroom, calling for Steve, saying...

"*You better get up here buddy...better hurry.*"

David met Steve as he was heading up the steps and said...

"*It's bad, man...Deanne, Wendi and Kristin are hanging from the ceiling fan.*"

David grabbed hold of Steve's arm to keep him from entering the room as Steve said...

"*Fuck all that shit Dave, now get your damn hands off me!*"

As Steve barged in the room, David heard him shout...

"*OMG*"

Rushing in the room after Steve, David stopped in his tracks. Deanne, Wendi and Kristin were sitting on the bed sharing a bottle of wine and looking surprised as Steve and David came crashing in, saying...

"*What in the hell is wrong with you two, I know this is our room Blue, but you guys knew we were in here.... you could've at least knocked.*"

Without another word, Steve grabbed David by the collar and threw him out of the room and against the hallway wall, shouting...

"*Dave, you punk ass, scary rabbit bitch...how in the buffalo fuck can you play a sick ass game like that? You had me about to lose it, man what the fuck is up with you?*"

David looked past Steve and wrestled Steve's hands off him, saying...

"*Steve, we've been friends for a long time, I'm telling you when I stepped in the room, they were all hanging from the ceiling...I swear, I wouldn't pull no sick shit like that.*"

Steve had his back to the bedroom door, which was maybe eight or nine feet away from the bed saying...

"*Well, Dave, they're sitting on the bed now...alive, and wondering what our problem is.*"

Suddenly, an odd feeling came over the room. Seriously, it felt like the air in the room was suddenly either sucked out, or made very heavy, and it almost felt like everybody was in a bubble.

Deanne looked over at David and Steve saying in a very frightened voice, that sounded like she couldn't breathe very well, and like she couldn't get out the words without struggling, saying...

"Do you feel that? What's happening?"

David and Steve tried to speak, when their speech actually came out, kind of slurred, and David ended up mouthing the words...

"I don't know...I can't move..."

Steve also mouthed a reply, saying...

"I can't...either..."

Just then Wendi stumbled out of the room into Steve's arms saying...

"What's happening? What's happening?"

Just then, the feeling of being in a bubble disappeared until there was nothing but an eerie silence, and then all of sudden, the bedroom doors as well as the bathroom door opened and slammed shut.

Steve, Wendi, Kristin, David and Deanne tried going towards the steps but were unable to move, except in the direction of the master bedroom, when Deanne cried...

"I gotta pee...I gotta pee."

Turning to Deanne, David said...

"You got to what?"

Kristin interrupted..., you heard her, she has to pee, people don't lose that bodily function just because weird ass shit happens."

David turned, saying to Kristin...

"We need to stick together, shit always happens when people split up, sorry Deanne...but you're gonna have to hold it."

Just then, the bathroom doorknob started turning. It was turning over and over again... almost like someone was trying to open it, but they weren't trying to open the door... it was actually turning in a rhythm.

It was turning back and forth, back and forth, in a rhythm at about the same tempo as the slow beat of the bass drum... like a beat to a song.

Deanne, Kristin and Wendi had inched closer to the bathroom door, and then froze. Their first thoughts were that someone had broken in David and Deanne's condo, though they couldn't figure out why someone would break in and be in the bathroom.

Deanne thought it was odd that the doorknob would be turning back and forth, especially since the bathroom door has no lock on it.

If someone was in there, they should've been able to open the door and walk right out.

While Deanne, Kristin and Wendi's movements were restricted, Steve and David couldn't move at all. That weird heavy-gravity feeling that was holding them down, still would not allow any of them to move.

David looked over at Steve, who was trying desperately to move out of the spot he was in but could not. The only movement David was able to make was in turning his head very slowly, and watching the doorknob turning.

Then, as the silence became thick, everyone heard it... singing. Voices, that sounded like a pair of young girls. At first none of them could make out the lyrics, and the only clear lyrics were the very last words at the end:

"Cold dead dancing".

The young girl's voices were singing in an almost nursery rhyme type style of singing, all the while turning the bathroom doorknob back and forth, to match the tempo of what they were singing...

"The Nun says, today brings pain,
And the night darkness until we open it up."

David grabbed the attention of everyone and opened his mouth to speak, but the sound that was produced was that of a mechanical voice in slow-motion, saying...

"What the hell are we going to do? We need to get the hell out of here."

The bathroom doorknob was still turning, back and forth and they were still singing this creepy song in a way that was kind of playful and taunting... for instance, kind of like when girls are teasing their younger brother or something.

The song almost sounded made up, by the way there was an automatic delay in the verse, when kids sometimes sing little made-up songs to be silly or playful, and at the end of the song, they were laughing, and giggling.

David turned his head, in slow motion, back and forth at the others to see if they were seeing and hearing the same thing he was.

David looked at Deanne's face and he could tell from the expression, that she was crying. The weird thing about it was, everything, the expressions, even the tears which ran down her cheeks were all in slow motion.

While everything for David and his friends seemed to move in slow motion, the song that the girls sung was in normal speed...

"When the Sister, Mary Jacalyn gets here there's gonna be cold dancing dead, dancing dead."

All at once, that heavy, dizzy weight that had been holding all of them down and making it so hard for them to move and breathe and talk, just lifted... just went away, like that.

When that feeling of that weight lifted, all of them could suddenly move again, and the air and gravity returned to normal.

From the moment of the loss of gravity and moving in slow motion, up until it lifted, lasted about thirty minutes.

Deanne and Kristin fell into the wall, while Wendi, David and Steve staggered, momentarily losing their balance, saying...

"What the hell just happened... Steve, check out the bathroom?"

Steve, went to the bathroom door, slowly and carefully, opening the door. The bathroom was empty, as Deanne came running and pushing her way past Steve and David, and saying to David...

"Blue, you keep that pretty ass of yours right by this door, and don't let anything come in on me!"

That's when Wendi and Kristin came up behind David, saying...

"Don't worry Dee, as soon as you're done, me and Kirstin have to pee too."

While Deanne was using the bathroom, Steve and David were whispering to one another saying...

"How could the bathroom be empty, Dave...we all heard them singing and the door knob turning!"

The upstairs was empty, except for Shone who was backed up against the door of the spare bedroom, growling.

Shone had either heard something or seen something… and from the direction in which she was looking as she barked, gave the impression that someone, or something was still upstairs, with them.

The air in the upstairs hallway suddenly felt hot and sticky, to the point that you could almost see a haze-like fog, trailing from the master bedroom door, past David, Steve, Kristin and Wendi, and going down the steps.

While David stayed at the bathroom door, he asked Steve to check out all the other rooms upstairs. As Steve walked down the hallway, he jumped as the sound of the toilet flushing startled him.

Wendi and Kristin however, were not affected, as they were anxiously crossing their legs and bouncing up and down waiting on their turn.

After what seemed like an eternity for Wendi and Kristin, the bathroom door opened, and Wendi brushed past Deanne, and ran into the bathroom as Deanne looked at Kristin and said to David…

"Out of the way Blue, girls on a mission."

Deanne stood embracing David, when the bathroom door open, and Wendi stood in the doorway wiping her hands as Kristin rushed past her, as Wendi threw the paper towel in the waste basket, saying…

"Okay, can we all get out here now?"

David looked down the hallway and then back to Deanne and Wendi, saying…

"Anyone see Steve?"

Deanne replied, saying…

"Huh…he came out of one of the bedrooms and headed downstairs; I thought you saw him."

David took Deanne's hand and looked at Wendi, saying…

"Okay, when Kristin is done, you two come on downstairs."

David, Wendi and Deanne started for the stairs, as David called out Steve's name…

"Hey Steve, what's going on man, where are you?"

Everything was still unsettling and spooky, as Deanne, Kristin and Wendi began talking about the way the girls' voices sounded, saying…

"Wendi, they didn't sound mean or creepy, or anything, they seriously sounded like two little girls who were just teasing us. It didn't feel or sound malevolent, or anything... even though it still creeped us all out."

Wendi replied...

"Dee, it all would make some kind of sense, but what were they doing in your house, and your bathroom of all places...and where did they go?"

David could tell that they were both still shaken up a bit, so he tried not commenting on anything as they reached the bottom of the stairs, where he cried for Steve, saying...

"Hey Steve...Steve."

No sooner had David called for Steve, did he emerged from the kitchen eating a sandwich with a drink in his hand, saying...

"So, you guys through watching each other pee?"

David walked up to Steve saying...

"Next time let somebody know when you're going to go off by yourself, okay, with all this creepy shit happening, hell I thought they grabbed your monkey ass."

Offering David half of his sandwich, which he did not take, Steve said...

"My bad, I wasn't even thinking, I mean, it is what it is...right?"

David walked slowly to the front door and turning the knob, discovered it would not budge as Steve said...

"Tried that when I got down here, it won't open, the windows won't budge either."

Wendi and Deanne walked up to Steve, as Kristin headed for the kitchen and after eye-balling his sandwich said to one another...

"We might as well get something to eat, it looks like we're stuck in here guys."

David followed everyone in the kitchen after he double checked all the windows along the way, saying...

"Is it just me, or am I the only one a little worried about the fact that we're trapped in here, and our cell phones don't work, and that there are some creepy ass spirits in here?"

Steve walked over to the cabinet and grabbed five glasses and poured several shots of vodka, into each one handing one to David.

Steve placed the others on the table and turning to Wendi, Kristin and Deanne, said...

"C'mon K-mart shoppers...we're all jacked up about everything, but what are we supposed to do, just sit here shaking like frightened little girls in a corner?"

David downed his shot of vodka as did, Deanne, Kristin and Wendi.

Every few minutes, David and Steve tried the cell phones, windows and doors, but were not able to get them to open.

Tired and exhausted, they all sat on the sofa with the television on low, drinking and talking.

About eleven o'clock p.m. everyone had fallen sound asleep, except David, who was coming around the corner in the living room, and who stopped because there was something very large and black by the dining room table.

Whatever it was, moved directly across the dining room floor til it was out of sight.

David looked in the half-lit room at Deanne, Kristin and Wendi who lay sound asleep, and snoring, while Steve was crumpled asleep in the chair by the front door.

David sat, sipping on another shot, smoking a cigarette wondering why, these things were bothering them when a loud noise which came from the kitchen woke everyone up, as it said...

"Alright kiddies, I've let you sleep enough. It's time to pay the piper and dance to the music!"

David started walking through the house with his gun in his hand and a drink in the other, saying in a loud voice...

"I am not scared of you, you motherfucker...C'mon."

David was trying to maintain some degree of control when something ran into the living room, causing Deanne, Kristin and Wendi to let out loud screams...

It was the Nun, Sister Mary Jacalyn! David could feel her eyes watching him, as she said...

"You! You little liar. You tell yourself you're not scared but you're about to piss and shit all over yourself."

David could feel all the little hairs on his arms and neck standing up. Just then Deanne began crying...

"I don't know who you are... why don't you please leave us alone."

Sister Mary Jacalyn hovered a few feet from the floor, over towards Deanne, saying...

"At last, someone who can speak up, it just so happens, it's a filthy cunt! Do you so-called men mean to tell me that you're gonna let this bitch show you that she has bigger balls, than you, and just think, I was on the verge of leaving you folks alone."

Steve stood up and said...

"Say, listen first off, you don't have to call our women names, just because you feel that way about yourself.

I'm not afraid you, why don't you just get the fuck out of here and leave us alone!"

Sister Mary Jacalyn hovered over within inches of Steve and dropped her head and then slowly turned saying...

"Aww, I'm so sorry. I didn't mean to bother you I'll leave."

With that, The Nun began hovering out of the living room towards the kitchen, as Deanne hugged Wendi, and Kristin saying...

"Oh my God, I can't believe she's gone."

Wendi, looking at Steve and David said...

"You did it baby, you made that old nasty ass bitch leave us alone."

For the first time, all day and night, there was something to celebrate. There was joy and excitement and a reason to cheer.

David reached out and shook Steve's hand, saying...

"Way to go Bubba."

Steve stood with a look of accomplishment on his face, saying...

"Just waited for the right moment, I mean after all, her old fake ass, didn't belong here anyway."

While the living room was the scene of joy and laughter, no one noticed that a gust of cold wind was blowing from the kitchen into the living room. Just then, a large gust of wind filled the living room, causing everyone to instantly be quiet.

There was loud laughter, a cackling which filled the whole condo as

Sister Mary Jacalyn appeared in the living room, dressed in a dingy white dress and wig, looking like a sick and decomposing Marilyn Monroe.

Deanne screamed as Steve stood up pointing at Sister Mary Jacalyn, saying...

"Hey! You were supposed to leave, what are you doing back here?"

Sister Mary Jacalyn turned to Steve saying...

"Was I really oh darn it, I guess I must have lied but honesty has never been my strong suit."

Sister Mary Jacalyn slightly bent her knees as a gust of wind caught her dingy white dress, and lifted it in the air, as she swished her ass, saying...

"Yes, I am naughty, and you thought Marylyn was the only one who could pull this off."

Sister Mary Jacalyn placed both her hands up to the sides of her cheeks, swaying her head side to side and saying...

"Pay attention girls, you just might learn how to bitch-a-size a situation."

Deanne, Kristin and Wendi ran to the front door trying to get out, as Deanne tried over and over again to unlock and open the door, but the door did not budge.

Wendi noticed a couple out walking and tried to get their attention by beating on the window, but the couple continued walking without turning their heads.

The pounding on the glass should've gotten the couples attention but when Wendi turned her head she noticed the Nun was standing at the window beside her, smiling and swaging her finger, saying...

"Don't you just hate it when people ignore you?"

Deanne began crying, while Wendi ran over to Steve, hugging him, saying...

"Do something Steve, we got to get out of here."

Just before Steve had a chance to say or do anything, David stepped in front of him and pointed his nine-millimeter pistol at The Nun and fired an entire clip in rapid succession at The Nun.

Steve reached up with his hand and placed it over David's hand, saying...

"Forget it dude, look, all the bullets are going through her and hitting the wall behind her."

David moved to the side and noticed the wall behind the Nun was full of bullet holes, then The Nun let out an ear-piercing cackling, and begun singing...

*"Adam caught Eve by the fur below,
that's the oldest catch I know
So sweet was the catch, and so good the chase,
that it's the oldest catch I know, I know...it's the oldest catch I know."*

Steve grabbed David by the arm and motioned for him to follow him. As they ran over by the front window.

Steve and David began snatching down the drapes and the blinds, as Steve said...

"The nasty ass bitch said that nobody could hear us, well, they'll just have to see us then."

As Steve was pounding on the window and jumping up and down, David grabbed one of the dining room chairs and began beating it against the window.

After what seemed like hours, David leaned up against the wall, exhausted while Steve urged him to keep trying to get out, as he threw a chair into the window, only to watch the chair smashed to pieces against the window.

Deanne, Kristin and Wendi, not knowing what to do and scared out of their minds turned and started running upstairs.

When David, noticed what Deanne, Kristin and Wendi were doing, and how they were making a mistake, he yelled to them, saying...

"No! Don't go up there!"

However, somewhere along the way, Deanne heard a voice at the top of the stairs whispering to her, saying...

"I bet you got a pretty fur that the fellows go crazy for. I bet you a penny you can't make it to the top of the stairs before I make you trip and fall."

Deanne tried ignoring the voices, until she did just that, tripped and fell. Wendi and Kristin stopped to help Deanne to her feet, saying...

"You okay Dee?"

Nervous and shaking, Deanne said...

"You won't believe me, but I-I just heard a voice telling me I was going to trip and fall, going up the stairs."

Not really knowing if running upstairs was a good idea, Deanne and Wendi stopped and stood on the steps before going any further.

Kristin was at the top of the steps crying, not knowing why they ran up the stairs in the first place, or where they were going to go, when a voice cried out to them...

"Girls!"

It was a real person's voice, not something that they imagined in their heads, but a real voice that was taunting and teasing them, saying...

"Deanne Kristin Wendi I'll bet you, that neither one of you three makes it out of here alive."

Wendi, Kristin and Deanne each looked at one another, horrified, and then they ran into Deanne and David's bedroom, locking the door behind them.

Realizing what they had just done, Deanne tried to turn the door knob, but it didn't open, so she began banging on the door and calling David's name, hollering...

"Blue...Blue, help us we're locked in here!"

David and Steve rushed upstairs after hearing Deanne's cries for help, began pounding on the door and trying to open it, but it would not open.

Just then, Steve hollered through the door to Deanne...

"Stand back!"

Backing up to the edge of the steps, Steve lowered his shoulder and with all his might put his shoulder into the door, and the door flew open.

As Steve and David entered the room, they saw Deanne, Kristin and Wendi huddled over by the bed crying and hugging one another, when suddenly, the bedroom door slammed shut, and there stood the Nun, Sister Mary Jacalyn.

"Oh no, not you again...what do you want!"

Steve cried out as he stood in front of Wendi, Kristin and Deanne, shielding them. David approached The Nun, pointing his finger at her and said...

"You! You're the one responsible for all of this, who the hell are you...and why won't you leave us alone?"

Sister Mary Jacalyn held out her hand and with that, David was stopped in his tracks, unable to move as Sister Mary Jacalyn slapped David upside his head twice, saying...

"You tries, and you tries, but you just don't listen, do you?"

As Sister Mary Jacalyn maneuvered in front of David, Steve withdrew the gun from his pocket, and as he raised it towards her, Sister Mary Jacalyn said sharply...

"Put that down, unless you wanna see me twist his head, off his shoulders."

Steve lowered the gun and let it drop to the floor, as Sister Mary Jacalyn continued...

"Responsible! Oh, you have no idea what I'm responsible for, or what I'm capable of.
Before I'm done, half of this city will have murdered one another, and condemned themselves to a life of prison and torture, just as I was, so many years ago oooh, I can hardly wait."

Sister Mary Jacalyn took her long, filthy fingers and caressed David's face, and then began squeezing David's face, as he grimaced in pain, as she shouted...

"Your ancestors condemned me to a hell hole, without a trial, and I intend to do all of their descendants, the same!"

Hoping to get her to loosen her grip on David's face, as blood began trickling from his nose, Steve took a step towards her shouting...

"You're a sick, twisted lying fuck... when this city was established, all that was here were German Catholics and Hungarian Gypsies. Heck look around... Wendi, Kristin and Deanne are Lutherans, I'm an Atheist and I know you got it wrong on Dave here, he's part Cherokee and part African American."

Sister Mary Jacalyn lifted David off the floor and throwing him to the other side of the bedroom said...

"You fool, I am speaking of the descendants of the residents of this city. How you ever got dominion over anything except a cesspool of piss and vomit, I'll never know.
We're going to play a little game, I am sending you back in time to a nightmare, and then we'll talk again."

Sister Mary Jacalyn, then clapped her hands, and with that the room was empty. David and Deanne found themselves back at the farm in Port Clinton, without any recollection of Sister Mary Jacalyn or the events that had just transpired, only a feeling that they were repeating some event in their lives.

Deanne walked past David who was sitting on the sofa reading a book which he had bought with him, as Deanne walked into the kitchen saying...

"Hey Blue, do you want me to make you some breakfast...I can make you eggs, waffles, and the left-over steak you didn't finish last night, and a tall glass of orange juice?"

David uncrossed his legs and sat up, saying...

"Mmm, Deanne, you know how to get my attention, don't you?"

While Deanne was in the kitchen getting the eggs and milk out of the fridge, David had snuck up behind Deanne and began kissing the back of her neck and loosening her apron string, saying...

"Or we could skip food altogether and go straight to something else."

Deanne smiled back at David, and said...

"I'll let you know when breakfast is ready, now quit playing."

David proceeded to walk out of the kitchen, when he stopped, and turned saying...

"By the way, when is everyone getting here today?"

Deanne responded, saying...

"Tim and Mary should be here by four-thirty, because they have the longest drive and, Steve and Wendi will be here around noon, and Kristin's on her way and should already be Columbus."

David finished breakfast and bought his empty plate into the kitchen and Deanne asked...

"How was breakfast?"

David nodded his head yes, saying...

"Honey, I know that this may sound crazy, but, I get the feeling that we've done this before. It's almost as if we've done all of this."

"You mean something like Deja Vu?"

Deanne said, as she loaded the dishwasher and started wiping off the range. David took a wine glass from the wine rack cabinet and poured himself a glass of wine saying...

"No. I mean what I'm feeling is more real than that. Do you remember how we got here, or do you remember getting up this morning?"

Deanne hung the dish cloth over the door handle of the range, saying...

"Well, come to think of it, I don't remember any of that...how we got here, going to bed or getting up. All that I really remember was walking into the kitchen to make breakfast, and where's Shone?"

Just then, a loud clap of the hands was heard, and David, Deanne, Steve and Wendi looked around the room, with a look of utter shock on their faces, as Deanne said...

"What in the hell just happened...me and Blue were just in Port Clinton... how did we get to Columbus?"

Wendi replied, saying…

"OMG!! It's like me and Steve closed our eyes and went to sleep or something, because we don't remember anything, until a few hours ago and now.

The Nun, Sister Mary Jacalyn replied, saying…

"Yes, Deanne and David, you were at the farm. I can send you anywhere in time or out of time that I choose. You people just don't get it, do you?
In what you call 'YOUR' reality, millions of people every day are sent forwards or backwards in time, and there isn't a damn thing you can do about it.
You see, you don't own this reality, and this is not your world. This stuff happens every day, to everyone.
You were meant to control and dominate everything in this world, but your weakness, and ignorance has you bouncing through realities like being in a marble pin ball machine.

Thousands of beings from other dimensions are all around you every second, every minute of the day, watching the simplest of things you do."

Steve, Wendi, Deanne and David all looked at one another and then back over at Sister Mary Jacalyn, when Wendi said…

"Are you saying that, everything that we experience is not real?"

The Nun walked over to Wendi and slapped her upside her head, saying…

"Now stick with me Oh, everything you experience is real, but the time and place where you experience it in, is not where you really are.
You ignored the smallest command which He gave, and the spiritual beings which surround you, they now control you.
We are able to send you backwards and forwards in time, keeping you confused and always keeping you an infant."

Deanne, clinging to David's arm, said to Sister Mary Jacalyn…

"You just said that these beings can't physically interact with us, so why are you able to?"

The Nun replied, saying…

That's because I'm not one of them, I'm on a whole other level. Outside of your may-fly existence, there are, Spirits, Powers, Immortals, Principalities and so on…depending on their taste and power, determines everything."

Steve sounding frustrated said…

"Tell us, is there anything that we can do to make you leave us alone for good. Honestly, I'm way past dealing with your old funky ass."

The Nun stared at Steve intently, saying…

"I shouldn't tell you, but what the hell, you'll never figure it out anyways. so, I'm going to show you something."

The Nun waved her hand in a circle motion, and suddenly Steve, Kristin, Wendi, David and Deanne saw, hundreds of beings, passing in front of them, and all around them. Criss crossing and passing through each other.

These beings were looking at Steve, David, Wendi and Deanne, staring at them as if they were animals on display.

Once more The Nun waved her hand, and everything was back to normal, there were no more beings, just The Nun, Steve, David, Wendi and Deanne, then Sister Mary Jacalyn said…

"Now you see, and now it's time for you to experience another reality you see, each time I send you to experience a different reality, it'll get longer and longer. More and more intense. Until, one time, you'll never come out of it.
You asked, is there a way to make all of this go away there is, but you will have to figure it out while you're experiencing your reality, and I doubt that you are smart enough for that."

Just then Steve snapped…

"Yeah, yeah, blah-bla-blah, bla-blah-bla-blah, I'm not buying all of this spirit dimension shit, I think this is all some kind of trick, but we'll get out of this, we'll find a way to."

Cutting Steve off, The Nun waved her hand and Steve, David, Wendi and Deanne were at the farm in Port Clinton.

Sitting at the living room table drinking and playing cards, with David and Deanne was Kristin, Mary and Tim, when suddenly, someone started pounding on the front door and the walls.

Wendi and Kristin screamed, as Steve, and David went to the door. Tim walked over near the front room window and eased the curtains back, to look.

Mary was in the upstairs bathroom, and came running downstairs, saying...

"Hey, what was all the noise about...I heard some loud banging.

Picking up the glass of water which she dropped, Deanne said...

"We don't know, the 'guys' are checking it out...well Steve and Blue are, Tim...seems to be checking out, Mari...marijuana."

Steve motioned for Tim to come over to the door where he was at, while David went to the back door, when Steve shouted...

"Hey everybody! I-I see somebody out there moving around."

David turned his attention to the front door unaware that someone on the other side of the back door had started to turn the door knob.

David stepped away from the door, only a few feet or so, when there was a loud crash at the back door and it flew open.

Standing there in a disgusting black habit was the Nun, Sister Mary Jacalyn, standing with the big man wearing the Ballerina's Tutu and holding an unlit lantern which was swaying back and forth as she said...

"Attention K-Mart shoppers! Are we ready to get down to the business at hand. I see that we are all here?
There are others who are coming along, so you'd best get use to how they look, because...how can I say it, uh their appearance takes some getting use to."

Mary leaned into David, saying...

"Okay, shit head, what the fuck is this all about, are we playing one of your twisted ass games?"

David turned and gave Mary the *'are you kidding me'* look, when Deanne interrupted her, saying...

"Mary, Blue had nothing to do with this...unfortunately, this is real!"

Sister Mary Jacalyn stepped in to the room, while the big man in the tutu closed the door behind him.

Sister Mary Jacalyn said...

"So, I see Mary-Mary and pothead finally made it. It wouldn't have been any fun without you two."

Tim looked at Mary, saying...

"Hey babe, do you know this freak?"

Mary replied to Tim, saying...

"Hell, no I don't know this bitch, and I don't like this shit either."

Mary's comments grabbed Sister Mary Jacalyn's attention quickly, as she turned to Mary saying...

"Okey-doke, the first thing we need to do is pair everybody off in groups of twos so let's start off by doing this.

Mary, Mary...you are the little slut, aren't you? Maybe you should smoke one of Tim's little Mar-je-wanna cigarettes and just shut the hell up."

Tim stepped in front of Mary and pointing his finger at the Sister Mary Jacalyn and said...

"I don't know who you are, but who in the hell do you think you are talking to us like that?"

Then Sister Mary Jacalyn walked towards Tim, and in a sharp tone said...

"You are going to find out who I am real soon. Yes, you'll get to know me real soon. Now as far as calling your wife, a slut well, 'it is what it is she is a slut.

I've watched all of you from the time you were in college, years ago
up to now, and you haven't changed I've seen all of your nasty, filthy,
dirty secrets, and not one of you can say anything."

Just then, Sister Mary Jacalyn started hopping and skipping until
she was directly in front of Mary's face, saying...

"SOUND BLAST TIME!
Mary, we're going to start off with you and David. Twenty-two years
ago, at a party, you slept with not one, but two of your relatives in
the basement of their grandparent's house.

Mary, you then traipsed upstairs to have sex with your husband
Tim, who was so stoned he couldn't tell whether you were his wife or
a fat little greasy, smelly pig.

On Thanksgiving Day, of the following year, while Deanne was waiting
for David to show up at her grandmother's house, you snuck into his
apartment while he was asleep and turning all the lights out, Dave
thought you were Deanne and boned your little tight ass.
To this day, you still fantasize about David's dark horse meat inside
of you so you see, you are a slut, now SHUT UP!"

For one of the first times in her life Mary found someone who had
her ticket, someone who made her shut all the way up.

Steve and Wendi turned in shock, and looked at each other, as
Deanne, looked at David, with a look of shock and embarrassment as
she asked...

"Well Blue! I asked you, I asked you if the rumor was true and you swore
it wasn't..."

David stood looking like the kid who was just caught with his hands
in the cookie jar, as Deanne slapped David's face hard, saying...

"You son-of-a-bitch!"

The situation was already heated and confusing without pitting friends, husbands and wives against one another.

Sister Mary Jacalyn knew this and got a lot of enjoyment making matters more intense.

Sister Mary Jacalyn turned to Kristin, Deanne's best friend, and then back to Deanne and said...

"Oh, nobody gets away especially not you Kristin, you're next bitch! Remember in college when the school was choosing one from the freshman class to award a scholarship to?"

Deanne looked over at Sister Mary Jacalyn nodding her head and saying... *"I-I don't understand."*

Sister Mary Jacalyn, sat down on the chair beside the window, crossed her arms across her chest, saying...

"Someone was so jealous that you were in the top three amongst those being considered for the award that they Sabotaged your chances and then embarrassed you on the side.

Deanne interlinked her arm with Wendi, saying... *"What—how do know so much about all of this?"*

The Nun then picked her teeth with one of her long finger nails, and drawing a maggot from her teeth, flicked it on the table saying...

"You remember, May 2ⁿᵈ, nineteen-eighty-four don't you Kristin?"

Deanne's mood immediately became sullen and she hung her head down, and then said...

"Oh no...

Sister Mary Jacalyn continued, saying...

"Remember how you and Kristin were sexually attacked in your dorm room, how Kristin, hit that cock sucking pederast, making him flee your room.

Ever since then, you've been kissing Kristin's ass as if she were your savior?

Kristin walked over to Deanne, and put her arms around her and looked at Sister Mary Jacalyn saying...

"Why are you doing this, bringing up something so traumatic and personal and then airing it in front of everybody."

Sister Mary Jacalyn looked at Kristin as she cocked her head to the left saying...

"Tsk, tsk, tsk still playing the part of the master manipulator, puller of strings, and the thimble rigging cunt from hell."

Kristin yelled at Sister Mary Jacalyn, saying...

"You don't know anything about me!"

Sister Mary Jacalyn, got up from the chair, saying...

"Oh, don't I? I know that you were jealous of anyone who achieved anything that you didn't have, that you would do anything to make them suffer for taking your good things away.

I know that you caused your father and his girlfriend's engagement to be called off, all because you thought she'd take your father's love away from you."

Kristin's voice grew louder, as Deanne interrupted Sister Mary Jacalyn, saying...

"Will you stop it...Kris is not like that, if it wasn't for her...you just don't know."

Sister Mary Jacalyn, turned to Deanne, saying...

"I'll tell you what I do know back in college, you were more popular than Kristin, and you were getting all the accolades.
This bitch you call your best friend, paid someone to rape and beat you up the only thing was, The guy got to your dorm too early, and Kristin was still there."

Deanne turned and looked at Kristin with a looked of disbelief on her face, saying...

"Kris, Kris, tell me that this isn't true?"

Sister Mary Jacalyn turned and looked at Kristin, saying...

"Go ahead you cunt, say it! really wanna hear the garbage that comes out of that trashy mouth."

Deanne snatched away from Kristin, and walked over and stood near Wendi, crying.

Just then Steve yelled out...

"Can't ya'll see what's going. This-this, 'Post Toasties' of the week here, is trying to get us all against each other, for her own twisted purpose...we gotta stick together, no matter what she says."

Sister Mary Jacalyn stood clapping and said...

"Oh yeah stick together, you all can hold each other's damn hands, toast marshmallows and sing Kumbaya all night too, but that's not going to do any of you any good.
We got things to get established before the night ends, and there is nothing that you can do to stop me.
I suggest that you make use of your time trying to find out how to get yourselves out of this, and to give you an idea of how things are, we're going to go back downstairs."

Before anyone could bat an eye, they were all downstairs in the living room, sitting on the sofa, as Sister Mary Jacalyn stood near the television, saying...

"Thought you'd like to know what you're up against."

Suddenly, the television all by itself begin changing channels, until it landed on the local news station.

'Good evening from Central Ohio's most complete news from WCCS. Tonight, our top story is the rash of murders and killings in the city. Neighbors in one northeast

Columbus neighborhood are in shock following a deadly shooting that rattled the community.

On Saturday night, Police were called to a shooting near N.E. forty-sixth and Livingston Ave. Police said thirty-four-year-old Detective, Marie Lopez was in her home and shot her thirty-seven-year-old husband.

Franklin county Coroner stated multiple gun shots at close range, killed the thirty-seven-year-old, Lopez.

"I was stunned,"

Said Captain Jones, who has worked with Detective Lopez for the past ten years. Lopez was pronounced dead at the scene. Police found Detective Lopez at the home and arrested her. Investigators said Mr. Lopez, appeared to be sleeping when his wife shot and killed him, still no motives for the murder was given.

"I don't know why she chose to shoot so many times at close range,"

Master Sgt. Marco Knight of the Columbus Police Department, said. Knight went on to say...

"It was senseless,"

Knight, who has lived next to the couple for seven years, said the couple had only lived in the home since last summer, and while both Knight and Lopez were law enforcement Officers, they worked out of different precincts.

"I'd watch a yard full of folks grilling, happy, dancing and they appeared to be happy," Knight said.

In a related incident, Columbus Police have identified a suspect they are searching for in connection with another murder, just hours before, and say he should be considered armed and dangerous.

Detective James Martin thirty-seven, is wanted in connection with the murder of his wife, thirty-five-year-old Melissa Martin.

Police Captain Lucas Jones stated as a result of the investigation into the murder, he is still at large, and wanted as a person of interest.

Officers arrived and found the victim, thirty-five-year-old Melissa Martin, suffering from gunshot wounds in the couple's bedroom. She was pronounced dead shortly after paramedics arrived on scene.

Police officials say the investigation indicated Mrs. Martin was shot once in the abdomen and once in the head, apparently as she slept. No signs of forcible entry were present at the scene.

Police officials did say several neighbors were awakened by the sound of gunshots shortly after midnight. According to one witness, a neighbor of the Martins for six years, stated, he worked the four-thirty to midnight shift at one of the downtown hotels, and was surprised to see all the lights on in his house when he arrived home.

The neighbor, who refused to be identified said, shortly after one a.m. he heard a shot, and because it sounded too loud, he looked out his bedroom window, where he was watching the late movie and enjoying a sandwich.

According to the witness, the first shot and the second shot were about five to six seconds apart, and he reported that after the second shot rang out, all the lights in the Martin residence suddenly went out.

Anyone with information on Detective Martin's whereabouts is asked to call the Columbus Police Homicide Unit at six-o-five-0-nine-eight-0 or Crime Stoppers at six-0-five-TIPS. Sister Mary Jacalyn stood next to Steve playfully touching his arm with her long grotesque fingernails, saying...

"What about it big boy,do you wanna make me go missing hehehe?"

Jerking away from Sister Mary Jacalyn, Steve shouted...

"All I want for you to do is to get the hell away from me and leave us alone!"

Sister Mary Jacalyn stood, pretending to be offended at Steve's remark, covered her lips with her hand, and lowered her face, batting her eyes, saying...

"Ooh, I like you, you like to play rough, uh? Well don't go getting too damn comfortable because I'm about to show you where you're heading, and we'll all see how tough you really are, now close your eyes lover boy."

Steve backed away from Sister Mary Jacalyn, until she reached out and caught Steve by his throat, saying...

"I said shut your damn eyes, or do you want me to have a bunch of filthy men that live in the hills, to have a go at Wendi?"

Whether Sister Mary Jacalyn's grip was that strong, or if Steve believed that she could do what she said, Steve closed his eyes tight, when suddenly everything went dark.

Not the kind of darkness you notice when you close your eyes, but a real cold darkness...........

Steve and Michael were waiting in the parking lot for Roger, they saw a crowd of young people standing on the west side of the road, in the parking lot of Jim's Sport's bar, apparently having just consumed a fountain of alcohol and a bucket of wings.

Steve and Michael could tell that some of them had a few too many, by the level and tone of their conversations, and the fact one of them was puking his guts up.

"I wish Roger would hurry up,"
Michael said to Steve.

Steve sensed Michael's apprehension concerning the young crowd across the street, and said...

"I'm ahead of you Mike, that's all we need right now is to get into it with a crowd of young drunk knuckleheads."

Almost as if they heard Steve and Michael, several from the crowd, crossed the street heading in Michael and Steve's direction.

Without thinking, Michael took his shot gun from the bed of the truck and slowly walked to the passenger side of the truck, hoping that the guys coming in their direction would see it and head in another direction.

Just when they thought things couldn't get worse, one of the young guys hollered at Steve and Michael, saying...

"Say, anyone of you guys got a lighter?"
Steve looked at Michael saying...

"Whatcha doing...they don't want a light, they just want to cause trouble."
Michael leaned his shotgun against the truck saying...

"No. We don't smoke."

As the young men were about twenty feet away, one of the guys responded, saying...

"Ain't no sense in being a dick about it, we saw you smoking from the other side of the street, besides, hunters always carry matches with them."

At that time Steve spoke up saying...

"Yeah, I got a light, but not for you.... it's kinda hard believing that out of ten-twelve folks, none of you would have a match, either."

When the men were directly in front of Steve and Michael, one of the guys revealed a knife with a blade about a foot long, looking at Steve, and saying...

"This is what I go hunting with."

That did it! Michael unzipped the case revealing his shot gun, responding...

"Well, that's a nice knife, but men use guns, we don't want any trouble, so just go on about your business."

One of the other young guys, whispered something in the ear of the knife wielder and the three young guys walked past Steve and Michael, shouting profanity as they walked.

Looking at one another Steve said to Michael...

"Damn, I hate that shit...another minute and I was about to show that young drunk punk what it feels like to have a long knife shoved up his ass."

Responding, Michael said...

"Well the girls have gone, I just hope Roger gets his slow ass here, before they decide to come back this way."

No sooner than Michael said that, Roger's Nissan pulled into the parking lot, as Steve shouted...

"It's about time man...we were about to leave your ass, what took you so long?"

Pulling his gun case and cooler from his trunk, Roger said...

"Hey Mike, Steve, man its only four-twenty-five and I said I'd be here by four, besides, we don't hunt until tomorrow...why are you blowing smoke up my ass?"

Steve took Roger's cooler and loaded it in the truck, saying...

"No big deal Rog, we just had a run in with a few young drunk eggheads and it got us all worked up."

Michael placed his shot gun back in the truck, saying...

"So, we all ready to get it on?"

Looking at his watch, Steve said...

"We got to stop at Theresa' and pick up the food."

Repositioning his cap, Michael responded...

"Oh yeah, we can't forget that."

Roger tapped on his cooler saying...

"Hey, why do we have to stop, I bought bread, lunch meat, and tomatoes... we got food, let's just get going."

While Michael was backing out, he turned to Steve and said...

"It's like this, we are going out for four days, and three of it's going to be in the rain, and hell man, we've got a crock pot full of white beans, a pan of corn bread, and eight thick pork chops."

Nodding his head Roger said...

"I thought you said the cabin didn't have electricity?" Stopping at the traffic light, Michael tapped Steve's arm and pointed to the three young guys who they encountered, saying...

"There's the guys we were talking about when you showed up."

Turning his head as they passed them, Roger said...

"Just a couple of punks that look like they'd be more comfortable butt-fucking a tadpole."

At first, there was silence in the truck and then Michael and Steve burst out in laughter, as Steve said..."

"Butt fucking a what?"

Steve, Michael and Roger continued on their four-hour trip, laughing.

Port Clinton, Ohio

David grabbed a poker iron from the fire place and slowly and quietly walked towards the stairs when he looked up and saw Tim and Mary coming down.

Shocked but expecting anything and everything, David's first thought, was that he was seeing things, as he said...

"Tim, Mary, what are you two doing here, you're supposed to be home in Wisconsin."

Tim was elated to see David, saying...

"Hey old buddy, sorry...but Mary and I were sitting in our living room, and boy, you wouldn't believe what we've been through."

David cautiously shook Tim's hand as they reach the bottom of the steps, saying...

"Let me guess, it was the Nun...right?"

Nodding his head, Tim said...

"Yeah, we were watching a movie when this old nasty Nun showed up out of nowhere and told us a lot of shit and the next thing we know...we're here, Dave, what's going on?"

Tim and Mary followed him into the kitchen and sat down, when Mary said...

"Oh, so, I don't get a hello or anything, I'm about to lose it here...how the hell did we get from Wisconsin to Port Clinton in the blink of an eye?"

David walked over and hugged Mary, saying...

"Sorry... hey Mary-Mary, I don't know what in the hell is going on. Me,

Deanne, Steve and Wendi were in Columbus at the house and the same Nun showed up, and a lot of weird shit started happening.

Look, I don't know what's going on, all I know is that, I've been trying to tell myself that I'm asleep and dreaming, but I know I'm not."

Tim got up and walked over to the window and then called David, saying...

"Look, you got company coming down your driveway!"

David walked over as Tim stepped aside, allowing David to see out of his front room window, who said...

"What in the world!"

Tim walked back over to David saying...

"Yeah that's what I was thinking...where the heck is her car, I know she didn't take a taxi here."

Tim and David looked at each other as Kristin was making her way up the driveway.

David and Deanne's driveway to the main house, has a long drive way of over three hundred feet, and then past a barn and then another hundred feet before reaching the house, and it appears that Kristin walked the entire stretch on foot.

As David and Tim waited for Kristin to walk up to the house, Mary asked...

"Where's Dee, Dave?"

David didn't want to tell Mary what happened with Sister Mary Jacalyn, but based on everything that's happened, keeping it from her would only make matters worse, and so he said...

"Kristin's on her way to the door, I'll explain everything then."

Mary snapped...

"Don't tell me that we're going through that shit again, because I don't know if I can take it this time. The last time it was people disappearing and coming out of the wood works and shit, this is not the dark ages, this is..."

David politely interrupted Mary as Kristin was walking in the door, saying...

"Welcome Kristin looks like you got the invite."

Kristin walked in and after looking around, said...

"Invite my white ass, I was sitting in my condo, working on some things when that old bitch showed up, where's Dee?"

Mary responded as she gave Kristin a hug, saying...

"That's what I asked him just before you walked in."

David walked over towards the fire place and placed Shone on a leash and led her out of the living room and into the den, saying...

"Just give me a sec, okay?"

Kristin and Mary both lived in Madison, Wisconsin, and both ended up in Port Clinton, Ohio at the hand of Sister Mary Jacalyn.

Mary and Kristin were making light conversation and Tim was at the kitchen table rolling up several joints of marijuana, when David came back in the room, saying...

"Okay everybody, earlier today, Steve, Wendi, Deanne and I were in Columbus at our condo, when Ms. Stinky breath showed up.

She explained that she was going to torture us, buy making us relive horrible nightmares.

At first, she had all of us one by one to go through our own nightmares, and then she said she was going to make all of us go through one together here.

Well Deanne coped an attitude and said some things that pissed her off, and she said that we were all going to appear here, but that she was going to make Deanne take the long way getting here, for pissing her off."

Kristin looked at Mary and then said...

"And that's okay with you Dave?"

David got up in Kristin's face saying...

"Don't go down that road Kristin, woman or not, you can get knocked on your ass too."

Kristin jumped back in David's face, as Mary tried holding Kristin, as she said...

"Oh, so you going to knock me on my ass, when all I did was ask you one simple question...you fucking piece of slug shit."

Just then the doorbell rang, and Tim quickly covered his marijuana and turned towards the door as David went to answer it.

Wendi entered the living room saying...

"Hey everybody, this is some fucked up shit, ain't it. Has anyone seen Steve?" Has Deanne made it yet?

Kristin walked past David and said...

"Is it alright if I go in the kitchen and start making something for everybody to eat?"

Giving Kristin his okay, David walked out of the front porch for fresh air, as Kristin walked off into the kitchen, when Mary and Wendi asked if they could do anything to help, as Kristin responded...

"Uh...no I got it from here, but I tell you, when I've made the sandwiches someone can open up several cans of soup and get it hot and set the bowls and spoons on the table."

Wendi quickly said...

"Okay, I got the soup, so Mary, do you mind setting the places around the table?"

Mary walked into the dining room, saying...

"I can't believe with all this stuff going on, we are really serious about sitting around and eating."

Tim walked over to Mary, saying...

"Mary baby, what else are we supposed to do...I mean, it's not like we can just leave anytime we want to, besides, I'm starving."

Mary pushed Tim gently away from her as Tim tried kissing her on the cheek, saying...

"Aww, my little pot head, you are always hungry."

A total of four hours passed since Tim, Mary, Wendi, Kristin and David arrived at the farm, and still there was no sign of Deanne, when Wendi said...

"It's been four hours now, Dave, do you think it'll do any good trying to call Dee on her cell?"

David stood up, and said...

"Wendi, I don't think Deanne's going to be able to answer the phone from where's she's at. Anybody want a drink, I know I need one, or two."

Tim, Kristin and Mary got up walking into the living room, towards the liquor cabinet.

Wendi was the only one in the bunch who didn't really drink, but she called to David saying...

"I'll take a glass of wine, what kind do you have Dave?"

David stuck his head from around the corner of the kitchen, looking at Tim, Kristin and Mary jockeying for positions around the liquor cabinet, shaking his head and saying to Wendi...

"Hey Wen, I got Chardonnay and sweet red, which one do you want?"

"*Normally, I'd drink the sweet red, but I think I'm going to upgrade to Chardonnay.*"

Wendi said as she walked over to the window, looking at her past messages, and looking at the sun going down and the darkness setting in.

Everyone assembled back in the living room, drinking their drinks and trying to make sense of why they were assembled and what was going to happen, when Wendi got up saying...

"*Dave, do you mind if I refresh my glass?*"

Heading around the corner to the bathroom, David said...

"*Oh no, Wendi help yourself.*"

Mary walked into the kitchen and hollered back to Wendi, saying...

"*Did you have a problem finding the wine Wendi?*"

Wendi yelled back...

"*No...why?*"

Mary called Wendi back into the kitchen, saying...

'*What's this?*"

Wendi stood in the kitchen and saw that every single cupboard door, cabinet and cutlery drawer were open, as well as the refrigerator was standing open.

Wendi looked on in surprise, and a thought that maybe Mary was up to her old antics of trying to secure the lime light, said...

"*No way, they were all closed when I was in here, and there's no way anybody else could have come in and done it because no one was in here except you and I.*"

While Wendi and Mary closed every drawer, refrigerator and cabinet door, Tim walked over to the window, saying...

"*There's somebody out there.*"

David joined Tim over at the window, and before they could look at what Tim was seeing, there was three loud knocks at the door.

Positioning themselves so that they could see, David saw a large man standing and waving at them, wearing a Halloween pig mask.

While they looked on, the man began turning the front door knob, and then there were three loud knocks at the back door.

David and Tim raced to the back door, checking to see that it was locked when Mary and Wendi came out of the kitchen, and Mary said as she walked to the front door and opening it saying...

"Are you guys just going to stand there, there's somebody knocking?"

Thinking it was Tim messing around, Mary opened the door to a large man wearing a pig mask.

Thinking it was Tim, playing around, Mary punched him in the stomach and mouthed *"good one"* and waved Tim inside, when Wendi hollered...

"Close the damn door, that ain't Tim!"

Mary had little time to react, when the large man stuck his foot in the door, preventing them from closing it, as Wendi hollered to David and Tim...

"Put something against the back door, somebody's trying to get in here!"

David and Tim raced over to the love seat and carried it over to the back door, tilting it and bracing it up against the door knob.

Wendi grunted, and Mary pushed as hard as she could, but the large man's foot was planted in the door way, when Wendi screamed, and Kristin ran out of the living room.

Thinking that Kristin had ran off and left them, David hollered...

"Kristin, get your chicken ass back in here and help...damnit!"

Just then, the large man's hand pushed through the door opening, as Wendi tried hitting and pushing it out, when out of nowhere, Kristin had crawled underneath Mary, burying a large knife in the large man's foot, who let go of the door and backed out of the door.

Kristin and Mary were at the front door and Tim and David at the back door. No one noticed that Deanne was standing in the middle of the living room crying, as Wendi turned to the sounds of Deanne crying and yelled...

"Dee!"

David turned in Wendi's direction and saw Deanne standing in the living room with Wendi and immediately left Tim and ran to Deanne, hugging her and kissing her, as Deanne said...*"We're gonna die, we're gonna die."*

David and Wendi attempted to calm Deanne down when the lights began flickering, and then suddenly went out.

Deanne and Wendi both screamed, as Kristin yelled...

Aww fuck!"

Ohio Wildlife Reserve Hunting Office
6:59 p.m.

Over the next few miles, Steve, Michael and Roger found themselves laughing and cutting up a storm until they arrived at the Ohio Wildlife Preserve registration office.

After checking into the reserve and signing for the cabin key, Steve, Michael and Roger headed for the cabin.

The cabin was furnished with the things any hunter needs, percolator for coffee, large and medium pot for cooking, four wooden chairs, a table and two set of bunk beds, with a medium sized outhouse, thirty feet from the rear of the cabin.

Michael, Steve and Roger laid the clothes out they were going to wear the next day, over the chairs, when Steve looked at Roger, saying...

"Dang Michael, you look like the poster boy for Bass Pro Shop. You know you ain't gonna get within range of a deer with that loud as new smell on your clothes, and what's with the black dog tags around your neck?"

Roger looked up at Michael as he flipped him the bird, saying...

"These are my lucky dog tags, wore them all through my time in Iraq."

After eating a healthy bowl of beans, chunk of corn bread and a pork chop, Michael, Steve and Roger settled in for the night and set their alarms for their early morning wake up.

Just as they were sound asleep, Michael was awakened by the sound of something in the woods, and woke up Steve, saying...

"Hey Steve, did you hear that? I have never heard that sound, what's making that noise?"

Steve listened for the sounds that Michael described, and at first heard nothing until he finally heard a disturbing wail, and said...

"What the heck is that! It sounds like a growl and a high-pitched scream all in one, doesn't it?"

For the remainder of the night, Michael lay in his bunk, listening to the noises, until it was time to prepare for the first day of hunting.

The plan was to go to the spot which was already picked out weeks earlier to set up their tree stands. The morning sun began rising as Steve, Michael and Roger sat patiently in their tree stands.

As the morning announced its arrival, Steve whispered over to Michael and pointed at the ground below saying...

"There's something moving out there."

Directly below the tree which Michael was perched in there was something on the ground. What Michael and Steve saw was, a half-body apparition.

Roger was in the furthest tree and was unable to see it, but because of Steve and Michael's preoccupation with it, he called out to Steve, saying...

"What are you guys looking at."

Steve turned in Roger's direction and said...

"The only way I describe it is, it's a half person. The torso is missing. It's just black, but almost see-through black."

Thinking that it was the dead portioned body of someone, Roger asked...

"How long do you think it's been dead? It's funny, but I don't remember seeing anything when we were rigging our stands."

Steve began lowering his stand to get a closer look, and said...

"Maybe it's me or the fog but, it looks like moving gas...like it's not a real person. I was looking that way and it just materialized, like 'poof'."

Michael turned to Steve, saying...

"Things don't just appear out of thin air...you didn't hear anything first?"

Steve stopped half way down the tree saying...

"It would've taken someone..."

Steve was interrupted when they all heard a bloodcurdling sound erupting from the clearing that froze everyone in their tracks.

This sound was unlike any other that they had heard, and it made every hair on their bodies vibrate and tingle.

The only way to describe it is, it sounded like a wild person with no knowledge of modern language being gutted alive. No words, just this high-pitched bloodcurdling scream.

Steve stopped and didn't move another inch, nor did Michael or Roger say a word. They all just sat there fixed on the clearing, and stared, when just as suddenly a second scream was let loose with even more force than the first.

By this time, Roger and Michael were sprinting and scrambling out of their tree stands and down the trees, shouldering their guns.

When Roger and Michael got to the base of the trees, they stood staring at the half-portioned body and Steve a few feet above it, frozen.

Steve maneuvered around the tree and jumped down, aiming his gun at the body lying on the ground.

Michael and Roger stood quiet with their eyes fixed on the ghastly lump, poking it with the tips of their guns.

Soon Steve, Michael and Roger slowly backed away from it and without anything being said… hurried towards Michael's truck as fast as their feet could carry them. When they were about a hundred feet from the truck, they heard leaves crunching, and the snapping of broken branches behind them.

Not knowing who or what was making the sounds, Steve stopped, pointed his gun in the direction and chambered a bullet, as Michael said to him…

"Whoa Rambo, let's just get to the truck first, we don't know who that is behind us, besides you might hit somebody, if you go off shooting without seeing what you're shooting at."

Roger had gotten ahead of Steve and Michael as they stopped and talked, and that's when they heard the screams and two shots. Turning and not seeing Roger, Michael yelled…

"Rog, where you at dude?"

There was no response from Roger, and as Steve turned to Michael the sounds behind them got louder.

At first it was just the sound of leaves being crunched and twigs being snapped, but then it progressed to the sound of water rippling through the woods, and dogs growling.

Even though Steve and Michael had guns in their hands, fear came over them, nonetheless, causing them to run.

As they ran through the woods, Steve yelled to Michael…

"Where the hell is Roger, did he answer you when you called him?"

As Michael made his way through the brush, several limbs snapped back, hitting Steve in the face causing him to drop his gun, and saying…

"Damn…aww fuck!"

Michael heard Steve yelling and stopped, saying…

"Hey man, you okay back there...sorry 'bout the branches, I thought you were right behind me."

Michael ran back to Steve and picked up his gun while Steve, who was bent over with his hands in his face, still cussing, said...

"C'mon dude, we got to get out of here, find out what's happened to Roger."

Wiping his face and taking his gun from Michael, Steve said...

"Aww fuck, Roger should've kept his happy ass with us, instead of going off to take a dump."

Then they heard voices, men yelling and a dull thumping noise as if someone was hitting a tree with something heavy. Steve and Michael stopped, looking behind them to find out if they could see who was behind them, when the brush started moving, signifying that something huge was coming directly at them.

The noise of dogs growling grew louder as Michael decided to shout out...

"We are hunters, and you're getting dangerously close to us, who are you?"

Steve grabbed Michael's arm, saying...

"What are you doing, you're going to mark us...are you stupid...didn't you see deliverance or other movies about people in situations like this?"

Michael looked at Steve saying...

"This ain't a movie, besides, we can't just go shooting without knowing what or who we're shooting at...just wait, give 'em a chance to identify themselves or back away from us."

Just then, Steve and Michael heard voices saying...

"They're this way, let the dogs loose!"

Steve sighted his gun at the brush, saying...

"If dogs come out of the brush heading at us, as much as I love dogs, these are going to be some dead ass mothers f***ers."

Just then four Rottweilers burst from the brush, in full charge at Steve and Michael and two tall figures followed as Steve took aim, fired and fired again.

Steve looked over at Michael wondering why he hadn't fired his gun, said...

"Shoot god-damnit!"

Then Michael grabbed Steve's gun, saying...

"What's your fucking problem you ass hole?"

Steve looked first at Michael and then in the direction in front of him, as Michael said...

"You stupid fuck...you just shot Roger!"

With a look of shock on his face, Steve looked closer at the lifeless body on the ground in the clearance, as Michael got up and walked towards it, bending down, saying...

Aww shit! Damn Steve, I can't believe this shit?"

Slowly getting up, Steve followed Michael and as he reached the lifeless body, he saw that there was a man lying dead, with a massive gunshot to the face.

Steve stood looking horrified and then all around him, saying...

"Where are the dogs, and the guys who came out of the brush?"

Michael grabbed Steve by the collar, saying...

"What in the fuck are you talking about, dumb ass, there are no dogs or other people coming out of the brush... just Roger who you managed to shoot."

Still horrified, Steve looked down at the body, saying...

"No...that can't be Roger, he was in front of us...he didn't answer, no, it can't be Roger."

Slamming Steve against the tree behind him, and then throwing him on the ground, Michael shouted...

"It was Roger god damnit...he stopped to take a dump and was behind us.... aww man."

In disbelief of what he was seeing, Steve crawled over to Michael, and the lifeless body of Roger, saying...

"Mike, you heard the dogs and the voices, we were running from them, you heard 'em chasing us...right?"

Michael examined the wounds to Roger, and seeing that half his face was blown off, said...

"Come off it Steve, all I heard was Roger yelling for us to wait up for him, shit...we're going to have to...god damnit Steve, you killed Roger."

Not knowing exactly what to do, Steve and Michael suddenly saw, two men with dogs in the brush, who spotted them, saying...

"There they are, let the dogs loose on 'em."

Steve tapped Michael and said...

"Let's get to the edge of the clearing up ahead so we have a better advantage...C'mon."

Michael and Steve made it to the clearing and waited for the two men and the dogs to come charging through the brush, but they never came.

Port Clinton, Ohio

Kristin looked at Mary and then said...

"And that's okay with you Dave?"

David got up in Kristin's face saying...

"Don't go down that road Kristin, woman or not, you can get knocked on your ass too."

Kristin jumped back In David's face, as Mary tried holding Kristin, as she said...

"Oh, so you going to knock me on my ass, when all I did was ask you one simple question...you fucking piece of slug shit."

Just then the doorbell rang, and Tim quickly covered his marijuana and turned towards the door as David went to answer it. Steve and Wendi entered the living room saying...

"Hey everybody, this is some fucked up shit, ain't it?"

Wendi asked...

"Has Deanne made it yet?"

Kristin walked past David and said...

"Is it alright if I go in the kitchen and start making something for everybody to eat?"

Giving Kristin his okay, David and Steve walked out of the front porch to talk, as Kristin walked off into the kitchen, when Mary and Wendi asked if they could do anything to help, as Kristin responded...

"Uh...no I got it from here, but I tell you, when I've made the sandwiches someone can open up several cans of soup and get it hot and set the bowls and spoons on the table."

Wendi quickly said...

"Okay, I got the soup, so Mary, do you mind setting the places around the table?"

Mary walked into the dining room, saying...

"I can't believe with all this stuff going on, we are really serious about sitting around and eating."

Tim walked over to Mary, saying...

"Mary baby, what else are we supposed to do...I mean, it's not like we can just leave anytime we want to, besides, I'm starving."

Mary pushed Tim gently away from her as Tim tried kissing her on the cheek, saying...

Aww, my little pot head, you are always hungry."

It's been four hours since Tim, Mary, Steve, Wendi, Kristin and David arrived at the farm, and still there was no sign of Deanne, when Wendi said...

"It's been four hours now, Dave do you think it'll do any good trying to call her?"

David stood up, and said...

"Yeah, I'm don't know if I'm starting to get pissed or worried, but I'm gonna pour me a drink, anybody else want one?"

Tim, Steve, Kristin and Mary got up walking into the living room towards the liquor cabinet. Wendi was the only one in the bunch who didn't really drink, but she called to David saying...

"I'll take a glass of wine, what kind do you have Dave?"

David stuck his head from around the corner of the kitchen, looking at Tim, Steve, Kristin and Mary jockeying for positions around the liquor cabinet, shook his head and said to Wendi...

"Hey Wen, I got Chardonnay and sweet red, which one do you want?"

"Normally, I'd drink the sweet red, but I think I'm going to upgrade to Chardonnay."

Wendi said as she walked over to the window, looking at her phone for messages and a signal, and looking at the sun going down and the darkness setting in.

Everyone assembled back in the living room, drinking their drinks and trying to make sense of why they were assembled and what was going to happen, when Wendi got up saying...

"Dave, do you mind if I refresh my glass?"

Heading around the corner to the bathroom, David said...

"Oh no Wendi, help yourself."

Mary walked into the kitchen and hollered back to Wendi, saying...
"Did you have a problem finding the wine Wendi?"
Wendi yelled back...
"No...why?"
Mary called Wendi back into the kitchen, saying...
'What's this?"
Wendi stood in the kitchen and saw that every single cupboard door, cabinet and cutlery drawer were open, as well as the refrigerator was standing open.
Wendi looked on in surprise, saying...
"No way, they were all closed when I was in here, and there's no way anybody else could have come in and done it because we would've seen them."
While Wendi and Mary closed every drawer, refrigerator and cabinet door, Tim walked over to the window, saying...
"There's somebody out there."
David and Steve joined Tim over at the window, and before they could look at what Tim was seeing, there was three loud knocks at the door.
Positioning themselves so that they could see, Steve and David saw a large man standing and waving at them, wearing a Halloween pig mask.

While they looked on, the man began turning the front door knob, and then there were three loud knocks at the back door.
David and Tim raced to the back door, checking to see that it was locked when Mary and Wendi came out of the kitchen, and Mary walked to the front door and opening it saying...
"Are you just going to stand there Steve, there's somebody knocking?"
Thinking it was Tim messing around, Mary opened the door to a large man wearing a pig mask, as she punched him in the stomach and mouthing *"good one"* and waved Tim inside, when Steve hollered...
"Close the damn door, that ain't Tim!"
Mary and Steve had little time to react, when the large man stuck his foot in the door, preventing them from closing it, as Steve hollered to David and Tim...
"Put something against the back door, somebody's trying to get in here!"
David and Tim raced over to the love seat and carried over to the back door, tilting it and bracing it up against the door knob.

Steve grunted, and Mary pushed as hard as she could, but the large man's foot was planted in the door way, when Wendi screamed, and Kristin ran out of the living room.

Thinking that Kristin had ran off and left them, Steve hollered...

"Kristin, get your chicken ass back in here and help...damnit!"

Just then, the large man's hand started coming through the door opening, as Steve tried bending it backwards, when out of nowhere, Kristin had crawled underneath both Mary and Steve, and burying a large knife in the large man's foot.

Letting go of the door and backed out of the door, Wendi and Mary managed to close the door and lock it.

Kristin, Wendi and Mary were at the front door while Tim and David were at the back door, no one noticed that Deanne was standing in the middle of the living room crying.

Wendi turned to the sounds of Deanne crying and yelled...

"Dee!"

David turned in Wendi's direction and saw Deanne standing in the living room with Wendi and immediately left Tim and ran to Deanne, hugging and kissing her, saying...

"Oh, Deanne baby, I was so worried about you, thank God you're here."

Just then, David looked over to his right and saw the Nun, Sister Mary Jacalyn standing near, laughing and pointing at David, saying...

"Time to wake up, wakey, wakey."

Suddenly David looked up and saw Steve standing in their living room.

Wendi hurried over to Steve, as she threw her arms around Steve, saying...

"It's about time your sexy ass got here...did you drive here or did...you know...?"

In between kissing Wendi and hugging her, Steve said...

"Baby, you won't believe it. We were hunting and somehow I ended up shooting and killing Roger, and then all of a sudden I'm here, with you."

Suddenly, the Nun, who was laughing hysterically pointed her finger at Steve and said...

"So, how did you like your little hunting trip wasn't it a blast! Just imagine, and you get to relive that over, and over again.
It's kinda like foreplay.until you climax. Want a smoke?"

Steve stood in disbelief, shaking his head and crying...no, no, no, as Wendi hugged Steve trying to comfort him.

Sister Mary Jacalyn pointed at Wendi, saying...

"To show you that I'm not a what do you call it heartless, I'm preparing a special little nightmare with all of you in mind, which I think you'll particularly love."

12
The Menagerie

Steve, David, Deanne and Wendi each looked at one another, wondering what they were going to do, and how they were going to beat Sister Mary Jacalyn, when Deanne threw her hands in the air shouting as she headed for the front door...

"Screw this shit! I don't care what you do and who you are, but I am not going to stand here and let you dictate what I will do and where I will go."

Sister Mary Jacalyn, cocked her head to the left, watching Deanne as she walked by, without turning her head, when Deanne reached the front door, Sister Mary Jacalyn clapped her hands and Deanne disappeared.

Wendi screamed and held onto Steve while David shouted...

"Where is she and what did you do to her"?

Sister Mary Jacalyn walked up to David saying...

"At last someone with some real spunk, unfortunately, I can't stand people who have spunk.

As for your precious Deanne, I can transport her from here to Port Clinton in a matter of seconds, but for your sweet little inamorata's insolent attitude, well let's say that she went to the store for some milk."

David looked Sister Mary Jacalyn in the face saying...

"Please, bring her back...don't hurt here, she's been through a lot."

Sister Mary Jacalyn rocked her head from left to right, saying in a sarcastic tone...

"She's been through a lot, he was abused as a child, his parents divorced when he was nine DAMN everyone goes through a lot, but it doesn't give you the right to sympathy."

David again pleaded with Sister Mary Jacalyn saying...

"Please, I'm asking you, please if you're going to send somebody somewhere, send us together.... please?"

Sister Mary Jacalyn, removed the head piece from her habit and looking at David, said...

"That was touching, I detected real sincerity in your words, you must really care for her, you know what?"

David lifted his eyes to meet Sister Mary Jacalyn's and said...

"You're going to send us together?"

"HELL NO!"

Sister Mary Jacalyn screamed, as she waved her hands as Wendi, Steve, and David disappeared.

There was no one left standing in David and Deanne's home except Sister Mary Jacalyn, Tim, Kristin and Mary.

Sister Mary Jacalyn looked around, smiled and drew the largest and nastiest bugger from her nose, covered with maggots and swallowed it.

Sister Mary Jacalyn again waved her hand and the front door slowly opened and then she whistled and Shone came running from upstairs, and followed Sister Mary Jacalyn out the front door, as it closed.

David walked into the kitchen in Columbus, and after looking around and looking out the kitchen window, he placed his keys on the kitchen counter, when he heard mysterious noises coming from the living room and went investigate them.

Walking into the living room, he noticed Sister Mary Jacalyn sitting on the coffee table with Shone's leash in her hand and Shone down at her feet. With a look of surprise on his face, David said…

"*So, where is Deanne, and will you please let my dog go?*"

Sister Mary Jacalyn responded, saying…

"I placed everyone else on hold, so that we'd have a chance to talk."

"*I don't see what we have to talk about, I mean you come into our lives, when we've done nothing to you and you scare and frighten innocent people…is that how you get your kicks?*"

David said as he held out his hand, snapping his fingers to get Shone to come to him.

Sister Mary Jacalyn looked at David and said as she let Shone's leash drop out of her hand…

"I can go on doing this for as long as I like, but occasionally, I try to give a poor sucker a chance to see if he or she is smart enough to figure out how to beat me. It doesn't mess up my resume, because I got an entire city, shit, and entire state to screw with, so are you up to the challenge?"

Looking at Shone and holding on to her leash tight, David said…

"*Up to a challenge…and just what are you talking about…it seems that there is little that we can do against you, so I don't see any benefit in bargaining with you?*"

Sister Mary Jacalyn began drumming her finger nails on the table top, expressing her boredom with David, saying…

"If you're finished with the blah-bla-blah, bla blah, I always wanted to say that.
We didn't use that phrase when I was living, but anyhow, I will consider leaving you and your friends and family alone, if you or any of them can figure out how to beat me, how to make me stop?"

David hesitated for just a moment and then said...
"What?"
Sister Mary Jacalyn raised her voice saying...

"Are you deaf, you maggot fucker, or are you naturally stupid. You are the one who has opened the tear in this reality. What you have to figure out is how you opened it and to close it."

Sister Mary Jacalyn walked up to David and smacked him hard upside his head, saying...

"Now pay attention."

David knew that he was taking a chance by irritating Sister Mary Jacalyn, but by this time he didn't really care very much, saying...
"All the shit you're doing to me and my friends and you got the nerve to wanna make a damn game out of it."
The facial expression on Sister Mary Jacalyn, suddenly changed to one of intense anger, as she flung a chair across the room, with a wave of her hand, as David backed up to the mantel place, saying...
"What you gonna do now...kill me?"
Sister Mary Jacalyn stopped and said...

"No, killing you is too easy, but if you piss me off again, I can speed things up I believe that you and your friends should suffer all you can. Nonetheless, you have three days before I make all of your nightmares a permanent part of your reality."

As David and Sister Mary Jacalyn were talking, a figure passed in front of them near the fireplace, and Sister Mary Jacalyn said...

"I got to go, you're about to have company, see you in three days."

David watched as Sister Mary Jacalyn disappeared like vapor, through the wall in the living room, and that's when he heard voices coming from upstairs.

He grabbed a knife from the kitchen and he and Shone slowly and quietly walked towards the stairs when he looked up and saw Tim and Mary coming down. Shocked but expecting anything and everything, David thought at first that he was seeing things, and he said...

"Tim, Mary, what are you two doing here, you're supposed to be in {Port Clinton."

Tim was elated to see David, saying...

"Hey old buddy, sorry...Mary and I were sitting in our living room, and one minute we're in Columbus, and the next we're in Port Clinton and now here in Columbus, you wouldn't believe what we've been through."

David cautiously shook Tim's hand as they reach the bottom of the steps, saying...

"Let me guess, old nasty looking Nun...right?"

Nodding his head, Tim said...

"Yeah, we were watching a movie when the old nasty Nun showed up out of nowhere and told us a lot of shit and the next thing we know...we're here."

Tim and Mary followed him into the kitchen and sat down, when Mary said...

"Oh, so, I don't get a hello or anything, I'm about to lose it here...how the hell did we get from Wisconsin to Port Clinton in the blink of an eye?"

David walked over and hugged Mary, saying...

"Sorry, hey Mary-Mary, I don't know what in the hell is going on, and you're not going to believe me, when I say we've already done and said all of this before.

Me, Deanne, Steve and Wendi were in Columbus and the same Nun, and a lot of weird shit started happening, then we ended up in Port Clinton with you and Tim.

Tim got up and walked over to the window and then called David, saying...

"Look, you got company coming down your driveway!"

David walked over as Tim stepped aside, allowing David to see out of his front room window, who said...

"Tim, I know it's Kristin...we already did this about an hour ago in Port Clinton!"

Tim walked back over to David saying…

"Yeah that's what I was thinking…where the heck is her car, I know she didn't take a taxi here."

Tim and David looked at each other as Kristin was making her way up the driveway.

David and Deanne's driveway to the main house, has a long drive way of over three hundred feet, and then past a barn and then another hundred feet before reaching the house, and it appears that Kristin walked the entire stretch on foot.

David and Tim waited for Kristin to walk up to the house, when Mary asked…

"Where's Dee, Dave?"

David didn't want to tell Mary what happened with Sister Mary Jacalyn, but based on everything that's happened, keeping it from her would only make matters worse, and so he said…

"Kristin's on her way to the door, I'll explain everything then.

Mary snapped…

"Don't tell me that we're going through that shit again, because I don't know if I can take it this time. The last time it was people disappearing and coming out of the wood works and shit, damn, this is not the dark ages, this is…"

David politely interrupted Mary as Kristin was walking in the door, saying…

"Welcome Kristin looks like you got the invite."

Kristin walked in and after looking around, said…

"Invite my white ass, I was sitting in my condo, working on some things when that old bitch showed up, where's Dee?"

Mary responded as she gave Kristin a hug, saying…

"That's what I asked him just before you walked in."

David walked over towards the fire place and placed Shone on a leash and led her out of the living room and into the den, saying…

"Just give me a sec, okay?"

Kristin and Mary and Tim all lived in Madison, Wisconsin, and ended up in Port Clinton, Ohio at the hand of Sister Mary Jacalyn.

Mary and Kristin were making light conversation while Tim was at the kitchen table rolling up several joints of marijuana, when David came back in the room, saying…*"Okay everybody, earlier today, Steve,*

Wendi, Deanne and I were in Columbus at our condo, when Ms. Stinky breath showed up. She explained that she was going to torture us, buy making us relive horrible nightmares.

First of all, we've already said and did all of this an hour ago, but the funny part is that, I can't stop myself from saying the same things I said.

Deanne pissed the Nun off, so she made Deanne disappear, and all of you were at the farm in Port Clinton, when the Nun sent me here."

Kristin looked at Mary and then said...

"And that's okay with you Dave?"

David got up in Kristin's face saying...

"Don't go down that road Kristin, woman or not, you can get knocked on your ass too."

Kristin jumped back In David's face, as Mary tried holding Kristin, as she said...

"Oh, so you're going to knock me on my ass, when all I did was ask you one simple question...you fucking piece of slug shit."

Just then the doorbell rang, and Tim quickly covered his marijuana and turned towards the door as David went to answer it.

Steve and Wendi entered the living room saying...

"Hey everybody, this is some fucked up shit, ain't it?"

Wendi asked...

"Has Deanne made it yet?"

Kristin walked past David and said...

"Is it alright if I go in the kitchen and start making something for everybody to eat?"

Giving Kristin his okay, David and Steve walked out of the front porch to talk, as Kristin walked off into the kitchen, when Mary and Wendi asked if they could do anything to help, as Kristin responded...

"Uh...no I got it from here, but I tell you, when I've made the sandwiches someone can open up several cans of soup and get it hot and set the bowls and spoons on the table."

Wendi quickly said...

"Okay, I got the soup, so Mary, do you mind setting the places around the table?"

Mary walked into the dining room, saying...

"I can't believe with all this stuff going on, we are really serious about sitting around and eating."

Tim walked over to Mary, saying...

"Mary baby, what else are we supposed to do...I mean, it's not like we can just leave anytime we want to, besides, I'm starving."

Mary pushed Tim gently away from her as Tim tried kissing her on the cheek, saying...

Aww, my little pot head, you are always hungry."

David grabbed Steve and they walked out on the porch as David said...

"Hey buddy. Do you remember being here and at the farm an hour ago?"

Lighting up a smoke, Steve said...

"An hour ago? No man, we were at home and then the next thing I know me, and Wendi are here."

David stood in front of Steve saying...

"Steve I'm serious, everything that, the conversations that they are saying... we've all gone through that an hour ago.

The Nun is keeping us repeating it over and over, how do you explain just showing up here?"

Steve looked David in the eye, saying...

"It's crazy Dave, I mean I don't have clue one as to what the fuck is going on...lets go back inside its cold as hell out here."

It's been four hours since Tim, Mary, Steve, Wendi, Kristin and David arrived at the farm, and still there was no sign of Deanne, when Wendi said...

"It's been four hours now, Dave do you think it'll do any good trying to call her?"

David stood up, and said...

"I don't think that Deanne could answer the phone from where she's at... you know, I told you all that an hour ago...I'm gonna grab me a drink?"

Tim, Steve, Kristin and Mary got up walking into the living room towards the liquor cabinet. Wendi was the only one in the bunch who didn't really drink, but she called to David saying...

"I'll take a glass of wine, what kind do you have Dave?"

David stuck his head from around the corner of the kitchen, looking at Tim, Steve, Kristin and Mary jockeying for positions around the liquor cabinet, shook his head and said to Wendi...

"Hey Wen, I got Chardonnay and sweet red, which one do you want?"

"*Normally, I'd drink the sweet red, but I think I'm going to upgrade to Chardonnay.*"

Wendi said as she walked over to the window, checking for a signal on her phone and looking at the sun going down and the darkness setting in.

Everyone assembled back in the living room, drinking their drinks and trying to make sense of why they were assembled and what was going to happen, when Wendi got up saying...

"*Dave, do you mind if I refresh my glass?*"

Heading around the corner to the bathroom, David said...

"*Oh no Wendi, help yourself.*"

Mary walked into the kitchen and hollered back to Wendi, saying...

"*Did you have a problem finding the wine Wendi?*"

Wendi yelled back...

"*No...why?*"

Mary called Wendi back into the kitchen, saying...

'*What's this?*"

Wendi stood in the kitchen and saw that every single cupboard door, cabinet and cutlery drawer were open, as well as the refrigerator was standing open.

Wendi looked on in surprise, saying...

"*No way, they were all closed when I was in here, and there's no way anybody else could have come in and done it because we would've seen them.*"

While Wendi and Mary closed every drawer, refrigerator and cabinet door, Tim walked over to the window, saying...

"*There's somebody out there.*"

David and Steve joined Tim over at the window, and before they could look at what Tim was seeing, there was three loud knocks at the door.

Positioning themselves so that they could see, Steve and David saw a large man standing and waving at them, wearing a Halloween pig mask.

While they looked on, the man began turning the front door knob, and then there were three loud knocks at the back door.

David and Tim raced to the back door, checking to see that it was locked when Mary and Wendi came out of the kitchen, and Mary said as she walked to the front door and opening it saying...

"*Are you just going to stand there Wendi, there's somebody knocking?*"

Thinking it was Tim messing around, Mary opened the door to a large man wearing a pig mask, as she punched him in the stomach and mouthing *"good one"* and waved Tim inside, when Wendi hollered...

"Close the damn door, that ain't Tim!"

Mary and Wendi had little time to react, when the large man stuck his foot in the door, preventing them from closing it, as Wendi hollered to David and Tim...

"Put something against the back door, somebody's trying to get in here!"

David and Tim raced over to the love seat and carried over to the back door, tilting it and bracing it up against the door knob.

Wendi grunted, and Mary pushed as hard as she could, but the large man's foot was planted in the door way, when Wendi screamed, and Kristin ran out of the living room.

Thinking that Kristin had ran off and left them, Steve hollered...

"Kristin, get your chicken ass back in here and help...damnit!"

Just then, the large man's hand emerged through the door opening, as Wendi tried bending it backwards, when out of nowhere, Kristin had crawled underneath Mary and Wendi, burying a large knife in the large man's foot, who let go and backed out of the door.

Kristin, Wendi and Mary were at the front door and Tim and David at the back door, no one noticed that Deanne was standing in the middle of the living room crying.

Wendi turned to the sounds of Deanne crying and yelled...

"Dee!"

David turned in Wendi's direction and saw Deanne standing in the living room with Wendi and immediately left Tim and ran to Deanne, hugging her and kissing her, saying...

"Oh baby, Deanne...you're here, oh baby, where did you come from, oh, I'm so glad to see you baby?"

Tim took all the cushions off the sofa and threw them to the floor, and pushed the sofa against the front door, while Mary and Steve moved the cushions against the wall of the living room.

The pounding on the doors suddenly stopped as soon as Deanne appeared in the living room. For an instant the house was filled with jubilee, but that was to be short lived as a voice, the voice of Sister Mary Jacalyn was heard saying...

"Remember, you have to figure it out, figure out how to stop me."

For the rest of the evening, everything inside was quiet and showed some signs of normalcy, when David said...

"Okay, we have work to do...Kristin, you're good at solving puzzles and shit, right?"

Kristin looked around at everyone and then back over to David saying...

"I don't know what you mean...yeah, I'm not a dumb ass, you know."

David went on to say...

"The Nun said that I have three days to figure out why she's here and how to stop here or else all the nightmares that we're having, she will make us experience them every day, forever."

Tim was sitting on the far edge of the sofa when he stood up, pulling rolling papers and a bag of marijuana from his shirt pocket, saying...

"Man, all this shit is messed up...I mean look, we are at the mercy of some funky ass Nun, who died centuries ago and we can't fight these damn ghosts or spirits, so, what are we supposed to do?"

David walked over to Tim saying...

"I hear what you're saying Tim, I don't know what to do or even how to feel about all of this, all I know right now is, it's happening, it's real and that 'Sally Fields, Flying Nun' reject is giving me three days to try and stop her."

Kristin walked over and sat next to Deanne, and as she sat with her, she looked at David saying...

"It's obvious, that someone here has been messing with an Ouija board, or with black candles or some other creepy ass-shit."

"I don't think it's that at all Kris, and besides, what good is it going to do, if we go all around the room with kind of thinking...we still have to figure out how to get out of this nightmare, and how to get rid of here."

Deanne said, as she got up and walked towards the bathroom, when Steve yelled out...

"Hold on Deanne! I think it's a good ideal if we stay together as a whole group or at least in pairs".

Turning around, Deanne said...

"Are you saying in the bathroom too?"

Nodding his head, Steve replied...

"Especially In the bathroom, it's better to be with someone, in case something happens."

Wendi, stood up and walked over to Deanne, saying…

"Hey, I'll come with you."

"It's not you Wendi but doing it while someone is in the bathroom with you, is hard…but come on."

Deanne said as they walked out of the living room into the bathroom around the corner.

Twenty minutes turned into an hour when David got up and walked out of the living room, saying…

"I'm going to see what's keeping Deanne and Wendi."

David no sooner left the living room when Steve chased after him saying…

"Yo buddy, where are you going?"

David stopped and said…

"To check on Deanne and Wendi, they've been gone almost an hour."

Steve grabbed hold of David's arm, saying…

"Look, man, look!"

David stood speechless as he saw Deanne and Wendi sitting at the dining room table talking, when he said…

"Damn Steve, I could have sworn they went to the bathroom."

Steve assured David that they have been sitting at the dining room table for a while talking, when Steve and David returned to the living room, and took a seat beside Deanne and Wendi.

Wendi took hold of Steve's hand, saying…

"Dee was just telling me about what happened to her, and I think everybody needs to hear it, go ahead Dee."

Deanne cleared her throat and looked at David, and said…

"Like I was saying to Wendi, when we were at the condo earlier in C-bus, you remember when the Nun made us all disappear?"

David and the others nodded yes, as Deanne continued…

"Well, what took me so long, was, first like I said, I was here all the time, watching ya'll, but you guys couldn't see or hear me.

When I opened up the front door to go outside, I ended up back at the condo again, with all of you, but you couldn't hear or see me."

Scooting to the edge of the sofa, Steve said…

"I wonder why we didn't stay there at the condo, I mean why did we all end up here?"

Looking over to Steve, Deanne replied...

"Because of me, you see, I walked out of the door here and we ended up at the condo, and then I tried to leave the condo, and we all showed up back here again.

The Nun explained to me that, she wanted all of us to experience this nightmare together, but if one of us tried to leave, that would throw all of us back at the start of the nightmare."

Kristin stood up, going to get another drink and said...

"So, in other words, if you try to leave, then we have to experience this bull shit from the beginning?"

Deanne shook her head, saying...

"That's right. The Nun said that, if any of us tried to leave, it throws us all back to the beginning, the problem is, no one but the person who tried to leave is the only one who'll have a memory of it.

The Nun said, she has millions of people doing things and experiencing things without any knowledge of it."

Tim, grabbed Deanne's attention, saying...

"That don't explain why me, Mary and Kristin are here, I mean, we live almost seven hundred miles away in Wisconsin, what do we have to do with anything?"

David replied, saying...

"I do...I know why. It's because when we had the Labor Day party here, and all that weird stuff was happening, and nobody saw and heard all that crazy stuff except me...yeah, that's gotta be it.

We were all together when it first happened, don't you see?"

"Rubbing David's back, Deanne said...

"She also said, that one of us, someone in our group here is causing all of this to happen, and that it spills over into our friends, and their friends, and that thousands in Columbus and Port Clinton are going through nightmares, without any knowledge of what is going on."

Tim took out a joint from his pocket and lit it, as Mary asked...

"Okay, so what are we supposed to do, just sit here and go through some stupid stuff, that don't matter anyway."

Wendi interrupted...

"Aww Mary I don't think that..."

Interrupting Wendi, Mary's voice got louder...

"I mean really, it's like, if one of us gets killed, or if one of us drives off a cliff or something, it won't really matter, because we'll just wake up somewhere, starting the whole nightmare all over again, right?"

Lighting up a cigarette and passing Tim back his lighter, David replied...

"I got a feeling that's not how this thing works. I remember when I was seeing all that crazy shit last year, some things were real, and others were not.

For example, all of us were here last Labor Day, and suddenly one by one everybody was disappearing, all except Deanne and Kristin.

The problem for us is, going to be figuring out what is real and what is not.

Just a few minutes ago, I was going to the bathroom to check on Deanne and Wendi, because I saw them going there, but Steve stopped me and told me that they were sitting at the table.

When I looked over there, there they were, sitting, even though I know I saw them going in the bathroom. So, you see, we are living out an illusion, or something...some of its real and some of it isn't."

Taking a deep drag, and coughing, Tim said...

"And people wonder why I smoke pot."

Kristin came back into the living room, saying...

"So, the answer to my question and Mary's question is...what do we do. Do we go through this day, as if some things matter and other things do not, knowing that at any time, things could vanish or not really be happening at all?"

David threw his hands up saying...

"I'm not the expert here, but I think all of us should always be with another person. Everything we do should be in groups of twos or fours, but I don't think any of us should be alone until we figure this out. Does that sound like a plan?"

Everyone shook their heads yes, when Mary said...

"There's one more thing, though, Dee said that the nasty ass Nun said that one of us in this room was causing all of this to happen, I'd like to know who it is."

Walking up to Mary, Deanne said...

"It could be any of us, and we wouldn't even know that we were causing it...but Blue is right, we should be in pairs, so that the other person can spot if we disappear or are doing or saying something creepy or whatever."

For the rest of the day, things seemed to be pretty normal, that is until, the night.

Mary, Kristin, Deanne and Wendi were in the kitchen, and David, Tim and Steve walked down into the basement to retrieve steaks, corn and Lobster tails from the freezer.

Since Mary was the least person you wanted cooking for you, Deanne suggested to Mary that she take care of the setting the table, getting the drinks ready, and making the salad, while Deanne, Wendi and Kristin focused on Potato salad, baked beans, macaroni and cheese and baked asparagus.

The steaks and lobsters were the domain of David and Steve out on the grill. There was little for Tim to do, so he acted as the 'runner' when he wasn't lighting up a joint and complaining about the cold.

Dinner turned out fantastic as everyone ate their fill and decided, instead of sleeping in separate rooms, that they would move the furniture around and retrieve the three sleeping bags from the attic and the two cots from the basement, and everybody would sleep downstairs in the living room.

There was little interest in playing social games, or that kind of thing, all that they wanted to do, was get some sleep and to get it over with.

The waiting is always the hardest thing to do, no matter what the situation…the waiting.

The night temperature was only expected to go into the low thirties, so there would be no need keeping the house too warm. David threw several large logs in the fire place, which he felt should last till morning.

Kristin curled up on the sofa, Tim and Mary were in sleeping bags, as was Wendi. Steve, David and Deanne slept on the three cots, and Shone, was in her dog bed by the back door.

Then it happened.

There was a soft…tic-toc, tic-toc, and then it grew louder and louder until it awakened Tim, Mary, Deanne and Steve, out of their sleep.

Deanne, being the one closest to the television startled first, saying…

"Oh god…its only four in the morning, what's all that noise?"

Mary, unzipped her sleeping bag and yawned, saying…

"Oh gosh, it's still dark out. Dee, I'm glad you're up because I gotta pee. Mmm, that sleeping bag was good and toasty, c'mon Dee."

Deanne sat on the edge of the cot, saying…

"Mary nobody's, stopping you, go pee, dang."

Mary stood up and walked over to Deanne, saying...

"You heard what the guys said last night, 'everybody in pairs'.

Deanne yawned, saying...

"Yeah ok, since I gotta go too."

Mary and Deanne walked to the bathroom, they made it their business to cut the overhead lights on.

Mary accidentally stepped on Tim, who said...

"Oh, man...where's everybody going?"

Looking over at David who was snoring, Steve said to Tim...

"Mary and Deanne are on their early morning pee run. Wow, I could use a little more sleep, do you know what time it is?"

Tim scrambled around in his sleeping bag trying to find his arm, and after a short comedy stretch, said as he laid back down and zipped the sleeping bag back up...

"I'm looking at a quarter past four."

Steve could see Tim getting cozy in his sleeping bag as he poked Tim, saying...

"Don't get too comfy all in there, when the girls are finished I got to go myself, so that means you are going too."

Tim stopped moving inside the sleeping bag for a moment, and grunted out...

"OK!"

Without incident, Mary and Deanne came out of the bathroom and sat down as Steve poked Tim again, saying...

"It's show-time."

Tim slowly unzipped his bag and came out of the sleeping bag with a joint in his mouth saying...

"Somebody say...smoke time?"

While Mary and Deanne started laughing at Tim, as Steve said...

"Man, you're a trip, you know that?"

Steve and Tim walked out of the living room to the bathroom, and as Tim was heading out of the living room, he lit his joint and did a little shuffle with his feet, singing...

"I'm walking, yes in deed and I'm smoking, a big fat joint, and I'm..."

Deanne, sat down on the cot, shaking her head and saying to Mary...

"Tim's got issues, you know that don't you?"

Mary looked up at Deanne shaking her head as she was settling in her sleeping bag, saying…

"I know, a big one…right between his legs."

Deanne fell back on her cot saying…

"Damn why did you have to go there, now I'm going have that image in my head."

Mary zipped up her sleeping bag, and laughed…

"He-he-he-he."

Deanne laughed as well and said to Mary…

"Aww girl, go on back to sleep, besides, Blue, packs all I need."

Steve and Tim were just walking into the living room as Mary and Deanne resettled into their sleeping bag, and cot, when Tim said…

"Instead of hitting the sack, we might as well go on and make breakfast, I'm hungry enough to eat the slime out of a slug's butt."

Steve laid on his cot, saying to Mary…

"Hey, Mary…you are going to have to take your man to see a doctor, and I'm not talking about a regular one either.…one of those special ones…he's sick."

Mary reached her hand out of her sleeping bag and rubbed Tim's belly, saying…

"What's a matter, my sexy man got the munchies huh? Well, in a couple of hours, I'll make you eggs, bacon, pancakes, fried potatoes and a big glass of orange juice."

Steve replied…

"You two need to quit it, now, you're making me hungry talking about all that."

Mary, Tim, Deanne and Steve all settled down and fell asleep within a few minutes of closing their eyes. As they slept, none of them paid any attention to the figure sitting at the kitchen table watching them.

It was Sister Mary Jacalyn watching them sleep. Sister Mary Jacalyn sat in the dim light watching them, as a large spider crawled across her face and stopped for several minutes on her left cheek, then crawled up her nose, and disappeared.

Deanne was awakened briefly as Shone began growling, and Deanne looked over to where Shone was lying, and whispered to Shone to be quiet.

As Deanne turned over on her cot to reposition herself, she caught a slight glimpse of a pair of red eyes staring at her from the dining room table, and paying it no mind, fell right to sleep.

The morning sun was beginning to rise, shining a faint light into the living room window, when suddenly, the front door burst open, wakening everyone.

Shone dashed out of the door barking, when David jumped up and bolted to the door, trying to catch Shone, who disappeared in the fog which had begun to set in.

David stood on the front porch looking as, Shone's barking could be heard, growing more and more faint.

David called her, bringing everyone to the door and the front windows.

David turned saying...

"Damn! Who opened the front door?"

Tim stood behind David as he stepped out on the front porch, saying...

"Not who, but what Dave...what opened the door. If you recall no one was near the door when it opened."

David hollered again for Shone, and thought...

"Shone was clearly chasing something, and she would come back once she was through."

David shut the front door and as he did, Tim said...

"Since most of us are up, we might as well look at eating breakfast."

Early in the morning on a farm just before daybreak, is a lot more serene than waking up in the city, the smells, sights, the view.

Deanne and Kristin were already in the kitchen by the time everyone was awake, pouring cereal, making eggs, grits, bacon and toast.

After grabbing a cup of coffee, Steve and David stood at the living room window looking out to see if the entire farm had been blown away overnight.

Curiously, Mary, Wendi and Tim ran to the big picture window that looks onto the front yard. There is however, one thing which was out of place...a strange truck was there.

No one appeared to be behind the wheel, though the engine was idling. The truck was... well, old, for one thing. Old-timey like from maybe the nineteen thirties.

You could picture Jethro behind the wheel, and Granny in the backseat, if you looked hard enough.

Everyone stared at the truck, bewildered, when Mary hollered into the kitchen asking Deanne...

"Hey Dee, your neighbor across the way, does he have an old blue, beat up truck?"

All at once, there was a loud, insistent banging on the front door. Mary and Wendi screamed.

Steve peeked outside the window to the left, very stealth-like, then turned back and looked confused, and shook his head, like...

"No one is there."

All at once you could hear everyone letting out a breath of relief. Even though everyone was aware that something was going to happen, no one was completely at ease.

Then every door in the house started banging — relentlessly. Rhythmic and terrifying, like all the doors were about to splinter and crack. There were two doors in the basement which reverberated at their feet.

The three basement-floor doors started shaking, causing a trembling and jerking on their hinges from the sounds coming from below. Finally, Deanne ran to the window either from a psychotic breakdown with reality or terror, crying...

"Who does that truck belong to oh, dear God, help us!"

Tim, David, and Steve ran to the window beside Deanne, and peeked out the picture window, but there is no one that they could see in the yard, but they could see all the doors in the front of the house from their viewpoint.

Just then, Deanne whispered...

"Look! It's Mr. Thomas from across the way walking by the truck with a shotgun in his hand."

Mr. Thomas looked puzzled, as he looked at the rear of his truck, and then he glanced at the window of the house and started up the steps.

Steve turned to Deanne and David, saying...

"According to the Nun, if we leave, we have to start this nightmare over, but what if someone from the outside comes is, what do you think that'll do?"

Deanne looked at David, and shrugged her shoulders, and said...

"I'm not sure what'll happen, but..."

Before Deanne could finish her sentence, Mr. Thomas, turned around and back down the steps and left in his truck, down the drive way.

Just then, Mary said as she opened the door, making sure not to go outside, hollered saying...

"Hey, old man!"

Steve jerked Mary's arm, saying...

"What do you think you're doing...if he comes back, what are we supposed to say to him, when he asks why we're all here and there are no cars?"

Jerking her arm away from Steve, Mary shouted...

"Get off me Steve...what do you mean what'll we say, we could say whatever we want, we need some contact with the outside."

David stepped up, in between Mary and Steve saying...

"Steve's right, and not because he's a man either Mary. If what Deanne says is true, us having contact with anything or anyone on the outside, will make us start this crap all over again."

Looking at David, Mary shouted...

"Oh, like you know, since when did you all of a sudden become an expert into this weird and crazy shit we're in?"

Trying to calm Mary down, David replied...

"I'm no expert, but I've been dealing with this shit longer than anyone here, and I feel that we have to figure out all this without dragging anyone else into it."

Then without a moment's notice, the wind began picking up and pushed the front door closed.

Like a tornado or the end of the world, the intense sound and roaring of a freight train could be heard, sounding so loud, until everyone was way too scared to even scream.

Then the shutters on the sides of the windows started banging until they came loose and were pulled off the sides of the windows and tossed into the yard and thrown around like leaves in the wind.

Tim hollered from the window on the far side of the house saying...

"Ya'll are not going to believe this...!"

Mr. Thomas's old truck just came rolling down the driveway, and there was no one behind the wheel of that thing.

Everyone had a clear view and especially with the outside house light shining on it.

Wendi, who still was standing at the front room picture window, cried…

"*Over here! I thought I saw a blur of something or someone running across the lawn towards the barn.*"

Steve and David were the first to run over to where Wendi was, saying…

"*Dave, can you get from the front of the house to the barn without being seen?*"

David stepped back from the window, saying…

"*No, not without being seen. I mean, you could use the walkway, but you'd have to be inside the house to use that, and then of course, the main door of the barn, is right there, but you can see it from here.*"

David and Steve were talking when, out of the blue, the wind died, and everything got calm.

Looking back in the driveway, Steve noticed along with Wendi and Tim that the truck was gone, and said…

"*Okay folks, it looks like the weird shit is starting to happen…Dave, Hey Dave where you going?*"

Turning around, everyone noticed that David was walking into the kitchen towards the door that leads to the walkway, which goes to the barn when Deanne yelled out…

"*Blue…Blue, you can't go out there baby.*"

David stopped and said…

"*Look I'm not going to sit in here and just wait for something to happen, you said we can't try to leave, well I'm not leaving, the walkway is attached to the house, I'm just trying to see if we can at least move around a little more or something.*"

Just at that moment Mary's cell phone began ringing, first hers and then Wendi's, then Steve's until they were all ringing.

When Mary answered her cell, all she heard was low, deep breaths.

On everyone else's cell phone, there was nothing except a deep chuckle and then the dial tone. Looking down at their phones, everyone noticed that the caller ID showed the number as 'six- six- six, six-six-six, - six- six-six'.

Wendi was the strongest Christian of the group and she began praying out loud, as Tim who was not a Christian simply said…

"*That don't mean nothing!*"

Wendi replied with nodding her head in agreement, saying…

"What do you mean, that don't mean nothing… all those six's…man that's the devil's number."

Tim walked over to the dining room table and laid his phone down, saying…

"All I'm saying is, that's the same to me as walking under a ladder or crossing a black cat. I know this is going to rub you the wrong way Wendi, but it's the same as holding the cross in your hand and praying for good luck, or whatever."

Wendi, Mary and Deanne stood in front of Tim, as Wendi responded…

"How can you even go there Tim, I know you claim not to believe in God, but faith is a very real reality for billions of people.

It's no daggone coincidence, of luck or any of that stuff, and based on what's happening to us, you'd best think about believing in God."

Steve and David stood near the dining table, as David shook his head, saying…

"Tim's in for it now, the boy just doesn't know when to shut his mouth, especially on certain subjects…whew!"

Tim turned to Wendi, Mary and Deanne saying…

"Nobody said anything about not believing in God, I believe that there is a being, a creator, I just said that I don't buy the…'fast and pray' attitude and God's going to come to your rescue.

He gave us a will, common sense and the ability and the strength to fight for ourselves, I mean look at the deep shit we're going through right now."

Just then Steve interrupted them, saying…

"Hey everybody, can we just put the brakes on for a minute. We need to shower, eat, and try to figure out what we're going to do about the mess we're in and how we're going to get out of it."

Nodding in agreement, David said…

"Alright, we have a shower upstairs and one down here. I think Wendi, Deanne, Mary and Kristin…"

"Where is Kristin?"

Deanne said as she looked around the living room.

"Did anyone see her leave?"

Wendi said as she walked over and hugged Steve, replying…

"She was here last night…I think, I can't remember her being here this morning."

Mary and Tim replied…

"I remember her being here last night…all day actually, cause we were looking at her when she arrived, walking up the driveway."

David replied as Deanne and Steve nodded in agreement…

"I don't remember her even being here yesterday."

Just then, Deanne said…

"Okay, that's why we need to stick together gang…I mean some of us remember Kristin being here and me, Blue and Steve don't remember her being here at all."

Tim lit a joint, saying…

"It's that broke down Nun messing with us, I-I felt as if something was watching me, all morning, I'm telling you, that damn Nun is here watching us, messing with us."

Deanne responded, saying…

"I agree with Tim, I've felt like we were being watched all morning too and when everybody's phones started ringing, mine didn't…I got a text instead."

David walked over to Deanne saying…

"You got a text…from who?"

"There was no caller ID number or anything, I just got a text with that six-six-six number saying…" "I'm here".

I didn't think that much about it since everybody a call this morning, I didn't think I was the only who got a text, until now."

Deanne said as she motioned for Wendi to join her in the Kitchen. Mary stopped Deanne and Wendi, saying…

"How are we going to do this, and what about Kristin?"

Stopping and turning, Deanne said…

"As much as this sucks, there is little we can do about Kristin, The Nun is messing with us and has some of us thinking that Kristin was never here, so, when she appears somebody stick close to her.

Wendi and Mary are going to cook breakfast, and guys, why don't ya'll take your showers first…just don't any of you drop the soap."

While Steve, Tim and David were cleaning up and shaving, Mary, Deanne and Wendi were preparing breakfast for everyone, and were going to shower afterwards.

By the time breakfast was ready, Tim, David and Steve walked into the dining room and each sat at the table seats apart from one another.

Not much conversation was heard from them until Mary, Deanne and Wendi entered the room.

Steve and Tim stood up to help Mary, Wendi and Deanne to sit the food on the table, when Wendi said...

"No, that's alright you guys go ahead and sit...we appreciate it, but we got this."

Sitting down, Tim said...

"MMM...that smells good."

All the food was placed on the table, Scrambled cheesy eggs, pancakes, homemade maple syrup, strawberry preserves, French toast, bacon, liver mush, grits, hot biscuits, orange juice, and coffee.

David looked across the table saying...

"I think more now than ever we need to ask prayer before eating...if everyone will bow their heads...

"Heavenly Father, we thank you for watching over our hearts, but we need you to come into this situation and make it right, and if not, then give us the power and heart to deal with it ourselves. We bless this food, and we thank Wendi, Deanne and Mary for their skills in the kitchen...Amen'."

Lifting his head up, Steve said, as heads bobbed up and down...

"Good job Dave, my man, touching.

Putting a lot on his plate, Tim asked Deanne and Wendi...

"What's this here, I've never eaten this before?"

Deanne replied, as she fixed her plate...

"Its 'Liver Mush'...Blue introduced me to it the first time I was in North Carolina at his Aunt's house, and I've loved it since...try a small piece Tim."

Wendi and Mary nodded their heads as they tasted liver mush for the first time, saying...

"Mmm good, Dave...it's good to see you showing good taste in something."

David sat with a mouthful and flipped Mary the bird and nodded to Wendi.

After breakfast, the women each took showers with the men watching the doors as they did, and to surprise, there were no incidents.

The weather outside was unseasonably warm, in the upper sixties, with a mild wind from the south east. Mary sat at the dining room table watching Tim roll up joints and placing them in a cigarette case.

David and Deanne were playing a game of cards with Steve and Wendi, when Mary looked over, saying…

"Gosh, I'm really getting bored, are we just supposed to sit here all freaking day, doing nothing?"

Deanne put her finger to David's lips as he was about to respond to Mary, and said…

"Aww, c'mon Mary, we might as well take advantage of some peace…who knows what we are in store for."

Tim joined in with Deanne, saying…

"Yeah babe, here hit this and chill out a little bit."

Mary very seldom would smoke marijuana with or without Tim, she preferred a mixed drink or a beer. Mary and Tim got up from the table and went into the kitchen for a cold beer, saying…

"Does anyone want something?"

Steve, David and Deanne responded, saying…

"Yes, three brews, Mary-Mary."

As Mary and Tim were making their way back into the living room with four beers, she heard a scratching noise coming from the basement door, and said…

"Hey Dave, you got rats or something down in your basement."

David grabbed the remote control and turned the music down and said…

"I got what in a gravamen?"

Walking deeper into the living room, Mary repeated herself saying…

"I said, you got rats or something down in your basement, I heard scratching noises like a rat or something."

David took a swig of his beer and sat the bottle down, saying…

"Be right back, let me see what's going on."

Steve stood up saying…

"Not so fast buddy, we got to do this on the buddy system, remember?"

David and Steve slowly walked over to the basement door and could plainly hear something scratching on the other side of the door.

Steve grabbed a large knife from the cutlery block as David slowly turned the door knob and opened the door.

Immediately as soon as the door opened, Steve and David stood in the opening looking, but there was no one or anything there.

David reached to turn the basement light on as Steve stood looking as if he were ready to recreate the charge of Santa Ana at the Alamo.

The at the bottom of the basement steps they saw a figure. It looked like it was a man. Then they saw his face...it was a woman, the Nun, Sister Mary Jacalyn, and she had the evilest smile they'd ever seen.

Her smile was so wide, it almost reached from ear to ear.

The Nun didn't say a word, all she did was point her long, decaying fingers towards Steve and David.

Initially, Steve and David assumed she was pointing at them, but soon realized Sister Mary Jacalyn was pointing behind them.

David and Steve turned and slammed the door hard, locking it and saying...

"All...God damnit!"

With Steve laying his back against the door, breathing heavy and saying...

"KRISTIN!"

David looked at Steve and then turned back around and sure enough Kristin was standing there with a blank expression on her face and bewilderment in her eyes, as David said...

"Kristin, where did you come from, where the hell have you been?"

Before Kristin could respond to David, Deanne, Mary and Wendi came running into the kitchen, and seeing Kristin, they all hugged her, as Deanne began crying, and saying...

"Oh my God Kris, oh my God, we've been so worried, you were..."

Interrupting Deanne, Wendi asked Kristin...

"Kris, what happened to you, you were with us earlier and then you were gone?"

Kristin and everyone sat on the sofa as Kristin said...

"All I know is, I think I was here this morning, and the next thing I know, I was bouncing back and forth from Madison, Wisconsin to here.

I saw everyone, but no one could see or hear me, and then the Nun, she, said…one of the seven here has to stop, elsewise, she will continue to torment us until we lose our right to remain in this reality.

She said, we will all continue to go through this nightmare until the person stops. She said she was pulled here from her reality to ours, and that the person responsible knows who they are, and that we have two more days to figure it out."

Just then Shone was at the front door, whining and whimpering to get in. David and Steve went to the door, to be certain that it was only Shone. David unlocked and opened the door and let her in.

Shone nudged up against David's leg and then ran over to Deanne who was sitting by the fireplace and jumped up on her.

For the next several hours, Deanne played with Shone on and off and seeing her energy and playfulness, took their minds off what was going on, until she became fidgety, signaling she wanted to go outside.

The overall feeling that everyone experienced wasn't that of the normal kind of bleakness that a country, farm setting generally offered. There was almost a kind of overwhelming sense of doom in the air.

Steve, David, Wendi and Deanne decided to break the boredom and the nothingness by playing dominos, while Tim and Mary sat huddled on the sofa, watching a movie. Just then Mary cried out…

"Something just grabbed my ankle."

Looking around to Mary, Deanne said…

"What's the matter Mary?"

Mary had scooted to the edge of the sofa, and was looking down at her feet, when Deanne replied…

"It was probably your nerves, girl."

Again, Mary cried out as she quickly put both feet under her, sitting on them, saying…

"I'm telling you, there's something under here."

Tim got off the sofa and, on his knees, looking under the sofa, said…

"There's nothing under here Mary, must've been the bottom edge of this blanket, rubbing against your legs, or something."

Tim sat back down on the sofa, when Mary screamed…

"Damnit…I can't take this shit anymore, we're cooked up in here, and can't go or do anything, damn creepy old ass Nun is messing with us, I'm going take my chances outside."

With that, Mary ran to the front door and opened it, stepping outside on the porch, when Deanne yelled...

"*Mary, don't! Get back in here!*"

Everyone got up from the table in time to see Mary standing in the doorway on the front porch with her arms outstretched, saying...

"*You see ya'll, all that 'we can't leave the house shit'...that was nothing but a bunch of crap.*"

Deanne, Wendi and David went near the door, as Deanne cried out...

"*Mary, just listen to me, back inside real slow, okay?*"

Tim walked over to the door, saying...

"*Wait a minute, I mean look, nothing happened, maybe Mary's right, maybe we can step outside, as you can see, nothing happened.*"

Before anyone could blink, Deanne vanished, and then Tim, then Wendi, then Steve, next Kristin, and lastly David vanished, but not before Sister Mary Jacalyn appeared to him, saying...

"*I instructed you not to try and leave this house, but like fools, you wish to tempt me...well, when you all come back, things will only become a little more difficult.*"

Just then, David grabbed a poker iron from the fire place and slowly and quietly walked towards the stairs when he looked up and saw Tim and Mary coming down.

Shocked but expecting anything and everything, David thought at first that he was seeing things, and he said...

"*Tim, Mary, what are you two doing here, you're supposed to be home in Wisconsin.*"

Tim was elated to see David, saying...

"*Hey old buddy, sorry...but Mary and I were sitting in our living room, and boy, you wouldn't believe what we've been through.*"

David cautiously shook Tim's hand as they reach the bottom of the steps, saying...

"*Let me guess, it was the Nun...right?*"

Nodding his head, Tim said...

"*Yeah, we were watching a movie when this old nasty Nun showed up out of nowhere and told us a lot of shit and the next thing we know...we're here, Dave, what's going on?*"

Tim and Mary followed him into the kitchen and sat down, when Mary said…

"Oh, so, I don't get a hello or anything, I'm about to lose it here…how the hell did we get from Wisconsin to Port Clinton in the blink of an eye?"

David walked over and hugged Mary, saying…

"Sorry, hey Mary-Mary, I don't know what in the hell is going on, but something seems strange.

Me, Deanne, Steve and Wendi were in Columbus at the house with the Nun, and a lot of weird shit started happening.

Look I don't know what's going on, all I know is that, I've been trying to tell myself that I'm asleep and dreaming, but I know I'm not."

Tim got up and walked over to the window and then called David, saying…

"Look, you got company coming down your driveway!"

David walked over as Tim stepped aside, allowing David to see out of his front room window, who said…

"What in the world!"

Tim walked back over to David saying…

"Yeah that's what I was thinking…where the heck is her car, I know she didn't take a taxi here."

Tim and David looked at each other as Kristin was making her way up the driveway. The beginning of the driveway to Deanne and David's front door was a long drive, five hundred feet.

You go past the barn and then another two hundred and fifty feet before reaching the front door, and it appears that Kristin was walking the entire stretch on foot.

David and Tim waited for Kristin to walk up to the house, when Mary asked…

"Where's Dee, Dave?

David didn't want to tell Mary what happened with Sister Mary Jacalyn, but based on everything that's happened, keeping it from her would only make matters worse, and so he said…

"Kristin's on her way to the door, I'll explain everything then."

Mary snapped…

"Don't tell me that we're going through that shit again, because I don't know if I can take it this time.

The last time it was people disappearing and coming out of the wood works and shit, damn, this is not the dark ages, this is..."

David politely interrupted Mary as Kristin was walking in the door, saying...

"Welcome Kristin looks like you got the invite."

Kristin walked in and after looking around, said...

"Invite my white ass, I was sitting in my condo, working on some things when that old bitch showed up, where's Dee?"

Mary responded as she gave Kristin a hug, saying...

"That's what I asked him just before you walked in."

David walked over towards the fire place and placed Shone on a leash and led her out of the living room and into the den, saying...

"Just give me a sec, okay?"

Kristin and Mary both lived in Madison, Wisconsin, and both ended up in Port Clinton, Ohio at the hand of Sister Mary Jacalyn.

Mary and Kristin were making light conversation and Tim was at the kitchen table rolling up several joints of marijuana, when David came back in the room, saying...

"Okay everybody, earlier today, Steve, Wendi, Deanne and I were in Columbus at our condo, when Ms. Stinky breath showed up.

She explained that she was going to torture us, buy making us relive horrible nightmares.

At first, she had all of us, one by one to go through our own nightmare, and then she said she was going to make all of us go through one together here.

Well Deanne coped an attitude and said some things that pissed her off, and she said that we were all going to appear here, but that she was going to make Deanne take the long way getting here, for pissing her off."

Kristin looked at Mary and then said...

"And that's okay with you Dave?"

David got up in Kristin's face saying...

"Don't go down that road Kristin, woman or not, you can get knocked on your ass too."

Kristin jumped back In David's face, as Mary tried holding Kristin, as she said...

"Oh, so you going to knock me on my ass, when all I did was ask you one simple question...you fucking piece of slug shit."

Just then the doorbell rang, and Tim quickly covered his marijuana and turned towards the door as David went to answer it.

Steve and Wendi entered the living room saying…

"Hey everybody, this is some fucked up shit, ain't it?"

Wendi asked…

"Has Deanne made it yet?"

Kristin walked past David and said…

"Is it alright if I go in the kitchen and start making something for everybody to eat?"

Giving Kristin his okay, David and Steve walked out of the front porch to talk, as Kristin walked off into the kitchen, when Mary and Wendi asked if they could do anything to help, as Kristin responded…

"Uh…no I got it from here, but I tell you, when I've made the sandwiches someone can open up several cans of soup and get it hot and set the bowls and spoons on the table."

Wendi quickly said…

"Okay, I got the soup, so Mary, do you mind setting the places around the table?"

Mary walked into the dining room, saying…

"I can't believe with all this stuff going on, we are really serious about sitting around and eating."

Tim walked over to Mary, saying…

"Mary baby, what else are we supposed to do…I mean, it's not like we can just leave anytime we want to, besides, I'm starving."

Mary pushed Tim gently away from her as Tim tried kissing her on the cheek, saying…

Aww, my little pot head, you are always hungry."

It's been four hours since Tim, Mary, Steve, Wendi, Kristin and David arrived at the farm, and still there was no sign of Deanne, when Wendi said…

"It's been four hours now, Dave do you think it'll do any good trying to call her?"

David stood up, and said…

"I don't think she'll be able to get your call from where she is. I'm gonna get me a drink, anybody else want one?"

Tim, Steve, Kristin and Mary got up walking into the living room towards the liquor cabinet.

Wendi was the only one in the bunch who didn't really drink, but she called to David saying...

"I'll take a glass of wine, what kind do you have Dave?"

David stuck his head from around the corner of the kitchen, looking at Tim, Steve, Kristin and Mary jockeying for positions around the liquor cabinet, shook his head and said to Wendi...

"Hey Wen, I got Chardonnay and sweet red, which one do you want?"

"Normally, I'd drink the sweet red, but I think I'm going to upgrade to Chardonnay.

Wendi said as she walked over to the window, dialing Deanne's number, and looking at the sun going down and the darkness setting in.

Everyone assembled back in the living room, drinking their drinks and trying to make sense of why they were assembled and what was going to happen, when Wendi got up saying...

"Dave, do you mind if I refresh my glass?"

Heading around the corner to the bathroom, David said...

"Oh no Wendi, help yourself."

Mary walked into the kitchen and hollered back to Wendi, saying...

"Did you have a problem finding the wine Wendi?"

Wendi yelled back...

"No...why?"

Mary called Wendi back into the kitchen, saying...

'What's this?"

Wendi stood in the kitchen and saw that every single cupboard door, cabinet and cutlery drawer were open, as well as the refrigerator was standing open.

Wendi looked on in surprise, saying...

"No way, they were all closed when I was in here, and there's no way, it was only you and I in there."

While Wendi and Mary closed every drawer, refrigerator and cabinet door, Tim walked over to the window, saying...

"There's somebody out there."

David and Steve joined Tim over at the window, and before they could look at what Tim was seeing, there was three loud knocks at the door.

Positioning themselves so that they could see, Steve and David saw a large man standing and waving at them, wearing a Halloween pig mask.

While they looked on, the man began turning the front door knob, and then there were three loud knocks at the back door.

David and Tim raced to the back door, checking to see that it was locked when Mary and Wendi came out of the kitchen, and Mary said as she walked to the front door and opening it saying…

"Is everyone just going to ignore the door, there's somebody knocking?"

Thinking it was Tim messing around, Mary opened the door to a large man wearing a pig mask, as she punched him in the stomach and mouthing *"good one"* and waved Tim inside, when Wendi hollered…

"Close the damn door, that ain't Tim!"

Mary and Wendi had little time to react, when the large man stuck his foot in the door, preventing them from closing it, as Wendi hollered to David and Tim…

"Put something against the back door, somebody's trying to get in here!"

David and Tim raced over to the love seat and carried over to the back door, tilting it and bracing it up against the door knob.

Wendi grunted, and Mary pushed as hard as they could, but the large man's foot was planted in the door way, when Wendi screamed, and Kristin ran out of the living room.

Thinking that Kristin had ran off and left them, Wendi hollered…

"Kristin, get your chicken ass back in here and help…damnit!"

Just then, the large man's hand pushed through the door opening, as Wendi tried hitting it and pushing it out, when out of nowhere, Kristin had crawled underneath both Mary and Wendi, burying a large knife in the large man's foot, who let go of the door and backed out of the door.

Kristin, Wendi and Mary were at the front door and Tim and David at the back door, no one noticed that Deanne was standing in the middle of the living room crying.

Wendi turned to the sounds of Deanne crying and yelled…

"Dee!"

David turned in Wendi's direction and saw Deanne rushing towards Mary.

To everyone's surprise, as soon as Deanne got in front of Mary,

Deanne balled up her first and punched Mary in the face, knocking her to the floor, saying...

"You stupid cow! Don't you know what you did? I told you that we could not leave the house, or we'd have to start this whole nightmare over from the beginning, and you walked out the door, and we had to start from the beginning.

Now, everybody...keep your fucking asses inside!"

Tim reached down to help Mary who had tears in her eyes, as she said when she got to her feet...

"Dee, I'm sorry...I don't remember anything, I don't remember going outside."

Deanne walked over and stood next to David, saying...

"I apologize for getting all jacked up, but we already went through this, and Mary, you walked out on the front porch and we just repeated yesterday morning a few moments ago."

Walking in the living room, Tim said...

"Hey everybody, did any of you guys feel this too?"

David, Wendi and Steve replied, saying...

"Yep".

Deanne sat on the sofa, next to Mary, rubbing her shoulders, saying...

"Just think Tim, a few minutes ago, didn't things seem a little familiar?"

Tim put his hand under his chin and rubbed it, saying...

"You know, I did have that Déjà Vu feeling.

"Rising to his feet, David said...

"You know, come to think of it, Deanne's right, because I remember the creepy ass Nun telling me, that since we couldn't pay attention and stay inside, that things were going to get more difficult.

I didn't know if it was real or a dream that I had, but it makes sense...we all got to stay inside and figure this shit out."

Everyone took their seats on the sofa, and for a few minutes, no one said a word, just complete silence, but the worrying kind of silence, suddenly, the entire house began rocking and shaking.

Deanne, Wendi, and Mary started screaming, as dishes began flying out of the cupboards in the kitchen, hurling themselves into the walls, and at everyone in the living room.

Removing a cushion from the love seat and using it as a shield, David hollered...

"C'mon...help me!"

Grabbing a cushion, Tim followed David into the kitchen, as David yelled back…

"We gotta get these cabinets closed…the drawer underneath the sink, there's a spool of twine, get it and tie the drawers shut."

While Tim made his way to get the twine, the flying dishes seemed to have a mind of their own. They were hitting Tim and David with precision on their knees and legs.

Once inside the kitchen, Tim found the twine and began tying the cabinet drawers, as David used his cushion to protect both himself and Tim.

Just when Tim and David secured the kitchen cabinets and drawers, they heard screams coming from the living room, and they ran to see what the problem was.

Once they arrived in the living room they saw, Kristin, Deanne, and Mary on the sofa and love seat which was four feet off the floor and spinning.

Wendi was pinned up against the wall by an enormous wind, coming from an open window in the living room.

David's initial reaction was to get the window closed and help Tim and Wendi and then Kristin, Deanne and Mary.

Suddenly, the front door opened and Mary, Deanne, Kristin and Wendi all were screaming and yelling.

David turned in the direction of the front door and saw a big man in a pig's mask enter, and then two small kids wearing hoodies were in the dining room.

Tim began yelling at David to watch out, as the man wearing the pig's mask was walking in the front door.

In the hand of the man wearing the pig's mask was a large olden type sickle, and the two small kids removed their hoodies and revealed misshapen bald heads, jagged teeth, and black eyes.

Just then, as the two small kids entered the house, they parted. The man in the pig's mask stepping to the left and the small kids stepped to the right and coming in the house was the old creepy Nun, Sister Mary Jacalyn, who stood in the center of the room.

As Sister Mary Jacalyn bowed her head, the wind stopped, and the sofa and love seat slowly lowered until they were on the floor.

With the women still crying and sniffling, Sister Mary Jacalyn said…

"It's good that you're all here, all except one how'd you like your little trip Deanne? You got to keep your eye on that cunt, Mary, she'll screw you guys up good, before it's over."

Mary stood next to, and holding onto Tim, saying…
"Where's Steve?"

"Now, let's us all have a seat in your parlor David, we've a few things to discuss.

David directed everyone to sit down, as he remained standing and said to Sister Mary Jacalyn…

"Look, whatever problems you have, don't involve me or my friends, just let them go and deal with me, huh?"

Sister Mary Jacalyn wagged her finger at David, saying…

"No…no…no…no…, as I told you, someone in your little fucked up group of friends has opened the portal of my reality, sucking me in here, so, no one is free to go, until it's discovered whom it is."

Suddenly, Sister Mary Jacalyn waved her arm and Steve appeared, standing near the fire place, saying…

"Listen, that sick game of making us appear and disappear, is getting old, bitch."

Sister Mary Jacalyn walked over to Steve, and in an angry tone, said…

"The only sick ass is going to be you, lover boy."

David walked in between Sister Mary Jacalyn and Steve, saying…

"Slow down partner, I got this. So, my question is, do you know who it is, or don't you?

It seems the only fair thing to do, is deal with the one who triggered all this, instead of innocent people."

Sister Mary Jacalyn turned and looked at David saying…

"INNOCENT! Was that meant to amuse me or something? Let me tell you what innocent looks like

Innocent looks like Kristin, who sold Deanne out to her parents, just to keep them from cutting her off financially, and set it up for her best friend to be rape.

Innocent looks like Mary, who pretended to be Deanne, and waited for David to get drunk just for sex.
"Innocent looks like Wendi, who lied to Steve, saying she couldn't get pregnant, all the while hiding the truth that she aborted his child...a boy at that!"
Innocent looks like Tim, who stole more than one hundred-ninety-three-thousand dollars from his company's fireman pension.
Shall I go on about these innocent fucking friends of yours, no Dave, we are going to play this little 'Jeu' out.

"David turned to look at each of his friends while Sister Mary Jacalyn exposed each of the dirty little secrets, that each one held secret.
Seeing the pain, and embarrassment in each of their faces, he turned to Sister Mary Jacalyn, saying...
"What about you, you're supposed to be a Nun, and look at how you act, look at how you talk...you're no Nun, you're not any better than any of us."
Sister Mary Jacalyn looked at David smiling, and said as she left the house...
"You almost had me there for a moment, but you see, I'm not supposed to act nice...you ass hole. Oh, I haven't forgotten about you Davey boy...

You masturbate to naked pictures of Mary, which you took from Deanne's college scrap book and Deanne who pretends to be so innocent wanna tell Davey boy about the nasty little games you play with the couple upstairs in your condo in Columbus?
So, you see, none of you are innocent."

Sister Mary Jacalyn then walked out the door, without an explanation.

Everyone raced to the window, looking to see which way Sister Mary Jacalyn went.

For about thirty minutes no one said a word, when Deanne said...

"Blue...what's the deal with jacking off to pictures of Mary? Do you want her or something, what's up with that?"

While everyone looked over at David, he said...

"Look Deanne that was way back when we first met."

Deanne snapped...

"That's bull shit Blue, those pictures of Mary, me and Kristin were taken two years after we began dating. What is it, is it her ass...what?"

David knew that he was caught in a lie, so he responded...

"Okay, it was only a few times, but what is this about the nasty games you're playing with the neighbors upstairs?"

Steve interrupted David and Deanne, saying...

"Okay, lets break it down a little bit. It seems funky ass knows and exposed all of our little secrets, so what are we supposed to do, turn on each other?"

Agreeing with Steve Wendi said...

"Look, we need to focus on the 'here and now', and not on shit that's going to keep us divided against one another."

It was a dark night. Clouds covered the moon, and the wind was whistling down the chimney and rattling the shutters of the farm house.

Deanne hugged David, saying...

"Oh Blue, I'm so sorry, I love you..."

David, hugged Deanne saying...

"I love you too Deanne. When we get out of here, I guess we all have things to clean up in our lives."

Later, when everyone had eaten and had fallen asleep, the remaining living room shutters slammed open with a loud bang, busting the window and waking everyone.

A wild wind whipped into the room, scattering papers and books every which way.

David, Deanne and Steve sat up, startled by the sudden noise.

Tim, Mary Wendi and Kristin were unshaken by the sudden noise while David, Deanne and Steve rushed over to the window to cover it up to prevent anymore cold air from rushing in.

Deanne was over by the sink picking up plants and debris on the window-sill, which was tossed by the wind, when suddenly, the broom came dancing across the middle of the floor from the closet, causing Deanne to yell...

"Blue!"

David and Steve turned in Deanne's direction to see what the commotion was all about, when the glasses, and cups in the dish strainer suddenly flew to the floor.

One by one, falling on the tiled kitchen floor, waking Mary and Wendi.

Through all the noise made by the window shattering and the dishes crashing on the floor, Tim and Kristin remained sound asleep.

As Mary and Wendi walked into the kitchen, Mary pointed to the floor and screamed. There beside the kitchen sink, on the floor was a dish of milk and a small saucer of cat food.

Deanne looked over to Mary and Wendi, saying...

"What?"

Wendi looked over to Deanne and David, saying...

"Do you guys feed Shone milk and cat food?"

Steve was busy picking up broken dishes as Deanne and David walked over to Wendi, inspecting the milk and cat food on the floor, when Deanne said...

"What the fuck!"

David stretched out his arm preventing Deanne from getting too close to it, saying...

"Okay, everybody! Do you all see this?"

Steve, Wendi and Mary, all nodded yes, as Tim walked into the kitchen as Kristin followed him, asking...

"What's all the fuss?"

Steve joined them in the kitchen saying...

"While you two were coping ZZZ's, the little old nasty ass Nun, has been up to her little funky ass mind games, look."

Tim and Kristin looked at the broken dishes and the cat food and milk on the floor, as Kristin said to Deanne...

"When'd ya'll get a cat?"

David looked over at Kristin, saying...

"We don't have a cat Kristin, damn, do you wake up dense, or do you have to take pills to get that way?"

Kristin stuck her tongue out and flipped David the bird, saying...

"Bite this!"

Deanne jumped in, saying...

"Gosh, will you two give it a rest. We need to find out, who amongst us is causing all this to happen."

Searching her coat pocket for her pack of cigarettes, Kristin said...

"My moneys on Dave here, I mean, this crap only starts either at Dave's condo, or here at his farm...right?"

Coming to David's rescue, Steve replied, saying...

"That is so like you Kris, Dave could no more be causing this than you can, or any of us for that matter."

Agreeing with Steve, Tim nodded his head, saying...

"Yeah, his right. Didn't the reject from the 'Flying Nun' say that all of us has our little secrets, we're hiding, so it could be any of us.

We all got something to hide, so, how are we supposed to stop this from happening, I mean we can't undo whatever we've done, right?"

Walking over and standing in the middle of the group, Wendi said...

"This is ridiculous, so we're supposed to expose every little dirty secret in front of everyone, somehow it's supposed to magically restore everything back to normal?"

Standing next to Wendi, Deanne put her arm on Wendi's shoulder, saying...

"One thing The Nun said to me while she was talking to me, was, after she was through messing with us, the person responsible would be revealed if we didn't find out who it was, and whoever it is would have to be willing to stop doing whatever it is that they've done."

The group continued over the next couple hours, arguing and accusing one another, not noticing that shone was at the front door growling, and then she began barking for all she was worth, and not at the door... she was barking and clawing at a spot on the floor.

Steve tapped David on the shoulder, drawing his attention to Shone's unusual behavior, when David got up and walked over to Shone in an attempt to quiet her down, saying...

"What is it girl, what are you barking at?"

David motioned over for Deanne to come over to him, saying...

"*Baby, you said we can't go outside the house, right? Now what about Shone, apparently, she needs to go outside, so if I let her out, will that make us repeat the whole damn morning all over again?*"

Shaking her head, Deanne replied, saying...

"*I don't think this applies to Shone, I mean she went outside chasing something a couple hours ago, and we didn't repeat the morning, so I'd say...let her out if she has to go.*"

Steve went over to David as he opened the door, saying'"

"*Hey partner, what's up?*"

David responded...

The dogs gotta go out, just letting her go, I'm not stepping outside."

"David opened the door and told Shone to go out, but she continued growling and barking wildly and clawing at the spot on the floor.

David and Steve looked at Shone and neither had a sense of what she wanted, whether she smelled something, or if something or someone was below them in the basement.

Whatever it was, it flipped David and Steve right the fuck out, who jumped backwards to the other side of Shone, as she jumped around clawing at the spot on the floor, but the fact still remained...Shone was going absolutely ape-shit.

All of a sudden as Shone was growling and clawing at the floor, the entire house began shaking. The sofa on which Tim, Mary and Kristin were sitting on started bouncing up and down, making Mary and Kristin scream.

Deanne and Wendi hollered as the pictures on the wall and the large spiral clock fell, crashing on top of the television and entertainment system.

Just then, Deanne and Wendi saw a white tail go past the other side of the coffee table and running in the kitchen, with Shone barking and chasing after it.

Steve turned to David, saying...

"*Hey dude, you got a cat or a racoon up in here.*"

Without thinking, David and Steve raced into the kitchen after Shone, and whatever she was chasing. As they entered the kitchen, Shone was viciously barking and drooling at what looked like a racoon who somehow got into the house.

Steve yelled to David, as he grabbed the broom, saying...

"What the hell is that...grab Shone's collar and I'll open the back door, so it can get out."

David held onto Shone who was still barking up a storm, as Steve positioned himself on one side of the fridge and tried to coax the animal from the top of the fridge to the open door.

The raccoon was so frightened by the chaos of Steve yelling, Shone barking and the broom being shoved at it, that it back tightly into the corner.

Every attempt Steve made to push the animal to jump to the door, the raccoon looking animal curled and wedged itself tighter and tighter in the corner space atop the fridge.

Seeing that it was doing little good, David yelled to Steve...

"Steve let's just back out of the kitchen, maybe it'll leave on its own."

Steve lowered the broom, while David pulled on Shone's collar, who was still in attack mode, pulling her out of the kitchen, when suddenly, as Steve made one last attempt to get the raccoon looking animal to leave, using the broom...it jumped from the fridge and bolted into the living room.

Steve heard the women screaming and Shone barking and knew, that he should've listened to David and let the raccoon looking animal leave the kitchen on its own, instead of that one last push with the broom.

As Steve entered the living room, he could see Kristin, Wendi, Mary, and Deanne standing on top of the sofa screaming, and David trying to hold onto Shone's leash as the raccoon looking animal ran upstairs.

As the animal ran up the steps, Steve looked over at David saying...

"What the hell is that dude?

Tim replied, saying...

"It's a raccoon, like you said."

David came from handing Shone's leash to Deanne saying...

"That doesn't look like any raccoon I've ever seen. It's got a head and face like a raccoon, but it's got a body like a cat, and raccoons don't have long bushy tails either."

Walking over to David and Tim, Steve said...

"Well, regardless of what it looks like, we're going to have to go up there and force it out the house."

Going back into the kitchen, David said...

"I've got an idea, Steve...wait just a sec."

Steve looked at David as he emerged from the kitchen with a can of wasp and hornet spray saying…

"Okay, dude, now I know it looks weird, and that looks nothing like a wasp."

Motioning for Steve to come over to the steps, he said…

"That thing is up in either the bathroom or the spare bedroom, because those were the only two rooms open.

Hopefully, it's in the bedroom, and while one of us opens the window, the other hits it with a shot of this, and that should make it head for the window, and then outside."

From across the room, Tim shouted…

"That's stupid Dave, all its gonna do is thrash around on the floor or something."

Disagreeing with Tim, David replied, saying…

"Tim, I'm hoping that once it gets a squirt of this in his face, he'll be looking for the first way out of here, besides, do you have a better idea?"

Jumping off of the sofa, Mary said…

"Well, whatever ya'll do, just keep that thing up there…I gotta pee and I don't want to come out the bathroom with that thing chasing my ass."

Chuckling, Steve said as he started up the steps…

"Don't worry Mary, your' pee-time won't be interrupted, we'll keep it up stairs."

David and Steve chuckled as they went upstairs, while Mary yelled to them…

"Yeah, funny Steve, I hope it bites you on your ass."

Steve and David stopped at the bathroom first and slowly looked all around, and upon not seeing the raccoon looking animal, closed the door, and headed to the spare bedroom, down the hall, on the right.

Steve heard David saying to himself…

"Good fucking deal. It's in here, the window leads to the roof, where there's a tree right next to it.

Now, I'll go open the window, you just make sure, it doesn't run back out of the room, and I'll hit it with a shot of this, and that ought to do the trick."

Out of all the things that have happened that day, the one thing that went right, was Steve and David were able to make the raccoon looking animal run out the window, onto the roof and shimmy down the tree.

David and Steve stood in the hallway talking, as Steve said…

"Dude, that was the ugliest looking raccoon I've ever seen, it looked more

like a cross between a cat and a raccoon...but anyways, after you hit it with a
shot of that, it broke camp quickly."

Just then, Steve and David heard Wendi scream, as they both ran
back downstairs.

When Steve and David got back downstairs, they noticed that
The Nun, Sister Mary Jacalyn was standing in the middle of the room
talking. When she noticed David and Steve, she said...

"Welcome boys, so glad you could join us, but tell me did you hurt my
kitty? I hope you didn't, because you should never hurt a woman's pussy."

Steve spoke up saying...
"Alright, now what do you want. All this crap you're doing, doesn't make
any sense?"
Sister Mary Jacalyn looked at Steve, saying...

"It's attitudes and spunk like yours that I hate, but I don't think
you're gonna like what's about to happen to you all.

I asked you all to figure out who among you has opened the door
to this dimension, and none of you have even tried, therefore, I said
that you all would go on a little trip...well, have fun."

Before Sister Mary Jacalyn vanished, she pointed to the living room
window.

Suddenly, Mary pointed out in the yard and yelled...
"Look!"
As everyone looked out into the yard, there were seven figures
walking up the walkway towards the house.

The closer these figures came to the house, the clearer they were,
until they reached the front porch and then suddenly vanished.

Steve turned in the direction of Sister Mary Jacalyn, who was no
longer in the room, when Wendi said...
"Oh my God...look everyone."
Though it was night-time, they were all looking through the
window and into another living room, but only this living room was
much clearer and brighter than Deanne and David's.

As they continued to watch in amazement, Deanne grabbed David's arm saying...

"Oh Blue, look...it's us, but how can that be, we're here."

Tim, Mary, Wendi, Kristin, Steve, Deanne and David, were all looking at themselves through the window into another house.

They were all dressed in the exact clothes which they were currently wearing.

Everything was an exact match, except for one thing, as Mary said...

"Kris, where are you at...everyone else is over there, except you."

Kristin replied, saying...

"Maybe I'm not going to be stuck in that crazy ass nightmare, like you all are."

David eased up next to Kristin, saying...

"I don't think so Kristin, maybe that creepy ass Nun, did something to you, I mean we're all here, looking at ourselves, all except you."

Just then a cold wind came up behind them, causing everyone to turn around, and as they did, Sister Mary Jacalyn was standing there, caressing that strange Raccoon looking like animal, saying...

"I told you all, that you needed to discover who among you is responsible for opening the door of my reality and close it.
Until you do, one by one, your counterpart which you see there, will permanently replace you here."

Steve was about to speak when David held him back saying...

"We get it, that we have to find out who among us is responsible but, how can we do that, if we're still having to deal with creepy ass animals and weird ass shit?"

Sister Mary Jacalyn placed the raccoon like animal on the floor and said...

"Shit happens, good, bad, whatever but you get no special dispensation, so that you can figure this out."

Sister Mary Jacalyn bent down as the raccoon like animal crawled up her arm and around her neck, as Kristin said...

"Excuse me…everyone is looking at their other selves, or as you call it their counterpart, but what about mine, I don't see myself anywhere over there."

Turning and looking at Kristin with a grimace, Sister Mary Jacalyn replied, saying…

"First of all, I will not excuse you, you over bearing, penny ass cunt. The reason your counterpart is not over there with the others is, because you are nowhere.and that means if there is no counterpart to exchange with, you go into the nothingness, into the nowhere, and you don't wanna think about that."

With a concerned look on her face and frustration in her voice, Kristin asked Sister Mary Jacalyn…

"That's crazy, people just don't go 'nowhere'…everybody has to go somewhere."

The raccoon like animal which was on Sister Mary Jacalyn's neck, made a strange sound as Sister Mary Jacalyn stroked it's under belly with her long deform fingers, saying…

"Oh yes they do, people go where they go. Have you not wondered about all the people who go missing each year, and how they are never seen nor heard of again and how their bodies are never recovered they are in the nothingness, and its gonna feel really good adding your ugly ass there."

David asked Sister Mary Jacalyn…

"How much time do we have before all this stuff starts, and how do we contact you once we solve this?"

Sister Mary Jacalyn, looked at David with a cocked grin, saying…

"Oh, lover boy, you've been on the clock for quite some time now, and as for contacting me you don't wanna do that, as a matter of fact, you don't even wanna think about, I'll contact you."

With Sister Mary Jacalyn's last sentence, she suddenly was no longer in the room, but only her shrill laughter was heard.

Mary, Tim, Wend, Steve, David and Deanne stood watching themselves through the window of another place, Tim placed his arm around Mary and began massaging her neck, when she said...

"Gosh Tim, you're hands are ice cold."

Tim was one of those people who always was really warm, but Mary commented that even his arms through his shirt felt ice cold.

Tim looked at Mary, saying...

"Huh...what are you talking about, I don't feel cold."

Mary asked Wendi to feel Tim's arm, saying...

"Do you feel that?"

Wendi reached out to touch Tim's arm and snatched her hand back, saying...

"Oh, wow Tim, you feel like you just stepped out of one of those walk-in freezers."

Checking his hands and arms out, and even putting his hands on his face, Tim replied...

"You guys must be tripping or something, I'm hot...not like burning up kinda hot, but I'm not cold at all."

Mary took a step back from Tim saying...

"You're fucking freaking me out right now Tim, you're ice cold."

Trying to diffuse the situation and change the subject, Steve said...

Well, it's probably nothing but shock setting in, we've all heard and seen some pretty jacked up things, but what we need to do is focus on how to get out of this nightmare and what to do about that nasty ass Nun, cause I refuse to believe that we don't have a chance."

Laughing and then shouting, Mary stepped in Steve's face saying...

"What about all of this, that you don't get Steve?" I used to think that you were the smartest one in the bunch.

I mean, this nasty ass bitch can make us appear and disappear, she walks through walls and shit, and you say you refuse to believe...news flash Steve, that bus left a long time ago."

Just as Steve was about to respond to Mary, the house began shaking and then everything went dark.

After several minutes, the lights came back on again, and Kristin had vanished.

13
Nothingness

September 4th
4:30 p.m.

Gasping for air, Kristin felt as if the very breath was being sucked out of her. The sudden darkness that Kristin found herself in, slowly gave way to traces of a dim milky light.

Inability to see quickly gave way to fear as Kristin called out...

"Hey guys, Dee, Mary, Dave...c'mon this is really messed up on so many levels."

There was no answer as Kristin again called out for her friends, but no one answered her.

Kristin thought to herself...

"Okay, we were in the living room and the lights went out, this is nothing but Dave and Steve fucking with me."

Time passed slowly for Kristin, who was trapped in a room without being able to see.

Kristin was trying hard to keep her sanity in check, but was slowly becoming more and more pissed off, at what she perceived as a twisted game.

Kristin felt out all around her with both hands, which did not touch anything or anyone.

Thinking out loud, Kristin said...

"I don't deserve this kind of shit."

Again, Kristin tried saying everything she could to get someone, anyone to listen or say anything to her, but there was nothing but silence.

Patting her pockets, Kristin searched her pockets for her cell phone. When she could not locate it, she searched for her cigarette lighter, but all she came up with was her house keys.

Frustration, then fear started filling Kristin's mind as she frantically grouped around in the milky haze, looking for anyone or anything, when her hands finally felt first a wall and next a light switch.

Nothing so small gave Kristin as much pleasure as when she found the light switch. Not thinking anything other than turning on a light, Kristin flicked the switch up...and nothing.

Kristin started yelling and cursing and then pounding her fist against the wall, in anger and frustration, when she heard a noise coming from the right of her, saying...

"Hello, is anybody there? I-I'm lost, and I need some help."

Kristin, who ordinarily doesn't perspire much, began dripping sweat.

"Fuck...Its hot in here...like I just went swimming."

Kristin thought. She tried to take control of her fear, but it was being somewhere where you aren't familiar with, trapped and scared was all too much for Kristin. Kristin thought to herself...

"I can't let this happen, I gotta calm down, and hold myself together if I'm going to get out of here."

Kristin's back was against the wall, as she began searching the entire room, inch by inch with her hands, without her back leaving the wall.

With the murkiness, came a sense of foreboding, and time, marked by luminous dials, passed with excruciating slowness.

Initially, Kristin didn't feel or sense the temperature change of where she was, but she suddenly found herself shivering in the damp, 34°F air.

Hours passed and still Kristin was groping around in the murkiness, not knowing where she was, or how to get out...until she heard squeaking noises from up above her.

Then something flew past Kristin, brushing her hair as it flew past her, causing Kristin to drop to her knees.

While Kristin was on her knees, her hand felt something that reminded her of grains of rice. Picking up some of the rice, Kristin noticed that there was a strong musky ammonia smell, and that's when Kristin realized that there were bats in the room.

All Kristin had was her sense of smell and touch to go on, with the murkiness, Kristin couldn't see her hand in front of her face.

Kristin tried, to get her eyes to adjust, either, because there's nothing for them to pick up on. Hard as she fought, Kristin was close to giving up, just curling up in a little ball and dying.

Kristin dozed off for brief periods, sometimes she just sat and cried, but that did not last long, because hunger was gnawing at her stomach.

Hunger pains, and thirst hit Kristin, with a force that she never felt in her life. There were times when Kristin was in college, she had to go hungry, but nothing like what she was experiencing.

When Kristin tried to get on her feet, she couldn't stand without becoming dizzy. Her head spun like she were on a merry-go-round.

The lack of water to drink, and Kristin's yelling and screaming, left her mouth dry and clogged her throat.

Three days had passed since Kristin found herself in that awful place, that she began to think she was dying. Soaked in her own urine and feces. Kristin wanted to cry but, she was so dehydrated to where there were no tears. There was nothing.

Just then, as Kristin was losing consciousness, she heard a faint voice in the murkiness, calling her name, saying...

"Kristin Kristin, can you hear me."

Kristin, struggled to lift her head, but was too weak and exhausted. Had Kristin been able to lift her head, she would have seen that the person calling her name was, Sister Mary Jacalyn, saying...

"OOH, you smell. You smell like rotten meat. You're not so tough, are you? I figured after three or four days, you'd be ball stinky and the sores that covered your body would be oozing with pus."

Sister Mary Jacalyn knelt down on the floor where Kristin lay and looking upward, a small dim light shone.

Sister Mary Jacalyn examined Kristin's dried, cracked lips, and sunken eyes in her head, saying…

> "Aw, you look good. People are literally dying for this look. You wanna hear some good news, you're not going to die. Tomorrow when you wake up, you'll be your old self again, but there's one itsy-bitsy catch you just won an all-expense paid trip to your own private hell."

Sister Mary turned, and as she turned, the raccoon looking animal jumped in her arms. Sister Mary Jacalyn stroked the animal saying…

> "That's my little pussy. Pussy, this little cunt here was all cocky and miss jump bad, now look at her. Oh, Kristin, stay with me now, because I've got news for you you're going to repeat each day over and over, and each day is going to get harder and longer isn't that wonderful?"

Kristin let out a small moan and slid back down on the floor in the corner, as Sister Mary Jacalyn vanished in the murkiness, laughing, saying…

> "Just wait til the morning he-he-he-he, just wait."

September 5th
5:30 p.m.

Kristin found herself in darkness, more like a murky atmosphere. She was able to see, but not clearly.

Immediately she called out for Deanne, Mary and even David, but no one responded, and Kristin yelled out...

"Alright you guys, where's everybody?"

Kristin hollered out, but no one responded. Next, Kristin began feeling all around her, hoping to resolve the feeling that she was not alone in wherever she was.

Kristin spent hours with her back against the wall side–stepping and groping in the darkness, but she felt nothing.

Of all the things Kristin feared, was not so much being alone, but the effects of not being able to take her insulin. Hunger was gnawing at her stomach, but more than hunger, was her need to use the bathroom.

Several more hours of groping in darkness and calling out, began to take its toll on Kristin as she squatted, pulling her pants down peeing and pooping.

The feeling that the lights would come back on and people would notice her, added to Kristin's sense of frustration.

Carefully stepping over what she had done on the floor and moving to her right, Kristin counted the steps that it took her to get from one side of the room to the next...

"Fifty-six three-inch steps and I should be at the other wall, which is, thirty-three-inch steps. I gotta be careful not to step in my own mess when I get over there...gosh, this is so messed up."

Kristin said to herself out loud, as she continued to walk the room. All Kristin had was her sense of smell and touch to go on, with the murkiness, Kristin couldn't see her hand an inch in front of her face.

Kristin tried, but she couldn't get her eyes to adjust, partially, because there was nothing for them to pick up on.

Hard as she fought, Kristin was close to giving up, just curling up in a little ball and giving up.

Kristin dozed off for short periods, sometimes she just sat and cried, but that did not last long, because hunger was gnawing at her stomach. In addition to the hunger pains, Kristin knew her sugar levels were very low, because of the hunger and disorientation she experiencing.

Suffering from dehydration and starvation, Kristin began feeling the effects of neuropathy to her feet from her diabetes episode. Kristin was in a desperate and dangerous situation, but for some reason her body, and mind would not let her fall down and die.

It was growing increasingly difficult to walk, and she had to have something to eat and drink. Kristin's breathing was growing more and more shallow, as she was reduced to crawling on the floor.

As Kristin continued to crawl, she felt something on the floor, a piles of wet rice. She thought at first, she must be in some farmer's barn or something, and then the stark reality that she was in a place called 'Nothingness'.

Kristin was so desperate for food, until she plucked a few grains in her mouth and nearly gagged at the taste.

The grains of rice she was eating had a strong ammonia odor and taste...and as Kristin continued eating she heard squealing bats overhead, and realized that she was not eating rice, but bat droppings.

The lack of water to drink, the wet bat droppings and Kristin's yelling and screaming, left her mouth dry, her lips cracked, and her throat clogged.

Three days had passed since Kristin found herself in that awful place. She began to think she was dying. Soaked in her own urine and feces. Kristin wanted to cry but, she was so dehydrated to where there were no tears. There was nothing.

The pus-filled blisters on Kristin's feet which were bursting open, both, itched and caused Kristin considerable pain, as she sat hopeless and helpless in her own feces and urine.

Kristin was so desperate during the night, that she tried dipping her shirt in her urine and soaking it, to sip on, but her cracked and bloody lips burned when the urine touched it, so she gave up on trying it.

Kristin's mind also was on its last legs. The other people that she could see, but not touch or speak to, would not or could not help her.

Kristin's mind began imagining that she was at her parents' home on Thanksgiving with all the trimmings.

Suddenly, something on the floor around Kristin began moving. Not the kind of moving of someone walking, but there was something on the floor moving...it was bugs.

Mice, roaches, ants, spiders and all types of beetles. Crawling all over Kristin's legs.

Kristin wanted to brush them off, but she was too tired, too weak to attempt to lift her arms.

The bugs crawled over her legs, and her arms, and up on her face.

They crawled in her nose and around her eyes and in her ears, causing her to jerk her face as they entered.

In her torment, Kristin's mind drifted back to the times when she was not a so nice person. A time, when she did and said hurtful things to people, but she couldn't take it all back, because she was understanding, there is a price for everyone to pay, for all the wrong done in a person's life, and *'I'm sorry'* doesn't live there.

Kristin was in a fix, she was in a place, a time, situation where mercy knew no one.

Kristin could feel her heart beat slowing down and her breathing becoming more and more shallow, and she knew it was only a matter of time.

Kristin continued to drift in and out of consciousness, barely able to hold her head up or to open her eyes, she began to softly cry.

Kristin thought of all the things she did and failed to do with her life, but more importantly, Kristin thought about how she was dying, and how she didn't deserve to die like that.

Kristin resigned herself to her fate and closed her dry, crusty eyes as best she could, waiting for the end, when she heard a faint voice in the murkiness, calling her name, saying...

"Kristin, Kristin wakey-wakey. Oh no, you don't get to die, you will grovel over the edge of death and just when you think it's over, you'll be refreshed to start all over this again."

Kristin, struggled to lift her head, but was too weak and exhausted. Kristin recognized that voice...it was Sister Mary Jacalyn, speaking as her raccoon-like animal ate the bugs which covered Kristin's body, and licked her wounds.

Just then, Sister Mary Jacalyn whispered in Kristin's ear...

"Wake up Kristin, it's not time for you to die just yet you're not so tough, are you? Where's your cocky-bitchy attitude now? All your life, you played the self-centered bitch, and now look at you."

Sister Mary Jacalyn bent down and with her thumb and index finger, spread Kristin's eyes wide open, and said...

"Is there anybody in there? Sure, there is, and I'm here to help you girl.
I told you that you were going to experience this over and over, until
I say enough is enough.
Are you ready for more, because more is coming well, you better buckle
your seat belt, because it's gonna get bumpy from here on out."

Sister Mary Jacalyn slowly vanished as Kristin could hear her laughing and singing...

"Just wait until the morning he-he-he-he, just wait."

Just then all the lights came on and Deanne said...

"Where's Kris...Wendi, Mary did you see where Kristin went to?"

Tim, David, Mary, Steve, Wendi and Deanne were still able to see their counter parts through the window, when Steve said...

"I think I have an idea where Kristin is..."

Deanne walked up to Steve, saying...

"Steve, I hate these games, just tell me where!"

Grabbing the bottle of Vodka from the bar and pouring a big drink for himself, Steve said as he took a huge swallow...

Nowhere, The Nun said she was sending her nowhere."

...the saga continues

Printed in the United States
By Bookmasters